Limping, and wincing w̶ toward the warehouse ruins. Mute watched, admiring the way the squad kept in formation, far enough apart that even a perfectly placed grenade wouldn't injure more than three of them. She suspected the helmets were fitted with air filters that would have made her neurostun grenades useless even if the wind hadn't been blowing the wrong way. She reached for a concussion grenade with her left hand while keeping her pistol trained on the ork. His armor jacket and pants looked like standard CAS issue with the insignia removed—which meant that the weakest spots were inside the elbow and behind the knee. She was waiting for a clear shot when Beef Patty came roaring through the rubble like an ugly comet, with Lankin and Magnusson in her wake. The troll stopped just beside Boanerges' astral form, dropped to one knee and aimed an assault cannon at the Step-Van. "Not so fraggin' fast!" she roared.

The ork in the lead stared at the mismatched trio—a hulking, leather-clad troll with a blond buzz cut, a dark-skinned elf fashion plate who was even taller, and a bookish-looking silver-maned human in an old but clean topcoat—and shook his head. "You're outnumbered," he drawled, "outgunned—"

Patty smiled, turned and fired at one of the barghests. The front half of the animal exploded, spraying everyone around it with blood, fur and small gobbets of bone and meat. The animal's haunches remained standing for a fraction of a second, then collapsed. The handler stared at the mess in horror. "But not outclassed," Patty announced.

SHADOWRUN™

A FISTFUL OF DATA

A Shadowrun™ Novel

Stephen Dedman

A ROC BOOK

ROC
Published by New American Library, a division of
Penguin Group (USA) Inc., 375 Hudson Street,
New York, New York 10014, USA
Penguin Group (Canada), 90 Eglinton Avenue East, Suite 700, Toronto,
Ontario M4P 2Y3, Canada (a division of Pearson Penguin Canada Inc.)
Penguin Books Ltd., 80 Strand, London WC2R 0RL, England
Penguin Ireland, 25 St. Stephen's Green, Dublin 2,
Ireland (a division of Penguin Books Ltd.)
Penguin Group (Australia), 250 Camberwell Road, Camberwell, Victoria 3124,
Australia (a division of Pearson Australia Group Pty. Ltd.)
Penguin Books India Pvt. Ltd., 11 Community Centre, Panchsheel Park,
New Delhi - 110 017, India
Penguin Group (NZ), cnr Airborne and Rosedale Roads, Albany,
Auckland 1310, New Zealand (a division of Pearson New Zealand Ltd.)
Penguin Books (South Africa) (Pty.) Ltd., 24 Sturdee Avenue,
Rosebank, Johannesburg 2196, South Africa

Penguin Books Ltd., Registered Offices:
80 Strand, London WC2R 0RL, England

First published by Roc, an imprint of New American Library,
a division of Penguin Group (USA) Inc.

First Printing, October 2006
10 9 8 7 6 5 4 3 2 1

Copyright © WizKids, Inc., 2006
All rights reserved

REGISTERED TRADEMARK—MARCA REGISTRADA

Printed in the United States of America

PUBLISHER'S NOTE
This is a work of fiction. Names, characters, places, and incidents either are the
product of the author's imagination or are used fictitiously, and any resemblance
to actual persons, living or dead, business establishments, events, or locales is
entirely coincidental.
   The publisher does not have any control over and does not assume any respon-
sibility for author or third-party Web sites or their content.

ACKNOWLEDGMENTS

Thanks to Seth Johnson, Sharon Turner Mulvihill, Tom Dowd, Robert Charrette and Paul Hume, and the gang at Adept Security: John, Paul, Doug, Sue, Vicky, Gail, Laurton, Sam, Richard, Vic, Alistair and especially Elaine.

NORTH AMERICA
AS OF 2060

Copyright 2005, WizKids, Inc.

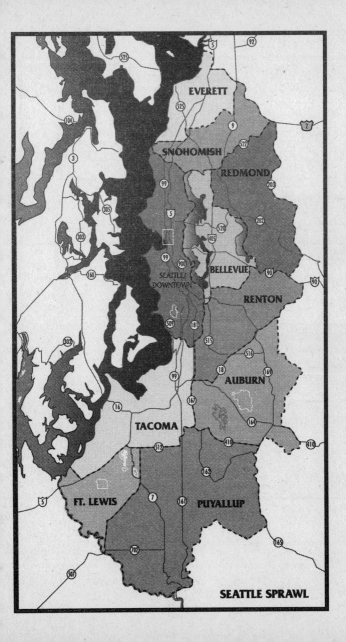

SEATTLE SPRAWL

1

It was all in the timing.

Mute sat on top of the elevator, watching the seconds tick by on her retinal clock and waiting for the signal from Mercurio Switch. The shaman sitting beside her looked up anxiously at the space above them—something Mute refused to do. She could feel that they were still descending, not climbing, which meant that the decker hadn't taken control of the security cameras. If she went through the trapdoor into the lift before Mercurio was ready, someone might get video of her and feed it into a pattern-recognition sensor. She was prepared to buy a new face, if necessary—not that it was easy to see hers through the chemsuit visor and respirator mask—but she knew software now existed that could recognize a walk or a way of moving, and she'd rather risk a relatively quick death, such as being crushed between the elevator car and the top of the shaft, than change *that*.

There was a quick flicker of multicolored symbols around the edge of her retinal clock display—confirmation from the decker that everything was going according to plan. Dr. Morales was in the lift with one wired bodyguard and an Aztechnology wagemage, as expected; the helicopter was on the roof, as arranged; the cameras were playing a loop of the inside of the elevator to anyone who might be watching in the security station. Mute held up three fingers while she removed the pin from the gas grenade *two*

and the leopard shaman's brown eyes began to glow faintly amber as she stared into the mirror they had set above the trapdoor and

one

the lights in the lift went out and

zero

Mute raised the trapdoor with her free hand, taking care not to move the mirror, and dropped the grenade into the elevator. Before it hit the floor she'd already grabbed her Taser from its holster, her boosted reflexes giving her superhuman speed. The shaman cast a stunball spell, which the elf wagemage tried to block, but the neurostun gas was already beginning to take effect. The elevator jerked to a stop, and the mage collapsed on top of Morales. Mute felt her weight increase as the elevator began to climb rapidly, and the bodyguard drew his smartgun and pointed it at the trapdoor.

Mute cursed silently. The vatjob was either obscenely healthy or protected by some sort of filtration system, and she was glad she'd brought a stun gun instead of a narcoject pistol.

The bodyguard, obviously tired of waiting for her to show her face, fired a burst of armor-piercing rounds into the ceiling of the elevator car. Mute heard the shaman shriek, and she dived headfirst through the trapdoor, firing as she fell. The Taser dart hit the bodyguard in the throat and he spasmed as the current coursed through his wired nervous system. He tried to bring his gun to bear on Mute, but his hand was jerking too wildly, and he succeeded only in spraying the walls with bullets as he tottered and fell. She grabbed his arm and found the switch to pop the clip from the gun, waited for a few seconds to see if the man was playing possum, and when she decided that he wasn't, pried the gun out of his grip and bound his hands with a set of plasteel restraints. She examined Morales, making sure that he was uninjured, then called, "Nasti?"

The shaman poked her head cautiously through the trapdoor. "Yes?"

"Are you hit? Is your suit punctured?"

"I don't think so."

"Check." Mute began patting down the wagemage and bodyguard, searching for anything that might be valuable to her or to her fixer—credsticks, Aztechnology ID, passcards, talismans. A moment later, Nasti slid through the trapdoor and closed it behind her.

"No holes," the shaman said. "How long does it take the gas to break down?"

Mute glanced at the glowing numbers above the door. "We'll be out of here before it does," she promised.

The Hatter leaned against the wall and sipped his tea as he watched Dr. Steinberg, one of Aztechnology's most brilliant mathematicians, talking to a small gaggle of undergraduates who'd come to hear his lecture. These conferences were great for recruiting, but organizing security for them was a nightmare—a nightmare that recently had been handed to the Hatter, along with a pay raise he considered barely adequate. Steinberg was regarded as an excellent lecturer, for a cryptographer, and a great advertisement for the megacorp's software R & D department. He was also skilled at spotting talented undergraduates. Unfortunately, it wasn't only mathematical talent that interested him. The Hatter didn't much care how many young women Steinberg invited back to his office for a personal interview; security at the Aztechnology Pyramid was excellent. Here in the conference center, though, the security station was off-limits to him and he'd been given only one mage and one low-level company man per Aztechnology scientist speaking at the conference. If someone wanted to try an extraction, he thought, all they'd have to do is—

His phone rang in his ear, and he grimaced. "Hatter."

"It's Carrington, Chief. Morales hasn't shown. The elevator seems to be stuck in the lobby. I've tried calling his bodyguard, but Runco doesn't answer."

The Hatter blinked. The elevator was supposed to have taken Dr. Morales and his guards nonstop from his last lecture to the basement car park, where Carrington was waiting to drive the mathematician back to the Pyramid. The Hatter nodded to Steinberg's bodyguard and hurried to the office, where he'd set up a dataline tap that enabled him to see through the building's security cameras. "Diaz!" he subvocalized as he ran. "What's happening with elevator number four?"

The guard in the security office took a few seconds to answer. The Hatter assumed he'd been up to his usual trick of trying to access the surveillance cameras in the women's changing rooms. "It's on its way down," he finally answered, his voice confident. "Got a clear picture of the three of them in there."

"What floor is it on?"

"Lobby."

"Let me know if that changes," said the Hatter, dumping his half-empty cup into a recycling bin without much regret. "And try to get Runco. Use the elevator's emergency phone if you have to."

As soon as the Hatter burst into his office, Diaz looked up with a slightly queasy expression. "I think we have a problem . . ."

His boss stared at the monitor for a few seconds. "No drek. That's a video loop. Somebody's hacked into the security system." His long fingers raced across the keyboard like two wired spiders, calling up images from the other elevators and all the exits.

The elevator doors opened, and Mute strode out onto the roof, carrying the still-unconscious Morales under one arm, glad that the mathematician was a dwarf rather than a troll. The Mitsuhama company men raised their guns at the sight of the chemsuited figures, but relaxed when Nasti called out the password. A combat mage jumped out of the helicopter and examined Morales to make sure there were no masking or tracking spells on him. A few seconds later, he nodded. "It's him," he said.

The team leader shoved his sidearm back into his holster, and snapped, *"Isoide kudasai!"* (Hurry!) Two of the men took charge of Morales and strapped him into a seat, and the Hughes Stallion lifted off and headed toward the Mitsuhama skyscrapers, with Mute and Nasti on board. "Where can I drop you?" asked the pilot.

"Hamlin Hotel," Mute told her, taking two rolls of stealth line out of a pocket on her belt.

The Hatter looked at the view from the helipad camera—another video loop, showing the helicopter idling—and shook his head in disgust. "Mitsuhama. They're on the roof. Or were."

Before Diaz could ask how he knew, the Hatter had one of Aztechnology's fastest deckers on the line and had instructed him to shut down all the elevators in the conference center and figure out who was controlling the cameras. Then he started barking orders at Carrington. "I don't care how many fragging flights of stairs it is! Get two of your men up to the roof! It'll be too late to catch the fraggers, but they might find something useful!"

Nasti looked down at the street in alarm, gripping the stealth line as tightly as she could. She'd never needed to use her catfall spell under conditions like these, and she tried not to calculate how far she'd fall if she missed the roof. She closed her eyes briefly as Mute jumped through the open doorway, then steeled herself to do the same.

She landed safely on the helipad, a little less gracefully than she'd hoped. Mute had already touched the catalyst stick to her own line, causing it to dissolve, and she chased after Nasti's tether and grabbed it just before it flew out of reach beyond the edge of the roof. A quick swipe with the catalyst stick, and it, too, disintegrated without any fuss. "They could have waited," the shaman grumbled as she removed her chemsuit hood. "Or at least slowed down." Her complexion had paled to a light tan, except where it was marked with fading black spots; Mute thought she looked like a player from a community-theater production of that ancient musical about cats, but didn't say it.

"Your first run?" asked Mute, removing her own hood. Nasti was surprised to see that she was smiling.

"Second," she admitted.

"Scared of heights?"

"No, I love heights. I'm scared of being found dead on Pine Street. I'd never live it down."

Mute's smile became a grin. "Mercurio said you were good."

To her surprise, the leopard shaman found herself grinning back. "You weren't bad yourself. You feel like a drink?"

2

As the Hatter had predicted, the guards arrived on the roof well after the helicopter had left, and they didn't find anything useful. The elevator containing the wagemage and the bodyguard had been on its way down to the third floor, where the first aid station was located, when the Hatter's decker finally regained control of the elevator system, and both were still unconscious when the doors opened. Aztechnology had pulled Steinberg out of the building immediately and had cancelled all its presentations for the rest of the conference, and the Hatter had been recalled to the Pyramid for the longest and most uncomfortable debriefing he'd suffered in years.

Four nights later, he walked into Hare's windowless apartment on the Pyramid's fifty-second floor for their weekly game of chess. The two men had been close friends since they'd met in chess club in college. Marc Herrera, a lecherous elf with teeth like tombstones and a dramatic cowlick, had been known as Hare since he'd first created a rabbit icon in his cyberterminal classes. Within a week after the two began hanging out together, a coed with a fondness for Lewis Carroll's books featuring Alice had dubbed the Roman-nosed Tom Mather the Mad Hatter. After Hare told him that he'd once read that "mad" had originally meant "dangerous," and "hatter" was a corruption of "adder," the Hatter had accepted the nickname—but he still took his revenge by planting some of his more creative homemade drugs in the coed's room and sending an anonymous tip to the school administration.

Hare was still jacked into his deck, a customized Fairlight Excalibur, when the Hatter rang his doorbell. Rather than unplug himself, the decker opened the security door using the room's electronics, switched the kettle on, and spoke through the trideo sound system. "It's your move," he said. "I'll be finished here in a few minutes."

The Hatter made himself a cup of tea, then walked over to the sofa and stared at the board on the coffee table before moving his queen to king four.

"Well, well, well," said Hare.

The Hatter raised a bushy eyebrow, knowing that the decker was watching him through the room's concealed cameras. "Want me to move you?"

"No—I've just found out who was playing around with the elevators and cameras in the conference center." The trideo screen flickered on and was instantly filled with lines of code.

"They used a deception utility," said the Hatter after studying it for a moment. "So?"

"Not just any utility." Hare highlighted two characters in one of the lines: an H and a G. "It's a work of art, and he signed it."

"HG?"

"You've forgotten the periodic table? *You?*"

"Mercury . . ." said the Hatter testily. The periodic table had been second nature to him long before he'd enhanced his already excellent memory with the best cyberware and biotech he could afford. His eyes widened as he made the connection. "Mercurio Switch? The shadowrunner?"

"If it wasn't, it's somebody using his software. But I'll bet it was him."

The Hatter nodded. "He'd be the team's third member. The forensic mages said there were two people on top of the elevator. One was a leopard shaman, but there aren't any leopard shamans working for Mitsuhama, and there can't be that many in Seattle."

"No," agreed Hare. "Though tracking one down might

be difficult; they're good at hiding. What about the other one?"

"The bodyguard saw somebody for about a second, but they were wearing a chemsuit, so he didn't see much. Human, light build, *probably* female, *probably* dark skinned with dark brown eyes and at least one datajack."

"Doesn't narrow it down much," remarked Hare. "Be there in a second."

A moment later, the elf walked out of the bedroom, his long, muddy brown hair even more disheveled than usual. "They've got you working as a Johnson?" he said sympathetically, sitting down on the other side of the chessboard and moving his knight.

"Not quite that bad," the Hatter muttered, "but I'm doing routine analysis, security clearances, updating our database and dossiers, that sort of drek. Long hours, no travel and no bonuses. I'd like to kill the fraggers."

Hare looked at him warily. "You know the rules," he said. "No vendettas. If shadowrunners are good enough to pull something like that and get away, they're worth hiring; you shouldn't waste them. We only kill the ones we catch red-handed. That's why people like Mercurio Switch leave their calling cards for us to find."

The Hatter grunted. "I need to do something to get back on top. Either that, or something that'll make me enough nuyen to go into business for myself." He knew that Hare swept his apartment regularly for bugs; it was one of the few places in the Pyramid where he could be sure that nobody was listening in.

"Do you have anything in mind?"

"Have you ever heard of GNX-IV?"

"Not that I can recall," Hare admitted after a quick search through his headware memory.

"It was an ORO R & D project. A way to reverse the effects of goblinization."

"You're kidding."

"The files are incomplete, so I don't know how well it worked, or what the side effects were, but it looked promising . . ."

"What went wrong?"

"The riots," said the Hatter sourly. "There were rumors that goblinization had been caused by an accident at some biotech lab. The story got around that this ORO lab was working on understanding unexplained genetic expression—you know, UGE—and somebody decided that meant the lab was really working on whatever made humans goblinize into orks and trolls. So a mob broke in and trashed the place. Smashed the computer, took the backups, killed the scientist in charge . . . and the samples in the lab just disappeared. Probably destroyed, but maybe stolen. But there was meant to be a vial of the cure on its way from the lab to the airport, to be flown to ORO headquarters in Aztlan. It never arrived, so it might still be out there somewhere—enough of it to try re-creating the formula, anyway."

Hare chewed his lip. "A cure for goblinization would be worth a fortune. The Japanese sales alone would be—"

"Check."

"What?" The decker looked down, and swore. "So why hasn't anybody else tried to track down this sample? It seems more likely that the scientists were fudging their results to get more money, or more mainframe time . . ."

"Others *have* tried, dear boy," the Hatter replied smugly. "They investigated after the riots, but if they found anything, that data was lost in the worldwide computer system crash of 2029 . . . and after that, they couldn't find anybody who remembered who'd driven the stuff to the airport, except that everyone claimed they weren't the one. One of the scientists *thought* it was a student who was working there as a lab assistant and security guard, but he couldn't remember his name or anything useful about him. Since then, most rookies in the section have gone through the copies of the old backup files that didn't succumb to the virus to see if they can find a clue as to who this guy was, something that everybody else has missed. Same as I did. But *they* didn't spend the last week getting lectured about how important Morales' work was, how useful it was for image enhancement and pattern recognition and that sort of drek. So I ran the last security recordings from ORO's

R & D lab through Morales' software to see if it turned up anything new."

"And?"

"I have a pretty good picture of the lab assistant, taken less than an hour before the rioters trashed the place. No audio, but he's walking to his car carrying a small case; you can even see the hazmat label. And I happen to know a *very* good decker—plenty good enough to hack into the Department of Motor Vehicles and see if he can match that photo to their old records without setting off any alarms. And together, maybe we can find this guy and ask him what happened."

"Or maybe he's already dead," said the decker. "It *was* forty years ago."

"Maybe," said the Hatter, reaching into the pocket of his hand-tailored suit and producing a datachip. "But he probably wasn't any older than eighteen or nineteen then; he'd be in his early sixties now. And if he was working in that lab, and driving company cars, he would have passed a security clearance, so he probably has a SIN. It's worth a shot, right?"

"I found three probables and another four possibles," said Hare, when the Hatter returned a week later. He placed a chip in the middle of the chessboard. "All the right age and height; after forty years, everything else is subject to change, and none of the photos are more than ten years old. I ran searches on these seven to see what else I could find. I haven't been able to get complete records from before twenty-nine, but all of the probables would have been students at about the right time, doing bio or chem, and they've been driving for as far back as the records go, without anything worse than a parking ticket. Two of the probables and three of the possibles are still alive. See what you think."

The Hatter nodded, and slotted the chip into his datajack without lifting his gaze from the chessboard. A minute later, he nodded. "Peter Nguyen," he said. "It's him. I'll bet on it."

"How much?"

"I'm a little short on cash at present, so . . . fifty thou?"

"You're that confident?"

"Army reservist, degree in pharmacology, worked for DocWagon for a few years in a crisis-response team, volunteered at Bridge Hospital, mainstream politics . . . Out of all of these, he's the one *I'd* have hired for a job like that."

Hare looked at him warily, then shook his head. Recruiting scientists—sometimes at gunpoint—was the Hatter's specialty. "No bet."

The Hatter smiled and shrugged. "As you say, it was forty years ago. The records are nowhere near complete: there might have been dozens of possibles who've dropped out of sight in that time . . . and I might be bluffing. But make it ten thousand, if you're nervous."

"One thousand. I've had a run of bad luck on the tables lately."

"Done. Mr. Nguyen lives in Covington. Shall we pay him a visit?"

Peter Nguyen looked his visitors up and down, making a quick and inadequate estimate of the cost of their suits, shoes and long coats. "Sorry the place is a mess," he said mildly, with a nod at the ancient sofa. The cats sitting there took a quick look at the guests and skittered off to their favorite hiding places.

Hare had established that Nguyen and his wife had separated barely a year after the last of their children had married, and that the workaholic Nguyen had moved to a smaller apartment and lived alone since then—except for three cats. Hare knew a little about them, too, from hacking into Nguyen's credstick records and taking a quick glance at his spending habits. Nguyen had extensive security coverage at the drugstore he owned, including an armed guard posted outside, but his home was protected by only door and window alarms and basic maglocks. The Hatter felt fairly sure that Nguyen wouldn't break the law by keeping any unlicensed guns more lethal than a stun gun or a narcoject—in short, the pharmacist was no threat to them. The apartment was clean and tidy, if somewhat shabby, and a faint scent of incense disguised any cat smells. The Hatter sat down gingerly on the sofa, removed his black silk top hat, and looked at his host.

Nguyen's appearance made the Hatter think of an Asian monk, maybe a Shaolin. In addition to being nearly bald, he looked much younger than his sixty-one years, and was obviously fit and alert. No cyberware apart from his eyes and a datajack. The Hatter managed to keep a pleasant smile on his pale face as he considered the best approach to getting the information he wanted. "Mr. Nguyen, we're sorry to intrude on you at home, but we're looking for people who worked at the ORO biotech labs in 2021. Were you ever employed there?"

Nguyen sat down in an ancient bamboo chair, and the largest of the cats crept into his lap. "The lab down in Puyallup? Yes, I was there for a while, back when I was in college."

"We're looking for something sent out of the lab the day it was destroyed. A courier was supposed to take a container to the airport to ship to another lab, but that container was never delivered."

Nguyen held up his hands as though surrendering. "Not my fault. The airport was sealed off before I even got close. National Guard had taken it over because of the riots. They'd been going on for a while by this time—we'd already lost the landline, nothing but our cell phones and radios, and were on emergency power when I left."

"You were the courier?"

"Yes, that's right."

The Hatter glanced at Hare, smiling broadly, then turned back to Nguyen. "What did you do when you discovered the airport was closed?"

"Drove back to the lab. But by the time I got there, the rioters had already broken through the fence and gotten inside. I wasn't armed, so I didn't go in. There was a security guard lying unconscious in the street outside, so I rushed her to the nearest hospital. There were troops guarding the hospital, so I let them know I was with the reserves. They teamed me up with a paramedic and promoted me to ambulance driver."

The Hatter nodded. "And the container? It was still in your car?"

"Yeah. I probably should have given it to someone at the hospital, but I forgot about it until they sent me down to Hell's Kitchen and I drove past the warehouse."

"What warehouse?"

Nguyen blinked, then smiled. "Monolith. They made the hazmat containers we used at the lab. I saw the logo on the sign outside, and I thought, if anyone could look after the stuff, they could. I'd been a hospital courier before I started working at the lab, so I knew they handled cell samples, medical waste, all sorts of risky stuff. I stopped the car for a minute and took it in."

"Do you remember who you spoke to?"

"The security guard on the gate outside. He wouldn't let me in, but someone came out from inside and I handed it over to her." He stroked the cat, his expression slightly sad. "All I remember about her is that she was a cute redhead, and she wore a white coat. Any other day, I might have asked her for a date. At least, that's what I told myself at the time."

"Did you ever go back there?"

Nguyen shook his head. "When I went back to the hospital, they found me a uniform that sort of fit, and a gun. For the next few weeks, I alternated between guard duty outside the hospital pharmacy and working as an orderly in the emergency room. Then I went back out on the streets and someone blew up the armored car I was in and I went back to the hospital as a patient." He grimaced. "That time is sort of a blur, but I don't think I'll ever forget the first day of the riots. It was insane, and the worst thing about it is . . . I can remember hearing someone say the crowds targeted our lab because we were doing genetics research, and they thought we might be responsible for goblinization. Hell, we were working on a *cure* for it, decades before anyone managed to sequence the genes. If it hadn't been for the rioters, we might have found a way to reverse the process."

The Hatter stiffened slightly. "How close do you think you were to a cure?' he asked, with forced casualness.

Nguyen shrugged, and began stroking the cat. "I don't know. I was just an assistant there—data entry, cleaning the glassware, that sort of thing. But the scientist who gave me the stuff to deliver seemed to think he'd made some sort of breakthrough."

"Dr. Sutter, wasn't it?"

"I think so. Sorry I can't be sure of the name. The guy in charge died, didn't he?"

"Yes. Heart attack, during the riot," the Hatter replied. "Mr. Nguyen, do you know if there was a data disk in the container with the samples?"

Nguyen shrugged, disturbing the cat, who grumped softly. "You know, it never occurred to me to look inside the container, but it wouldn't surprise me. We couldn't send data through to the head office with the landline down. Dr. Sutter might have put the data in the container as a backup."

"Yes, that would make sense," said the Hatter. "We're hoping that if we find Dr. Sutter's notes, our scientists may be able to pick up where he left off. Maybe even find a cure."

"For UGE?" replied Nguyen warily.

The Hatter hesitated for an instant, wishing he'd thought to check whether any of Nguyen's children were metahuman. He noticed framed photos above the trideo set and zoomed in on a picture of a girl who was either an elf or an elf-poser. "Perhaps eventually," he said. "But our immediate goal is to build on this existing research to learn how to alleviate some of the . . . allergies . . . that afflict so many metahumans. To sunlight, for example. If we can relieve those . . . well, that would make life much better for many people."

Nguyen nodded. "Yes, I can see that."

"But we're going to need more research before we can put something like that on the market," said the company man, warming to his theme. "And research is expensive, and if the execs think somebody might beat us to this cure, they might shelve the whole project as not worth the risk. So it's important for us to know exactly who else knows what was in the container, or where it might be."

"Someone from Monolith might," said Nguyen. "If any of them are still alive, of course. I know the warehouse isn't there anymore. But this was a pretty awful time in my life, and I've really never discussed it with anyone else."

"Excellent," said the Hatter, beaming. He reached into his coat and, with one smooth action, drew his silenced smartlinked Fichetti and shot Nguyen in the forehead. "And you never will."

3

It took Hare less than an hour to pinpoint the location of the ruins of the abandoned Monolith warehouse in the Puyallup Barrens, but a week to compile a thoroughly incomplete history of the site. "It may be a dead end," he admitted as he set up the chessboard. "Shiawase bought Monolith two years after the riots and shut the place down, said it wasn't worth repairing. There aren't any staff records after that."

"So Shiawase has the info?"

"Maybe not. Nguyen knew what he was doing. Among other things, Monolith was licensed to dispose of medical waste and biohazard material, and that included storing stuff pending destruction. So they had a secure storage facility—underground." He grinned. "In an emergency, such as an angry mob heading their way, it would be sealed off, probably with quick-drying concrete. The warehouse was badly damaged in the riots, but there's nothing to indicate that a secured part of the facility was ever breached."

"Would Monolith have admitted it if had been?" the Hatter grunted.

Hare wrinkled his nose as he considered this. "I think they would have. If there was a risk that something nasty had escaped, Monolith would have been better off warning the emergency services and blaming it on the rioters or the volcano rather than keeping it to themselves and getting caught later."

"So you think the stuff could still be down there."

Hare tapped his prominent front teeth with a long finger while he stared at the board. "I can think of only two other possibilities. One is that Monolith saw that the hazmat container was addressed to ORO and they sent it on its way after the riots, and any record of the transaction has been lost. The other is that Monolith destroyed it." He moved his king pawn two spaces. "This whole thing is a long shot, but it shouldn't cost too much to find out what happened. The warehouse site's available for six thou; we can probably get it for five if we make the right noises about hiring locals. A little more to dig up the floor and see if the storage facility is still intact . . . security, transport . . . we can probably do it for under ten thou, and I've seen you drop more than that on a pair of aces."

The Hatter grunted again, and moved his own king pawn. "Who owns it? Shiawase?"

"Puyallup District Council. They're not going to ask any questions."

"Any squatters?"

"Most likely, but we can get rid of them easily enough. Send in a truck, take them somewhere for free food and booze . . . we'll be finished before any of them get back. No trouble at all."

The snake was barely visible in the dust. No, not *the* snake, Boanerges realized, but Snake. Or maybe SNAKE, because despite her apparent size, he was definitely in her realm, not the other way around.

Don't move, she hissed.

I had no intention of moving, Boanerges replied. *I won't tread on you.*

No. The place you are now. Your nest. If you leave, it will be bad for all I protect. You must learn its secrets, and decide what to . . . Boss? Boss?

The street shaman opened one bleary green eye and peered at the curtain of his medicine lodge. It was always dark inside, and Boanerges was only human, with natural eyesight, so he reached for the flashlight beside his lumpy futon mattress and shook it until it emitted a beam. No

point in wasting energy on a light spell this early in the . . .
He peered at the old clock standing amid his collection of
candles. Eleven forty-seven, unless he'd forgotten to wind
it again. And he guessed that it was probably morning,
because it smelled and sounded more like day than night—
not that it was easy to be sure in the Crypt, where many
of the denizens were allergic to sunlight, the kitchen was
open twenty-four seven, and the only ventilation came from
the occasional air elemental summoned by the apprentice
mages.

"Boss?" Pierce repeated while thumping on the
doorframe—a rather tentative thump for the muscular ork,
a wannabe drummer more noted for his energy than his
talent. "You awake?"

"Yesss?"

"Some'un here wants to see you," said Pierce.

"Does he need healing?"

"Not yet, he doesn't."

Boanerges opened his other eye, stretched, scratched,
brushed his dreadlocks away from his face, and reached for
his much-patched jeans. The dream was already beginning
to fade, but he could still smell the hot sandy red-pepper
smell of the desert, rather than the familiar cold musty
odors of the Crypt, and he felt oddly reluctant to put his
dirty feet down on the dusty floor. When he did, though,
he encountered nothing more dangerous than his ancient
moccasins. "What's he like?" He knew that Pinhead Pierce
was nowhere near as stupid as his nickname suggested.

Pierce grinned toothily as the shaman emerged from behind the curtain, still blinking, barefoot and fumbling with
the buttons on his jeans. "Human, Anglo, too clean to be
living on the streets, not clean enough for corp," the ork
replied. "Wearing a heavy coat, and it's a warm day upstairs. Kinda pale, like he mostly works nights or indoors.
No smartlink, but he's got a jack an' his eyes look funny.
Sumatra had a look at him in astral, and he's not wired
below the neck." He shrugged his massive shoulders. "My
guess is he's a hired gun, an' a cheap one."

"Did he say what he wanted?"

"He was snoopin' around, so Sumatra and me cornered

him when he started comin' down the ramp and asked him
what he was after. He said he'd been told to look and see
if anyone lived here. I asked him why, and he said he was
just doin' what he was paid to do. That bit I believe."

"Where is he now?"

"Sittin' on the ramp. He asked if anyone was in charge
here, and I figured that was you."

The snake shaman nodded, and grabbed his much-
scuffed boots, an ancient military-issue greatcoat with its
original colors now obscured by graffiti and grime, and a
pair of bulletproof mirrorshades—all gifts from grateful patients. Fully dressed, he followed Pierce through a poorly
lit maze of rickety cubicles toward the ramp.

It was eleven minutes before noon, and most of the
squatters who lived in the cavernous sublevel of the ruins
were nocturnal for one reason or another. The intruder was
sitting halfway up the ramp, sweating slightly in the hazy
sunlight and peering into the darkness. Sumatra, a beady-
eyed ork, lurked in the shadows below him, chatting
blandly with the man. Boanerges saw a plastic shopping
bag floating like a disembodied head a few meters behind
the man; when he peered into the astral, he saw the bright,
ephemeral form of a city spirit that Sumatra had summoned. "Hoi," said Boanerges, squinting as he stepped into
the light. "Can we help you, chummer?"

The man stared at Boanerges, taking in his dirty black
dreadlocks, sallow complexion and multicolored coat, then
held his hands up, palms outward, to show that they were
empty. "I'm not looking for any trouble."

"What *are* you looking for, then?"

The man hesitated. "I just needed to see if anybody was
living here."

"Why?"

The man swallowed nervously. "To tell them to move
out. The place has been sold."

Pierce guffawed, Sumatra snickered and Boanerges con-
tented himself with a serene smile. "Now, who would want
to buy this dump? And why?"

"I don't know."

Boanerges nodded. "Did they pay you in advance?"

The man hesitated, and Boanerges saw Sumatra's face became briefly ratlike. Confident that Sumatra had cast an influence spell on the visitor, Boanerges waited for his answer. "Half in advance," said the human automatically.

"Certified credstick?"

"Yes, but I left it at the office. Area like this, I—"

"We . . . *I'm* not after your money," said Boanerges. "Do you know who you're working for?"

The man stared nervously at the two orks, wondering why he was unable to stop himself blurting out the truth. "Just a guy. Human, an inch or two taller than me, light brown hair, blue eyes. Didn't tell me a name, but he looked rich. Good suit, coat, gloves, gold wristcomp, pocket secretary . . . even wore a top hat. Looked like he was on his way to a wedding or a funeral, and talked a bit like a lawyer."

"Corp lawyer?"

"Maybe, but I can't guess which corp, or where he's from. He wasn't Asian, but he didn't exactly sound local either. English, maybe . . . though that might've been fake or a chip. But he was awfully well dressed for a Mr. Johnson, with an expensive haircut or a makeover spell . . ." He wound down, with a glance askance at Pierce's jagged and largely self-inflicted Mohawk. "And his money was real enough."

"You'd never seen him before?"

"I'm pretty sure I'd remember if I had. The clothes, anyway."

"And your name?"

"Foote." He swallowed. "Sam Foote."

"Have you ever worked for a corp, Mr. Foote?"

"Olympic Security. Two years, before I decided to go into business for myself."

Boanerges nodded, wondering what you had to be caught doing to get yourself fired from Olympic Security without going directly to jail. "How much do you think this Mr. Johnson knows about the job?"

"I *think* he knew a lot more than he was telling me, but I'm not sure. He had one hell of a poker face. I don't know where the money was coming from, and maybe he didn't either, but I can tell you one thing—he wasn't somebody you try to frag around with. If I was you, I'd get your butts out of here. It's not like it's prime real estate or nothing."

Boanerges shook his head slightly. "I'm afraid you're wrong about that. Have you ever heard of the Crypt?"

Foote's eyes widened slightly. "I've heard a little. This is the Crypt?"

"Yes."

"How many people you got living here?"

Boanerges smiled. "I haven't done a head count recently, but several dozen. Some of them can't be exposed to sunlight without intense pain. But this place isn't just a squat, or a sanctuary. It's a school for street kids. It's also my medicine lodge, and a clinic." He waved at the painted snake that coiled, caduceus style, around the concrete pillar beside the entrance. "We offer both magical and medical healing, and we have patients who cannot be moved. More important, though, if we were to move, how would people who need us, find us?

"So I'm afraid that we *can't* move, and we won't, and any attempt to move us will cost your employer far more than this land could *possibly* be worth. Please relay this message to him—or better still, let me speak to him."

Foote hesitated. "I don't have any way of reaching him. I'll have to wait for him to contact me with the rest of my payment. Look, I'm just a messenger. I don't want any trouble . . ." He jumped slightly as Pinhead growled. "I mean, I don't want anybody to lose their home or anything, but maybe you could make some sort of deal with this guy. Is there some way he can contact you?"

Boanerges peered over the top of his shades to look him up and down, then turned to Pierce. "Do you have a booking agent?"

The drummer blinked, then recited one of his e-mail addresses. Foote tapped it into his wristphone, then nodded and walked backwards up the ramp—still unaware of the city spirit that hovered above the ruins, or the watcher that Boanerges conjured up and sent after him.

"He wasn't lying," said Sumatra once Foote was out of

earshot. "He may've been lied to, but he believed what he was saying."

Boanerges nodded.

"Do you think he'll be back?" asked Pierce.

"Him? No. I think they'll send someone a little more persuasive." There was the faintest hint of a hiss in Boanerge's voice, and Sumatra took a half step back. "I can't imagine what it is they want here, but this is our home, and it's worth defending."

Foote walked into his cubicle-sized one-room office to find the Hatter already waiting for him, sitting on the shabby sofa and reading the latest stock market report on his pocket secretary. "How did you get in?" the investigator blustered.

"You need a better lock," said the company man, not looking up. "And what's that poison in your desk drawer for? Cleaning your guns?"

"It's bourbon."

"You *drink* that? Voluntarily?"

"Only when I've had a bad day," grunted Foote, sitting down heavily in his old synthleather chair and plugging himself into the tabletop computer to download images from his opticam. "Your vacant lot isn't vacant. There's at least three people living there, and they're probably telling the truth about there being dozens. They've even got a small farm—well, a vegetable garden—growing in the ruins. You ever heard of the Crypt?"

"Of course. Shadowrunners and other crooks go there to lick their wounds when they've nothing better. It's in that building?"

"Under it, more like." He copied the images to a chip, which he threw to the Hatter. "The skinny human with the dreads is the boss. A magician of some sort, probably a shaman. The big pale ork with all the drek in his face is Pinhead Pierce, plays drums in a couple of clubs when they're desperate and busks outside shops until somebody pays him to leave. The other ork I don't know. They gave me a contact number, if you want to negotiate with them."

The Hatter smiled and reached inside his coat. "I don't think that will be necessary," he began, then blinked as a watcher spirit, shaped like a snake with a huge mouth, appeared on Foote's shoulder.

"Now hear this!" the watcher blared. *"Any attempt to relocate us from our home will cost you more than the land could possibly be worth!"* It looked at the Hatter expectantly.

The company man hesitated, his hand still on the butt of his slivergun. "Tell your master," he said smoothly, "that we own that land now, and he has until noon tomorrow to move. If he does not, it will cost him much more dearly than he imagines. Can you remember that, or do I need to repeat it?"

The watcher faded away, leaving the Hatter fuming. He considered shooting Foote as he'd planned, but he hadn't counted on the possibility of a magical witness. He'd already disabled all the security devices he'd found in the investigator's office, but he had no way of being sure that the watcher had really gone, or that he wasn't being observed magically or astrally. "I was never here," he told Foote, "and you've never heard of the Crypt. You are likely to live much longer if you erase all records of the address, as well as these photos, and any photos you may have been foolish enough to take of me. Can *you* remember *that*?"

"Sure," said the investigator, trying to sound braver than he felt.

The Hatter nodded and tossed him a certified credstick. "Buying yourself a better grade of liquor would probably increase your life expectancy, too," he added. "This should be more than enough. And you'd better replace that lock, too."

The last remaining bookstore in Pike Place Market was scarcely larger than Mute's bathroom, but it was packed with antique comics, books and magazines, as well as a small collection of fiction chips and disks. Mute was examining a signed first edition of *The Chrysalids* while stroking the shop's cat, but she looked up as soon as she heard the door open, then looked down again as a bald, ebon-skinned dwarf approached her. The dwarf looked around at the store—empty apart from the cat and the manager—and murmured, "Good book?"

"Yes." She nodded at the manager, who disappeared behind a curtain. There was a click as the door locked. "What's the job?"

The dwarf, 8-ball, stared at the cat. "You remember that squat we hid in after that Brackhaven run went sour?"

"That hole down in Puyallup?"

8-ball nodded. "Doc Czarnecki called me. Some fragger's bought the land and wants to kick everyone out. No more clinic, no more illegal data tap, no more sanctuary for runners who've been ratted out to security . . ."

"Did you ever find out who was behind that?" asked Mute softly. It had been more than a year since she, 8-ball and Sumatra had smuggled a decker inside Brackhaven Investments' offices, then escaped to find their rigger and getaway car gone and their escape route cut off by armed guards. The decker, Mandy Mandelbrot, had been mowed down while they were diving for cover. Sumatra had been wounded, and had fought to remain conscious long enough to summon a hearth spirit to provide concealment while they ran. Mute and 8-ball had all but dragged him back to the lift, then blasted their way through a third-floor window and rappelled to the ground. The rigger, Mercedes Benzene, had never been seen again.

8-ball shook his head. "I still can't believe that Mercy would have done that to us—especially not to Mandy. I thought it might be their fixer, but that doesn't make sense either. Maybe someone in the building got lucky, realized the car didn't belong there . . ." He didn't sound convinced. "I guess we'll never know. Anyway, Czarnecki said they needed help, so I said I'd be there. They can't afford to pay us, but I've stayed there when I couldn't afford to pay them, either. It should only be a day or two, and I don't have anything better to do right now. How about you?"

Mute nodded. "Count me in."

*   *   *

Hare studied the pictures Foote had taken and shook his head. "I don't recognize any of them, but I'm not an expert on magicians. How about you?"

"No," said the Hatter, sprawling in one of Hare's armchairs. "There's an ork named Pinhead Pierce on our resources database; if it's the same one, and he certainly matches the description, he works as a bouncer at the Big O sometimes, and plays the drums when they let him or need to clear the place. There used to be an illegal jackpoint at the club, so he probably knows some shadowrunners, and may even have worked as muscle on a few runs, but I don't think we need to worry about him. We don't have a name for the other ork; I've run the picture through the facial recognition software, but it's not clear enough to come up with any positive matches, just a list of possibles. The magician who lives there is supposed to be strictly a healer, but a good one, so Lord alone knows why he lives in that dump . . . He may have set up some magical defenses, so we may need a magician as well as some muscle."

"Who were you going to use? Genocide George and his team?"

"No. If it's a shadowrunner hangout, they might have friends down there, and even George charges extra for shooting his friends." "Genocide George" Sequoia was a Makah warrior who'd been discharged from his tribe's military and become one of Seattle's most trigger-happy mercenaries: he'd once blown a hole in a teammate's abdomen with an assault cannon so he could get a better shot at one of his enemies. "And word is he's just pulled off a big job against Mitsuhama and is resting up. I did think of hiring a gang, but the place is in neutral territory between the Forever Tacoma, Black Rain and Reality Hacker zones: I assume nobody wants it very badly. I've had some contact with the Reality Hackers, but I don't think they'll risk going in armed, and gangers are terrible at keeping secrets. No, there's a squad of mercs I've hired before. They're strictly cash up front and expenses, no percentage, and they don't ask any embarrassing questions. And they're from way out of town, so they won't have any sentimental attachment to this place. There wasn't a magician on their team last time, but I'm sure we can find one they'll work with if they can't."

"What about the one you've been dating? The blonde with the legs and the pheromone glands?"

"I don't mix business with pleasure, and Elena's strictly for pleasure. Have you managed to find plans for the building?"

"Lost in the crash," said the elf apologetically. "Do you want to send a drone over? Infrared and ground-penetrating radar should give us a pretty good map. I can make one disappear from stores for a while without anybody noticing. Do your mercs have someone who can fly it?"

"Their rigger, Griffin, is pretty good." He looked around the tiny sitting room. "If this works, you can get out of this closet. Move upstairs a few floors. Maybe even get a window."

Hare snorted, and picked up his deck. "This is all the view I need," he said. "Though some more scenery in the bedroom occasionally wouldn't go amiss. How soon do you want the drone?"

"The mercs will start arriving at midnight. Wallace, the commander, and Griffin will be on the first flight; I'll speak to them then." He glanced at the chessboard on the table between them. "Fancy a quick game?"

It was an hour after sunset when 8-ball drove his heavily accessorized Land Rover over the litter and rubble outside the Crypt and parked it between the remnants of two inner walls, glancing frequently at the satellite navigation receiver and radar readouts on his dashboard as he positioned it. "Worried about the feng shui?" asked Mute, yawning.

The dwarf grinned, and flicked a switch. A heads-up display appeared on the windshield, and he checked the rangefinder before moving the vehicle forward another half a meter. "Grenade launcher," he explained. "Minimum range. You want to get your stuff?"

Mute grabbed her small backpack. Unlike the weapons specialist, she preferred to travel light, the better to move quickly and quietly. With her free hand, she picked up one of 8-ball's cases, and barely managed not to grunt from the effort. "What have you got in here?"

8-ball glanced at the case, looking at the notches on its rim. "Assault cannon."

"Is that all?"

"And the ammo, of course. I may have put a few grenades in there as well." He picked up another two cases, and hauled them out of the back of the Land Rover. "This one's a little lighter . . ."

Mute wrinkled her nose at this sexist remark, considered that he might also have been taking a shot at the fact that she was human, and followed him toward the entrance. A concrete ramp was set against the sublevel's east wall, and Pinhead Pierce and a purple-haired dwarf girl who looked barely old enough to shave were leaning up against the painted pillar near its foot. The ork greeted the shadowrunners with an extravagant salute. 8-ball looked at the dented baseball bat in Pierce's right hand and the big revolver tucked into the waistband of his ancient cargo pants. "Is that thing loaded?" he asked.

Pierce looked down at the Warhawk as though he'd never seen it before, tucked the bat under his left elbow, drew the revolver with his right hand, broke it and looked into the cylinder. "Nah," he said finally. "Didn't think so."

"You ever fired it?"

"Yeah, but never *at* anyone. But I'm pretty sure I didn't reload."

"Where did you get it?"

"Took it off some fragger at the O a week ago. Figured he couldn't use it anymore anyway, not with two broken arms. Been meaning to pawn it, but haven't gotten around to it yet."

8-ball shook his head. "I have some ammo for that in one of these cases; I'll give it to you later. When I do, you keep the gun in your right hand, okay? Not in your pants."

"Okay."

The weapons specialist sighed and turned to the dwarf girl, who was gripping a Remington Roomsweeper and looking nervous. 8-ball hoped that it was loaded with gel, not shot; knowing Boanerges' distaste for lethal weapons, that seemed likely. "Is *yours* loaded?"

"Yes, sir."

"Safety on?"

"Yes," she said, then looked. "Yes," she repeated.

"What's your name?"

"Didge."

"Short for Dr. Digitalis," Pierce explained, chuckling. He glanced at 8-ball's face and decided that making short jokes in front of the weapons specialist was probably a bad idea. He coughed softly and stared up the ramp at the cloudy sky.

8-ball ignored him. "Do you know who I am, Didge?"

"No," she said quietly. "But *he* did, and you know who *she* is, so I thought you had to be friends. And we're not expecting any trouble tonight. No outsiders ever come here at night."

That, 8-ball reflected, was mostly true. "Okay. Where's Boanerges?"

"There's a meeting in his lodge," said Pierce. "You're to go straight in."

8-ball nodded. "Where should I put these? I wouldn't want the kids to start playing with them."

"Leave them with me."

The dwarf put his cases down behind the pillar. Mute did the same, then shrugged her pack onto her back. 8-ball led the way into the underground shantytown, a multicolored labyrinth of cubical dividers, cartons and crates and other scavenged or stolen building materials, decorated with posters and printouts and painted in a variety of styles. It was dark in the maze except for the illumination leaking out around the curtains that gave a vestige of privacy to the residents' quarters. Both shadowrunners could see in infrared, and there were faint heat traces of other people on either side of the serpentine corridors. "You been here recently?" asked Mute.

"I grew up here, and spare me the height jokes. I've heard them all before." He turned left at a crooked T-junction and kept walking until they heard raised voices. The dwarf paused. "Lankin," he muttered sourly.

"Long Lankin?"

"Yeah. You know him?"

She shook her head. "Is there anyone in this biz you *haven't* worked with?"

Instead of answering, 8-ball drew back the threadbare smoke-colored curtain and they walked into a crowded, candle-lit medicine lodge. Long Lankin, the tallest and blackest elf Mute had ever seen, was standing as he addressed the gathering, making a case for negotiating with the intruders. His head was slightly bowed, not in respect, but to avoid bumping it on the ceiling. "If they'll give us more time, you can find another place."

"Snake wants me to stay here," said Boanerges softly. "The rest of you can move, if you feel you must. I'm staying until she tells me to go."

There was a moment's silence before a short ugly ork in a once-white lab coat, who Mute recognized as "Cutter" Czarnecki, the street doc, asked, "What about transport? The hospital's not going to be easy to move, not to mention our patients."

"We get them to pay for transport," said Lankin. "A bus and a truck should be enough, and cost much less to hire than they must have spent buying this land—"

"That's assuming they *have* bought it," interrupted a redheaded elf in faded jeans and a "Cthulhu for President" T-shirt. "This guy Foote didn't show us any proof of that."

"You want us to call Lone Star and check, Ratty?"

The redhead unzipped his cyberdeck case, giving Lankin a nasty grin. "Do you know what they call you in England, Lank?"

"Ratatosk, you make a good point," said Boanerges patiently. "Can you hack into the council's database and find out?"

"No problem," said the decker, and Mute stared at him in amazement. Ratatosk was a legendary figure: Mercurio Switch's most promising student and protégé, and one of the best freelance deckers on the West Coast. Mute looked around the room at the others gathered there: an androgynous blond troll in studded leather, Sumatra the street shaman, two middle-aged human males (one Anglo, one

Native American), a neatly groomed dwarf with bandaged fingers, and a black-clad Japanese elf woman of almost breathtaking beauty.

8-ball cleared his throat. "This is it? Where's the rest of your coven?"

Boanerges shrugged. "Kaneda and Joji are in Japan, Caitlin's in the Tir, Marlowe's in Everett preparing for an astral quest . . . Jinx and Mish are doing a stock take of the herbs and the medicines. So there's only the six of us, but it *was* short notice. I'm glad you could make it. Did you bring any food?"

"I brought weapons," said 8-ball shortly. "And Mute, here—best infiltration and extraction specialist I know. Mute, you know Boanerges and Sumatra; have you run with any of these other chummers?" When she didn't answer immediately, he nodded at the mixed group sitting on rugs on the floor. "The scrawny redhead is Ratatosk. The big blond is Beef Patty."

The leather-clad troll gave a friendly smile, and 8-ball turned to the silver-haired Anglo in the lined coat. "This is Professor Magnusson, Maggie to his friends. The Space Needle impersonation is Lankin, whose rep I'm sure you know. The short guy with the Zeiss eyes and the damaged digits is Zurich, tech wiz, and the human chummer with the extra holes in his head is Crane, best rigger ever to be dishonorably—"

"We've met," said Crane curtly, then shrugged. "Long time ago, and in another country. No hard feelings?"

"No," said Mute. "Was that—"

"Why I was drummed out? No, that happened later; my CO and I had a small disagreement about my taking out a plane without authorization. But at least I didn't sell the one *I* stole." He extended a hand, and after a slight hesitation, Mute shook it.

8-ball smiled. "And last but not least," he finished with a flourish, "the lady nearest the door is Yoko Aruki."

Mute clenched her teeth to prevent her jaw dropping, and was glad that the poor light and her dusky complexion made it difficult for anyone to notice whether she was blushing. Dozens of street samurai and ninja wannabes had spent millions on cyberware trying to emulate Yoko Aruki, the stealthy and reportedly bulletproof warrior-adept who could use almost any small object as a shuriken, and had once killed a yakuza oyabun while he was surrounded by a dozen elite bodyguards. Mute bowed and took a deep breath before righting herself. "Honored to meet you all."

"I'm afraid honor is all we can offer," said Yoko wryly. "And shelter, and healing for those who need it. There are another twenty-seven people living here at present—you'll have met at least two of them on your way in—but very few of them have any sort of combat training or experience, and most of that is with a knife or a stick. Maybe half of them could manage to look intimidating. I'm hoping that will be enough."

"You don't know why these people want the land?"

"No," said Ratatosk. "That's been the main topic of discussion so far."

"There's one obvious possibility," said 8-ball. "This isn't the only squat in the area, but it's the only one between here and the freeway that's weatherproof and lightproof enough for many of the people here. This location is good protection for people who are allergic to sunlight, or to being seen, particularly by Lone Star or the corps. If whoever this is can shut us down, this would make an ideal base for clearing out a huge part of Puyallup—large enough for an airport or a military base."

"Or anything else the sararimen don't want in their backyard," said Lankin. "A prison farm. A toxic-waste dump."

Boanerges shrugged. "I hope you're wrong. This place was pretty toxic when I first came here, and we've put a lot of work into making it livable, even bringing in clean soil for a garden. The background count is almost down to zero now, though I hate to think what's in some of those drums and containers we have lying around up above. I keep asking Pierce to move them, but he likes the different tones they make when he plays them."

"Can we use those to create barricades, or traps?" asked 8-ball. "It would be subtle, since they just look like rubbish."

Boanerges looked at Yoko. "This is out of my line of

expertise. We can handle magical security, if you'll take care of the physical."

The adept nodded. "Okay. 8-ball, you said you brought weapons?"

The snake shaman shook his head as he looked at the armory spread over three of the dining hall's rickety tables. One assault cannon, two AK-98s, two smartguns, six pistols ranging from Predators to derringers, a shotgun, a stun gun, a stun baton, a crossbow, a machete, a short sword, three survival knives and a small case of grenades as well as a large collection of potentially lethal cooking and gardening utensils. "Do we need all of these?" he asked.

"It's not enough," said Yoko almost simultaneously. "Not if we want to scare them into negotiating. If everyone has a gun . . ."

Boanerges shuddered. "That sounds like a recipe for a massacre. Mutually assured destruction. Most of the people here have never even fired a gun before."

"I'm hoping they won't have to *fire* them. Those who have training should get live ammo; the rest will be better off with gel, or blanks, especially as there's no way we can armor everyone who's here." To Yoko's disappointment, no one contradicted her.

"Even the kids?" said Boanerges.

Yoko sighed. "Okay. No guns for under twelves who have an adult who'll protect them. How many does that leave out?"

"Six, maybe seven or eight . . . something like that. Ms. Hotop would know better than I do, since she's in charge of educating all the kids here."

"That should be okay. I don't want to have to kill anyone, but if we can do enough damage to their vehicles that they have to walk back . . ."

Beef Patty grinned. "I'd like to see them try to call a cab down here," she said.

"I'd rather not be responsible for any of the opposition getting killed, either," said Boanerges, shaking his head. "And if they try walking through this neighborhood at night looking as though they've got anything worth stealing . . . there's plenty of chipheads around here who'd gut someone for a warm coat or a pair of shoes, and a few body shops that'll buy secondhand eyes with no questions asked. Let's make sure they have a safe way out."

"We're not going to have to worry about it; if they're professionals, they'll have a back-up plan," 8-ball replied. "Or good DocWagon coverage. But gel rounds would be a good idea anyway; less chance of friendly fire casualties. I should be able to get them by morning, if you can tell me what calibers you need, and a few extra vests and helmets, but that many guns . . . that'll take serious fragging time and/or money."

Boanerges turned to Beef Patty. "Could we get guns from your friends in the gang?"

"I can ask," said the troll, "but I dunno. The Black Rains are a bit twitchy after that drive-by drek last month. Asking them to reduce their weapons supply might make things worse."

Ratatosk snapped his fingers. "Doc, do you still have that jackpoint here?"

"Sure, next to the library."

"Great. Give me half an hour; I have an idea where you can get your guns."

4

The honeymoon suite at the Renton Inn was decorated in a fake Scandinavian style that instantly set the Hatter's teeth on edge, but the price included good electronic and magical security as well as a huge bed and a trideo screen that was even wider—and it was far enough from the Aztechnology Pyramid that there was little danger of the mercenaries guessing who the Hatter worked for, or of the Hatter's superiors finding out what he was doing in his spare time. Hare had carefully isolated the trideo from the hotel's network, and the squad's mage was sitting on the bed staring into astral, watching for spells or intruders. Griffin, the squad's rigger, stared at the aerial photos on the huge screen and traced the site of the former Monolith warehouse with a laser pointer. "There's not much left above ground," he said. "No roofing, nothing left of the second floor except some rubble, but some stretches of wall are still standing. Highest near the corners, as is to be expected; these bathrooms are mostly intact except for the roof. It seems unlikely the toilets are still in use, but the showers probably are; these look like rainwater tanks. No electricity, though . . . at least, no lights or heat above ground. The brighter spots are vegetation; they may be trying to grow some of their own food. This box may be a car, probably an SUV; they've camouflaged it pretty well, but if you enhance it a little, you can still see the tire tracks and the warmth of the engine.

"This is the ramp you told me about, northeast corner of the sublevel. I can't see any other exits, though the stairwell here may still be useable. The buildings around this are in even worse shape—no roof, no basement, not even much left in the way of walls—but they're unoccupied, as far as I can tell."

Hare smiled to himself. He had already checked out the buildings surrounding the Monolith lot: ruined warehouses, small factories, and a lunch bar. All had been officially vacant for at least twenty years, and so thoroughly stripped that they were no more than crumbling shells. "What about the radar?"

Griffin nodded, and a new image flashed onto the screen. "Ground-penetrating view shows no tunnels except for the sewer pipes and other standard conduits—maybe big enough for a snooper drone, but not for people. We can't get a very good picture of the underground levels, unfortunately. Most of the stuff down there is almost invisible to radar; some metal, a little concrete, but not much structural apart from those pillars, which you can see here. They're probably the only thing holding the roof up. But *this* is interesting: some sort of vault or bunker under the middle of the floor. Metal-lined, and while I can't tell you how deep it is, from above, it looks the right size to be a cargo container." He scratched his aquiline nose. "Anyway, that'll give you a good idea of the scale of that level. Room for a hundred bunks, easy."

"Go back a few slides," said the Hatter. "The low-angle view. I thought I saw something in the background, another building . . ."

Griffin scrolled through the images. "That?" he said, indicating the edge of a funnel-shaped structure.

"Yes."

"I have a better shot of that . . . here. It's a cooling tower from an old power station."

Hatter nodded. Several geothermal power stations had been built on the lava flow from the 2017 eruption of Mt. Rainier, but later abandoned.

"How tall is it?"

"Seven or eight floors."

"Intact?"

"Seems to be. It was built to withstand any subsequent eruptions, and so should be pretty robust."

"Thanks," said the Hatter, and turned to the mage the mercenaries had brought with them—an attractive young woman named Lori. She was round-faced and short for an elf, scarcely taller than the lanky rigger who looked at her with obvious affection, and her straight, shoulder-length haircut hid her ears: she could easily have been mistaken for human, and presumably didn't care. "If you looked at the site in astral, could you tell us how many people really *are* down in that cellar?"

"If it's not too thoroughly protected, yes."

"Good," said the Hatter. "We may be able to provide them with food, transport . . . anything that would entice them to leave without a fight. Makes it easier on everybody."

Ratatosk had never liked the look of Lone Star's icon in the Matrix—an adobe-colored square block marked with the Lone Star insignia. The architecture, an old-West–style fort complete with cannons, went beyond mere ugly functionalism to being distinctly forbidding: it gave the impression that visitors were as likely to be greeted with gunfire as with assistance.

Of course, few people went there looking for the sort of assistance that Ratatosk was seeking.

The icon of a large red squirrel—Ratatosk's custom-designed representation of the interface between his brain and the Matrix—slipped through the gate into a bustling representation of Seattle's South Main Street circa 1884, and headed for the sheriff's office. Ratatosk checked that the secret door hidden behind the wanted posters hadn't been removed or booby-trapped with intrusion countermeasures— popularly known as IC, or ice—then tapped in the appropriate code. In the Matrix, the squirrel sniffed at the wall and scratched gently at the crack between two boards. The posters parted like curtains, and the squirrel scampered into a dim corridor. Ratatosk had entered a Lone Star host through a backdoor access.

He found the appropriate dataline and zoomed along it

to a datastore protected by low-intensity IC in the likeness of giant Gila monsters patrolling its adobe walls. The squirrel produced a small card from an invisible pocket and flashed it past an arrow slit in the wall. The steel door swung open, and he scrambled inside the store.

The datastore looked like a nineteenth-century library, the books on its shelves ranging from thin dime novels with bright yellow covers to huge, iron-bound, chained and padlocked Bibles. Ratatosk felt that the tarantulas, rattlesnakes and Gila monsters scuttling around the floor and along the shelves rather spoiled the illusion. He knew these creatures represented probe IC that would check his credentials each time he tried to read a file inside the datastore; if he fragged up, or even if he tried to read too many files, the probe IC would summon Lone Star deckers armed with special utilities that would let them track Ratatosk to his jackpoint and stun him. The deckers' icons mostly looked like the classic movie cop Dirty Harry in Lone Star uniform, and many of them had a similar attitude—preferring to attack with a lethal version of the black hammer utility first and perform autopsies later.

Ratatosk cautiously opened a small file drawer. If the metaphor held, this would be the library's card catalog, an index that would point him to the directory he needed. He discovered that the list of passwords that guaranteed access to the information he wanted was kept in a locked cabinet. The squirrel icon plucked a stiff hair from its tail and picked the old-fashioned lock; when the door swung open, Ratatosk found himself standing at the edge of a large bubbling tar pit.

He swore silently as he analyzed the security measures. The gray-level tar pit IC could infect his deck with a viral code that could not only crash his deck but corrupt everything in its memory. Worse still, there was probably even more dangerous black IC under the graphite-colored surface, monofilament-sharp slivers of code that could shred his software and tear all the way through to the interface between the datajack and his brain, burning out circuits and neurons alike and potentially causing a fatal stroke. Ratatosk had seen too many victims of black IC and black hammer, with blood and worse leaking from their ears, to take any unnecessary risks.

On the other hand, he mused, the password file would not only enable him to upload the schedule he'd come here for, it would allow him into other local Lone Star datastores for as long as the passwords remained valid. If he didn't set off any alarms, that might be as much as a week . . . and he could trade that information with other deckers, for other passwords or nuyen. He took a deep breath, and decided the risk was worth it.

The squirrel leaped lightly to a solid-looking patch of ground, using its tail for balance. It crossed the tar pit carefully, testing each patch of ground as if it were climbing through the tiny branches at the top of a tree, watching for triggers that might suddenly turn into damaging viral codes in the guise of dire wolves or saber-toothed tigers. He had a slow program loaded, one powerful enough to make the IC move as sluggishly as a glacier, and a seriously damaging attack utility in reserve, but hoped he wouldn't need either; he'd always preferred to rely on stealth. After what felt like an hour of nerve-jangling paranoia but was only seconds of real time, a bursting bubble of tar revealed the corner of a small book. The squirrel plucked it out of the tar, produced a silk handkerchief from another hidden pocket, and wiped the cover clean (removing any IC in the process) without getting anything stuck to his russet fur.

Ratatosk opened the slim volume and scanned the few pages for likely-looking passwords. The words kept trying to move around, but the squirrel stroked the book cover, and they settled into place. Ratatosk decrypted the file contents as quickly as possible and searched for the passwords he needed. He chose keywords cautiously until he had three likely-looking logon IDs and passwords—the most he could try without the risk of bringing a posse of defensive deckers down on his head. Hoping that none of the passwords had been corrupted by the scramble IC, he leaped out of the tar pit and back into the library. Quickly scanning the shelves again, the squirrel chose a padlocked ledger in Wells Fargo green—the file of transport schedules. He ran a claw over one of the passwords, which morphed into a key. He tried using this to open the ledger, but it remained locked: insufficient authorization.

Ratatosk swore silently again, thankful at least that the book's leather cover hadn't morphed into a ravenous mouth full of teeth, and tried the second logon ID and password. This combination gave him read-only access, but that was all he needed to download the file: unlike last week, this time he wasn't inside Lone Star trying to edit a criminal record. The ledger sprang open, revealing lines of names and figures in neat copperplate script.

Seven seconds later, he logged off. Everything went black for a moment, and then the shadows slowly assumed recognizable shapes. Ratatosk felt momentarily disoriented as he tried to remember where he'd left his body. "You okay?" asked a huge troll.

The decker blinked, and remembered that he was in the Crypt's magical library, with Beef Patty standing guard over his meat. "Fine," he said, then took a deep breath and added, "Let's go."

"The bad news," Ratatosk said when he returned to the meeting in Boanerges' colorfully cluttered medicine lodge, "is that the land *has* been legally sold, to the Giuoco Piano Company, which is owned by the Fedorov Family Trust. Neither existed until last week, and both are registered in Konigsberg . . . which means that there's no way we can find out who really owns them, because Konigsberg's commercial confidentiality laws are murder and their databases are in sealed systems. The contact details on the district council's database are for the trust's law firm, which is also based in Konigsberg, and represents a few hundred shell companies. And before you ask, they paid up front with a certified credstick.

"The *good* news is that I think I can get us the guns we need, tonight."

"Where from?" asked Yoko.

"Lone Star."

"You want to rip off *Lone Star?*" asked Lankin, obviously appalled.

"Not exactly," Ratatosk replied, grinning. "Just a few

slightly bent cops who have a sideline using Lone Star property. You know how any weapons that get confiscated are supposed to be destroyed? Well, some of them aren't exactly destroyed. The man who runs the junkyard picks out the weapons with good resale value and finds buyers for them. His understanding with the cops is that these guns'll either go to collectors, or get shipped outside the UCAS, so they never get used in a crime locally and Lone Star never has to explain why they weren't melted down as required by law. He backs this up by having the cops who deliver the confiscated weapons to his yard also transport to the buyers the guns that're being sold—that way, in addition to getting their cut, the cops know where the weapons have gone, in case they ever *are* used again in a way that Lone Star finds embarrassing. The cops who make the run think of it as a perk, and management either doesn't know about it or ignores it. Same with the city. Anyway, the van is plainwrap, and we don't hit it on its way to the junkyard, when it's on official business—we ambush it on the way back, when it's supposedly deadheading but is actually carrying a load of illegal guns. If we can do it without damaging the cops or the vehicle, they won't even report it. Of course, the only surefire way to do that is with magic."

Yoko considered this. "You're sure there's one of these deliveries happening tonight?"

"Pretty sure. Deliveries to the junkyard get made a couple of times a week, and there's one leaving the evidence storeroom at four a.m.; I checked the schedule. The *last* delivery included some military weapons they took from those Humanis fraggers they convicted last week—plenty of time to pick out the good stuff and find some buyers by now. I think it's worth a chance." He shrugged. "Unfortunately, I don't know where the meet is happening, so we can't ambush them; we'll have to tail them from the junkyard to the meet. So we'll need two cars."

Yoko nodded. "Okay . . . but if the buyers are already there, and they're already armed, just keep driving. I'd rather try buying weapons from the all-night pawnshops than have any of you fail to get back by sunrise. Maggie, do you know any sleep spells?"

"Of course," said Magnusson mildly without looking up from his pocket computer.

"Sumatra?"

"Only stunbolt," said the rat shaman apologetically.

"Okay." She looked around the circle. "8-ball, you're the team leader. Ratatosk, you cover them from the Matrix. Let's roll."

Cooper yawned. He disliked night shifts, but he also disliked day shifts and most other forms of work, and at least the night shift paid better. Particularly these milk runs to and from the junkyard. He'd had the Roadmaster on autopilot on the way there, and even though he was yawning his head off he switched it to manual for the return journey so the unauthorized detour wouldn't be recorded. It was raining heavily enough that the autopilot would have slowed the van down to walking speed anyway, even though there were hardly any other vehicles in sight at this hour.

Godley had gone back to sleep as soon as the van had been unloaded and loaded, but that was his right as a sergeant and Cooper knew he'd wake up as soon as they reached the rendezvous with the buyer so he didn't miss out on his cut. He looked at the map projected on the dash; another seven klicks to the Stuffer Shack, the buyer and some coffee that was slightly better than the drek they served at the station. He waited until he could see the familiar double-S sign through the rain, barely a block ahead, then thumbed the radio mic and told the dispatcher they were taking fifteen minutes personal time. Godley stirred and opened one bleary eye. "Are we there?"

Cooper sped up as he swung into the parking lot, then decelerated and came to a screeching halt a few centimeters from a concrete barrier. "We are now. No sign of the contact, though."

Godley closed his eye again. "Wake me up when he gets here," he muttered. Cooper snorted, pulled up the collar of his armor jacket and stepped out into the rain.

Magnusson switched on the autopilot, picked up his old-fashioned binoculars and peered through the back window of Patty's Superkombi as the gray Roadmaster receded into the distance. "They've stopped at the Stuffer Shack on 136th Street East and the driver's gone in," he said into his earplug phone. "His partner's still in the van, but I can't see him clearly enough to cast a spell. Don't know whether this is the meet or just a pit stop."

"Understood," replied Ratatosk, still in the library at the Crypt, and jacked in. It took him only a few seconds to locate the Stuffer Shack's CPU, take control of the security cameras, and isolate the Panicbutton so that any calls for help would go unanswered.

"Anyone else in the lot?" asked 8-ball.

"One three-door Jackrabbit and an old Americar," said Magnusson. "If either is the buyer, the load must be fairly small."

"See you there," said 8-ball, tromping the accelerator. The two vehicles had been shadowing the Roadmaster from the time it left the junkyard, with one following and one a few blocks ahead. The dwarf looked at Sumatra, who was hunched over in the passenger seat, and grinned. "It's showtime."

Pinhead Pierce rolled the rusty drum into place, blocking a gap in the wall, then thumped once on the lid and listened with the air of a connoisseur. "What's in these things?" asked Beef Patty, who had picked up a half-empty drum under each arm and was walking across the rubble.

"Dunno."

"Can we empty them out?"

"That'd ruin the sound. I spent months puttin' this set together!"

Patty shook her head. "Hey, d'you know what they call someone who spends all his time hanging out with musicians?"

"A drummer, right?" said Pierce. "Ha-ha. If I had a nuyen for every time I'd heard *that* one, I coulda bought this place myself."

The troll smiled as she dropped the drums and pushed them into position. "You ever considered working for a living?"

"What for?" Pierce picked up a length of wire and began stringing it across a gap in the wall. "I got all I need right here. Never had anythin' else, so I don't miss it. 'Sides, you can't be a great musician unless you're hungry—or even a great drummer, before you say it. You can't let a day job or anything else stop you goin' where you need to go. What do *you* do when you're not hangin' around here? Apart from killin' people?"

Patty shook her head, then picked up another two drums. "I stop people killing my friends, and my friends stop people killing me."

"Friends are good," Pierce agreed, "but no one's tryin' to kill me."

Patty grunted. "Not yet, maybe. Hand me that entrenching tool. No, the thing that looks like a shovel. Yeah, that one."

The Roadmaster's windows were too heavily tinted for Sumatra to see through, and 8-ball's thermographic vision showed only that there was someone warm inside. 8-ball tested the passenger-side door, which proved to be locked. The same for the driver's side and the cargo doors. The dwarf took out his maglock passkey just as a cop came sprinting back toward the van, a cup of coffee in his right hand and the remote key for the car in his left. He hesitated for just a moment before dropping the cup and reaching for his gun, giving Sumatra enough time to cast a stunbolt spell, which he cast with all the force he could summon and no regard for the drain. The cop hit the ground, and Sumatra wavered as though he were about to do the same, but grabbed on to the side of the van. "Grab the keys," he muttered.

"You okay?" asked the dwarf, as he pried the keys from the cop's fingers and ran back toward the passenger-side door.

The shaman nodded weakly, then looked up as the Superkombi drove into the parking lot, blocking the exit.

"Okay," said 8-ball. "Get down in case someone starts shooting." He drew the narcoject pistol out of his belt, and raised his wristphone to his chin. "Maggie? Get over here and get ready with the magic fingers." He kept the pistol trained at the door, but there was no sign of movement, so he risked a quick glance at the Stuffer Shack. No one else seemed interested in venturing into the downpour. 8-ball reached into a pocket for two folded caltrops, flicked them open with a skill born of long practice and ran across the parking lot, dropping one spike each behind the front passenger wheels of the American and the Jackrabbit. The caltrops were of toughened transparent plastic—difficult to see even at the best of times, and almost invisible in water—and sharp enough to shred ordinary tires. The Roadmaster, he knew, would have runflat wheels, and the spikes wouldn't even slow it down. Magnusson came running across the parking lot. 8-ball pressed the button on the key chain to unlock the doors, Sumatra swung the door open, and Magnusson hit the cop inside with a stunbolt before he'd even opened his eyes. It made no apparent difference. Sumatra closed the door again, being careful not to slam it, and 8-ball muttered, "Grab the other cop, put him back in his seat. We don't want anyone running over him."

The ork shrugged, picked up the unconscious body and ungently dragged it toward the driver's side of the Roadmaster, while 8-ball opened the cargo compartment and stared inside. "Not bad," he said, quickly opening two duffel bags. "A couple of silenced HK-227s, a Skorpion, and . . ." He counted quickly. "Six FN HARs. Eight guns and a piece of drek, and no ammo."

Magnusson shrugged. "It'll do. I hope we won't have to use them, though if you and Yoko could give a few quick lessons . . ."

"There's a shotgun in the cab," said Sumatra, "and they've got pistols, stun guns, armor vests—"

"No," said the 8-ball. "If we take those, they'll have to report that they were robbed, and there'll be an investigation. This gear doesn't officially exist anymore, so they're not going to tell anyone it's gone."

Sumatra let it drop, though he clearly wasn't happy about it. "What about the buyer?" he asked. "Whoever it is is bound to be carrying money, and maybe some guns as well."

"I suggest we get out of here before that becomes an issue."

"Right," said 8-ball, picking up the heavier of the duffels. When he'd loaded both bags into the Land Rover, he tossed the keys to the truck into the Roadmaster's cab and shut the door. "Pleasant dreams," he said, smiling.

The shadowrunners were a block and a half away when a Eurovan pulled into the parking lot and four orks in camouflage armor jackets climbed out and surrounded the Roadmaster.

For security reasons, the mercs had flown in on five different flights, meeting up again in the cheap hotel the Hatter had booked for them. They'd all stayed in worse accommodations before, but even the largest bedrooms were small, and while the ceilings were high enough for ogres or elves, the building obviously hadn't been designed for trolls, and Crabbe had bumped his head trying to get through the doorway. The rooms hadn't been designed for meetings either, thought Quinn sourly, but she knew that it would be a mistake to ask the mercs to gather in the bar.

She looked around and mentally did a roll call. She was relatively new to this team, and she was still amazed by the motley mix of humans and metahumans Wallace, their leader, had managed to gather around himself. Hartz was eating something that stank like pepper spray; she didn't know whether it was characteristic of all ogres, but it seemed that if he wasn't actually on duty, he was feeding his misshapen face. Dutch was sitting upwind of him, sharpening his second-best knife. Quinn considered him one of the best at knife-work she'd ever seen—and that was saying something, considering how many places she'd served where knives were the enemy's primary weapon. Crabbe was dozing beside the door, sitting up because there wasn't room on the floor for his three-meter frame and beautifully curved horns. He would have been difficult to miss at any time, even without his habit of drawing attention to himself by affecting a muscle shirt and board shorts in any weather. With the ogre, the ork and the troll checked off her list,

Quinn looked around the room for her fellow humans. Lewis was sitting at the writing-desk, reading an old-fashioned paperback book—or photographing the pages and storing the images in his headware memory for later reference. Knight was cleaning the gun in his gleaming custom cyberarm. Kat was asleep with her eyes open but switched off; her hand razors slid out as she dreamed, then retracted. Wallace, Lori and Griffin were still at the meet with the Johnson, so that left four team members unaccounted for. "Has anyone seen Lily?"

"Here," said the dwarf from behind the telecom. She raised her manicured hand so that it was visible, and waved.

"Okay. What about Carpenter, Severn and King?"

"King and Carpenter are waiting for the pups to pass through Customs," said Dutch. He yawned—always an impressive sight, because his mouth was huge, and his sharp tusks protruded almost to the tips of his pendulous earlobes. "A vet's looking them over. King called in, said they'd probably be another half hour, an hour at the outside. He couldn't decide whether the vet was scared of the barghests, or just hadn't seen very many in his career so was taking his time. Severn was on the same flight, and he's hanging around to catch a ride with them."

Quinn nodded. She trusted Severn; he and Hartz had served with her in the Desert Wars. She was mildly irritated that King had reported to Dutch rather than to her, but the ork had been Wallace's exec before she'd been recruited into the company, and King seemed to have an old-fashioned prejudice against female soldiers, especially good-looking ones. Or maybe it was only female officers he disliked, or redheads, because there seemed to be no friction between him and Kat, or Lily, or Lori.

Well, she thought, that was everyone accounted for, if not exactly present and arguably not correct. It bothered her that Wallace didn't require his team to show even a minimum of military discipline when off duty. Between the nonregulation haircuts (Griffin's shaggy blond mane and Lily's braids) and the nonregulation footwear (Lori's moccasins, Kat's sneakers, and Knight's cowboy boots) it was hard to tell if they were even prepared to go into combat.

But she didn't doubt their loyalty to Wallace and to each other, even if she wasn't sure what most of them thought of her.

"Okay," she said, with only a hint of a sigh. "Everybody check their gear, then grab some sack time. Reveille at five hundred hours, breakfast in the dining room at five fifteen, and room service is *not* an option. Dismissed."

The squatters lined up along the street ranged in age from a seventy-one-year-old retired teacher to two of her twelve-year-old pupils. Yoko appraised them, careful to keep her expression neutral; she'd taught unarmed combat techniques to children younger than this, but for this class had imposed an age requirement. Five of the teenagers— Akira, Leila, Easy, Hook and Pike—were promising students; a few others had attended some of her self-defense classes before becoming bored or scared.

It was darker outside than it was in most rooms of the Crypt; the sliver-thin moon wouldn't rise for hours, gray clouds obscured most of the stars, and there were no working streetlights for several blocks in any direction, most of them having been used for target practice. This left most of the humans in the class at a decided disadvantage, but Yoko had long suspected that fair fights were almost as rare as military intelligence. She hefted a meter-long stick in her left hand as she walked along the line, and said, "I'm hoping that none of us will have to fight, but the people who are trying to oust us will approach us assuming we will resist. They'll probably have better armor than we do, and more guns, and better night vision than some of you. The only advantages we have are that there'll be more of us and we know the ground.

"Other members of the coven have gone to obtain guns, which will be given to the sentries. Someone else will train you in using those. As for why we are here . . ." She drew her favorite knife, a powerful weapon focus, from her belt with her right hand. "Most of you have knives of some sort. If you have one, wear it from now on." She sheathed the knife again and raised her club. "Each one of you should be able to find a good, solid stick, about this length.

Keep it handy. A stick extends your reach, and you can hit with one of these much harder than you can with your fists. Not only will it hurt them more, it'll also hurt you less. You can hit the soft parts of a body with your feet and hands, if you insist, but for the hard parts, you use a tool. If someone points a gun at you and you can't reach him with a stick this long, do this"—she dropped the club and raised her hands—"and hope that he won't shoot an un-armed person. If you have room to use a sword or a spear, then he has room to use a rifle, so that advice still applies. Don't draw your knife unless there's no other option, and don't throw it unless you're sure of damaging something vital, such as the spine—otherwise, you're just disarming yourself and giving him another weapon."

Didge raised a hand. "How do you hit someone in the spine?"

"From behind," she said shortly. "And the only circumstance under which that's justified is to protect someone else, and it assumes that your knife can get through his armor. Now, his head, chest and groin are where he's likely to have the most armor, so you're much better off going for his limbs and trying to disarm him. Armor isn't much use against an armlock.

"In case any of you *do* get into a corner where fighting looks like the best option, I'm going to teach you a few tricks. Most of this is bastardized Escrima, Filipino stick and knife fighting. If you don't think you can fight like that, to protect yourselves or your friends or your children, then go back downstairs and see if there's any other way you can help. I won't hold it against you: I'd rather know who can and will fight before I put you, or anyone else, in danger."

She looked along the line. No one flinched, not even the gray-haired teacher. "Okay, then. Leila. Try to take this stick from me."

Perhaps the only one of her kind in the entire Seattle sprawl, Leila was a Night One—a European elf metavari-ant. Yoko still felt a mild jolt of surprise every time she saw the girl, whose skin covering of fine midnight blue fur matched her eyes. Leila gripped her club nervously, then

rushed at her. Yoko parried her blow, then used her stick
as a lever to put Leila in an armlock, being careful not to
hurt her or to use any abilities that only adepts could learn.
A quick twist and Leila's club dropped to the street.

"Can we see that again?" asked Didge. "In slo-mo?"

Yoko released Leila, who retrieved her club and walked
back to the line, rubbing her wrist. "Okay," the adept said
to the dwarf. "Your turn."

Getting to the top of the cooling tower from the inside
had taken Carpenter nothing more than a grapple gun,
climbing gear and a refusal to look down: the tower had
been designed to be earthquake proof and was still structur-
ally sound after all these years. Turning it into a secure
sniper's nest had taken a little more effort, but the end
result was a platform that hung from the rim of the tower
and a carved, narrow gunport allowing Carpenter to watch
the Crypt while presenting the smallest possible target. The
sniper had tethered himself to the platform and had his
smartlink-adapted rifle fastened to his belt with a metal
lanyard. He was also equipped with a hooded urban-
camouflage cape, a pack full of ration bars, several bottles
of water and an almost machinelike patience.

He watched through his telescopic sight as an attractive
dark-skinned human woman in a charcoal jumpsuit guided
a Land Rover through the ruins. When she seemed satisfied
that it was in the correct position, an ork with multiple
facial piercings and a leather-clad troll with a severe buzz
cut set about covering its tracks, placing nailed boards
across any pathways wide enough for vehicle access. A bald
black dwarf in an armor jacket climbed down from the
Land Rover, followed a few seconds later by a shabbily
dressed ork.

"Chief?" Carpenter subvocalized, as the dwarf and the
woman draped the Land Rover with camouflage netting,
then carried two heavy duffel bags to the ramp and down
into the sublevel. "Looks like they've brought up reinforcements, and they don't look like squatters. At least two of
them move like they're wired or boosted. And I can see
two sentries—a dwarf and an ork. Over."

There was no reply for a few seconds, and the sniper wondered if his radio was working. "Chief?"

"I read you," said Wallace. "Sorry—the pups were making a racket. Been cooped up too long." He looked over at King, who was feeding his pet barghests. He had removed his gloves so he could scratch their ears. The rawboned sergeant felt his commander's gaze burning into the back of his neck, turned around and hastily put on the rest of his armor and climbed aboard the Step-Van. "The mage says they've set up astral defenses, too," Wallace continued, "but nothing that'll keep the pups out."

"Any idea why this pit is worth so much? Over."

"Nope. Ours not to question why, remember?"

"Yeah." Carpenter peered through his sight at the troll, drawing a bead on the back of her neck. "Over and out."

5

There was a thin yellow line of sunlight barely visible on the horizon when Akira heard the approaching vehicles. For a moment, he thought he might be imagining it. He'd been on guard for less than ten minutes, and awake for no more than twenty. But he poked his head up from behind the wall and looked around until he could see the trucks. He fumbled for the radio Zurich had given him, and breathed, "Someone's coming."

"How many?" asked Yoko, looking up at Boanerges.

"Clever," muttered the shaman. "Just when we're at our weakest." City and hearth spirits went their own way at sunrise and sunset, the metahuman sentries who were allergic to sunlight had just been relieved, their thermographic and low-light vision no longer giving them any edge.

But hardly surprising, thought Yoko. She peered down at the diagram they'd drawn of their defenses, noting that Akira was watching the northwest corner.

"Can't tell," said Akira, over the radio. "There's a small truck, and another car or van behind it. No lights."

"Easy?"

"Hear them, but can't see anyone yet."

"Jinx?"

"Same here."

"Pike?"

"Nothing here," said Pike, who was watching the southeast corner and already sounded bored.

"Okay. Stay under cover, and for frag's sake, don't shoot anyone. Akira, I'm sending someone up to check it out." Yoko put the radio down and thought. Sumatra and Magnusson were sleeping off their spellcasting from earlier that morning, and none of Boanerges' students knew any spells that would be useful in combat. Several of the students were also allergic to sunlight, as was Sumatra—or so he claimed. She suspected the rat shaman's only recurring medical problem was an allergy to honest work.

"I'll go," said Boanerges, as though reading her mind.

"No."

"We know they have at least one mage on their team," said the shaman. "The watchers spotted her when she flew over in astral. She didn't come close enough for them to attack, but she would have seen them, and she might have seen our sentries, too. And I'm protected by a deflection spell, in case anyone starts shooting."

Yoko drew a deep breath. "You said I was in command of the muscle, right? Well, your muscles are staying down here until the sun's fully up and you can conjure a city spirit to protect you."

Boanerges glared at her. "Who taught you about magic?"

"You did, Master," she said without a hint of sarcasm. Boanerges had initiated her into the Crypt's coven years before and taught her to develop her astral vision, and she'd picked up more than a smattering of magical theory in the process. "Send up another watcher to get a report, if you like, but you're also the best healer we have, and you're staying down here until I know what we're up against. Mute!"

Mute, who had been lying motionless on a mattress with her eyes closed, was instantly awake. "Yes?"

"Go up to the northwest corner and take over from Akira. And take a rifle."

Mute picked up her silenced Browning and a clip of armor-piercing sabot rounds, then followed the adept's orders. Boanerges and Yoko watched her stride out of the medicine lodge and disappear into the corridors. "Think you can move that quietly?" asked the adept softly.

"You probably could, but not me—not without a stealth spell," said the shaman. "I've heard librarians make more noise. I guess I'll go see if Doc needs any help."

"Good idea," said Yoko. "Zurich can't fight until his hands have healed, and Crane's still on painkillers." The rigger was recuperating from a clash with one of the Seattle Seoulpa Rings and was planning to leave town as soon as he was well enough to fly, hoping to get beyond the reach of the Korean organized crime syndicate. "But don't knock yourself out; we may end up with some people who *really* need help."

"You think it'll come down to a real fight?"

Yoko grimaced. "I hope not. A standoff will be more costly for them than it is for us; we've enough food to withstand a siege for a few days, and enough water, thanks to the rain." 8-ball had bought several boxes of ration bars, MREs and other packaged food on his way back from the run that morning rather than depend on the Crypt's meager stores, food creation spells, and the drek the squatters had collected while Dumpster diving. "It depends on what their budget is, and how badly they want this place. But I think it'll come down to negotiation; that's why I brought Lankin. He could cut a deal with a dragon and not get burned."

"What sort of deal?" asked Boanerges, sounding unhappy.

"Help to find a new place for the Crypt that's big enough and safe enough. Transportation. Maybe some food and bedding thrown in. More time, so we can get word out on the street that you've moved. That sort of thing. Let's face it: it's not the location that makes this place so important to so many people."

"There's no point in offering sanctuary if no one knows where you are," Boanerges replied sharply. "And here in the Barrens, we have no trouble with any of the syndicates—we're under their radar, or their cost-effectiveness formula—and almost none with the gangs. We've spent years building the reputation of this place; it means a lot to a lot of people, and not all of it can be moved easily. The vegetable and herb gardens, the lodges, the magical circles . . . they're going to take money and a lot of time to rebuild. But it's not just that. For a lot of people, knowing they have a bed here is the only stability and security in their world. This place has seen . . . seen so much happen, and *absorbed* it. You can feel the good memories, if you're quiet for long enough. The people we've healed, the kids we've taught, the magic we've performed—there have been good times . . ." He shook his head. "I just wish I knew who's really behind this piano company drek, why they want the place, where the money is coming from—"

"I can tell you one thing about them," interrupted Magnusson without opening his eyes. "They play chess."

"What?"

"I've just realized where I'd heard of Giuoco Piano before. It has nothing to do with music; it's a chess opening." The magician rolled over on the thin mattress and picked up his pocket computer. "And Fedorov was a grand master," he said a moment later. "They're chess players. And it's their move."

Mute cautiously poked a metal mirror around the edge of the wall and angled it so that it showed the advancing vehicles: even her expensive cybereyes didn't allow her to see around corners or through concrete. The Step-Van in the front was a matte black with no visible logos; the other vehicle was smaller, and the Step-Van blocked her view of it, but to her enhanced hearing it sounded like a multi-fuel four-wheel-drive SUV, probably a Gaz-Willys Nomad. Both vehicles stopped half a block away, their engines still idling, and Mute wondered what they were waiting for. She switched her sight to thermographic, and a hint of movement overhead caught her attention. She looked up, filtered out the sound of the trucks, then grinned savagely. There was a small drone hidden in the low cloud cover above the Crypt, quiet enough to be undetectable by anyone with merely human vision and hearing—probably a Condor, a hydrogen-filled balloon with some electronics, using its turboprop just enough to hold its position. She used her image magnification to zoom in on the small heat source above, then aimed her silenced smartgun at its center. Her first round nicked the gasbag, causing a slow leak; the second shattered one of the cameras, and the third ignited the hydrogen.

Griffin winced as the infrared picture from the Condor winked out. "They're shoo—" he began, then froze in midword. Lori passed her hand in front of his eyes, then remembered that the rigger's cybereyes would track even if the brain was out of action. "Griff?"

No reply. Quinn, sitting next to the rigger in the back of the Step-Van, looked over queasily. "Dump shock?"

"I think so," said the mage, looking him over in astral. "No sign of a magical attack. I think they got the drone."

"Drek." Quinn thought a moment. Wallace had ordered them to keep radio silence until they emerged from the vehicles, but it looked as though the squatters had started the fight without waiting for them to arrive. "Chief? I'm not getting anything on-screen from the Condor. How about you?"

"Nothing here," Wallace replied, after a quick look at the screen on his wrist computer. "Not even a status bar. What does Griff say? Was it jammed or brought down?"

Quinn relayed the question to Lori, the only member of the group who lacked a headware radio. "He's coming around now," said the mage, relief plain in her voice. "No signs of physical damage. But I think he was trying to say 'They're shooting' when he was dumped."

"Either that, or he was commenting on their footwear," said Quinn dryly. "Wallace? Shall I ask Carpenter if he can see any guns?"

Wallace thought for a moment. The sniper had made two reports since taking up his position in the cooling tower, and hadn't mentioned any weapon emplacements. The guy Mr. Johnson had sent in for initial recon hadn't even seen any handguns. "Tell Lori to turn her radio on; I've got a question." The elf mage was a valued member of the team, but her distaste for technology sometimes irritated him. "Lori, could you bring a Condor down with a spell?"

"Me? Probably not. But in theory, it'd be a snap. A

fireball or lightning bolt would be easiest, and an air elemental could—"

"Thanks. That's all I needed. How's Griffin?"

"On the Richter scale?" the rigger replied as he tried to sit up. "Bad hangover. You want me to send up the other drone?"

"No, not yet. Did you see anyone shooting at you?"

"I saw someone pointing a pistol, but didn't hear any shots or see any muzzle flash. She'd have to be a fraggin' good shot, at that range, or extremely lucky. But I was recording; the cameras may have seen something I missed."

"Okay. Everyone armor up and get ready. Lori, is any of the magical drek they've set up going to stop you doing that gun-counting spell of yours?"

Mute watched as the vehicles drove onto the garbage-strewn lot to the north of the Crypt, noticing that the driver of the Nomad positioned the SUV so that the Step-Van was between him and the Crypt, which suggested that the black van must be pretty heavily armored. She heard the doors on the far side of the van slide open, then a soft, all-too-familiar howling.

Barghests!

Mute stiffened, then gritted her teeth and waited for the invaders to emerge from cover. A moment later, a figure appeared at either end of the Step-Van. They wore urban camouflage fatigues; their faces were hidden by security helmets, and their hands by heavy gauntlets, but one was too big to be anything but an ork, while the other seemed human scaled. Both carried AK-97s, with stun guns, survival knives and a few grenades clearly visible on their web belts. Mute waited until they were halfway across the road, then fired a shot at the ork's ankle. The ork yelped as the armor-piercing bullet tore through his boot; then he dropped to a kneeling position with his gun at the ready. The human dropped to the roadway, supine, looking for a target. Mute heard Easy laugh, and the human fired a shot in her direction before the ork barked out an order. *"Cease firing!"* he snapped. *"Who's there?"*

Boanerges' astral form appeared on the sidewalk almost instantly—a powerful-looking figure in silver and white robes, much more muscular than his scrawny meatbody, with dreadlocks that seemed to move like a gorgon's crown of snakes. "We *live* here," he said. "Who are *you*?"

"This isn't your property," said the ork calmly. "We're here to escort you from the premises."

"To where?"

"You're free to go wherever you want."

"We don't want to go anywhere. This is our home."

"Not anymore. Look, chummer, we can move you if we have to."

"Who says you have to? Who are you working for?"

"The legal owner of this land!"

Boanerges smiled. "We've been here for more than twenty years, and possession is nine-tenths of the law."

"Dead people can't own property," the human subvocalized into her throat mic.

The shaman could not have heard the words, but his astral form detected the finer shades of the emotional content, and he stared at her, his eyes suddenly reptilian. "Indeed," he replied.

The ork shook his head. "Enough of this drek. You, Dreadlocks, you want to see what you're up against here? Okay. *Go, go, go!*"

The vehicle doors opened, and another nine mercenaries poured out, all with guns at the ready—except for the dog handler, who had a leash in each hand and a carbine slung on his back. The jet-black barghests sniffed the air and howled again, this time more piercingly.

8-ball shuddered. The cameras in the Land Rover were fixed, without a view of the street. He grabbed the radio. "What can you see?" he asked Mute, trying not to sound as though he were pleading.

"Eleven armored, ten rifles and two barghests. Guessing three orks, a dwarf, a troll; the rest look human. Probably merc, not corp."

The dwarf turned to Yoko. "Permission to go—"

"No."

"There are three kids up there with handguns, against

eleven of *them*! Mute can't take on that many alone, and what're we going to do if they take hostages?"

The shadowrunners looked at Yoko expectantly, and she sighed. "Okay. Patty, you've used an assault cannon?"

"Sure."

"Take that and your smartgun. Use the cannon on the trucks, if you have to, but not on the people. Lankin, Maggie, go with her. 8-ball . . . you get Pike and Easy. I'll get Jinx. The rest of you stay here. Make sure those mercs don't get down the ramp. Okay?"

The dwarf nodded, picked up his smartlinked AK-98, handed the remote control for his car over to Crane and followed Yoko up to the surface.

Limping, and wincing with every step, the ork advanced toward the warehouse ruins. Mute watched, admiring the way the squad kept in formation, far enough apart that even a perfectly placed grenade wouldn't injure more than three of them. She suspected the helmets were fitted with air filters that would have made her neurostun grenades useless even if the wind hadn't been blowing the wrong way. She reached for a concussion grenade with her left hand while keeping her pistol trained on the ork. His armor jacket and pants looked like standard CAS issue with the insignia removed—which meant that the weakest spots were inside the elbow and behind the knee. She was waiting for a clear shot when Beef Patty came roaring through the rubble like an ugly comet, with Lankin and Magnusson in her wake. The troll stopped just beside Boanerges' astral form, dropped to one knee and aimed an assault cannon at the Step-Van. "Not so fraggin' fast!" she roared.

The ork in the lead stared at the mismatched trio—a hulking, leather-clad troll with a blond buzz cut, a dark-skinned elf fashion plate who was even taller, and a bookish-looking silver-maned human in an old but clean topcoat—and shook his head. "You're outnumbered," he drawled, "outgunned—"

Patty smiled, turned and fired at one of the barghests. The front half of the animal exploded, spraying everyone around it with blood, fur and small gobbets of bone and meat. The animal's haunches remained standing for a fraction of a second, then collapsed. The handler stared at the mess in horror. "But not outclassed," Patty announced, then muttered into her throat mic, "and you didn't say nothin' about not using the cannon on the dogs."

Lankin shook his head. "I apologize for my companion. Subtlety is not her forte."

Mute smiled, and shot the second barghest through the eye with her silenced pistol. The creature whimpered and fell over dead. The handler stared, then dropped the leashes and unslung his carbine with the growl of an animal in pain. Boanerges' astral form vanished from sight. Magnusson cast a stunbolt at the handler, who dropped the gun and fell on top of it. "He's not dead!" the magician yelled, but his voice was drowned out by the roar of gunfire.

Pike spun around as he heard 8-ball come running through the rubble, and squeezed the trigger of his pistol just far enough to activate the laser sight. The beam passed over 8-ball's head and placed an orange dot on the crumbling wall of the old decontamination showers. The dwarf glanced at the gun, then shook his head. "Aim lower next time," he suggested. "Come on. Yoko wants you out of there now the—"

The distinctive boom of an assault cannon made the rest of the sentence unnecessary as well as inaudible. Pike ducked and scrambled away from his post, following 8-ball past the blocked-off stairwell toward the ramp and doing his best to keep his head down. Though barely thirteen years old, the lanky elf was already two meters tall. "What if this is just a diversion?" he asked.

Carpenter stared through the sight at the elf and the dwarf as they hurried through the ruins. "Chief? I've got a peach of a shot."

The city spirit manifested in the form of a trash can, and was the most beautiful sight Boanerges could remember seeing. "Guard and concealment on my three friends over there," the shaman gasped. "Now!"

*   *   *

"Cease firing!"

The commander's voice was painfully loud over his men's headware radios, and clearly audible over the shooting. 8-ball's head jerked around; then he turned to Pike. "Get downstairs, and tell Yoko I'll be back soon."

"What?"

"That voice. It sounded familiar." He switched his helmet mic on. "Mute, are these fraggers wearing any insignia? Any badges?"

"No, nothing in infrared or visible light. Maybe in UV . . ."

"How about their belt buckles?"

There was a moment's silence, then, "The leader has three stars in a circle embossed on the buckle. One of the humans has a smiling cat face. That's all I can see from here."

"Thanks." As quickly as he could, he ran toward the north side of the lot. Pike hesitated, then followed him as quietly as he could.

The mercs stared at the empty space where Lankin, Magnusson and Patty had been standing a moment before, then looked around warily, waiting for new orders or new targets.

"Wallace?" came a voice from the ruins.

Wallace blinked. "Who's there? Show yourself!"

"If you promise not to shoot."

The mercenary commander grunted. 8-ball poked his head up from behind a bullet-riddled rusty drum, then removed his helmet to show his face. Wallace stared at him for a moment. "8-ball? What're *you* doing here?"

"I was going to ask you the same question," said the dwarf, grinning. "I used to live here. *You're* the one who's a long way from home."

"We've got a contract," replied Wallace heavily. "How about you?"

8-ball scrambled up on top of the drum, and sat in a lotus position. "Nope. Sometimes I fight for free when the cause is good." He looked at the soldiers: one dwarf, one troll, the rest human or ork. None wore visible rank insignia or name badges, and 8-ball wasn't close enough to make out the emblems embossed or engraved on their belt buckles. "Any of the old team still with you?"

"King and Lewis. And Griffin. I don't think you ever met my new exec, Quinn. She was with us in Damman— well, not exactly *with* us, but she was there."

"The Mighty Quinn? Royal Marine Commandos? Only by reputation," he said carefully, and saluted her. "What happened to Baker?"

"Disappeared."

"Carpenter?"

Wallace hesitated a little too long. "He's still around."

8-ball nodded. "And the rest of the old squad?"

"Some got jobs. Some got married. Some got killed." He shrugged, and raised his visor so that 8-ball could see at least part of his face—a chin like a concrete block, a huge pair of tusks, a mustache like a dirty yard broom and a nose that even Picasso would have found difficult to draw. "Me, I'm too lazy to get a job, too ugly to get married . . . nearly got killed, once or twice, though. How about you?"

"A few times," 8-ball admitted. "Nearly killed, that is, not married. Wallace . . . I gotta tell you, if you come any closer, there's going to be more shooting. There's a lot of people down there, and a lot of guns . . . but no soldiers. Some of them couldn't hit the side of a tank from the inside. Some of them are only kids. Is there some way we can do this without people—yours and ours—getting killed?"

Wallace glanced at where King lay between the bodies of the dogs. "It's a bit late for that, old friend. I've got one man down already and several injured, and you know what happens if we default on a contract."

The dwarf nodded, his expression sour. A mercenary team that refused to honor a contract tarnished not only their own name, but that of the profession. The commanding officer would become an unemployable pariah, and would probably be killed either by his own men or by other commanders. The two old soldiers were silent for a moment, then 8-ball asked, "This contract . . . what exactly does it say?"

"The owner wants the property evacuated by whatever means prove necessary."

"So if we go peacefully . . ."

"Fine and dandy. I didn't get into this biz to kill kids."

"I know. What if they take stuff with them?"

"They can take every fraggin' brick for all I care. Nothing in my contract about that."

"Just the land?"

"Uh-huh. 'Course, we've got to make sure it *stays* vacant until the new owner gets here. What he wants it for, or how long he'll be here . . ." He shrugged. "Frag me if I know, chummer. You think you can talk them into going quietly?"

"Most likely, if we have somewhere to go. But not this minute. Some of 'em need healing, some will want to pack and some are allergic to sunlight."

Wallace looked up at the cloudy sky. "This is sunlight?"

"Hey, it's not raining. Welcome to Seattle. So, is there any time limit on this contract?"

"They're not paying us by the hour," the mercenary replied, then subvocalized into his headware microphone, "Griffin?"

"Here, Chief."

"What time's the sun set?"

"Just a sec . . . eighteen twenty-six."

Wallace glanced at the clock readout on his retinal display: 0737. "Think you can have your people out of here by nineteen hundred hours, 8-ball?"

"Possibly."

"Because we're coming in at nineteen fifteen. We won't stop anyone leaving, but anyone trying to enter will be turned back."

"Wakarimasuka," the dwarf replied. "Good to see you again, Wallace." He turned and walked back to the ramp.

Wallace watched him, then lowered his visor. "All wounded, fall back! Hartz, Lily, take King back to the van. Everyone else, hold your positions. Quinn, you're in command."

* * *

Carpenter peered through the telescopic sight as 8-ball tramped back toward the ramp, where Pike and Boanerges were waiting. "Quinn?" the sniper murmured.

"Here."

"I heard they got King. That right?"

"Yes."

Carpenter nodded, centered the crosshairs on the back of the shaman's head and squeezed the trigger.

6

Magnusson winced as Beef Patty stepped on his foot yet again, and tried hard not to grunt with the effort as he and Lankin held up the wounded troll and helped her to stagger back to the ramp, still concealed by the city spirit. Boanerges looked at her blood-soaked leathers and shook his head.

" 'Mokay," muttered the troll through a mouthful of blood.

"Drek. Maggie, get her to the doc. I'll be there in a moment."

Magnusson nodded wearily, and he and Lankin half led, half carried the still-protesting mercenary down the ramp and around a corner to Czarnecki's improvised surgery. A moment later, Boanerges felt something smack into the side of his head; he stumbled forward, then dropped onto all fours, dazed. Pike turned around at the noise, and ran toward him. "Sensei? *Sensei!*"

Boanerges grunted, and put a hand up to the side of his head. It came away wet with blood. He stared at this for an instant, tried to stand, then rolled down the ramp an instant before Carpenter fired again. The bullet ricocheted off the concrete, narrowly missing Pike. The elf turned to see who was shooting, and a bullet punched through his secondhand armor vest, tore through a lung, bounced off his sternum, and careened back through his heart before coming to rest between two vertebrae. Pike spun around and fell, and never felt his head hit the ground.

An eye for an eye, thought Carpenter, and reached into his pocket for another clip.

Lori looked at King's armor, then at his face as Hartz removed his helmet. It confirmed what the barghest handler's biomonitor had already told her. "He's okay," she said. "None of this is *his* blood; he doesn't seem to be bleeding at all. I'm not sure he was even hit."

Wallace, who had removed his boot to examine his injured ankle, looked up sourly. "Magic?" he asked.

"Yeah, a stunbolt. No physical damage. It just puts you to sleep in a very definite way. I saw it coming, but I couldn't stop it."

The commander shook his head. "If he's okay, let him sleep. They killed Bruno and Sylvie, and that's gonna hurt more than anything else."

Lily and the mage peeled off King's armored fatigue jacket, examined the khaki T-shirt underneath it and determined that it wasn't stained with anything worse than sweat and mustard. "How're *you* doing, Chief?" asked Lori.

"Well, I may never play the violin again."

"Good. I've heard you sing karaoke. Bruno had more musical talent than you do."

Wallace grinned despite the pain in his foot and reached for the medkit. He looked around the Step-Van's cargo bay. It was cramped and cold and generally made for a lousy field hospital, but at least the walls were proof against small-arms fire. As long as the squatters didn't bring out the assault cannon again or any heavier artillery, they should be safe. He looked at Knight, who'd taken a bullet in the back of the right knee and was definitely out of the fight, then glanced down at the hole in his own boot and swore. There was at least one annoyingly good shot among the opposition.

Try as he might, he couldn't quite bring himself to think of them as the enemy.

Boanerges tried to pick himself up, and suddenly found

himself surrounded by Yoko, Magnusson and 8-ball. "What . . ."

Magnusson grabbed the shaman's chin, turned his head and examined the mess. "You've lost part of your ear, and you may be concussed," he said. "It seems that quickened deflection spell of yours was only partly effective. I won't know any more until we shave the side of your head."

"How's Patty?"

"Not good," the mage admitted. "I think everyone must have been aiming at her. One bullet hit her in the jaw, and at least half a dozen hit her chest. None of them penetrated her armor, but the blunt trauma would've been enough to kill a couple of ordinary-sized people. She has a few cracked ribs despite her bone lacing, and we're afraid that she may have inhaled a couple of teeth. Doc Czarnecki's checking her now for internal bleeding. But Lankin doesn't seem to be hurt, and I wasn't hit at all."

Boanerges glanced at Lankin, who looked down at his long red leather coat. There were two bullet holes in the side, just below the armpit—one an entry wound, the other an exit. "Doesn't she have DocWagon?" he asked.

"She let it lapse," the shaman replied. "She was having trouble paying the bills. Who shot—"

"There's a sniper," said 8-ball. "South of here, and in an elevated position, probably in the old power station. He's killed Pike. At least, I think he's dead, but I'm not a medic, and if the sniper is who I think it is, I'm not in a hurry to go back outside and check it out."

"You know these people?" asked Lankin.

"Some of them."

"Small world."

"Big war," replied 8-ball flatly. "We went on a couple of peacekeeping missions together, which mostly meant finding weapons and destroying them. Thanks to Wallace, their CO—the big ork out there—we usually managed to do it without any casualties on either side. He's an honorable man, and his men just about worship him because they know he won't endanger them unnecessarily or leave them behind. We'd better hope that nothing happens to *him*, because they'll take it personal.

"His new second-in-command, Quinn, is a different matter. I only know her reputation, but she's supposed to be a fraggin' good soldier, special-forces training and cyberware. Rumor has it that she's never lost a fight, from a barroom brawl to a major offensive. Downside is, she's an adrenaline junkie, and she doesn't believe in taking prisoners—which is why she's now a merc instead of posing for recruiting posters back home.

"Wallace has given us nearly twelve hours to vacate; I don't know what you want to do with them. Quinn probably wouldn't have given us twelve minutes."

"Is Wallace his first name, or his last?"

"Both. His mother's probably the only one who could call him by his given name and live. But Wal's not the immediate problem; the sniper is."

"Do you know *him*, too?"

8-ball shrugged. "I've met him a few times, if it's who I think it is. There was a sharpshooter in Wallace's company named Carpenter; they've known each other forever, or thereabouts. Might even be cousins or something. Anyway, give him a good rifle and time to sight it in, and he can hit almost anything at one or two klicks range . . . and that's as close as most people want to get to him. Except for Wallace and King, the chummer with the barghests. They go back a ways, too."

Boanerges closed his eyes and was silent for a moment. When he opened them, his expression instantly changed from pained to stricken. "Pike's dead," he confirmed, trying to swallow. "He must have died almost instantly. Fraggit, he was only thirteen . . ."

"He was taller than you are and carrying a gun," said 8-ball. "That's all a sniper would have noticed, or cared about, and if he'd heard that some of his own squad were down . . ."

"Down, maybe, but not dead!" Magnusson protested.

"He might not have known that, either. And stunning these guys isn't going to do us much good, unless you can stun them all and keep them restrained. They're not going to go away, and they're not going to wait forever. I've bought us some time; what are we going to do with it?"

"Can we get the kids out, at least?" asked Yoko.

"With the sniper out there?" Boanerges said softly, closing his eyes. "And even if we do, is there any safe place for them to go?"

Severn winced as Lori examined his wounds. "It's not *that* bad," he protested, his Welsh accent stronger than usual. "It's not like it went . . . Ouch!"

"It's nicked the renal artery," said the mage. "You're going to need serious healing if you don't want to lose that kidney. I hope you still have the other one?"

"Yes!"

"Good." She looked at his broad back, trying to find a spot hairless enough to place a tranq patch, then slapped it onto his bicep above the dragon tattoo. Then she looked up at Wallace and shook her head. "I can give him some painkillers and antibiotics, remove the bullet, patch up the hole and cast a healing spell, but he really needs a hospital."

"I'm fi—" Severn began, then closed his eyes as the patch took effect.

"What about Knight?"

"He'll be okay, if you don't need him to walk. Or stand. But that knee will have to be reconstructed or replaced."

The ork sighed. "He was thinking of getting new legs, anyway, to match his arm. Griffin can drive them both to Good Samaritan. Everyone else okay?"

"Within reason. And speaking of reason . . ."

"I was just about to call him," said Wallace wearily. He walked to the front of the Step-Van and grabbed the phone from the dash. "Mr. Fedorov?"

The Hatter was eating breakfast in his apartment when his wristphone began vibrating. He'd gone to bed after hearing the briefing from Griffin, sent his latest mistress home at midnight, taken a sedative just after two a.m., and woken again at five thirty. Getting back to sleep, he knew, would be impossible—he felt like a preschooler on Christmas morning. So he'd gotten up and made himself a pot of tea while he waited for the sunrise.

He put his cup down and rubbed his eyes, then glanced at the name and number on the screen of his wristphone and switched the scrambler on. "Yes?"

"Mr. Fedorov? This is Wallace. We're meeting heavier resistance than we expected. They've shot down your drone, killed the dogs, and put two of my men into the hospital. They're much too well armed and well trained to be ordinary squatters. Is it possible that some other organization is interested in this site?"

The Hatter repressed the urge to scream obscenities. His office was soundproofed, but that didn't mean that it wasn't bugged. "Are you saying that you need reinforcements?"

"No . . . I don't think so. But I was wondering whether we might get further, at less cost, with a carrot as well as a stick."

"What do you mean?"

"They claim that hole is their home, that there are kids down there, and that too many of them can't come out in sunlight. They might be lying, but if that's all they want, then maybe offering them some form of assistance would be enough to get them to go peacefully. I don't think they'll ask for much—"

"No!" the Hatter snapped. "We *own* that land. If we let squatters think that they have a right to it just because they were there before we were, what sort of precedent would that set?"

Wallace counted to ten silently before he could trust himself to speak civilly. "Any special instructions on what I should do with the bodies?"

"Leave them where they are. You're close enough to Hell's Kitchen that Lone Star won't be a problem. We're going to be demolishing the building anyway; we can bury them underneath it. Just make sure you move all the survivors out of the immediate area." He yawned. "There's a squat near Petrowski Farms, isn't there, with a soup kitchen? Dump them there, if you can get them all into your van. When do you think you'll have the place secured?"

The mercenary chewed his bushy mustache. "Twenty-one hundred hours, if you want us to clear any out booby traps.

Maybe an hour earlier if you'd rather do that yourself." He looked around as Lori leaned over the seat, her expression haunted. " 'Scuse me a second." He put the phone on hold. "Trouble?"

"Carpenter's shot one of the squatters. A thirteen-year-old elf boy. Carpenter says he was armed."

The ork groaned. "What do the squatters say?"

"They say he's dead."

7

8-ball and Patty had set up an improvised pistol range at the back of the Crypt by rearranging some of the temporary walls and makeshift furniture, making sure there was no one who might be hit by bullets passing through the partitions. Then they'd given every squatter five rounds of gel ammunition, handed them Lankin's silenced Fichetti, and watched them shoot. The dwarf watched silently as Leila fired her five shots, managing to hit the roughly human-shaped form painted on the far wall of the gallery with every one—three of them in the chest. "Not bad," he said encouragingly. She looked at the grouping, then slid a throwing knife out of her sleeve and threw it, hitting the target in the right eye.

8-ball grinned, then tried to look stern. "I hope you have another knife," he said.

"Of course," she said, as though he were stupid to have thought otherwise.

"More than one?"

"Want to frisk me and find out?"

The dwarf was still trying to think of a safe reply when Lankin walked up and squatted beside him. "You seem to know this Wallace pretty well, 8-ball," he said. "Well enough to predict what he's going to do?"

8-ball considered this as he watched Leila walk up to the target and extract her knife. "I know what he was planning to do. What he'll do now that he knows I'm here . . ." He shrugged.

"What do you think he had planned?"

"He usually starts off by sending drones overhead so he knows where the sentries are, to make sure it's not an ambush. Mute shot down his first drone, but he'll have more—armed, probably. He has a mage in his team, so she'll have checked out the area from astral as well. He approached from the north because Carpenter was watching from the south, so we have to watch our backs all the time." He smiled at Leila as she walked out. "He knows he has enough people to take and hold the ground level, so he'll do that first. He'll be watching all the exits, and he'll also be looking for places to drop in a gas grenade in case he decides to stun us or smoke us out. I'm not saying he'll do it, but he might, and those helmets have air filters built in as standard. They'll be carrying concussion grenades, too—but they're using jacketed ammo, not gel, and if they see anyone with a ranged weapon, they'll give them one warning before they shoot, but they won't wait long for a reply. They might use the tasers if they see someone with nothing more than a club or a knife, but I wouldn't bet on it.

"Anyway, they'll take the ground level—and we might as well let them, because it's too difficult to defend—then probably repeat the procedure, sending drones down and some watchers, until they know what sort of force they're likely to meet. Wallace doesn't like wasting money, but he'd rather lose any number of drones than a soldier. Then, *maybe*, they'll come down in force. Of course, if he wants to surprise us . . . I don't know what he'll do. Let Quinn lead the attack, maybe." He shuddered.

"What is she likely to do?"

"I wish I knew . . . no, scratch that. I'm not sure I *do* want to know." He looked up at the water-stained concrete of the ceiling. "Do you think the guys who bought this place are going to care if the roof's intact? You wouldn't exactly need a bunker buster to bring it down on top of us."

Lankin also looked up, and his face turned slightly green.

"I still have no idea why anyone would go to the expense of buying this pit. Would she *do* that?"

"She might threaten to, and I wouldn't want to call her bluff. And this 'pit' is my alma mater, college boy."

Lankin straightened up. "No offense," he said insincerely. "That was a pretty good job of negotiation you did out there, by the way."

"Don't know if it'll do any good," said 8-ball with a shrug. "Wallace isn't the problem. I wish I knew who hired him."

"Ratty's working on that," said Lankin. "I don't know how much he'll find."

"Where is he?"

"Using the jackpoint near the library."

"I think I'll see how he's doing. 'Scuse me."

Ratatosk was sitting on the library's cardboard floor with his legs folded into a lotus position. The space was barely six feet square and was defined by curtains of heavy material hung from the ceiling. The library's contents consisted of three or four dozen well-used hardcopy books, an equal number of datachips along with a battered reader, a small collection of telesma, an enchanting kit and a cracked vase holding three dusty dried flowers—some resident's idea of decorating—all arranged on shelves built from concrete blocks and particleboard. He was jacked into his deck, and his eyes were closed. 8-ball peered at the small vidscreen, which showed the shimmering interior of a datastore from Ratatosk's point of view, then cleared his throat loudly.

"Yes?" the decker asked a moment later, his voice coming both from his lips and the deck's speaker.

"Shouldn't someone be guarding your body?"

"I knew you were there, didn't I?"

"What if you set off an alarm and they trace you?"

"What're they going to do? Send in troops?" Ratatosk smiled, though his eyes remained closed.

"Okay, then. What if you hit some black IC and need the doc?"

"Unlikely. The stuff I'm scanning now is strictly low security. Did you want something?"

"Do you know who hired Wallace yet?"

"No."

8-ball sat down, leaning up against one of the rickety bookshelves. "I thought of some leads you could try following up. Those vehicles and the drone that Mute took out might belong to Griffin, or they might belong to the employer. Same with the weapons, but not the barghests. They would have trained those fraggers themselves. And transporting dangerous animals like those . . . that'd be difficult to do without leaving a trace."

"True," said the elf. "Any idea where they would have come from?"

"They could've been working anywhere, but their home base is somewhere in the Confederated American States. Try the airports around Memphis. Probably flew out in the last forty-eight hours."

"I'll see what I can dig up. Thanks."

"No problem. Um . . . d'you mind if I ask you a personal question?"

"No. I can always refuse to answer."

8-ball smiled. "Why are you here? You didn't grow up here, and I've never seen you hide here or come here for healing . . ."

"Yoko asked for my help."

"That's all?"

"Yes. We were lovers for a while. She knows that if she asks for my help, I'll come running."

The dwarf raised his eyebrows. "That must keep you busy," he said dryly. "They say you have a pretty big harem."

Ratatosk didn't reply.

"So what's the story with Lankin?"

"You'll have to ask him. Or Yoko."

8-ball snorted. "No, thanks."

"All I know is that they were lovers once, too; I don't know when. I've heard that she left him, and that that was a first for him and he's never completely gotten over it. But that may just be idle gossip. I can't think of any other reason why he'd be here."

"Okay. Thanks."

"Not a problem. I'll let you know if I find out anything about the barghests."

8-ball nodded. "If the mercs get in, can you use a gun? Someone told me you were a pacifist."

Ratatosk raised his cyberarm, palm out to show the smartlink, then extended his spur. "I used to be, until some fragger shot me with an assault cannon. Ten or twenty centimeters to the right, it would've blown my heart out through my spine. After that, I thought that since I was in a dangerous biz, I'd better be dangerous too."

The dwarf smiled crookedly. "A wise foreign policy."

He walked back to Boanerges' medicine lodge, where Yoko was meditating. "We need to do something about the sniper," she said as soon as she saw him. "He's not only keeping us pinned down, he's really bad for morale with Pike's body out there. Sumatra went into the astral and checked out the cooling tower; he's there, all right, but he's behind cover, and it's almost a kilometer away. You're the weapons specialist; what do we have that has that sort of range?"

"Only the assault cannon. Or magic. Either way, he has the drop on us—unless there's another exit he doesn't know about?"

"We could clear the stairwell, given time, but that would give the mercs another way in. Sumatra has an invisibility spell; if he can maintain that long enough, it would give someone a chance to get out and take a shot at this . . . Carpenter?"

8-ball nodded. "It had better take only one shot. If Carpenter gets a chance to return fire . . ."

"How good are you with an assault cannon?"

"Not as good as Patty. Maybe half as good as Carpenter is with a rifle."

"Patty's too badly wounded. It's going to have to be someone who's faster than this sniper—and not so big that it takes four of us to carry her back in if she's hit."

"Then I guess it's me," said 8-ball unhappily, "unless someone has a spell that'll take him down and keep him down for at least the next twelve hours?"

Yoko looked up as she heard footsteps on the dirt floor

outside. Pierce and Boanerges entered the lodge a moment later, the ork propping up the wounded shaman. "Mute and Jinx are still out there, and Pike, and we can't bring them back in until we do something about that sniper," Boanerges mumbled.

Yoko shook her head. "He has a clear shot at anyone who goes up the ramp."

"Maybe not that clear," said 8-ball. "Sensei, how tall are you?"

"What? One eighty-five or so. Why?"

"And Pike was two meters or thereabouts. If the sniper's shooting through a chink in the wall, and around what's still standing upstairs, I think he's got a pretty restricted field of fire. He hasn't taken a shot at me, and I don't think that's because he recognizes me; I suspect he can't see anything that doesn't raise its head above the level of the drums we've got around the place."

"You're suggesting that when we go outside, we should crawl around on our bellies?"

"Well, Napoleon said that an army marches on its stomach."

The shaman winced at the pun. "That's—"

"Can you get a clear shot at *him*?" asked Yoko. "Without him seeing you?"

"If I can blow a big enough hole in the side of that tower . . ."

"I have a better idea," said Boanerges. "Does the tower have a roof?"

"No," said the dwarf after a moment's thought. "It's basically a big chimney. Why?"

"Then we can get a clear shot. Where's Magnusson?"

Carpenter listened sullenly to the reprimands, then repeated, "They killed King. I heard you say so. Somebody had to—"

"He isn't *dead*! The *dogs* are dead, sure, but he's only sleeping! They hit him with some sort of stun spell, that's all!"

The sniper was silent for a moment as he absorbed this. "No drek, Chief? Honest?"

"Ask Lori, if you don't believe me," said Wallace, careful not to raise his voice. "What exactly did you hear Quinn say?"

Carpenter blinked. "She said he was down. King, I mean. He loved them dogs," he muttered.

"I know, but . . . don't shoot anyone else until I give you the order. Okay?"

"Okay, Chief. Over and out."

Wallace leaned back in the Step-Van's passenger seat and stared at the ceiling. "What a fraggin' mess," he muttered.

"I don't understand," said Lori.

The ork turned his head to look at her. She was the squad's newest recruit, and he realized that she might not have been told some of the details of his history. "King's his cousin," he said. "Or second cousin, I think, but they were more like brothers. King's real name is Carpenter, too; Elvis Carpenter. That's why people been calling him King since we were in school; Carpenter was usually known as Woody.

"Anyway, the three of us grew up together. King's older by a couple of years, but he taught us how to swim, how to fish, how to track animals and live off the land, how to shoot . . . " He grimaced. "Actually, Woody was a better shot about five seconds after he first picked up a gun than King is ever likely to be. He was a pretty smart kid too— at least compared to King and me— until some fraggin' idiot shot him in the head. Since then . . ."

He saw Lori's shocked expression slowly mutate into something much worse—pity. "You?" she said.

"Yep. Hunting accident. I've been looking after him ever since. So's King, even though it wasn't his fault. Well, okay, it was his father's gun I was using, and he probably shouldn't have taken it, but still . . ."

"You both feel responsible."

"Fraggin' right we feel responsible. And now I'm responsible for the kid he just killed."

"No, you're not."

"I'm the CO. I gave him that gun and put him there. I should've known what he'd do when he heard that King was down; I *did* know. That makes me responsible, in my book. Hartz!"

The ogre appeared behind Lori a moment later. "Yeah, Chief?"

"You patched up?"

"Uh-huh."

"Good. I'm going to tell Carpenter to stand down. You'll be relieving him."

Yoko waved to Sumatra, who was lying down in the corridor between Boanerges' and Mish's medicine lodges. The ork closed his eyes, and his aura traveled out of his body, manifesting at the top of the ramp. Carpenter aimed at the astral form and his finger tightened on the trigger; but Wallace had commanded him not to shoot, and he never disobeyed a direct order. The ork didn't seem to be armed, anyway, nor doing anything at all threatening . . . He was just walking around, occasionally glancing up at the sky as he slowly made his way to the street.

"No one has shot at him yet," said Magnusson. "Let's do this."

"Are you sure you can maintain this spell?" Yoko asked Boanerges, as Magnusson shed his lined coat. "You look like you're about to fall over."

Boanerges nodded. Magnusson gritted his teeth while he still had them, and waited for the spell to take effect. The medicine lodge seemed to be growing, and its colors shifting down the spectrum. He took a few seconds to reorient himself, then flapped his wings experimentally, then jumped, flapped again and managed to perch on Yoko's hand. "Are you sure you can fly all the way to the tower?" she asked. "And don't say 'Nevermore.'"

The raven dipped its head once and flew away—quickly, if a little awkwardly. Yoko looked at the two magicians and sighed.

There were three mercs positioned along the north side of the block, and all aimed their rifles at Sumatra's form as it reached the sidewalk. He held his palms up, showing that he was unarmed, and looked at Quinn. The merc was so heavily wired that her aura was barely visible, but the rat shaman could almost smell her hostility. "A question from Boanerges," he said. "He apologizes for not being able to speak to you himself, but he's still in surgery after being shot. Could you let us pick up the body of the kid your sniper killed?"

Quinn's jaw tightened. "You're sure he's dead?"

"Boanerges took a look at him in astral. So did I. No aura left. He's fraggin' dead, all right."

"What are you going to do with him?"

"I don't know," the ork admitted with a shrug. "There's no earth around here deep enough for a grave, but we can't just leave him lying around. We'll improvise some sort of coffin, I guess, until we can work something out . . . unless you could lend us a body bag? Extra large?"

"I think we can do that," said Quinn through gritted teeth.

"And the sniper?"

"We've already told him to hold his fire until he's fired upon."

"Thank you. Also, some of our people wish to leave now—mostly children, and some of their parents. Will you promise them safe passage?"

Magnusson flew over the wasteland between the Crypt and the tower, staying low in case Boanerges failed to maintain the spell and he suddenly found himself back in human form. The shaman was an old friend of his, as well as head of their coven, so he trusted him . . . but Magnusson had treated Boanerges' wounds, and he wasn't sure that the shaman was as fully recovered as he claimed. He kept flying as fast as he could, looking down only when he saw movement through his peripheral vision. He spared a quick glance at the mercs positioned around the block, hoping that none of them would waste a shot firing at him.

"Safe passage? If they're unarmed, we'll do even better than that," said the merc coolly. "We'll give them an escort. Where do they wish to go?"

"No thanks," said Sumatra. "How do we know you won't take them as hostages? Come out with our hands up, or you kill the fraggin' kids? No thanks."

Quinn tried hard to think of a persuasive answer to this, and finally said, less convincingly than she would have liked, "Of course we'd prefer it if you all came out with your hands up. That way nobody gets hurt, either on your side or ours. But we . . ." She drew a deep breath. "Do you really think we'd murder children?"

"What do you think you're doing by kicking them out of their fraggin' home? Without any transport, and carryin' everything they own on their backs? You think there's any safe place to go around here, anywhere they wouldn't be mugged for a couple of blankets and a change of clothes?"

Carpenter stared through the telescopic sight at the body of the skinny elf and suddenly realized what was bothering him. His pistol was still clenched in his hand; no one had tried to take it. That, he was sure, could mean only one of two things—either the gun was a toy, or the ork who'd just come out of the building was an illusion of some sort. Which meant that he was a magician, or somebody else down there was.

Carpenter had never liked magicians. He remembered his mother telling him, Bible said thou shalt not suffer a witch to live, and he was pretty sure that applied to wizards as well. He was prepared to make an exception for Lori, because King and Wallace obviously liked her and Griffin seemed crazy about her, so what she was doing had to be more like faith healing or miracles or something, but he didn't even feel comfortable around her, and not just because she was so fraggin' pretty, maybe even prettier than Quinn, and he liked Quinn a whole lot.

He sneered as the saw the ork walk back toward the ramp, standing proud and tall as though he owned the place. Had to be an illusion, he thought, and suddenly wondered, could you scare an illusion? Would it flinch if you fired at it?

He smiled at the thought, then shook his head. Not *at* it;

Wallace had ordered him not to shoot anybody. But *near* it . . . that must be okay. He aimed at a rusty drum a couple of meters behind the ork, and fired.

His rifle was fitted with the best silencer available, and no sound came back to him as the bullet penetrated the barrel. The ork didn't even hesitate. Carpenter aimed at another drum, this one where the ork would see it if it actually could see, and squeezed the trigger again. This time, there was a spurt as fluid began pouring out of the drum, and a gratifying reaction from the ork—it stared, apparently horrified, then vanished completely.

Magnusson was close enough to the sniper nest to see the rifle barrel protruding from the side of the cooling tower. He hovered for a moment, chanting in Aramaic as a centering technique to reduce the drain from the spell, then cast a full-strength lightning bolt at the gun. Boanerges had told him that disabling the rifle was the priority; it was unlikely that the gunman would have any other weapons to hand with a long enough effective range to be a problem. Unusually, he hadn't specifically said that he didn't want the sniper harmed.

The powerful charge hit the silencer and was conducted through the metal. The lenses in the telescopic sight shattered, the chambered round exploded, and the electronics in the smartgun system fused. The current was also carried through Carpenter's metal lanyard to his belt, and through the wiring of his smartgun link, along his arm, up his neck, and all the way into his retinal link. He was flung backwards off the platform and hung there head down, dangling from the tethers that attached him to the platform, and blacked out without hearing the thunderclap.

Sumatra's body sat up suddenly, eyes wide with panic. *"Toxic!"* he yelled.

8

Boanerges, already pale from blood loss, looked as though he'd turned to bone. Yoko stared anxiously at him for a moment, then turned to Sumatra. "Where?" she demanded.

"Upstairs," said the rat shaman. "Some sort of water spirit—it was confined in one of the barrels, but that fraggin' idiot in the tower shot a hole in the barrel, didn't he? I don't know how powerful it is, but it's *real* fraggin' angry!"

Boanerges nodded wearily. "I can't fight it and concentrate on this spell. Go and tell Magnusson to get down; he's about to change back."

"Go out there? With *that* thing rampaging around?"

"I'll go out first, but I can't fight it *and* be sure of maintaining the shapechange spell. I can't concentrate on both things for long, and I'm nearly—"

"Dead?" suggested Yoko heavily.

"You can't fight a toxic spirit with cannons or kata," Boanerges told her. "And Jinx and Mish don't have enough training." He turned to Sumatra. "Tell Magnusson to get back here as quickly as he can, because if I *can't* beat it, it'll be up to the two of you."

The rat shaman nodded, though his expression suggested he was trying to swallow something not meant for human consumption. He lay back down, and his astral form floated out of his body again, then waited cautiously at the bottom of the ramp until he saw Boanerges' aura ascend above the ruins and confront the spirit.

The toxic spirit had taken the form of a great mud-colored water serpent, as though in deliberate parody of Boanerges' totem. No, not a serpent, Sumatra realized. An enormous leech. There was no sign of Boanerges' watcher spirits, and the rat shaman guessed that they'd already been destroyed by the monster. Revolted, Sumatra sped away toward the cooling tower in search of Magnusson.

Boanerges grabbed the front end of the spirit and squeezed, just behind where the head would be if it were a snake, and the creature whipped around and wrapped its tail around Boanerges' throat. "This is not your domain," said Boanerges. "Go!"

"It was," replied the toxic, in a voice like a handful of poisonous mud. "And it will be again, very soon."

Magnusson was five meters above the potholed road when Sumatra manifested in front of him. "Get down!" the ork said, frantically waving his arms. "Bo—"

Magnusson didn't wait to hear the rest of the sentence, but he wasted a second looking for a softer place to land, and suddenly realized that he was no longer a bird. He landed heavily on all fours, feeling the breath jarred out of him by the impact, and crouched there waiting for the power of speech to return and making a mental note to learn a catfall or levitation spell. "Wha—what's happened?"

"There's a toxic spirit. Boanerges is trying to banish it, but I don't think he's winning."

The mage nodded and rolled over onto his back. "Watch my meat. I'll—"

"Are you crazy?" the shaman spluttered. "You can't leave your body *here*, unguarded!"

"We're half a klick from the Crypt," said Magnusson, breathing hard. "Even if I *could* run that far, I'd get there too late to be of any help. Either I leave my meat here, or you'll have to go back and fight the toxic."

Sumatra looked at the mage and realized that he was right. Magnusson was a forty-some-year-old academic, a professor of hermetic magic; he hadn't worked the shadows since before his first marriage, nearly twenty years ago, and he'd never been an athlete. "Okay," he said reluctantly. "I'll go. My meat's back there, anyway."

Magnusson merely nodded, picked himself up off the street, and brushed himself down. "Good luck," he said, but Sumatra was already gone.

Boanerges gritted his teeth as the toxic spirit slithered out of his grasp, leaving his hand feeling diseased. The creature tightened its grip on his throat, and the shaman's attempts to grab it failed. Boanerges felt himself weakening; apart from his wounds, he was nearly exhausted from the effort of maintaining the shapechange spell for so long. He continued to struggle, knowing that while he and the toxic were locked in astral combat, it would be unable to attack anyone else . . . and with only a few magically talented novices available to try to stop it, it might be able to do the mercenaries' job for them, sending many of the Crypt's denizens fleeing and killing the rest.

Boanerges felt his vision start to blur and darken as his magical power ebbed under the spirit's onslaught. It had wrapped loops around his wrist, now, as well as his throat, and his attempts to dislodge it were having no apparent effect. He rallied his remaining strength and brought his hands up to his face, then bit into the creature. The taste of its astral form was foul enough to send a shock through his body—it was like trying to eat a burning tire flavored with cyanide—but the monster seemed to burst in his mouth like a blister, and the loops around his hands retracted. Even the stranglehold eased slightly for a moment, and the shaman thought he might have damaged the spirit badly enough that it would flee and try to regenerate. But instead, the toxic wound itself more tightly around his throat. Boanerges clawed at it, but this merely seemed to sear his fingers as though he was stirring acid with his bare hands.

Then, suddenly, the thing seemed to disintegrate. Boanerges turned around, expecting to thank Sumatra, or Magnusson . . . but instead, he saw the astral form of a stranger, a moon-faced young elf woman with shoulder-length black hair. "Thanks . . ." he gasped.

The astral form smiled, becoming prettier in the process. "Don't mention it. Lucky I just happened to be in the neighborhood."

"I don't . . ."

"Okay, I was spying on you, and I saw . . . no, it was as though I *smelled* that . . . What *was* that thing?"

"A toxic spirit. Either it was trapped inside that barrel somehow, or the toxic spill was enough to attract it."

She nodded. "I've heard of them, but I've never seen one before. You looked as though you needed help."

Boanerges didn't need to ask whether the mage had summoned it; it was obvious from her aura that her only contact with it had been the coup de grâce she'd just delivered. "Yes," he said. "I—"

Sumatra's astral form suddenly came hurtling through the sky at the speed of thought and rammed into the elf mage like an avalanche.

Hartz trudged into the cooling tower, stared up toward the iron-gray sky with his eyes set to maximum telescopic magnification, then reached for the small military-grade binoculars in his pocket. Carpenter still hung from his tether, the ruined rifle dangling from the lanyard on his belt. Hartz looked at him through the binoculars, shook his head despairingly and subvocalized into his headware microphone, "Chief?"

"Here."

"Carpenter's . . . well, he's either dead or unconscious. I'm going to climb up and see, but he's not looking good."

"What happened?"

"Fragged if I know. No sign of a bullet hole. Magic, maybe."

Wallace grimaced and looked at Lori's motionless body. He'd have to wait for her astral form to return before he could send her out to check on the sniper. "You sure the area's secure?"

"I think so. Nobody's shot at me yet."

"Okay. I'll have Lori scan the area as soon as I can;

she'll be able to tell whether he's dead." He shook his head. Griffin hadn't returned from his run to the hospital, which meant there was only the one van—and moving that away from the site would leave everyone there with no aid station and no backup. "Can you carry him back here if he's still alive?"

"Yeah, I think so."

"Good. I'll send—" He looked around the cargo bay. "Crabbe over with a medkit. Over and out."

The troll scrambled to his feet, keeping his head bowed to avoid banging it on the Step-Van's ceiling, and reached for his helmet. Wallace glanced at his wristcomp: 0806;—just over eleven hours left before they went in, and three men down already. He wondered how much of his squad would still be in fighting trim by sunset.

Lori was too startled to defend herself from the unexpected attack, but she quickly recovered and was about to hit her assailant with all her strength when Boanerges shouted, *"No! Stop!"*

Both combatants paused and stared at him. "She's one of—" the ork began.

"She just banished the toxic," said Boanerges. "She may have saved my life." He turned to the elf mage. "Again, thank you, and my apologies."

The mage hesitated. "Don't mention it. If that thing had stuck around, it would've been bad for everyone. And I don't want to have to kill any of you. But we've said we'll see this place evacuated one way or the other, and we will."

Boanerges nodded. "I believe you," he said unhappily. "But I'd rather we keep the truce as long as we can." He looked at Sumatra grimly.

The rat shaman wasn't stupid. "My apologies," he said, holding his arms wide as though being crucified. "If you want a free shot . . ."

Lori hesitated, then shook her head. "You're his teacher?" she asked Boanerges.

"Yes."

"Then I can see why he tried to defend you. Apology accepted."

"Thank you," said Boanerges, and Sumatra followed suit a few seconds later, though without the same warmth. The snake shaman's astral form returned to his meatbody, and Lori and Sumatra's astral forms were left watching each other warily for a few seconds.

"He's not going to give this place up," said the ork. "You'll have to carry him out. Are you prepared to do that?"

"Are *you* prepared to see him killed over a worthless piece of land?"

"He's my teacher, and I took an oath to defend the coven he leads. And if this land is so worthless, why is somebody paying you to kill for it?"

I wish I knew, thought Lori. Instead of answering the question, she flew back to the Step-Van and her physical form. Wallace looked around when he heard her move, and waited for her report.

"They were just attacked by a toxic spirit," she said. "I think it was attracted by a chemical spill—a stray shot must have hit one of the barrels. I helped them banish it; it was a danger to us, as well."

Wallace didn't answer.

"The watchers they had up as guards over the entrance have gone. I'm sure they'll put new ones up before long, but they seem to be running out of magic—and magicians."

Wallace grunted. "Can you get down into the bunker, see who and what is there?"

"I don't know. They probably have someone watching the entrance in astral, and there's enough pure earth on their roof that I'd have to plow my way through it—not to mention the four hermetic circles drawn up top. And wouldn't that be violating the cease-fire?"

Wallace shrugged. "I don't know, but it probably isn't worth the risk. Hartz just radioed in; Carpenter's unconscious, maybe dead. Can you go and check on him? And if there's no watchers guarding the entrance when you come back, tell me."

Magnusson walked cautiously through the ruined buildings, using his astral vision to peer into every shadow in search of possible threats—not just mercs, but also scavengers, thrillers, devil rats and feral dogs. He was wearing his oldest pair of jeans and a hooded gray sweatshirt, both safely nondescript but cleaner than the average squatters' usual garb. And an observant eye would have noticed that he looked well fed and well groomed, and wore sturdy walking boots of real leather. He might as well have been carrying a neon sign saying "Mug me" in three languages. He wished he'd thought to bring a gun and wear heavier armor: he wasn't much of a shot, but the black-handled ritual knife that he wore on a thong around his neck had a blade barely longer than his middle finger, and you couldn't bluff with lightning bolts and stunball spells unless your attacker already knew you were a magician.

He was picking his way through the weeds and rubble of the abandoned recycling plant a block south of the Crypt when something crunched loudly underfoot. He froze, then looked down. It was a piece of toughened transparent plastic, with a vaguely streamlined shape, and appeared not to have been there long. He squatted down to examine it; he'd heard that Mute had brought down an ultralight drone, and this was very likely a part of it. And drones were often armed. He looked around in the hope of finding a usable weapon, and caught sight of a dull metallic sheen amid a patch of weeds. As quietly as he could, he walked over to where the object lay and picked it up. It was roughly the same size and shape as two medium-sized plates, and there was something oddly familiar about it. He thought for a moment, and realized why: it reminded him of one of his favorite stories, "A Saucer of Loneliness."

Magnusson smiled, and examined the object more closely. There were lenses set into one side, and snapped-off plastic struts—one of them long enough to serve as a handle, so that the thing could be wielded like a mace. It wasn't much of a weapon, but it had more reach than his knife, and one of the technical types in the Crypt might be able to get some useful information from it. Feeling slightly more confident, he crept up to a pile of rubble on the northern edge of the Crypt and cautiously scanned the area. There were two mercenaries standing guard, one on either southern corner of the block: there was a clear line of sight between them, and Magnusson rightly suspected they could also be seen by their counterparts on the northern corners.

Wishing that he'd learned an invisibility spell, or that he was protected against gunfire by a quickened deflection spell like Yoko and Boanerges (his hard-won ability to reflect spells back on their caster wouldn't save him from bullets), he sized up the guards and calculated his chances of being able to run between them and make it to the ramp without being gunned down. They were depressingly small, but bringing at least one of the sentries down with a sleep spell would improve the odds. Unfortunately, his centering technique required speaking aloud and drawing attention to himself, so he ruled that out, and there was no safe place where he could see both of them at once, so a stunball was—

One of the sentries glanced in his direction. Magnusson wasn't sure whether the merc had seen him—the visored helmet made it difficult to tell—but it spurred him into action. Without bothering with centering measures to reduce drain, he cast a powerful stunbolt at the human, who immediately collapsed. Without waiting to see how the other merc would respond, Magnusson scrambled out past the rubble and into the street, running faster than he'd done in more than twenty years.

Hartz had nearly reached the top of the cooling tower when Lori manifested on the platform above him. "Frag!" he snapped, gripping the rope tightly. "You nearly gave me a coronary!"

"Sorry," she said. "Wallace told me to see whether Carpenter was alive."

"And?"

"His aura says he is, though he's in bad shape. He's been hit by some sort of spell that did a lot of physical damage. Probably a lightning bolt."

Hartz sniffed. There was a faint odor of ozone, as well as burnt flesh, gunfire and an approaching rainstorm. "Can you help him?"

"I can stabilize him; I'm not sure I can do much more

than that without getting him to a hospital." The sniper was a poor candidate for magical healing even under ideal circumstances; he'd had so much cyberware implanted over the years that he barely had any essence remaining. "And you'll need to get him down first."

The ogre swore again as he clambered up onto the tilted platform. "Can't we just call DocWagon? This sounds like a job for a medevac chopper."

"We have to get him down first," she said firmly. "Our employer doesn't want us drawing attention to this place. Unless you can think of a good cover story."

Hartz grunted as he hauled Carpenter back over the platform's low railing, thankful for the extra strength his muscle replacements lent him. "Not one that anybody would believe," he admitted. "Y'know, it's days like this I almost wish I'd never slugged that sergeant."

Dutch stared as Kat fell over, and looked around to see where the attack was coming from. When he saw a tall man sprinting across the road *toward* the Crypt, it took him half a second to link the two events together and, despite his boosted reflexes, another quarter second to bring his gun to his shoulder and aim at the intruder. *"Halt!"* he shouted. "Who—"

The man glanced at him without breaking his stride, and Dutch found himself fighting to stay awake. He blinked, then looked around to see where his target had gone. To his surprise, the man was still on the road, moving more slowly than before. Dutch wondered if he'd been hit by the same spell, or gas, or whatever was affecting him . . . "Stop!" he yelled.

Magnusson looked at the sentry, who was still standing—if a little unsteadily. He froze for an instant, then fell to the ground in the hope that the mercenary wouldn't shoot a man who was already down.

The ork peered at him uncertainly, and lowered the gun. Magnusson risked another stunbolt, muttering in Aramaic in the hope of reducing the drain to a manageable level, and was relieved to see the merc pitch forward and collapse

full length onto the road. The magician picked himself up
and staggered wearily onto the sidewalk despite his legs
feeling like water and his feet like lead bricks. Climbing
over the knee-high wall of the derelict warehouse required
an almost superhuman effort, and once on the other side,
the urge to lie down on the compost heap was almost over-
powering. He continued to stumble along, doing his best to
avoid the beds of herbs, chard, carrots and potato plants,
until he snagged his foot on a trip wire and landed face-
first in mud. When he looked up, his vision seemed to be
filled by the muzzle of a rifle.

"Maggie?" said a wonderfully familiar voice somewhere
in the distance. "Frag, Prof, you look like drek. Are you
okay?"

Wallace ground his teeth as yet another report came in
of a man down, and glanced at the tactical map projected
on the windshield's heads-up display. Crabbe and Hartz
were bringing Carpenter back, Griffin was still too far away
to be of any assistance . . . He called to Lori, who appeared
a moment later. "Are you okay to go out again?"

"What is it this time?" she asked.

"Not what—who. Kat and Dutch. They're both down.
Sounds like it's the same magician. Some truce."

"Carpenter was the first to break it," said Lori flatly.

Wallace shrugged. "I remember a preacher in Sunday
school told me that if everyone believed in 'an eye for an
eye and a tooth for a tooth,' the whole world would end
up blind and toothless. I guess Carpenter was asleep that
morning."

The mage looked at his tusks and attempted to smile. "I
don't think anyone could ever accuse you of being
toothless."

The ork snorted. "That's not what worries me. If it
comes down to a war of attrition, I think they may be
winning."

"If it comes down to magic, they will," said Lori, suddenly serious. "I've had a look at the plants they're growing
on their roof. Some of them are food, but there's a remark-
ably healthy herb garden in there as well—the sort of herbs

that talismongers pay a fortune for. And the soil's been magically cleansed of contamination, and that takes meta-magic. You remember that we were told this place is a school? I think they're teaching magic; there's at least three magicians down there, and I don't know how many more we might be facing." She shrugged. "I'll go check on the sentries."

Magnusson collapsed face-first onto a mattress in the corridor and lay there for a moment, then rolled over and looked up at the trio who'd helped him down the ramp— 8-ball, Pinhead Pierce and a human teenager he didn't recognize. "Thanks," he mumbled.

"Don't mention it," said the dwarf, looking at the object he'd had to pry from the magician's fingers. "Where did you get this?"

"Block south of here. What is it?"

"Looks like the instrument package from a Condor drone," 8-ball replied. "Crane would know for sure."

"Can we find out who owns it? Are there any serial numbers inside, or anything like that?"

"Should be, if they haven't been removed. Are you okay?"

Magnusson shook his head. "Nothing a lot of sleep won't fix."

"You've got about ten hours. If you're lucky."

The magician closed his eyes. "How's Boanerges?"

"Fragged. Looks even worse than you," said Pierce with his usual level of diplomacy.

"Mish and the doc are looking after him," said 8-ball as reassuringly as he could. "Sumatra's conjured up a couple of watchers and is taking a break. Pierce can you take this to Crane and Zurich and ask them to have a look at it? Akira, can you go to the kitchen, get me some drinking water?" He watched the teenagers leave and shook his head. "Yoko's standing guard, keeping a watch in astral. That toxic really took it out of Boanerges, so we'd better hope they don't hit us with anything magical. Not for a few hours, at least."

The magician closed his eyes. "Should we start evacuating the kids? The ones who can stand the sunlight, at least?"

"If it was up to me . . . yes. If Wallace says he'll take them to another squat, then I believe him. We might even persuade him to run the elves and the orks somewhere they'll be welcome."

"You think it'll come to that?"

"I think they'll be safer somewhere else than here, and I'd like to give them that option. I know Boanerges is a big fan of Gandhi—you know, the nonviolence guy—but I don't think passive resistance is going to work this time. If I were you, I'd start packing up the library and the enchanting stuff, maybe even as much of the hospital as we can. Or you get ready to kill everyone who comes down that ramp. Either way, I think we should get the kids out now."

Crane and Zurich sat on opposite sides of a folding table under a magnifying lamp (both scrounged from a bring-out-your-trash day in Auburn) taking the instrument package apart with their multi-tools, while Pinhead Pierce pedaled a jury-rigged bicycle generator to power the lamp. The Crypt's electricity supply was mostly drawn from the few working streetlights in the area; it was notoriously unreliable, and much of it was consumed by the small refrigerators in the clinic and the kitchen. Czarnecki had commandeered all of the library's fully charged battery-powered lamps for the surgery, leaving readers with nothing but candles. Zurich had insisted on having reliable light for the precision work he needed to do, so he'd dragged the bicycle generator from the kitchen into the library, hooked it up to the lamp and drafted Pierce to provide the energy.

"It's from a Condor, all right," said the rigger. "Some interesting modifications to the sensor package, too. That radar looks military, but it's not standard UCAS issue."

"Hmm." They continued dismantling the electronics, noting the serial numbers they found, until Zurich did a double take and held the radar unit closer to the magnifying lens, comparing it to diagrams displayed on his retinal link.

"You're right. This interrupter is an Aztechnology design, but it's Aztlan mil-spec, not meant for corp or civilian use."

Crane nodded. "They're mercenaries," he said. "They could have stolen the equipment, salvaged it, bought it on the black market . . . If you looked at all the components in all the drones I've used over the years, you'd think I'd been everywhere."

"I still think it's worth checking these serial numbers," the dwarf replied. He looked over at Ratatosk, who was sitting on the floor still plugged into the Crypt's only jackpoint. When the elf didn't acknowledge that he'd heard them, Zurich slid down from his chair and walked over to look at the screen on the deck. Instead of the view of the Matrix that he'd expected to see, the monitor showed greatly accelerated video of cases and crates being loaded into vans. The camera angle was too high for Zurich to spot any landmarks, and after watching for nearly a minute, he asked loudly, "What is this?"

"Sea-Tac," said Ratatosk, not looking at him. "8-ball suggested I check to see if anyone transported any barghests from the CAS. You can't do something like that without a drekload of official paperwork, so if you know where to look, it's not difficult to find the paper trail and start tracking back."

"Any luck so far?"

"A little. They flew in on a commercial cargo flight, landed just after three a.m. Signed over to an Elvis Carpenter, who had all the papers he needed to get them in and out without a quarantine period. That can't have been cheap, but he paid it himself with a certified credstick. I'm just hoping I don't have to go looking through his bank records to see who paid *him*. If he's one of the mercs, he'll have accounts in datahavens with ultraviolet security codes. *Got* it!" he chortled, as the video slowed down to half-normal speed.

"Got what?" asked the sweaty Pierce, still laboring away on the bike.

Zurich peered at the small screen. Two heavy mesh cages were being loaded by forklift onto the back of a dark gray Gaz-Willys Nomad. "Can you get the license?" he asked.

"Working on it," said Ratatosk, keying in instructions. Physical security at international airports was better than that on most federal buildings and some military bases, with all vehicles going in and out having to pass through at least three automated checkpoints and the records being kept indefinitely. So the data they wanted existed, but accessing one of these datafiles was difficult, and risky even for a decker of Ratatosk's skill; deleting or editing one was nearly impossible as well as pointless, because multiple backups existed in carefully isolated systems. If they could get to the info, it would be accurate. "Just hope it's not rented."

"We have some serial numbers from the drone that Mute shot down," said Zurich. "I'll leave them on the table; can you check those when you've finished?"

"Okay."

"Can I stop now?" asked Pierce.

While the Crypt's internal structure seemed perfectly chaotic, an astute observer would have noticed a few patterns. Humans, the least likely to be susceptible to sunlight, tended to cluster in the cubicles nearest the bottom of the ramp. Most elves set up their quarters along the west wall, while orks and trolls gathered in the southeast corner. As a result, the height of the doorframes and the lengths of the improvised beds tended to increase the farther they were from the ramp, which sometimes gave newcomers the strange feeling that they were shrinking as they walked away from the light.

Akira's room was a fairly typical single sleeping cubicle: roughly two meters by three, with its walls and bed improvised from pallets and crates. The inner walls were lined with several thicknesses of posters for a little soundproofing and, unlike some, they actually reached the mottled ceiling. The dirty concrete floor was covered with flattened cartons; the curtain across the doorway was an old microfiber blanket worn too thin to provide much warmth. The mattress on the narrow bed was a slab of plastic foam; the pillow, a calico bag stuffed with rags; the bedding, a sheet, a stolen Japanese flag, a thermal blanket and whatever spare cloth-

ing he had that didn't smell too bad. Lankin had borrowed
the room so he could check his investments on his pocket
secretary in privacy, and was considering buying more Mitsuhama shares when the "Incoming Call: Gardiner" message scrolled across the bottom of the screen.

Lankin hesitated for a fraction of a second before activat-
ing the scrambler and accepting the call: it was rarely a
good idea to keep a fixer waiting. "Yes?"

"Lankin? Johnson wants a PR on the FB job."

The elf was too good an actor to wince or let his smile
falter. "I'm recruiting another member for the team. A
good covert ops spesh who can get into the factory ahead
of us, or get us out if things turn ugly. The job'll happen
on schedule." Lankin was masquerading as a highly placed
civil servant from the Caribbean League, in Seattle to buy
a Federated-Boeing Executive Commuter with military
armor. The plan was for him to smuggle a rigger into the
factory to steal the plane and fly it to Cascade Ork territory, with a decker and a mage doing their best to stop it
being tracked electronically or magically.

"It'd better: you need the nuyen. Who's the spesh?"

"Mute."

Gardiner actually looked impressed. "How big a cut does
she want?"

"We're negotiating now. And I may have found the per-
fect people for that job in LA next month. A weapons
specialist and a warrior adept. I'll tell you more later."

Griffin pulled up behind the Step-Van and was greeted
by an obviously irritated Wallace. "About time you got
back," the ork growled, and nodded at the Nomad. "Can
that make a return trip on autopilot?"

The rigger shook his head. "On these roads? No way.
After it gets to the highway, maybe."

"Frag. Okay, set it for manual. King'll have to drive; I
need you here. I want a drone up in the sky as soon as
you can put it up there—one that can shoot back, if necessary. We've had another three men taken out since you
left."

"You're kidding!"

"I fraggin' wish. Kat and Dutch have been hit with some sort of sleep spell, not a scratch on 'em, but Carpenter . . . something fraggin' near fried him. Lori's managed to stabilize him, but she's exhausted; I asked her to wake up the sleeping beauties, and she said that if she tried, she'd probably fall over too. So we've put Carpenter in a stabilization unit and I'm letting Lori rest up, because we're bound to need her again."

"King's awake?"

"Not yet, but he's had more time to sleep it off, and I can't spare anyone else. 'Sides, you know King. Ordering him to drive Carpenter to the hospital is probably the only way to stop him going redshirt and rushing into that place to find the fragger who cast the spell. And then I'd be another man down, and I'd have to tell *both* of their mothers."

"King has a *mother*?"

His commander glared at him. "Yeah. And you don't want her angry at you, believe me."

"I'll bet."

"And 8-ball will have some nasty little surprise waiting for whoever's first down that ramp—assuming they can get past that sentry. That's why I want it to be another drone, not one of the squad. Got that?"

Griffin nodded. "I can have a rotodrone in the air in four minutes. Light machine gun and grenade launcher. What sort of grenades should I load?"

The ork sighed. "Concussion and neurostun. And gel rounds—for now. Did they give us gel rounds for the machine gun?"

"I'll check. I know we asked for them."

"You sound as though you don't trust our employers."

"Have we *ever* had one who gave us exactly what we said we needed to do a job and didn't try to cut costs somewhere?"

Wallace thought about this for a moment. "I don't remember one," he admitted. "But I don't think Mr. Fedorov is spending his own nuyen, and this stuff isn't war surplus. Most of it's too new. I smell corp money behind this, and lots of it."

"Me too." The rigger looked around at the wasteland. "Who do you think 8-ball's really working for?"

*   *   *

Despite his injuries and obvious signs of exhaustion, Boanerges insisted they meet in his magically shielded medicine lodge rather than Czarnecki's clinic. 8-ball looked uneasily at the shaman's bandaged head and his unusually dull eyes, then at the way Magnusson leaned on the lodge's elaborately painted wall. "How is Patty?" asked Yoko.

"Mish is watching her," said Czarnecki, his tone and expression making it clear that he believed that he should be—and watching Boanerges as well. "She cast a healing spell on her, and I taped her ribs and wired her jaw. Fortunately, her lungs seem undamaged, and I don't think she's lost much blood."

"Is she conscious?" asked Boanerges.

"She was. I wanted to call DocWagon, but she won't leave until you do. I had to give her a sedative to stop her coming to this meeting, even though she can't talk."

"How soon will she be able to move?" asked Lankin.

"She could probably fall out of bed without magical assistance," said the medic coldly.

"I'm not talking about fighting," said Lankin. "Could she walk a few blocks, then drive?"

"In a few hours, maybe. Why?"

"Her van's parked a few blocks away," Lankin replied. "If we're not going to trust the mercs to take the kids to safety, she could drive them. It would keep her out of danger, too, and free up a bed for the next patient."

Boanerges opened his eyes a little more widely. "You think we need to start evacuating?"

"I think we'll have to. The best we can hope for is to negotiate for some form of compensation. How many of those mercs do you think we're likely to be able to kill if they come storming down the ramp?"

"*What?* I'm hoping we don't have to kill any!"

"Then you'd better hope *they* haven't worked that out," said Lankin grimly. "I know this may be difficult for many of you, but you'll have to try thinking like a corp. Do you know what our lives are worth to a corp? Nothing. They don't enter into the equation at all. Same with the common law that says this place is ours because we've been here more than four years. Any corp knows we can't win a court battle, any more than we can beat those mercs without taking a lot of casualties.

"But do you know what the mercs' lives are worth to that same corp? Probably between two and five thousand nuyen each. That's the main difference between a live mercenary and a dead one to them—a few thousand in funeral expenses and hush money. They expect mercs and shadowrunners to have their own medical and life insurance. The good ones do, and they figure the rest are disposable. Now, if they do an assessment and decide that we can kill, say, five mercs, that's ten or twenty thousand nuyen extra expense. If we say that we'll evacuate peacefully in exchange for, oh, two hundred each, that's a saving of a few thousand for them . . . but only if they believe we can and will kill those five mercs. And I think getting the kids out of the way is a good way to show them that we're ready for a real fight."

"He's right," said Ratatosk, to Lankin's astonishment. "At least, he's right about thinking like a corp. I traced the license of the Nomad that picked up the barghests from the airport. It belongs to Aztechnology, and it's not listed as stolen. The drone also looks like it came from Aztechnology; it has Aztlan military-issue radar and infrared. I don't know how often they do a stock take of their drones at the pyramid, but I'm pretty sure that if one of their trucks went missing for more than twenty-four hours and was picked up by the scanners at Sea-Tac, it would've sounded some alarms and someone would've called Lone Star to cover their butts. They haven't, and that means that someone with authorization checked the car out of the pyramid. The only people who could do that are Aztechnology employees."

"Or a team of runners with a first-rate decker," countered Lankin.

Ratatosk shrugged. "Maybe. But it seems like a lot of trouble to go to for a couple of trucks and a few drones. 8-ball, is there a decker in that squad?"

"I don't know. The only ones I know are Wallace, Griffin, King, Lewis and Carpenter. Quinn I know only by reputation. Of those, Griffin is the closest they had to a tech wiz, and his specialty is hardware, not programming. They could've hired someone . . . but I think Ratatosk's probably right. There are cheaper and easier ways to get the stuff."

"Unless it's an attempt to make it *look* like Aztechnology's behind this," said Sumatra.

"Behind what?" asked Boanerges. "Whatever it is they want this place for, they're not going to be able to say it's part of Aztechnology if it isn't—not for long, anyway."

"They might be planning a massacre," said Sumatra darkly. "If that got out, it'd be really bad PR."

8-ball shook his head. "If that's what they wanted, they picked the wrong team of mercs. I've known plenty who wouldn't have hesitated before they came storming in to wipe us all out."

"And the massacre of a few dozen squatters wouldn't even make the major newsnets," said Lankin. "Not enough people would care. If there was any blowback at all, which I doubt, the CEO would just pin the blame on the mercenaries and maybe sacrifice someone in middle management who was supposed to be in charge. The guys higher up the pyramid wouldn't even lose their annual bonuses. No, whoever's paying for this, whether it's Aztechnology or not . . . they really want something that's here."

"Or somebody," said Sumatra slowly. "Maybe it's not the land at all. Maybe it's one of us."

9

The Hatter checked his pocket secretary for messages as soon as he managed to escape from his nine a.m. meeting, and read the report from Wallace as he walked back to his office. He hit the Reply button before the door had finished sliding shut behind him. "What's this about a toxic spirit attacking your mage?" he demanded.

"It didn't attack her," said Wallace—quietly, because Lori was sleeping in the cargo compartment behind him. She'd cast a stabilizing spell on Carpenter as soon as Crabbe had brought him back, but she was sufficiently worried about his condition that she'd insisted on riding in the back of the Nomad with him. King, though still groggy from the aftereffects of the stunbolt, had managed to drive them to Good Samaritan in good time without any mishap. Once Carpenter had been checked into the ER, Lori had staggered back to the Nomad and lay down on the stretcher, and was fast asleep by the time they returned. Wallace and King had carried her, still on the stretcher, back to the Step-Van and laid her beside the still-unconscious Kat and Dutch. "She attacked it. That's not what's knocked her out. It's all the healing spells."

"The shaman in the Crypt didn't summon it?"

"She doesn't think so; it was attacking one of them, and she says it nearly killed him. I think she'd know if any of the shamans there are toxics."

"Nearly killed him," the Hatter murmured thoughtfully. "And you have three men in the hospital now?"

"Yes. Carpenter's still on the critical list; the other two are stable and won't need any transplants or prosthetics— well, no new ones."

The Hatter glanced at the digital clock on the screen and nodded. "Understood. Keep me posted." He broke the connection and stared at the computer monitor on his desk with obvious distaste. His morning's work was to double-check the résumés of applicants for jobs that required a computer security clearance, and it was tedious work. He knew that any decker good enough to be worth hiring would probably have hacked into the records of his school and any previous employers to give himself a more respectable history, and all he was expected to do was to weed out the less successful forgeries. He also knew the job wasn't entirely a punishment; it was a necessary precaution, and he had the right abilities and mind-set to do it well, but it was much less exciting or rewarding than the work he'd done before that humiliating incident with Morales. "Nearly killed him," he repeated thoughtfully, then punched in an address he hadn't used since his days as a Mr. Johnson.

"One of us?" repeated Boanerges. "Why would Aztechnology be interested in any of us?"

No one spoke for several seconds; then 8-ball sighed. "Okay. Who *else* here has been on a run against the Pyramid that they might want to kill us for?"

Sumatra, Zurich, Ratatosk and Crane slowly raised their hands, and Pierce hesitantly followed suit. "I was only guardin' the meat," he said. "I don't think they coulda known I was involved. 'Sides, we didn't actually manage to steal anything—the team was lucky to get out alive."

"How recently do you mean?" asked Lankin uneasily.

"How long can a corp bear a grudge?" Ratatosk replied.

"It was six months ago, and they couldn't have known I'd be here! I've never been here before . . . and if they wanted to kill me, I'm not that difficult to find."

The decker silently conceded that that was true. Lankin, a former Fuchi company man, was well over two meters tall and a flashy dresser. He lived a life of luxury in a custom-built apartment in the Elven District, drove a Merlot-colored convertible Saab Dynamit and ate regularly at the exclusive elf-biased restaurant Icarus Descending. Even his creditors and ex-girlfriends had no trouble locating him. Ratatosk turned to Yoko and raised an eyebrow inquisitively.

"Not in more than a year," she replied. "I've done three runs *for* them since then, all of them successful. I don't think this is personal."

"Unless someone's been betting against you," Pierce suggested.

Yoko shook her head. "I haven't had to defend my title in more than a year. I'm flattered by the suggestion, but sending a team of mercs after me—after any *one* of us— seems like rather serious overkill. There must be some other explanation."

"Maybe," said Lankin neutrally. "Maybe it's not Aztechnology. I heard somebody stole a shipment meant for Mitsuhama last week—close to a million nuyen worth of magical gear, which you can be sure they want back. And there was a Seoulpa courier they found dead behind the Downfall a few nights ago, minus the case cuffed to his wrist . . ."

"And the wrist," said 8-ball. "His whole arm and both his eyes. At least, that's what my fixer told me. She might have been exaggerating."

"Whatever the explanation is," said Lankin, "I still think it's imperative that we evacuate as many of the children as practical. They'll be much safer in another squat, and I think it'll improve our negotiating position . . . and in a best-case scenario, if we do manage to keep this . . . place," he said before Boanerges could object, "they can come back when the shooting has stopped and the mercenaries have gone."

Boanerges looked around the room, stopping when his gaze fell on Yoko. "If we can arrange some kind of transportation, I think we should give them the choice," the adept said. "I don't want them hurt, and I don't want anyone to say we've been using kids and noncombatants as human shields. I want everyone who stays to be willing and able to either fight or work in the clinic." She turned to Czarnecki. "You've been here nearly as long as any of us, Doc. What do you think?"

The ork was silent for a moment. "I'm not a fighter. One of the first things they teach us is 'First do no harm,' and I've been trying to obey that one for a long time now. I don't want to have to kill anyone. I don't even want to carry a gun. But if you're going to fight, you'll need a medic. And where else are you going to find one if I leave? Where is anyone in this area going to find one?" He looked at Boanerges. "I'll stay. I can find work for a couple of stretcher bearers, and someone to keep things clean, but I agree the kids should go. And I'll want to know everyone's blood type; if they don't know it, they come to the clinic now and get tested." He turned to Lankin. "If and when I have to leave, I want a vehicle that I can use as an ambulance. Can you do that?"

"I'll add that to our list of demands," Lankin assured him.

Boanerges glanced at Magnusson. The magician grimaced. "Why are you asking me?" he said. "This isn't my home, and it never was—nor my school, nor my hospital, nor even a place of refuge." He looked around the medicine lodge, at the murals laboriously created from colored sands and powdered crystals and other pigments, chosen not just for their magical properties but also for their brilliant hues both in the visible spectrum and in infrared, and all of them scavenged from the wasteland south of the Crypt. "I have a good apartment, I teach in a fine school, I have DocWagon, I have no need to hide from anyone—except my ex-wives' lawyers, of course, and even they haven't bothered me recently. This place is a dump, a hole, a pit; everything you do here, you could do somewhere else . . . except maybe finding raw materials for talismongers. I'll grant you that it's a good location for that. That aside, though, there must be a hundred other squats in the metroplex where you could do the same sort of good work. I don't feel any particularly strong tie to the *place* . . ."

"Do you, to *any* place?" asked Boanerges.

"Not enough to risk dying for it, but let me finish, please. I swore an oath of fraternity when you allowed me to join the coven, and here, *you're* the professor. The dean, even. If you say stay, I will stay. I will heal those who need healing, and if you say fight, I will fight."

"Snake told me to stay," said the shaman. "She didn't say why, or that anyone else had to . . . but thanks. Lankin, 8-ball—I'm going to go up in astral and ask if the cease-fire still holds. If it does, I'd like the two of you to negotiate safe passage for everyone who wants to leave; and Lankin, anything extra you could persuade them to give us would be welcome, of course. Ratatosk, in case it *is* the land they're after, see what you can find out about the history of this place."

Wallace marched back to the Step-Van—still limping slightly, but doing his best to hide it from 8-ball and Lankin. He sat down heavily on the bench seat and hit the Redial button on his phone. "Mr. Fedorov?"

The Hatter was examining a particularly opaque résumé and was only too pleased to be interrupted, though he managed to hide this. "What is it now?"

"Some of the squatters—kids, mostly—want to leave while it's still light, but there's no safe place within walking distance, especially not if they're carrying all their dr—uh, belongings. There's also one of their number who may be too badly injured to leave under her own power. They want a van, one they can use as an ambulance. I said I'd ask my employer."

"A van. I'm sorry, but do I look like a charity? Do I *sound* like a charity?"

"I don't think they're expecting an executive transport. Any old junker would do, as long as it can run for a couple of days, and it *might* help move them out of here faster," said Wallace, trying to keep the exasperation out of his tone. "I don't think they trust us to drive them anywhere, but if they can choose where to go, it'll stop them coming back . . . most of 'em, anyway. It could save you nuyen in the long term."

"I'll look into it. Are they asking for anything else? Rooms at the Hilton and dinner at the Edge, maybe?"

"No," said the ork, deciding not to mention some of Lankin's other ambitious requests.

The Hatter thought for a moment. "I have a meeting in a few minutes. I'll call you when it's over. I may be able to arrange something."

Yoko was waiting beside the painted pillar at the bottom of the ramp as Lankin returned underground, bowing his head to avoid bumping it on the ceiling. "How did it go?"

Lankin shrugged. 8-ball, walking down the ramp behind him, looked glum. "Wallace said they'd ask for a van, but he didn't sound too hopeful," said the dwarf. "As for the other stuff . . . I'm not sure I'd want to accept gifts from the fragger who's running this show. He sounds like the sort of scumbag who used to give the natives blankets infected with plague."

"Smallpox," Lankin corrected him. "You get plague from rat fleas. But I concur with your assessment of his character."

"Thanks."

Yoko nodded. "I need to talk to you," she told Lankin. "In private. 8-ball, can you stand guard for a moment?"

"Sure," said the dwarf, drawing his smartgun and leaning against the pillar. He glanced over at Akira, who was standing rigidly beside the other, gripping an assault rifle so tightly that his knuckles were white. 8-ball found himself hoping that the gun was set to single shot, not full automatic fire, and was glad that Mish had summoned a hearth spirit and ordered it to guard the sentries against any accidents. "You ever used one of those before?" he asked, nodding at the rifle.

Akira glanced at the bokken—a wooden sword—propped up against the pillar within easy reach. "Guns are too noisy."

"I think that's one of the reasons Yoko gave it to you,"

8-ball replied. "If anyone does try to get in, you can alert everyone else even if you miss. Who's your sensei? Kaneda?"

"Yes," said the teenager, obviously proud of being one of the swordmaster's students. "Who was yours?"

"Kaneda gave me my sword, and Yoko's taught me some taijutsu, but I'm not an adept like them. I don't have your reach either, and I prefer not to wait until the fraggers are close enough to step on me before I can hit 'em, so I carry this instead." He patted the Ingram smartgun at his side. "It may not be as honorable as a sword, or as pretty, but it's kept me alive this long despite some other people's best efforts—and most of *them* couldn't give a drek about honor, either."

"Who taught you to shoot?"

"I did. Some Humanis drek tried to make me dance by shooting at my feet—"

Cleaning up Underworld 93 after a big concert was a dirty job, but the management didn't worry about SINs if you were prepared to work for half the going rate, and sometimes there was stuff left lying around that was worth scavenging—if you could smuggle it past the security guards, who always demanded a cut. Some of the other cleaners boasted of having found BTL chips, drugs, weapons, even certified credsticks, and one had gathered a large collection of women's underwear and T-shirts. 8-ball had never managed to keep anything more valuable than a disposable cell phone, but he'd managed to save up enough to buy an armor vest, a good pair of boots that actually fit, and an old Dodge Scoot—all on the black market, of course. He'd also picked up a good amount of gossip about shadowruns, and when all else failed, there was the perennial game of Name that Stain.

It was a few minutes after three a.m., and 8-ball had just finished his shift. He'd gone into a Stuffer Shack to buy a Nukit meal and a couple of beers to take back to his doss at the Crypt and was paying for his purchases when he heard a slurred voice behind him say, "You sell that drek to kids now?"

Joey, the clerk, looked down at 8-ball, then up at the

face of the man standing halfway down the aisle, a baseball cap pulled down to shade his eyes. "No, mister. He's not a kid. He's a dwarf."

8-ball knew he should just walk away, but Joey had plugged his credstick into the reader and was waiting for the transaction to finish—often a slow process because of Puyallup's tenuous connection to the Matrix. Instead, he glanced over his shoulder and noticed the Humanis Policlub symbol tattooed on the man's bulging bicep. The man smiled and drew a short-barreled revolver from the back of his waistband. With the smooth motion of someone doing something for the thousandth time, he shot out both the Shack's security cameras, then aimed at the clerk's face, the orange dot of the laser sight flicking across his eye before stopping on his forehead amid the constellation of pimples. Joey gulped and froze, too scared to reach for the pistol under the counter. The man looked at the back of 8-ball's T-shirt, and laughed. "Underworld 93, huh? You a musician, Dopey?"

"N-no, m-mister, he's—"

"I didn't ask you," said the man darkly. "So, Dopey, if you're not a musician, what are you? A dancer, maybe?"

8-ball turned around. He was armed with only a knife, a small but sharp one that he'd made himself. It wasn't balanced for throwing, and in any case the man was wearing a heavy sleeveless vest that probably had armor plates under the pockets. Before 8-ball could speak, the man fired a shot into the floor between his feet, causing the dwarf to jump.

"Not bad," said the man, firing again—this time hitting the floor a few centimeters from 8-ball's right ankle, causing him to take a hasty leap to the left. The next shot, predictably, hit the floor to 8-ball's right. The dwarf jumped again. The man's apparent drunkenness didn't seem to be affecting his aim, but 8-ball allowed himself to hope that it might have slowed down his thought processes. He kept a close watch on the beam from the laser sight as the man aimed at his face and fired again. 8-ball fell forward onto the floor, and reached for his knife. Six shots, he thought. Please let him not have a backup gun.

The man squeezed the trigger again, and the hammer thudded onto an empty chamber. He blinked as though baffled, then reached into his pants pocket for some spare ammunition. He was still fumbling with the loose bullets when 8-ball hurtled down the aisle and drove the point of his knife through pocket, hand, and thigh muscle. The man yelled from the pain, and Joey snapped out of his funk and drew the Roomsweeper out from under the counter. The man stared at him, and then the front of his baseball cap and the upper part of his face disappeared, splattering the window, the shelves, and 8-ball's bushy Afro with blood, splintered bone and gobbets of brain.

"He shoots! He scores!" Joey crowed, then looked at his surviving customer. "You okay, chummer?"

"Sure," said 8-ball thickly. He retrieved his knife and wiped it clean, then picked up his beers and his taco platter and staggered out into the rain to his bike.

He washed his hair twice that night, and once again the next morning, but it still didn't feel clean, so the next day he shaved it all off.

"And that's how I got my name," 8-ball finished. "Then I went and bought myself a Roomsweeper of my own. I never wanted to be in a situation again where the other fragger had a gun and I only had a knife, or even a sword. Since then, I've learned to use as many weapons as I can lay my hands on, from rocks to rocket launchers."

Akira shrugged. "I still prefer swords."

"I'd prefer it if we all had swords, sure," said the dwarf. "But do you think fighting was any cleaner back when the katana was the ultimate weapon? It wasn't. Life then was . . . a lot like me."

"Huh?"

"Nasty, brutish and short."

Haz had been conceived, born and raised in the fallout-contaminated wasteland known as Glow City, and was the ugliest individual the Hatter had ever seen outside of his nightmares. He was massive even for a troll, with heavy dermal plating encasing his huge torso, but the skin of his elongated head was oddly smooth, and there was something disturbingly childlike about his face and his tiny horns. His arms and legs were short, his feet and hands gigantic. His huge, wide-set eyes watered constantly, making the Hatter think of crocodile tears. It took him only two gulps to down the bowl of soup that the Hatter had bought him, then he reached for the mug of soy beer. "Nice coat," he said between swallows. His own outfit consisted of a tattered chemsuit poncho over a pair of shabby drawstring pants and an old Seattle Slugfest T-shirt. His huge feet were bare, and the Hatter decided he didn't want to know what they might have trodden in.

They sat in the back room of the Joke, protected from spies by the biofiber mats on the floor, walls and ceiling, and the Hatter's state-of-the-art bug jammer and white noise generator. "You want the name of my tailor?" the Hatter asked blandly.

"I got other priorities," the shaman replied, thumping the empty beer mug down on the table. "What's the job?"

"Have you ever heard of the Crypt?"

"The squat down near Hell's Kitchen?"

"Yes."

"Yeah, I've heard of it. What about it?"

"I want the squatters out of there."

"What's in it for me?"

"You get to keep the van that brought you here and whatever you can scavenge from the site—including the bounties on anybody who might be hiding out there."

Haz snorted. "Thanks for the food," he said, standing.

"It used to be a dump for medical waste," said the Hatter quickly. "The shaman who lives there now has cleansed the site of contamination, but there could still be a lot of toxic material in the barrels lying around the place."

The poisoner shaman bared his jagged teeth. "Where I live, chummer, a few barrels of toxic waste is small change. You should come down there sometime. It'd make a man outta you."

"Like you?" The Hatter shrugged. "Name your price, then."

Haz stared down at him. "What if I said a dirty bomb in the middle of Bellevue?"

Another shrug. "For one day's work? Be serious. What about a vial of a new resistant strain of VITAS-3?"

The poisoner's mouth hung open for a few seconds. "Drek," he muttered.

"No drek."

"You really got it?"

"Not on me, of course," the Hatter said blandly. "But I can get it for you. Some friends of ours have been using it to thin out some rebel encampments. You can't put up much of a fight, or even make a speech, when you're busy puking your guts out. Of course, it'd be even more effective if you could put it in the air-conditioning unit of a building during, say . . . a Green Party convention." He looked at the monstrous troll, watching the doubt in his eyes being overpowered by an obscene mutant strain of glee, and barely managed not to smile at the toxic's gullibility. "Do we have a deal?"

"Yeah, why the frag not?" said Haz. "You're probably full of drek, but I like the way you think."

When the meeting was over, Yoko led Lankin to the nearest empty room, which happened to be Akira's, and sat on the bed, while Lankin hovered in the doorway for a moment before gingerly perching on the handmade kneel stool. "How bad is it?" the adept asked.

"Worse than I imagined," said Lankin, looking around at Akira's quarters and his meager collection of possessions. The place reminded him of an emergency room cubicle during a power failure on a busy Saturday night. "You actually lived in this dump for *how* long?"

"A couple of years, I suppose, if you add up all the time I spent here. I didn't grow up here, unlike a lot of people: I just came here to hide, and stayed to learn. And you know that wasn't what I meant."

"Our odds? Right now? I'm not a small-unit tactician. The dwarf would know a lot more about that than I would."

Yoko sighed. "Don't play games. How badly in debt are you? And to whom?"

Lankin tried to smile, but something went wrong with

the procedure and he grimaced instead. "Drek. I can't lie to you, can I?"

"That never stopped you trying."

"Touché. Well, if I sold the apartment and the car and the art collection, at market value, and to only one customer apiece . . . that'd take care of all but about a hundred thou."

Yoko's face remained impassive.

"Or two, maybe," said Lankin. "A quarter mil, at worst. Come on, Yoko, you know how I work. I have a run planned for later in the week that should net me fifty thou, and another next month that's worth even more. And if I need to, I can sell everything I own two or three times over, for enough up front that I can cover most of the debts. I may even find another sucker who'll buy the whole building; it's worked before. Then I go into hiding for a while. If worst comes to worst, there are still some cities where they don't know me, not that I want to leave Seattle, of course . . . unless you'd like to come with me?"

Yoko ignored the suggestion. "Who do you owe?"

"You."

"I'm serious."

"So am I. That's why I'm here, Yoko-chan."

The kunoichi smiled insincerely. "I didn't know I was *that* good."

"You were—it was—and you know I'd give anything to have you back. But that's not what I mean. If it weren't for you, my creditors probably *would* have killed me by now. None of them are really scared of me, but they know *your* reputation, and they're worried that you might avenge me."

"And where did they get that idea?"

"I . . . may have been guilty of some slight exaggeration here and there."

Yoko sighed. "If that's kept you alive, I suppose I can forgive you that."

"It's definitely helped. Most of my creditors know I'll come good in the end, even pay the interest . . . in favors if not in cash. But there are some who aren't that patient."

"Yaks?"

"Do I look *that* stupid? No. I check everybody I borrow from to make sure they're not *that* well connected. Not that the yakuza aren't scared of you, too . . . but I wouldn't want them to think they could use me as the bait in a trap to get you." He blinked as an idea hit him. "You don't think that ork could be right, do you? About it being one of us that they're after, not the place? Specifically, you?"

"It doesn't seem likely," said Yoko. "It doesn't *feel* right. If the yaks, or one of the corps, were doing this for revenge, they'd make it *look* like revenge. They wouldn't bother being furtive about it. Just the opposite; they'd make it obvious, an object lesson."

"As long as it couldn't be proven in court," said Lankin wryly. "Where would we be without plausible deniability? But if not one of us, what could be here that a corp would want?"

"Evidence?" suggested Yoko after a moment's thought.

"What sort of evidence?"

"I don't know. Maybe someone's buried under the floor. Or maybe Sumatra's partly right—maybe it's someone here, but not one of us."

"What do you mean?"

"If you had something that a corp wanted, what would you do with it?"

"Call them and make a deal."

"What if you didn't know what it was worth? Or what if the price you put on it was so high that they decided it was cheaper to hire a pack of mercs and hunt you down?"

Lankin snorted. "I'm not an amateur. I make sure I know what *everything* is worth to somebody. And I hide copies of any useful data and make sure that if I die, it—" He stopped suddenly.

"What if you *were* an amateur? A beginner? Most of the kids here want to be shadowrunners one day . . ."

"I can see why," said Lankin, looking around the cubicle. His closet was at least half as large again, and smelled much better. "You think one of them might have stolen something that's worth a lot more than they know?"

"Stolen or found, or seen or heard . . . but yes, it's possible. A pocket secretary, a wristcomp, a micro-camcorder, even a chip or a material link . . . They might not seem to be worth much at first glance. The small-time fences these kids mostly deal with might not know what to do with them, but their owners might be prepared to kill for them."

"You want me to grill the kids," said Lankin. It wasn't exactly a question.

"You're the expert," said Yoko. Lankin had been one of Fuchi's best interrogators before the corp had collapsed. "Almost everyone comes into the kitchen at some time, and it's the best place to hear who's been doing what. But be gentle."

"Of course." He stood, still keeping his head bowed. "What do you do in this place if you catch them stealing from each other?"

"Depends what you mean by stealing. People who come here rarely have anything more than they can carry on their body, and everyone soon knows who owns what. Boanerges has rules against hoarding food and drink; you can keep a small quantity for yourself, but anything over that limit is up for grabs. And if you take something and sell it without the owner's permission, and can't make reparations, you're likely to be out of here as soon as the court finds you guilty. But if you take something without asking, but return it undamaged, that's bad manners at worst.

"Of course, if you get a reputation for bad manners, it's a good idea not to train in the dojo, because people might not pull their blows, and you might have to wait a long time for healing. And a repeat offender might be ostracized, which around here is taken pretty seriously. Apart from shelter, the most important thing most of these people have is each other."

Lankin nodded. "What about sex?"

"Maybe when this is over," said Yoko, rolling her eyes, "but only if you promise not to get all possessive and monogamous again, okay?"

"I *meant*, where do these people have sex? Privacy must be hard to find."

"Soundproofing is another luxury we can't afford here," the adept replied dryly. "The rest of it comes down to manners," and suddenly she was off the bed, with the side of her foot less than a centimeter from Lankin's chin. "And I'm one of 'these people,' and we think good manners are very important."

Lankin swallowed very carefully. "Point taken," he whispered.

The old multifuel minibus was audible from several blocks away on the deserted streets, and when Haz stepped out of the cab, he saw the orange lights of two laser sights sweeping across his armored torso. He held up his huge hands and bellowed, "Fedorov sent me!"

The door of the Step-Van opened, and Wallace emerged, his gun still trained on the troll's chest. "What are you doing here?"

"Didn't he tell you? This is the van the fraggers in there asked for."

"He spared no expense, I see," said the mercenary sourly, as he looked at the smoke trail that had followed the minibus down the street. "Okay, step away from the door. Hartz, keep an eye on this joker while I check the car. Griffin, call Fedorov, ask him to describe the vehicle and the driver." *If he can,* he added silently. He looked in the cab, then in the cargo bay. The minibus's seats had been removed, though Wallace wasn't sure whether that was to create more space for passengers, or because they were worth more than the rest of the rust-eaten vehicle. Every other nonessential component with resale value was also missing, including the radio and autopilot. A few seconds later, Wallace emerged, glad of the air filters in his helmet. *No wonder the driver's eyes were watering,* he thought. "Griffin?"

"The description matches," said the rigger, over the radio. "He says he bought the cheapest big van he could find that would actually run. Got it from a junkyard."

"And the driver?"

"That matches too. Fedorov says he lives there."

Haz smiled. "He said the squatters would be more likely to trust me than some guy in a uniform."

Maybe they will, Wallace thought, *but I don't.* He wished Lori weren't sleeping off her fatigue; he would have liked her to scope this guy out. "What's your name, laughing boy?"

"Haz."

"Griff, ask Mr. Fedorov if he got this joker's name."

"I already did," Griffin replied. "He says his name is Haz."

"Okay. Call 8-ball, tell him their carriage awaits. Chauffeur-driven, with room for about a dozen economy-class passengers. No hostess service or in-flight entertainment." He looked down at the wheels and refrained from kicking the worn tire, wondering whether it even had a spare.

Griffin radioed back less than a minute later. "He says they're having a meeting to pick the ones who want to leave. He doesn't think they'll need the chauffeur; in fact, they'd rather do without."

"Did Fedorov say they had to let him drive?"

"No, not that—"

"Fine. Don't bother asking him." Wallace raised his visor and looked at Haz, who was singing softly to himself. "They say they won't need a driver, thanks. You can take a walk. Get a breath of fresh air."

Haz nodded, and continued singing as he walked toward the Crypt. A toxic spirit came racing toward him through astral space, and Wallace shuddered without knowing why.

The kitchen and dining hall made up the largest open space in the Crypt, but even standing room was difficult to find when most of the inhabitants crowded in there to hear Boanerges speak. The street shaman stood on the least rickety of the tables and looked around at the gathering with gloomy affection. "As you may have heard," he began, "Lankin, 8-ball and I have been trying to negotiate with whoever has bought this land. They're not making many concessions. We have until an hour after sunset to be out of here completely, but they've also given us a van we can use to take anyone who wants to leave to a safe place, at least until this blows over. But only one van, with room for maybe ten people and their stuff. If you want to drive rather than walk, or take more than you can carry in a bag

and can stand the sunlight, this may be your best chance
to get out safely. Everyone is free to go if they choose, of
course, but priority for the transport goes to young children
and their parents." He glanced at 8-ball, who climbed up
onto the table beside him and coughed loudly.

"I know it's dangerous out there, but the mercs have
asked that you not openly carry any weapons," the dwarf
said dryly, "so keep those in your bedrolls or backpacks;
don't let them see them. We'll also need a driver, and possibly a mechanic, from what Mute's told me about the van.
The driver will be making a few trips, but the mercs won't
allow him or her back into the Crypt."

There was some faint murmuring, but no one stepped
up. "Okay, don't everyone volunteer at once," said 8-ball.

An old woman in faded denim and polar fleece raised
her hand. "If there's going to be trouble, I'd like to get my
children out of here," she said, "but I can't leave them in
a strange place while I act as taxi driver."

Boanerges nodded. Angie Hotop, a retired grade-school
teacher, had moved into the Crypt after being evicted from
her apartment, and had fallen in love with the above-
ground garden. Her "children" were not her descendants,
but the Crypt's entire preteen population. Boanerges, who
had never understood why her pupils called her the
"Gravedigger," wondered how many of them would go
with her willingly. "That makes sense. Any drivers willing
to go?"

"Preferably someone strong enough to push the van if it
breaks down," said 8-ball a few seconds later. He looked
straight at Pierce, who did his best to avoid his gaze.

"Where are we going to go?" asked a young girl.

Boanerges sighed. "That's up to Ms. Hotop, but right
now the best option is the squatter camp near Petrowski
Farms. There's a soup kitchen there, and no racial bias:
they dislike everyone more or less equally."

"I'll drive the van," said Crane awkwardly. "Can you
give me a couple of minutes to pack my gear?"

Boanerges nodded. "You can have ten. Ms. Hotop, can
you get the kids and your stuff ready, and meet Crane back
here by then?"

"Can we make it fifteen?" asked the teacher, who'd had more experience in trying to herd children.

"Fifteen," said Boanerges. "And anyone else who wants to leave before sunset—speak to Crane or Ms. Hotop, and they'll work out a roster." He sighed inaudibly. "Okay, we're done here."

8-ball cornered Pierce as they filed out of the hall. "You've been a roadie, haven't you? Surely you can drive a manual transmission."

"Can we talk about this later?" asked the ork, trying to dodge past him. "I'd like to get to the can before the kids start lining up."

8-ball stepped aside, then followed him toward the alcove euphemistically known as the downstairs bathroom—a stolen Porta-John, a compost toilet hidden inside a cardboard spiral, and a trough filled during wet weather by seepage from the rainwater tank. "You can't possibly drive any worse than you shoot," the dwarf said. "And you don't seem to have a major problem with sunlight. Why are you staying?"

" 'Cause I'd rather be shot than spend a couple of hours with the Gravedigger," Pierce replied. " 'Sides, I'd feel like a coward, an' a louse. I'd rather be the next one carried out of here than the first to walk. Got it?"

"Someone has to go," said 8-ball. "No one would have thought you were a coward. And nothing personal, Pierce, but I'd rather Crane had decided to stay, and not just because he can shoot. You're safer out there than in here, and he isn't. In fact, he's going to be in much deeper drek."

"What?"

"Why do you think he came here? He went up against Pok Moon, and they don't call his syndicate the Divine Revenge Ring for laughs. They're staking out his apartment and his garage; he was lucky to get out alive with what he had in the car, and he had to dump the car before they traced it and get a friend to drive him here. He was going to head off for another city when he'd finished healing."

Pierce digested this unpalatable news slowly. "Could Pok Moon have hired those mercs outside?"

"I guess so, but it's not likely. They've put a bounty on his head, but it's only ten thou, and Wallace and his squad would cost at least twice that much a day, not including expenses. No, I think this is something else." He lowered his voice. "Look, you want to go on a run when this is over?"

"Sure!"

"We're getting a team together to hit Crane's place. Most of the stuff is still there, because the place is booby trapped to hell. Crane's told us how to get past the traps and move the stuff out; we just have to take care of any Seoulpa who may be waiting for him to get back."

The ork's eyes lit up until they were almost gleaming. "You're serious?"

"We can find a job for you, even if it's only guarding the meat. But there's one thing you'll have to do first."

"What's that?" asked Pierce warily.

"Not get killed."

Easy looked at the shabbily dressed troll as he made his second orbit of the block, singing an old-fashioned–sounding song. Then she glanced at her "mirror," the human merc standing guard on her corner. He was also watching the troll, though his gun was still pointed at the sky. The troll segued into another tune, then ambled across the sidewalk and stepped over the remains of the brick wall onto the Crypt's ground-level rooftop garden. The sentry stiffened and brought the gun down slightly, but didn't shoot. Easy turned around to watch the troll, who was looking around as though lost. She considered challenging him, but reached for her radio instead of aiming her gun. "Intruder alert!" she whispered.

Yoko, in the dining hall, picked up the radio. "How many, and how armed?"

"One. Troll. No weapons. I—"

Haz turned around and grinned, and Easy was hit with the full force of the toxic spirit's terrifying power. Whimpering with fear, she dropped the radio and gripped her Roomsweeper with both shaking hands, trying to raise the muzzle high enough to take a shot at the troll. Her nerve failed her before she could get her fingers to cooperate fully, and she ran from her camouflaged sentry post onto the sidewalk.

Lewis saw the pistol before he saw the girl holding it and immediately lowered his rifle and fired a three-round burst at her chest. Quinn turned at the sound of gunfire, and with a speed and accuracy borne of special-forces training, military-grade cyberware, and two tours of duty in the Desert Wars, fired another two shots—one in the head, one in the side.

Yoko shook the radio. "Easy? *Easy?*" She waited for a second, then dropped the radio on the floor as she ran toward the ramp.

10

At first, Boanerges thought the clattering sound was his alarm clock: it took him several seconds to recognize the staccato rhythm of a rattlesnake, a warning from his totem. He woke suddenly, rolled off his bed and onto his feet, and ran out of the lodge. He could sense—almost *taste*—the danger, clearly enough that no one needed to tell him which way to go.

His feet bare, he ran through the twisting corridors toward the ramp as quickly as he could, leaving his lined coat hanging beside his bed.

Mute was watching Haz make his way cautiously toward the ramp when she was suddenly distracted by the sound of rifle fire. "Yoko?" she subvocalised, and waited two heartbeats for a reply.

8-ball was in the dining hall, stripping and cleaning one of the submachine guns they'd taken from the Lone Star contraband shipment; he'd seen Yoko rush out of the room and bent down to pick her radio up from the floor. "Not here."

"8-ball? Shots fired. And there's an intruder heading for the ramp. Troll."

"Fired by who?"

"Whom," she replied automatically, then, "I'll check." She signed off and used her mirror to peer around the edge of her shelter. The guard on her corner, a dwarf, was nervously trying to look in every direction, and the human merc was staring at something to her east. Mute's thermographic vision showed that the muzzle of the merc's gun was hot; at least one of the shots fired had come from her. "Easy?" Mute subvocalized.

No reply from Easy's radio. Mute glanced at the troll and chose the merc as the more immediate threat, holstered her pistol, unslung her assault rifle and aimed at the merc's spine.

Rove leaned against the pillar at the bottom of the ramp and yawned. The gun was getting heavy, and when he'd volunteered for guard duty, it was because he'd hoped to be assigned to watch Ratatosk as he ran the Matrix and maybe pick up a few of the decker's tricks. He wasn't sure he wanted to be a decker—in fact, he'd never decided what exactly he wanted to be, though he knew that he didn't want to work in the family's garden and greenhouse growing plants that all looked the same to him. Something a little more exciting and profitable, with lots of travel, involving lots of hardware but not too much time spent in the open.

When the toxic spirits oozed down the ramp toward him, Rove was trying to think of a really cool street name he could use if he became a rigger. He looked around when he noticed a new stench, worse than anything he'd ever smelled in the Crypt's bathrooms or even its kitchen. Akira, who was standing on the other side of the ramp, looked up.

"What the frag is—"

"Look out!" Akira yelled, firing at one of the spirits. The bullet passed through the spirit without leaving a hole, and the monstrosity materialized as a vaguely humanoid mass of foul-smelling sludge and descended on him like a tsunami. Akira dropped his rifle and took up his wooden sword while Rove was still blinking.

"I don't see—" he began, and then the second spirit materialized and he was suddenly enveloped by a wave of corrosive fluid. He tried to scream, but snapped his mouth shut as the foul liquid filled it, searing his tongue and throat as well as his face. He tried to close his eyes, but the acid was already eating away his eyelids.

Akira struck the toxic facing him with his heavy hard-wood stick. The surface of the training sword bubbled and smoked as the chemicals burned it, but Akira continued to slash at the spirit, using the extra reach the sword gave him to maximum advantage. The toxic retreated slightly, and the third spirit hurled a blast of psychic venom toward the young man. Instead of fleeing in terror, as Easy had done, Akira stood his ground and struck at the second toxic again.

It dematerialized and hesitated for a moment. Its orders were simple enough—find the shaman Boanerges and lead Haz to him, removing any obstacles it encountered on the way—but it was suddenly uncertain how this should best be done. The other sentry didn't seem to pose much of an obstacle anymore; he was writhing on the ground as another spirit's caustic secretions burned away his skin and his clothes.

Akira stared at the remaining two toxics, waiting to see whether they would materialize again. He spared a glance at Rove, sickly aware that there was nothing he could do to help him until the spirit was magically dispelled, or moved on for reasons of its own. Suddenly, he was enveloped by a gas so foul and pungent that he could scarcely bear to keep his burning eyes open—and then the toxics materialized again, and closed on him like a pair of horrific jaws.

Angela Hotop was walking toward the ramp with five children in tow. It was fewer than she'd hoped for, but all that she'd been able to get ready by the deadline. Once these were in the van, she thought, with the driver watching over them, she could go back and try to catch some more of her pupils . . . and maybe even some of the younger teenagers who secretly were looking for a way out but had been even more scared of looking uncool or cowardly in front of their friends than of the mercenaries outside.

They were nearly at the foot of the ramp when she saw a human form writhing on the ground so completely enshrouded in a fluorescent green slime that she couldn't recognize him. She ordered the children to run back to the kitchen and get help, then dropped her suitcase and ran toward the ramp.

8-ball looked at the small screen on his pocket computer, then turned to Pierce. "You know this guy?" he asked.

The ork shook his head. "Nope. Face like his, I wouldn't forget in a hurry."

"Not without brain surgery," the dwarf agreed. He twiddled the trackball until the crosshairs were positioned half a meter ahead of the troll, glanced at the rangefinder readout, and pressed the Send button. The grenade launcher in the back of his Land Rover fired, and the concussion grenade exploded just beneath Haz's jutting chin.

Most of the nerves in Rove's face and hands had been eaten away by the corrosive spirit, but there was no release from the agony until he finally slid into unconsciousness from lack of air. The toxic disengaged itself as soon as its victim stopped struggling, and looked around for fresh prey. Akira was backed up against the wall and doing his best to keep the other two spirits at bay with the remains of his sword. Seeing no clear angle of attack, and aware that Haz and a fourth spirit were approaching from the surface, the spirit dematerialized and oozed down the ramp.

The blast from the grenade made no impression on the spirits at all; Akira was temporarily deafened by the explosion, but concentrating too hard on his own fight to really notice. He was unsure whether he was doing any real damage to the spirits, but they certainly seemed to be reacting as though his blows hurt. Even if they were only playing with him, he was at least delaying them, and he was confident that Boanerges or Magnusson or some other magician would soon arrive to dispel the abominations . . . and then one used its power of binding to root him to the spot, while the other retreated out of range of his sword to blast him

with stream after stream of corrosive fluid. Unable to parry
the attacks, he tried to dodge, but the toxins inexorably ate
away the flesh of his fingers and his face.

Haz, at the top of the ramp, looked around to see where
the grenade had come from, and noticed the hole in the
camouflage netting draped over the car. He considered re-
taliating with a fireball, but he was still reeling from the
concussion and fuzzily aware that the drain might knock
him out. Instead, he lurched down the ramp, with the
fourth toxic spirit hovering behind him.

Wallace swore loudly when he heard the shooting outside
the van, and quickly looked at the tactical display. His five
sentries were still roughly in position, and their biomonitors
indicated that they were still alive, if breathing a little fast.
"Quinn! Report!"

"One of—" his exec began, but the sentence was cut off
by the sound of a nearby explosion. She instinctively
ducked, and Lewis, who was even closer to the top of the
ramp, dropped to his knees and held his gun over his head.
"Quinn?"

" 'Mokay," she murmured, looking around cautiously.
"Lewis?"

The sentry muttered something, and Wallace glanced at
his biomonitor readout. Heartbeat up, but otherwise nomi-
nal. "Griffin?"

A window appeared on the monitor, showing the aerial
view from the rotodrone. Wallace saw Lewis pick himself
up, and noticed the body near his feet. "Thanks. Can you
zoom out? Where the frag is that—okay, I see him," he
said, as the picture widened to show the top of the ramp
and Haz beginning his unsteady descent into the depths.

"Chief?" said Lewis shakily. "We just—"

"She had a gun in her hand," Quinn interrupted,
"and—"

"I can see it," Wallace replied. "Are you—"

"She's dead! She's just a kid, and she—"

"—hurt? And who fired the—"

"—wasn't shooting or—"

"—she was running toward—"

"—fragging grenade?"

"It wasn't either of—"

"Actually, I think it was a nonfragging grenade," Griffin interjected.

"You didn't fire it?"

"No."

"Neither—"

Wallace turned down the volume on Quinn's and Lewis' radios to a murmur. "Griff, is that machine gun loaded with gel?"

"Yes. They gave us one belt of gel, one of explosives, and three jacketed, all but the gel mixed with tracers. Did you ask for explosives?"

"No." Wallace grabbed what little remained of his patience. "I want suppressing fire if anyone comes out of that hole. *No one* is to get to the sidewalk. You got that?"

"Wilco. Uh . . . does that include the woman in the northeast corner?" He panned with the camera until the monitor showed Mute, her rifle at the ready.

"Drek. Yeah, her too."

"And Haz?"

"Yes," Wallace replied, staring at the screen. He wasn't sure whose side the troll was on, whether he was working for Fedorov or the Crypt or only for himself, but he wasn't one of *his* team. He thumbed a switch and addressed the entire squad. "This is Wallace. Until further notice, ground level of the area bordered by the sidewalks is a no-go area for everyone. Is that understood? Our side, their side, armed, unarmed, young, old, *everyone*."

Griffin stared at the view through the camera mounted on the rotodrone's machine gun, aligned the crosshairs on Mute and pressed the firing button.

Angie Hotop ran through the toxic spirit's astral form without noticing any more than a vague sense of unease, a faint impression of clamminess and sour sweat. The spirit considered chasing her, then noticed the huddle of children the teacher had left behind. Gleefully, it dived into the center of the crowd, spraying a nauseating stench of advanced decay in all directions. The children scattered, screaming—some back to the kitchen, some toward the ramp, others into the maze of corridors.

Ms. Hotop bent over Rove's acid-etched body, then glanced over her shoulder as she heard panicked children running toward her. She looked up the ramp and saw Akira locked in a desperate battle with two creatures of sludge and slime. They reminded her of paintings of malignant water spirits that had terrified her as a child. Beyond him, silhouetted against the gray sky, was the monstrous form of a deformed troll lumbering down the ramp toward her. Four children ran past her in blind panic, hurrying toward the exit—and the troll, who was charging in the other direction. The troll decided they were too small to be worth his attention; he roared at them as he swatted them out of his path, but didn't look back once they were behind him.

Ms. Hotop looked up and down the ramp, paralyzed for an instant by indecision as much as fear, before summoning all of her courage and deciding to follow the children who'd left the relative safety of the Crypt. She took a few tottering steps toward the troll, but another toxic spirit materialized in her path, falling on her like a wave of acid.

This is fun, the toxic spirit thought with sadistic glee as its victim writhed in agony for a moment before lapsing into unconsciousness. The spirit hovered over its broken toy for a moment, waiting for it to move again, then headed farther into the underground area. It saw another woman standing firmly in its path, watching it, her aura glowing brilliantly—partly from the quickened spells tattooed onto her body, but mostly from her own enhanced power. When the spirit blasted her with its toxic breath, she didn't run, or even flinch. "You don't belong here," she said with an eerie calm. "Go. Now."

The toxic spirit wavered. It could go past her, or it could turn and follow some of the other children through the corridors . . . but that would feel too much like a retreat. Though she could obviously see its astral form, the elf woman didn't seem to be the shaman it had been told to kill, and despite her obvious magical power, she wasn't trying to dispel it, cast any spells to destroy it, or create any sort of magical barrier that could stop it. It hurled another blast of terror, but the elf remained unmoved: her serene smile even widened slightly. The spirit sensed someone else approaching, then suddenly felt a magical hand grab its aura and try to disrupt it.

The toxic turned its attention to the newcomer, and instantly recognized the shaman it was sent to destroy. Unable to break free of Boanerges' magic, it engaged him, trying to suck the shaman's power into itself. Boanerges held on, despite feeling weaker than he had at any time since before his initiation. He hadn't fully recovered from his encounter with the first toxic spirit, or from the exhausting drain of the healing spells he'd been casting . . . but there seemed to be no other way to stop the monstrosity from attacking the Crypt's mundane population, who had no defense at all against it.

Yoko glanced at her teacher, wondering if he needed help, and then she heard the high-pitched screaming of children, and the clatter of automatic fire. Boanerges caught her gaze, and nodded minutely, and Yoko squeezed past him and ran toward the ramp. Another spirit re-formed into a nearly human shape to block her path, but the adept hit the physical form with all her strength, and more important, all her willpower. When the spirit didn't immediately disintegrate, she continued to punch, ignoring the pain from her hands. The spirit, already hurt in its fray with Akira, hastily dematerialized and tried to slip past her in search of easier prey, but Yoko's reach extended into the astral, and dealt it a final fatal blow.

Yoko turned to look up the ramp. An ugly troll, halfway down from the surface, seemed even more monstrous in astral than he did to normal sight. Another toxic spirit hovered over Akira's and Ms. Hotop's acid-etched bodies, sticking to the hideous troll like a bodyguard. "Pretty pretty elf," said the toxic shaman through loosened teeth, as he lurched toward her. "Pretty pretty skin. I like pretty pretty skin."

Yoko didn't reply.

"Like the way it smells when it burns," the troll continued, tears streaming down his hollow cheeks. "Like the sounds of the pretty pretty bubbles it makes as it blisters. Like the pretty pretty colors it turns."

Yoko faced him, her damaged hands at her sides. "You like it? Come here and get it, if you think you can."

Haz threw back his head to laugh—and in that fraction of a second, Yoko threw the first weapon she found in her pocket, a pen, at the shaman's right eye. Haz blinked reflexively, and the pen went through his leathery eyelid as well as the eyeball. Before he could react, Yoko closed the distance between them and hit him in the throat, crushing his larynx. As Haz began to drown in his own contaminated blood, Yoko hit him again with her other hand, breaking his neck and paralyzing him. Knowing that this might not be enough to stop him casting a spell, she slapped the end of the pen, pushing it into his brain. A toxic spirit engulfed her, but she ignored it as she delivered the coup de grâce.

Griffin, watching the Crypt through the rotodrone's cameras as the machine patrolled the edges of the site, zoomed in on the four figures running from the top of the ramp. He fired a burst of gel rounds at them as they headed for the street, following it up with a concussion grenade. A fraction of a second before the grenade exploded, he did a double take and swore. If the rangefinder reading was correct, the tallest figure was no more than 140 centimeters tall—which meant they were either children or improbably skinny dwarves. The grenade landed between two of the runners, one of whom had already been brought down by a gel round. The other staggered a few meters more toward the sidewalk before collapsing, leaving two still running. "Griffin here," he said rapidly into the radio. "Two heading for you—but they're not armed, and they look like kids!"

Wallace looked at the picture. "Tasers!" he commanded.

Lewis, still kneeling over Easy's dead body, immediately dropped his rifle and drew his stun gun as he looked up, scanning the ruins for signs of movement. Quinn switched her rifle to her left hand as she reached for her own stun gun. A girl stumbled onto the sidewalk on the east side; she looked around as darts flew past her from either direction, and dropped to the ground. A boy came running after

her, was hit by Lewis' second shot, and fell to the street,
convulsing. Lewis ran toward them, his stun gun at the
ready; no one else moved for several seconds. The merc
pulled the dart out of the boy's body and snapped plastic
restraints around his feet, before turning his attention to
the girl. She looked up anxiously, seeing her face reflected
in his tinted visor. "Are you okay?" Lewis asked. When
she didn't answer, he holstered his stun gun and picked her
up. "Caught both of them," he said over the radio. "What
do we do with them now?"

"Is anybody else coming?" Quinn asked the rigger.

"Not unless they're invisible," Griffin replied. "There's
three unconscious on their patch—two kids and a woman."
He zoomed in on the two children who'd been knocked
down by the concussion grenade. "Lori, you awake?"

"No, but I can probably wake her if it's important,"
said Wallace.

"Well, if she could take a look in astral, make sure the
others are still alive . . ."

The commander repressed a sigh. "Lewis? Make sure
those kids don't go anywhere; Crabbe will come pick them
up. If they're okay, we'll put them in the Nomad until we
know what the frag is going on. Griffin, see if you can raise
8-ball—but keep watching that ramp."

Boanerges could feel the magical power being drained
from him and his physical strength beginning to fail; his
vision blurred, and even breathing felt as painful as bones
breaking. The toxic spirit seemed to be made of nothing
but gangrenous sinew and berserk rage, and Boanerges had
little of Yoko's fighting skill. When the monstrosity was
finally disrupted, Boanerges had to fight off the urge to lie
down and rest. He staggered forward to the ramp and
peered up toward the exit. He was in time to see Yoko
disrupt another of the toxic spirits with a power blow
backed by the strength of her will and charisma—and to
see her collapse as the last remaining spirit retaliated with
a blast of corrosive slime. The physical form loomed over
her for a moment and continued to spray her with toxins.
Boanerges hesitated, then looked at the other bodies on

the ramp. Angie Hotop's aura showed that she was scarcely alive, perhaps even clinically dead. The body near hers was even more terribly damaged, barely recognizable as Rove. Akira, lying a meter farther up the ramp, was unconscious, but his aura was stronger. The troll was as cold and dead as the concrete he lay on. Yoko's aura revealed that she was still alive, barely, but the toxic spirit was obviously determined to keep damaging her body until there was no hope of healing her. Desperate to save her, Boanerges ran up the ramp toward them. To his amazement, the spirit dematerialized and slipped into the concrete floor.

Boanerges knelt over Yoko's body, aware that the toxic might be waiting in ambush, but he would rather risk anything than leave Yoko lying there. He cast a stabilizing spell, not caring that the fight with the toxics had left him so weak that he could barely manage to channel the needed mana, and without pausing to meditate to reduce the drain. Blood poured out of his ears as he concentrated, and as Yoko's heart began beating again, his own slowed . . .

slowed . . .

stopped.

11

Cutter Czarnecki walked past Beef Patty's bed, the largest in the clinic, and picked up her chart. He took care to avoid her legs, both of which hung over the end. Most of the clinic's secondhand equipment had been made long before UGE, when few patients grew to more than two meters tall; even elves and orks found the beds uncomfortably short, and Czarnecki was glad he'd never had a giant come to him as an inpatient.

Czarnecki sniffed. Like all good healers, he knew that smells could tell as much about a patient's health as the way they looked or sounded—and this acrid stink, cutting sharply through the disinfectant smell of the clinic and the mustiness of the damp and sunless Crypt, was new and extremely worrying. Still staring at the chart, the doctor reached for Patty's hand in the hope of finding a pulse through her dermal plating, and recoiled from the touch of something that felt *wrong* even through his latex gloves. He looked at his patient and saw something crouched over her body—something with the look of a corpse that had lain in wet ground too long, with eyes the color of a *Staphylococcus aureus* infection. His years as a street doc had almost completely cured Czarnecki of squeamishness, but he found himself gagging as the toxic spirit seemed to decay into a seething gray-green ooze, covering Patty's bandage-shrouded face and chest. He stumbled back until he bumped into the next bed, then looked over his shoulder.

Mish had returned to her medicine lodge, and Jinx was on her lunch break, but Magnusson was sleeping on the army-surplus cot in the far corner. Czarnecki unclenched his teeth long enough to gulp out, *"Maggie!"* but the mage didn't stir.

The toxic spirit's lambent eyes fixed themselves on Czarnecki's, and the ork felt a blast of fear worse even than the nausea. He tried to climb backwards over the bed, which collapsed underneath him with a metallic clatter. Magnusson rolled over and opened his eyes. He snapped out the first few words of an Aramaic exorcism ritual, then cast a spiritbolt spell that disrupted the toxic instantly, leaving nothing behind but a residual stench and fresh wounds on Patty's body and face.

Czarnecki untangled himself from the mess on the floor and bent over the troll, examining her wounds. "These look like acid burns," he said. "What was that? Some sort of elemental?"

"A toxic water spirit," replied Magnusson, sitting up and swinging his feet off the cot. "Swamp or river, I think. You'd better get Boanerges; he knows more healing spells than I do." He hastily conjured up a watcher spirit and sent it off with an order to fetch the street shaman. "How bad is she?"

"She's stopped breathing. I think she inhaled enough of that stuff to drown her—and I hate to think how much damage it's done to her lungs, even if it's not still in there. It isn't, is it?" He fished his stethoscope out of his coat and listened for a heartbeat. "Nothing," he said, making the word sound like a curse. "I'm going to try CPR—unless you have a better idea?"

Magnusson shook his head, watching helplessly as Czarnecki pounded on the troll's armored chest, then looked up as Crane rushed into the clinic. "Quick!" the rigger panted. "Something's . . . Yoko's badly . . . burned, I think . . . and Akira and Rove and the teacher and . . . Boanerges is . . . is . . . I think he's dead."

The mage turned pale. "Boanerges is dead?"

"I think so."

"Where are they?"

"On the ramp. I didn't know whether we should move them."

"Do the burns look like this?" asked Czarnecki. "I'm going to have to open the chest."

"Yeah. They look like that. You've got to—"

"One patient at a time, please," said the ork. "There's a tray of surgical implements in the autoclave. Can you bring it here?"

"The what?"

"I know what an autoclave is," said Magnusson, "but if there's anything that can be done for Boanerges . . . I think that should take priority."

"Don't tell—"

"He knows more healing spells than the rest of us combined; what we know, he taught us. If we can save his life, how many more can *he* save?"

Czarnecki scowled at him, but he straightened up and nodded. "Okay. I'll come. Someone had better get Mish and Jinx." He grabbed his black bag, and wearily followed the others as they hurried back to the ramp.

"I put the kids in the Nomad, like you said," muttered Crabbe as he clambered back into the Step-Van and removed his helmet.

Wallace nodded. "Did you lock it?"

" 'Course. I guessed that was why you wanted 'em in there, not the other piece of drek that just drove up." He looked at Wallace, his expression unusually grave. "And I picked up the body of the girl that got shot, too."

"Dead?"

"Yeah. When Quinn shoots somebody, she don't frag around. Little hole right in the temple, exit wound big as my hand."

Wallace looked at the troll's gauntlet and decided that had to be an exaggeration. "Where did you put her?"

"Beside the other van. We got a body bag for her? Normal size?"

"Sure."

"She's still holding on to that Roomsweeper. Don't think I can get it out of her hand without breaking her fingers, but I took the ammo out. Here." He held out a fistful of gel rounds. "They're all there. She hadn't fired the fraggin' thing."

Wallace didn't reply.

"Lewis's in a bad way," the troll continued. "You want me to relieve him?"

"How bad?"

"He's holding on to his stun gun like it was some sort of . . . drek, what do they call them holy things?"

"Cross?" suggested Hartz, without opening his eyes.

"Icon?" replied Wallace.

"Whatever. I don't think he's going to pick up his rifle again anytime soon, and as for firing it . . ." He shook his head.

The commander grimaced. Crabbe was barely literate, and in most situations he tended to rely on his strength, toughness and intimidating appearance. This and his broad hillbilly accent led most people to underestimate the troll's intelligence; but he was a good judge of character, and difficult to fool. "Thanks. I'll tell him you're coming."

"I'll bag that body first." He donned his helmet again. "It's hard to tell now, shape her face is in, but Lewis thinks she wasn't any more'n fifteen. Looks even younger to me, but what do I know 'bout human girls?"

Wallace nodded. "The body bags are in with the chemsuits." He watched as the troll opened the ammo box and removed one bag from the pack, then closed the box quietly to avoid waking Lori, Dutch and Kat. As soon as Crabbe had closed the door behind him, Hartz turned to his commander and said, "We going to do anything about the kids on their side of the sidewalk?"

"Don't *you* start," Wallace growled. Hartz was known for his ruthlessness, his short fuse and his antipathy toward children. Wallace didn't quite believe the rumors that the ogre had once eaten a prisoner of war when their rations ran low, but he'd never seen him worry about the welfare of an enemy before.

"It's just you know Lewis's going to ask."

The commander nodded, and activated his radio. "Griffin? You got through to 8-ball yet?"

"No answer," the rigger replied.

"Tell him I want a meet. I want to know what's going on. They can send someone in astral if they don't trust us not to shoot."

"Will do."

Wallace closed the channel and looked at Hartz. "Given the choice of letting them take care of their own wounded and wandering onto their territory—which 8-ball and the magicians are bound to have booby trapped—to get their people and use up our medical resources taking care of them . . ."

The ogre held up his hands. "Hey, I'm not arguing. I just thought I'd mention it before Lew—"

"Duly noted," Wallace replied, cutting him off. The ogre subsided, closing his eyes again.

Czarnecki held a mirror over Boanerges' mouth while he listened through his stethoscope in the hope of finding at least a faint heartbeat. "I think he's gone," he muttered. "No carotid pulse, no evidence of respiration, and bleeding from the ears is never a good sign." He put the mirror away and took a tiny flashlight and a cotton swab out of his black bag, then shone the light into the snake shaman's all-too-human-looking eyes. He tried turning his head from side to side, then ran the swab lightly over the corneas. "Pupils don't restrict, no oculocephalic or corneal reflexes . . . How's his aura?"

Mish peered over his shoulder, her tears splashing onto Boanerges' chest. "I can't see one." She looked around at Jinx and Magnusson, who shook their heads.

"I'll slap a trauma patch on him, though I don't think it'll do any good," said Czarnecki. "What do you think happened?"

"He was badly wounded by the toxic spirits, and he cast a spell that required him to channel more mana than his body could take," said Magnusson gravely. "I think he must have cast a stabilizing spell on Yoko. *Her* aura still shows traces of it. How is she?"

"She'll live. Those chemical burns look nasty, but they're already beginning to heal." He reached for her wrist and saw her gold-plated DocWagon bracelet. "Pity Boanerges doesn't have one of these. Should I call them, get them to pick her up? They have better facilities than I do."

"Do you think they'll land here?" asked Jinx. "Doesn't this count as corporate territory now?"

"If they park or land in the street, we can probably persuade the mercs to let us carry her that far," said Czarnecki. "They're supposed to be getting us out of here, dead or alive. Maggie? I guess you're in command now. What do you say?"

"Me?"

"You were initiated into the coven at the same time as Yoko, right?"

"Yes, but she's been through more degrees of . . ." He trailed off. "I'm an academic, not a combat mage! What about 8-ball? He knows tactics, and he knows the people outside; he's been doing a good job negotiating with them . . ."

No one spoke.

"*He's* not dead too, is he?"

"No," said Jinx. "I saw him in the kitchen on the way here."

Magnusson sighed with relief. "Okay. Crane, go and get everyone we need for a war council in the medicine lodge, ASAP, and I'll hand command over to 8-ball there. And get someone to stand guard here, and the strongest stretcher bearers you can. We're taking these people back to the clinic." He turned to Mish and Jinx. "What healing spells do you know?"

"Antidote, cure disease, and healing," said Mish between sobs. "Boanerges was teaching me a diagnosis spell, but he . . ." She choked, and wiped her eyes.

Jinx shrugged. "I can treat recent injuries, but that's all."

"Same here. Remind me to learn that stabilizing spell if we get out of here alive." Magnusson bit his lip. "Okay, triage time. I'm going to call DocWagon and see if they can help Boanerges. I'll pay whatever it costs. Doc, your first priority is keeping him alive until they get here. If you can, he can save . . . well, Snake alone knows how many more. But if you think we can heal Yoko ourselves and there's half a chance that she'll come around before sunset that way . . . then she stays here."

"What?"

"She heals fast; you can see that. It's one of the advantages of being an adept. And if she were conscious, I think she'd choose to stay, and I think it's what Boanerges was willing to die for. I don't know whether that was him thinking, or Snake, but either way . . ."

Czarnecki stared at him incredulously.

"If you want to overrule me on medical grounds, go ahead. You can explain it to her when this mess is over."

The medic hesitated. "How fast *can* she heal?"

"I don't know. Ask Ratatosk or Lankin. But with our help, I'm hoping we can get her back on her feet before we have to leave. How bad are the others?"

"Both sentries are in bad shape," said Czarnecki sourly.

"Does anyone know their names?"

"Akira and Rove," said Jinx. There was something about the way her voice softened when she said Akira that made Magnusson feel twenty years younger for a fraction of a second. The street doc gave no sign of noticing it.

"One of them—Akira, right?—is badly burned," Czarnecki said, "but there's no sign of internal injuries; I think he'll pull through. The other's much worse off—third degree chemical burns to more than half his body. Ms. Hotop had gone into tachycardia, but her heart's beating normally now. Most of her burns are to her face, neck and hands, but she's seventy-something years old and badly in shock; she'll heal slowly, if at all. I'm not sure I can save her eyes, either. And I couldn't do anything for the troll even if I wanted to."

"Okay," said Magnusson "I'll take care of Yoko. Jinx, Akira's yours. Mish, do what you can for Ms. Hotop and Rove. Both of you, pace yourselves—make sure the drain doesn't knock you out, too, or you won't be any good to anyone. Doc, watch these two and make sure they don't keel over, do what you can do about the burns, and keep the painkillers ready for when our patients wake up."

Crane came running back with Pierce, 8-ball, Leila and Sumatra. "Do you know any healing spells?" Magnusson asked the rat shaman, without much hope.

"Nope. Sorry."

"Frag. Okay, put up a couple of watchers and a fresh hearth spirit on the ramp in case they hit us with any more of those toxics. Pierce, Leila, get something we can use to carry these five back to the clinic. We're also going to need a couple more mattresses in there. Crane, grab one of those guns; you're on guard until someone else volunteers. 8-ball, you're in charge of choosing volunteers, but first, can you try to call the mercs and ask if we can get clearance for DocWagon to send an ambulance to pick someone up?"

It was a solemn group that gathered in Boanerges' medicine lodge ten minutes later. Magnusson looked unutterably weary from the drain of spellcasting, and Ratatosk was bleary-eyed from multiple dump shocks. Lankin, Crane, Zurich and Sumatra leaned up against the walls and listened uneasily as 8-ball reported on his communications with Wallace. "Wait a second," said Lankin, interrupting. "You called a DocWagon for Boanerges and Patty and *left Yoko here*?"

"Yes," said Magnusson. "She was stable—thanks to Boanerges—and already beginning to heal."

"What makes it your decision? You're not her next of kin, either of you, and who put you in charge anyway?"

"It was a medical decision," the mage replied. "And the coven of the Crypt has a hierarchy—a chain of command, if you prefer. Of the members who are here and conscious, I was next in line. I don't want the job, and I've put 8-ball in charge of all nonmagical and nonmedical matters. And I don't think Yoko has any next of kin."

"Only Boanerges," said Ratatosk. "At least, that's what she told me last time we went on a run together."

"No family?"

"None that she'd talk to. Her family sold her. I don't know whether any of them are still alive—I'm not sure *she* knew—but it seems unlikely. The yaks don't usually forgive people who they see as reneging on a deal."

Lankin's mouth hung open for a moment before he recovered his composure. He looked at 8-ball, who nodded. "Wallace said he'd let the DocWagon make the pickup as long as there was no media coverage, so we passed that along to DocWagon. The cease-fire's on again, and the sidewalk is neutral ground. We managed to get Boanerges into the ambulance without stepping onto the street; Wallace said if he catches us doing *that*, we're not to return. They're entitled to shoot us if we try, and call it self-defense. He's promised to use stun guns and gel rounds as much as possible," he finished dryly.

"Wallace has caught two of the kids and is holding them in one of the vans, but we can pick up the people who're lying upstairs inside the perimeter—which includes Mute. He says their mage has assensed that they're still okay, just stunned." He smiled crookedly. "I've sent Pierce outside to pick them up, and asked Wallace what they wanted us to do with the troll. He said he wasn't part of his team and we could stick a pole up his butt and use him as a scarecrow on the farm for all he cared."

"Do you believe him?" asked Zurich.

"I think so. If the troll *was* one of the squad, Wallace wouldn't have let him come in alone like that. And if he'd known what the troll was doing, he would've taken advantage of the chaos immediately, not given us time to recover and regroup like this."

"And poisoner shamans aren't team players," Magnusson agreed. "I'm surprised anyone managed to recruit one—or even that they tried. Giving one free rein would pretty much preclude anyone using this land for anything cleaner than a waste dump." He turned to Ratatosk. "Any data on what they *do* want the land for?"

"Nothing useful yet," replied the decker in an apologetic tone. "I've been doing my best to run a search, but your Matrix access here isn't exactly reliable; I'm lucky to go more than half an hour without getting dumped." He didn't think it was necessary to mention that it had also taken him three attempts to send the file of Lone Star passwords and logon IDs to his fixer. "All I've found is that it used to be a warehouse for hospital, lab and medical supplies, with equipment for sterilizing and recycling some of the gear, and included a small biohazard-containment facility. It belonged to Monolith, who were bought by Shiawase after this place was abandoned as economically unfeasible. No connection to Aztechnology that I can find. I'm waiting to see if the searches dig up anything on the former staff; some of them might have gone over to Aztec—" He broke off as Pinhead Pierce shuffled into the medicine lodge, with Mute holding on to his arm for support.

"Sorry for interruptin'," the ork said. "I tried to take her to the clinic, but she said she'd cut my balls off if I didn't bring her here first."

"Are you okay?" asked 8-ball, looking her up and down. "You—"

"I feel better than I probably look," said Mute, letting go of Pierce and standing unsupported for a moment before sitting down. "Lucky they're using gel rounds, so no bones broken. I was lying in the mud, playing dead, waiting for someone to get close enough for me to get a clear shot. None of them did."

Magnusson nodded. "Are the kids okay?" he asked Pierce.

"Out cold, but no holes in 'em," the ork replied. "Like she says, gel rounds. Cutter's looking them over now." Uninvited, he sat down.

8-ball quickly brought them up to date. "Is Boanerges going to make it?" asked Mute.

"I don't know," said Magnusson. "They tried to resuscitate him in the DocWagon. His heart is beating, but it's irregular; he's in a coma, and they've had to put him in a stabilization unit and take him to a hospital to see if they can detect any brain activity. Patty seems to be stable, though her lungs are badly damaged and may need replacing, and she won't be talking for a while."

Lankin shook his head. "Replacing? Who's going to pay for that? Do you think I can persuade the mercs to cover our medical bills on top of everything else?"

"I've paid for the DocWagon," said Magnusson. "And I'll pay for any treatment Boanerges needs. We can sell the library and the magical gear for a few thousand. If Boanerges recovers, we'll start the coven again somewhere else, from scratch. If not . . ." He shrugged.

Lankin rolled his eyes. "It's a pity you didn't think of this a few hours ago. You could've bought or rented some other dump like this and moved, and nobody would have died!"

"Where would you find a squat this large, this lightproof, that wasn't already occupied?" asked Mute softly. "And if we evicted the squatters who were there before us, how would that make us any better than Aztechnology?"

"I'm not talking about morality! I'm talking fragging *survival*! Two kids are dead, Boanerges is probably dead, Patty and Yoko might not make it, and for what? I say the sooner we get everybody out of here, the better!"

"Snake told Boanerges to stay," said Magnusson. "He couldn't ignore that."

"So people have died just because he had a *dream*? About a *snake*?"

"*The* Snake," said Sumatra suddenly. "Not *a* snake. And Boanerges' dreams weren't just ordinary dreams."

"All sorts of people dream about snakes," said Lankin heavily. "And they can mean all sorts of things. There was some chemist, once upon a time, who dreamed about snakes and decided they were trying to tell him how some molecule was formed. Freud had an even simpler explanation for what snake dreams meant. And I can think of three religions who say we were kicked out of paradise because someone listened to advice from a snake. I—"

"Snake didn't ask *us* to stay," interrupted Sumatra. "Just Boanerges. And she didn't say for how long. Maybe she just wanted him to stop the poisoner."

Everyone fell silent as they tried to think of an answer to this. "I can't believe Snake would sell Boanerges' life so cheaply," said Magnusson uncomfortably, nearly a minute later. "And it wasn't defeating the toxic that killed Boanerges. It was saving Yoko."

"And I'm grateful for that," Lankin replied, "even though he *was* the one who put her in danger to begin with. But the toxics have been defeated, now, and Boanerges *has* left the building, possibly permanently, and even if you choose to believe that he was getting his orders from Snake, you heard what Sumatra said. That doesn't apply to us. 8-ball and I've gotten the best compensation deal possible out of the new landlords, so I say we start packing up and leaving *now*."

Magnusson nodded. "You're free to go, of course."

"I will—but I'm not leaving Yoko here."

"Then you'll have to wait until the deadline," said 8-ball firmly. "Or until she wakes up and decides for herself whether she goes or stays."

"That's—" Lankin looked around, hoping for support.

Sumatra scratched his ear. "Yoko made an oath to the coven," he said uncertainly. "So did I. That doesn't mean I don't think you're right about going . . . but for me, it's not that simple. Besides, how much do you think Aztechnology, or whoever it is, has already spent on getting this place?"

"Buying the land, hiring the mercenaries, transporting them, equipping them . . . at least thirty thousand so far," Ratatosk replied.

"Which means there has to be something here that's worth more than that," said the shaman. "And I don't think it's the land, and if it's not one of us . . . if it's something we can find and take it with us, find a buyer . . . we can pay the medical bills and have a bit left over to divide between everybody here."

"A few hundred each," Lankin scoffed. "How long will that last?"

Pierce laughed. "We don't all eat at the Edge, chummer. Most of us could get by on a hundred a month, even without this place."

"And if everyone clubbed together, we could probably rent a warehouse or something like that, somewhere," 8-ball suggested. "Drek, I know I've risked my life on runs that scored less, sometimes a lot less. Any idea what it could be?"

"This place has been a squat for nearly thirty years," said Lankin. "It must have been picked clean by now."

"Unless there's something buried under the floor, or in one of the pillars," said Zurich.

"What sort of thing?" asked Lankin.

"I don't know. A mass grave? An insect spirit hive? Dunkelzahn's body?"

"Maybe it's a material link that's just become valuable," Magnusson mused. "Or something else that has magical uses that weren't known about thirty years ago. Something a forensic mage can use as evidence." He closed his eyes.

"Or a backup copy of data lost in the Crash," Ratatosk offered. "The facility's the right age. Maybe there's not a link to Aztechnology at all. Maybe it's embarrassing to Shiawase or some other corp, and Aztechnology wants to use it for blackmail. You know how much money there is in blackmail, Lank."

Lankin managed not to snarl. "That sounds a lot like wishful thinking, Rat, and it smells like something even worse."

"We have, what, just over six hours left before we have to decide whether to try to withstand a siege, or cut our losses and run?" said the decker. "And it's thanks to you and 8-ball that we have that much time. We might as well use it."

Magnusson opened his eyes again and looked at Lankin with a faint smile. "You're free to leave, if you choose . . . but if you're thinking of trying to take Yoko out of here before she regains consciousness, I'd advise against it. I've just sent watcher spirits to the healers and the sentries, telling them that she's not to be moved without direct orders from 8-ball or myself. And as a mark of respect for your obvious power of persuasion, the watcher is now standing guard over her, and it will tell me if any attempt is made to take her."

Before Lankin could react, Mute drew her smartgun and pointed it at the ceiling. "I'm heading that way myself," she said blandly.

Lankin looked around the group, then stormed out of the medicine lodge. Mute ran after him, and a moment later, Ratatosk stood and followed them. "I'd better get back to work," he said. "See if my search programs have turned up anything new. If they haven't, there must be something in Aztechnology's databanks. Sayonara."

*   *   *

When the decker returned to the jackpoint in the library, he was not at all surprised to see Lankin waiting for him. "Why didn't you back me up in there?" Lankin fumed. "You know Yoko's going to be safer outside."

"Maybe," said Ratatosk, sitting in a lotus position and removing his cyberdeck from its cushioned bag. "But I also know Yoko well enough to be sure that she'd have chosen to stay. She's loyal to the—"

"Oh frag, not you too!" Lankin groaned. "You're a decker! You don't believe in all this mystical drek about oaths and visions!"

"I don't know enough about it to say," Ratatosk replied, his tone mild. "And you ought to know better. The shamans can't make me experience it, any more than I can see in astral, and so I don't really understand it—but they can't see and understand what I see in the Matrix, either. Unlike you, chummer, I respect Yoko's opinion and her right to believe what seems right to her, whether I understand it or not."

"Don't call me chummer, you piece of drek! You don't even fragging care if she lives or dies, do you?"

"Of course I do. But she'll live or die by her rules, not mine. I'll come running anytime she asks for my help, though it's not often she needs it."

"And that's fine by you, isn't it?"

" 'From each according to his abilities, to each according to his needs.' " Ratatosk quoted. "Mute and Cutter and the magicians in there with her can do a better job of looking after her than I can—or than you can, for that matter. Even if you care more, which I doubt, they know what they're doing. I'll take competence over obsession anytime—and so would Yoko. Do you think we're the only lovers she's ever had who would've come on a run like this when she asked? There's probably more than I could count, and I'm pretty good at large-number theory. I think she picked us because we're the best at what we do. If that's not enough for you, I'm sorry, but your ego isn't my problem."

"You're a great one to talk about ego! Do you care about anybody else apart from yourself, Rat?"

Ratatosk looked around the improvised library alcove—the jury-rigged jackpoint, the floor of pressed cartons, the sagging shelves and assorted lighting fixtures and other shabby furnishings put together from other people's discards, the enchanting materials scrounged from the wasteland, the texts salvaged or stolen or copied. "You think I'm here for the money or something?"

"Something, yes. I'm not sure what it is, but I can make a few guesses."

"Guess away." The decker looked past him as he heard footsteps. A moment later, Didge pushed the curtain aside and poked her head into the alcove.

"Ratatosk? Do you mind if I watch?" She did her best to sound as though she wasn't begging. Unlike most street kids, the dwarf knew exactly what she wanted: to become the hottest decker around. In the Matrix, it wouldn't matter what height she was.

"No. I was just about to log on, and Lankin was just leaving." He smiled as Lankin stalked out, and plugged a cable from his modified Slimcase into one of his datajacks. "There's no hitcher jack, but you can watch the vidscreen."

"Thanks."

12

Sumatra lay down on his mattress and closed his eyes. 8-ball, Crane and Zurich stood around his meatbod while the rat shaman's astral form burrowed its way through the floor. "Do you really think there's anything down there?" the rigger asked.

Zurich shrugged. "The only other reason I can think of for someone wanting this land badly enough to spend that much money on it, is that something's about to crash on it. A satellite, a plane, an iridium asteroid, something—and no one can predict where something's going to impact with *that* kind of accuracy, even if they've planned it. Unless they're using magic."

"If that's it," said 8-ball, "we'd better get the frag out of here anyway."

They waited in silence for several minutes until Sumatra opened his eyes again. "There's something down there," he said. "Some sort of container—I guess you could call it a vault—roughly in the middle of the floor."

"How big?"

"A bit wider than my arms, maybe twice that long, and about up to here," he said, running a hand along the bottom of his sternum. "About half of that is empty space, cased in something manufactured. Metal and concrete, I think, and a drekload of it before you get through to pure earth. Nothing's alive down there."

"How thick is a drekload?" asked Zurich dryly.

"Not quite up to my elbow," said the shaman, holding up a large hand, fingers extended. "It's fraggin' dark down there, can't see for drek, even in the empty spaces. There's a bit of a background count, some sort of toxic drek, but nothing alive. Nothing magical, either, or anything that was handmade with any sort of feeling, so I think we can rule out the Ark of the Covenant or the Holy Grail. And if anything down there still has enough life left in it to be a material link, I didn't pick it up.

"Of course, that doesn't mean there's nothing valuable— it could be full of plutonium, or old-fashioned money, or anything like that. I could try a catalog spell, but that's only going to help if I have some idea of what I'm looking for."

"Did you find a door, or some other opening?"

"Nope. I think it's been sealed pretty thoroughly, but not magically locked, or anything like that."

"Hazmat storage," suggested Zurich. "It makes sense. Could you find it again?"

"I think so. Give me a minute to rest and I'll look again. It's not directly under here, I can tell you that much, but if it's under any of the lodges, or the library, it'll be a snap. If not, I'll have to use you as landmarks. You got any ideas on how we're going to open it if we find it?"

"Do you have any spells that'll do it?"

"Only powerbolt. You'd do a lot better with shape-charges—or maybe a pick and shovel, at least against the concrete."

Zurich sighed. "I'll see if there's anything around I can turn into a metal detector. That'll tell us how much metal we have to deal with." He walked out of the lodge and headed for the clinic. 8-ball watched him go, then turned to Sumatra. "Pick and shovel?"

"There's gardening drek upstairs, and I saw Patty with an entrenching tool."

8-ball shook his head. "Okay. But the first person to start singing 'Hi-ho' better be wearing their running shoes."

Lewis removed his helmet as soon as the Step-Van's door closed behind him. As a younger man, he'd been handsome enough that some people mistook him for an elf, though he was barely 180 centimeters tall, and some vestiges of this usually showed on his clean-shaven face. Now, though, he looked so tired and drawn that he more nearly resembled a zombie. "Crabbe said you wanted to see me, Chief."

Wallace nodded, noting that the soldier had his rifle slung and, as Crabbe had said, a firm grip on his stun gun. "Yeah. I was about to go see to our, uh, prisoners. You feel up to walking and talking at the same time?"

"I think I can manage."

"Good. Hartz, keep an eye on the sleeping beauties." Wallace grabbed his helmet and walked out to the back of the Nomad with Lewis following close behind him. "You know, one of the first things I learned about tactics was that no plan survives contact with the enemy."

"You think these people are our enemy?" asked Lewis. "Even the children?"

"You've seen kids with guns before," the ork reminded him. He stopped, and leaned up against the side of the Nomad. "Frag, I had kids shoot at me in the desert, and I bet you did too."

"Not girls."

"How'd you know? Did you see them all?"

"Not clearly," Lewis admitted. He turned and stared at the ruins. "We've killed two teenagers, taken two young kids captive . . . I wonder if their morale's as low as ours."

Wallace shook his head. "Better not let anyone else hear you talk like that. They might think it sounds like mutiny . . . Mr. Christian."

Even though Wallace couldn't see it through his visor, he knew the human was smiling his crooked smile. Lewis had been an altar boy for a mainstream religion, and while a phobia of public speaking had prevented him becoming a preacher, he was the closest the squad had to a chaplain. "I'm not going to mutiny, Chief, but I think this might be my last mission. How've we been reduced to this? We were soldiers once. We were protecting our country, or at least we thought we were. What are we now?"

"Still alive?"

"Is that enough?"

"It—" Wallace hastily censored himself; he knew Lewis disliked swearing almost as much as blasphemy. "Beats the alternatives. We're not all as confident as you are of getting into heaven, Lew." He looked down at his shadow, then at the wasteland around them. "It'll be over soon, anyway, and we can go home. Look for some other sort of work then, if that's what you want to do . . . But right now, I still need you here. If you think morale is bad now, imagine what it'd be like if someone deserted."

"Especially if you had to shoot them."

"I didn't say that. And I wouldn't shoot you. Well, not to kill, anyway."

"Thank you."

"Thought about what you'd do if you quit?"

"A little. I have a brother-in-law working for Ares, who says he can get me a job as a security guard."

Wallace grimaced, but he kept his tone neutral. "Well, it's your decision, but I'd hate to lose you. Let's see how you feel when this is over. Now, we've got plenty of water for these kids to drink, if they'll take it from us; pity there isn't enough to wash them too. And they look like they haven't been eating that well. What have we got to feed 'em?"

Leila was badly allergic to sunlight, and usually slept during the day—but like many of the Crypt's residents, she'd been too keyed up to sleep. By noon, she'd given up on lying on her lumpy mattress and was wandering around the basement looking for something to distract her. She'd worked out with the Wing Chun dummy until her once-white gi and once-black track pants were damp with sweat, and been unable to go upstairs and wash because the shower stalls were being used as a temporary morgue. Instead, she'd put on her other clothes—a black synthleather jacket, tight black jeans and T-shirt, and knee-high boots—and wandered out to the kitchen. She walked toward the water purifier, and nodded to Lankin as she passed him. "You look as though you'd rather be almost anywhere else."

Lankin stared at the ersatz coffee in his mug and shrugged. "Wouldn't you? No, don't tell me. You grew up here."

"You could say that," she said as she decanted herself a cup of cloudy-looking liquid, then sat down opposite him. "Do you mind if I ask you a question?"

"If I can ask you one."

"How tall are you?"

"Why?"

"I asked you first."

"Two hundred and seventy-four centimeters, last time I was measured. Or maybe it was two seventy-six. It was a while ago."

"College basketball?"

"Yes, but don't pretend you remember me. You couldn't have been more than three or four at the time."

"It was just a guess. I've heard a little about you, the way you work. How do you get away with it when you're so easy to recognize and so easy to find?"

Lankin looked at her fine blue-black fur, and realized that her interest might not be entirely academic. "I buy mask spell foci from talismongers when I need a new look, and I have a modest collection of fake IDs, but to be honest it's rarely a problem. There're a lot of ways to survive, even thrive in this world, and you've just got to decide how you want to live. I figured I had a choice between trying to hide who and what I am, or use it. I was born with the gift of gab, and the intelligence to make it count for something, so I decided to use my appearance to my advantage. People get excited about being associated with someone as unique as me, and that's my angle.

"There's an old saying that you can't con an honest man. That's not actually true, but the *best* cons depend on your victim being just as crooked as you are, but not as bright— or at least too crooked to go to the cops if he realizes he's been stung, and preferably too embarrassed to warn his friends. So you let someone think he can double his money or better, but you make sure he knows that it's illegal. It used to be gambling or prostitution, and now it's insider trading or funding a shadowrun. Or letting him believe he's buying stolen or counterfeit goods. But make sure he believes you can deliver—and the best way to do that is to have a reputation as a winner, and *look* like a winner.

"The reputation isn't as difficult as it sounds: you can have accomplices recommend you, or actually pay off once or twice and know the winners won't be quite as secretive as the losers. That's how pyramid schemes work, and they've never managed to stamp *them* out.

"Now let me ask you something. Have you been on any runs?"

"Nothing very big," Leila replied. "I've helped shadowrunners get away from skiptracers, and gone with Pierce on a couple of structure hits. And we've done some stuff for Chopsticks Chen—shoplifting, courier work, a couple of warehouse B and Es—but I think the most I ever got from that was these boots."

"Chen? Skinny ork with really long tusks? Calls himself the Great Fence of China?"

"Yeah. He fences most of the stuff we pick up: he's convenient, and he doesn't ask questions. You know him?"

"Yes, unfortunately. He was selling bootleg trid movies and counterfeit perfume in parking lots when I was your age. 'All guaranteed stolen,' he used to say. I'm surprised he's still alive."

"I'm nineteen," said Leila stiffly. "Stop making it sound like I'm six."

"Sorry. Where's he based, nowadays?"

"Shop on 204th Street. I don't remember the name, but the front is full of fake antiques. Chen comes in sometime in the middle of the afternoon, and he's usually there all night."

"Guards?"

"Not usually, unless he's out back. Why? You think he's got something worth stealing?"

Lankin shook his head slightly. "Probably not. Do you know where Pierce is?"

The icon for the Aztechnology host was a near-perfect trid representation of the real-world Pyramid, apart from the absence of the perpetual cleaning crews swarming over the steps. Ratatosk knew that this detail, as well as air traffic to and from the helipads, was shown on some real-time computer model somewhere in both versions of the Pyramid, but Aztechnology had good reason not to broadcast this information. Some of those helicopters might be targeted by assassins, and while the windows and exterior walls were said to be impenetrable, one team of shadowrunners had once managed to extract an Aztechnology magical researcher by opening a forty-fifth-floor window from the *inside* and escaping in the window cleaners' lift.

Like the Pyramid, the Aztechnology system was composed of multiple tiers. Ratatosk didn't know of any trapdoors into the Aztechnology online hosts, nor did he have any up-to-date passwords. With a cloak utility disguising his icon as a gray-suited sarariman, he entered the grid through a system-access node sculpted to resemble Tihuanaco's Gateway of the Sun, and found himself inside a bustling market for Aztechnology merchandise. Most of the persona icons swarming around moved as slowly as tortoises, including the four Jaguar Guards patrolling the area. Ratatosk looked around for the equivalent of a door with a "Staff Only" sign, and saw a SAN next to a sculpted icon of an Aztec priest's palace—decorated with nuyen symbols in gleaming platinum, as well as masks of Quetzalcoatl, the plumed serpent. Special facilities for preferred customers with excellent credit ratings, Ratatosk decided. He looked warily at the masks, then examined the lock on the door. The serpents' eyes flashed red as the decker slipped a sleaze utility into the keyhole; then the glow faded as the system accepted the software as a genuine platinum credstick backed up with a retinal scan. "Welcome, Dr. Gray."

"Thank you," said Ratatosk, and looked around the chamber. No colorful bustling market ambience here; this was a bank, all polished brass and hardwood and plush. He ducked into a cubicle, sleazed through the order form into the subprocessor and began interrogating the system until he'd located the directory he needed. An instant later, he was standing in a cavernous underground parking lot. There was only minimal sculpture here, little effort wasted on making things look attractive—not much more than a huge gray space filled with the icons of different vehicles. The decker looked at the icon of a clipboard hanging on a support pillar, and smiled. As he suspected, the clipboard was a datafile, a booking schedule for the vehicles—complete with the names and phone numbers of those who'd borrowed them. He scanned it for IC, and found it protected by nothing more than a low-rated scramble program. Shaking his head, he began decrypting the data, then downloading it—until a shadow fell across the printout, turning the characters to gibberish. He spun around and saw a hare standing behind him. The icon had enormous buck teeth, a face made up largely of scar tissue, ears that added another half meter to its height, and huge mad red eyes.

The March Hare grinned. "What's up, doc?" he asked, and produced a huge cartoon shotgun from behind his back.

13

Ratatosk stared at the icon of the gun. The twin muzzles looked as big as a pair of manholes, and he hastily began uploading his armor software. Hare was quicker, and Ratatosk shrieked in pain as he was blasted by a black hammer utility that ripped through his icon and sent a current through to his meatbody. An instant later, Ratatosk's sarariman disguise reshaped itself into the form of a Viking shield. This absorbed some of the next blast from the gun, but not enough of it for the decker to believe that he could survive another attack.

Hare looked at the squirrel icon and the Norse runes on the shield, and laughed with delight as he recognized his opponent. "Ratatosk! You know, I always hoped we'd meet someday." Before Hare could fire again, Ratatosk unloaded the armor program and replaced it with a cloak. The black hammer's next attack missed as Ratatosk disappeared behind the pillar, and then behind the icon of a white Toyota Elite. Hare scanned the room, trying to relocate him.

"Do you ever watch old movies?" Hare asked. "Some of the best fight scenes ever are set in parking garages like this one. Like *Highlander*."

He fired another blast with the black hammer. Ratatosk evaded the attack, dodging furiously and hoping that he could get into position to counterattack while he waited for the datafile to finish downloading. If he jacked out now, he might not get enough of the data for it to be useful.

"Mask of the Phantasm. Tomorrow Never Dies. Blood-Soaked Brothers III." Hare fired again. "Pity these cars don't explode," he mused *"Naked Killer.* Did you ever see that one?"

Ratatosk uploaded his attack program and popped up from behind the icon of a bronze minibus. "Which version?" he asked, as the icon of an art-deco ray gun appeared in his hand. A translucent energy field appeared around Hare just in time to absorb the beam.

"The one without the happy ending, of course," said Hare cheerfully. "The one where they die. I was *sure* you'd have seen it. You're a man after my own heart."

"Actually, I was aiming for your head," said Ratatosk, shooting again.

Hare evaded the attack easily. "Sorry," he said. "It's duck season." He returned fire, and Ratatosk felt himself flying backwards into a darkness as cold and deep and terrifying as drowning. He fought to keep his eyes open, even though there seemed to be nothing left to see.

Sumatra's astral body popped up from the concrete floor like a rat swarming up a rope. "Here," he yelled, as he manifested. He waited impatiently until 8-ball came running into the cubicle and drew a cross under his foot, then peered at the satellite navigation reading on his wristphone.

"Okay," he said. "So it looks like it's about six meters long. Want to try the next corner?"

Sumatra looked to the west. "I think Mish's medicine lodge is over there, and she's not going to be happy about you digging that up. Whose room is this?"

8-ball looked around at the handmade glaive leaning in one corner, the clothes piled on the extra-long army surplus cot, and the color printouts from *Playelf* that lined the walls. "Pike's, I think."

"Well, at least *he* won't object to us digging up the floor."

"No," said the dwarf. "But we should probably get someone in to sort through his stuff first, see if there's anything worth taking."

"Did he have a family or anything?"

"Somewhere, I guess. Yoko might know. She was his sensei." He picked up the glaive—an iron bar ground to a rough edge with a corner clipped off to make a point, welded to a length of galvanized metal pipe—and hefted it experimentally. "Can't help thinking we should be using this as a grave marker, like they did with the swords in *Seven Samurai*. Not that we have time to dig him a grave."

"I thought that's what we were doing," said Sumatra dryly. The Crypt's dead were usually left outside the church, temple, synagogue or mosque of their choice in Puyallup; those who hadn't made a choice were taken to the nearest Salvation Army fortress. Police medical examiners identified those with SINs and attempted to contact their families, while the SINless were cremated as paupers. Their only memorial service consisted of planting a tree or bush in the garden, with a few prayers or eulogies usually followed by a wake. The best-loved had epitaphs chiseled into the brick and concrete walls by their friends. "Do you really think we're going to find anything down there that's worth the effort?"

"Probably not," 8-ball admitted, "but we've got about six hours left, and I hate sitting around and waiting. 'Sides, if we only went after sure things, we'd be sararimen, not shadowrunners."

The rat shaman nodded. "I'll try the *south*west corner next," he said, and sank back into the concrete floor.

Mute reached for her smartgun as Didge came running into the clinic. "What—"

"Ratatosk," said the dwarf. "I think he got hit by some black IC. He's jacked out, but I think it's more than just dump shock. He looks pretty bad."

"Is he conscious?" asked Magnusson, who was lying on the dropcloth-covered floor with his eyes closed, recovering from the drain of the healing spells he'd been casting.

"Sort of."

The mage sighed. "Doc? Do you make house calls?"

"Not today," replied Czarnecki. "If he can't walk, see if you can get someone to carry him."

"I can walk," said Ratatosk more or less truthfully, as he lurched into the room, grabbing on to the plastic shower curtain rod stretched across the doorway for support. It was a trip of barely fifteen meters from the library to the clinic, but the decker seemed exhausted by the effort. "I won't say I've never felt better, but I'm not about to die on you."

The street doc looked at him suspiciously. "Not if I have anything to say about it, you aren't. Sit down and let me look at you. Was it black IC?"

"Just killjoy, I think," said the decker, moving unsteadily toward a plastic and metal chair older than his grandmother. "Another decker caught me in their system."

"A rabbit icon," said Didge. "He knew you. Do you know him?"

"I haven't run into him before," said Ratatosk. He lifted his datajack onto his lap.

"No jacking in," said Czarnecki, touching his throat to take a pulse while shining a mini flashlight at the elf's face. "No using cyberware if you can help it. These your own eyes?"

"Yes."

"Thought so. The bloodshot effect's a little too realistic. Bad headache?"

"I've had worse, but not by much."

Czarnecki nodded. "Killjoy, my butt. You think I've never seen black IC damage before? You're lucky your brain wasn't completely fried. Do you know where you are?"

"The Crypt. Puyallup."

"I don't need to ask if you're dizzy. Any ringing in the ears, or visual disturbances?"

"Some. It seemed darker than it should outside, and brighter in here, and . . . I feel like . . . I don't know. Like I've shrunk, or everything else has grown. Is growing. And you keep fading in and out."

"Do you remember the date?"

"October . . . something. Twelfth?"

"Year?"

"2063."

"Your birthday?"

"No. I mean . . . July twentieth, 2036."

"You're *how* old?"

"Twenty-seven."

The ork shook his head. From what he'd heard about Ratatosk, he'd assumed that he just aged slowly, like most elves, and was in his forties at least. When Czarnecki was twenty-seven, nearly thirty years ago, he was still living with his mother so he could pay off his student loans. His car, his first, was twelve years old, and he'd had only two sexual relationships worth mentioning in confession. "Hope you manage to get to thirty," he said sourly, and asked several more questions while he continued the physical examination. "Okay," he said, when he was finished. "You're a little disoriented, but you don't seem to be hallucinating in any serious way, or to have lost any memory or motor function. If I were you, I'd get your scrawny butt out of here and go get a full scan and workup done. Best I can do meantime is to give you some painkillers for that headache and tell you to rest. Anything more will take magic, and we're a little short on that."

Ratatosk looked around the overcrowded clinic. "How's everyone else doing?" he asked softly.

"Yoko's doing better than I had any right to hope," said Czarnecki. "Healing incredibly fast, even for an adept getting healing spells. Those tattoos she has—they're quickened spells, aren't they? Some of them, at least?"

"Yes," said the elf, "but I don't know which ones, or even which spells. And she's had a nano-symbiote treatment; that probably has a lot to do with it."

The street doc blinked. "I've heard of those, but never came across one before. Are they as good as they say?"

"Sure, if you can afford it. I've thought of getting it done myself."

"How much do they cost?"

"Hers cost her sixty thou, not including the extra cred she has to spend on food. That's a lot less than I've spent on this arm—probably less than Lankin spends on shoes."

"And about ten times as much as all the gear in here,"

said Czarnecki sourly; then he shrugged. "Mind you, if we tried keeping anything with resale value in this place, we'd need more doors, with locks, and Boanerges won't stand for that sort of drek."

"Have you heard how he's doing?" asked Ratatosk softly.

"No."

"What about the others?"

"Akira's going to make it," said Jinx, who was lying on the floor between two of the cots. "His aura's actually gotten *brighter* since this morning. I think he's been Awakened."

"He's a magician?" asked Czarnecki, surprised.

"A magician or an adept. I don't think he could've held off those toxics if he hadn't been able to assense them. Rove and Ms. Hotop aren't doing as well . . . but neither of them were as strong as Akira or Yoko to begin with."

"What about the kids who were shot with gel rounds?"

"They're badly bruised, and scared, but nothing worse than that. They're conscious now, and one of the older kids is watching them."

"I've taken up enough of your time," said Ratatosk, standing. "I'll leave you to it."

"Go find a bed and get some rest," said Czarnecki. "Let me know if you think you're getting worse. I'm sorry, but walking wounded will have to wait."

"Cheapskate Chen?" said Pierce between mouthfuls of thin vegetable soup. "Yeah, I know him. Why?" he asked with the wary air of a man suddenly wondering whether it's too late to invoke the fifth amendment.

"How good is his security?" asked Lankin, unwrapping a small block of chocolate and breaking off a chunk for himself before placing the remainder on the table between them. The other diners looked over hopefully, but none of them spoke or approached him.

"He's prob'ly got a gun or two under the counter, and he uses one of the bouncers from Pualani's Pink Pagoda when he needs muscle," Pierce replied. "It's right across the road, and I think he's a regular there."

"I gather you're not talking about a restaurant."

"The sign outside says it's a noodle bar," said Pierce, finishing his soup and reaching for the chocolate, "but it has rooms upstairs, and a lot more waitresses than it needs. I suppose it depends how well you tip. But the bouncers are pretty tough, and if Chen has any kind of alarm system, it probably rings a bell there. You thinking of hitting the place?" he asked softly—and rather incredulously.

"No; I think a phone call should be enough," said Lankin. Though a master at buying low and selling high, Chen was strictly small-time, his dreams of becoming a fixer hampered by his miserliness and his aversion to taking risks . . . which also stopped him leaving anything of value in his shop for more than a few days. If he had any sort of security other than a part-time bodyguard and the protection he paid to the Yellow Lotus Triad, it would have been bought cheaply from a shadowrunner desperate to sell.

Intimidating him wouldn't even be a challenge.

The 38 Special was one of the best cafés in the Aztechnology Pyramid's residents' mall. On a clear day, clients had a view of Lake Washington and Council Island, and sometimes even a glimpse of the mountains farther east. The Hatter didn't much care about the view, or the art-deco furnishings, but he liked the food and the staff knew him—and they often sold him valuable information they'd overheard at other tables. The Hatter sipped at his tea and pretended to be reading the daily newssheet while he looked around the café to see who was talking to whom. He noticed Hare walk up to the hostess, and leer at her cleavage while she nodded toward the Hatter's booth, and pretended to study the menu as the decker walked toward him.

"We may have a problem," said Hare without preamble, as he sprawled across the bench on the other side of the booth. "There was an intruder in the system. Ratatosk. He was downloading the sign-out sheet for the vehicles."

The Hatter sipped at his Earl Grey tea, which suddenly seemed to taste of metal dissolved in acid.

"I don't think he'll be back in a hurry," said Hare, but

his tone wasn't reassuring. "I hit him with black hammer, fried his bod as well as his deck. Unfortunately, he jacked out before I could finish him off—or finish tracing him."

"How many other cars were checked out?"

"Not including ours, fifty-six. Most of them routine stuff, but I suppose the data could still be worth stealing." He didn't sound convinced. He smiled at the waitress who brought him his carrot cake and pot of tea, and smiled even more broadly as she walked away.

"So what makes you think he's snooping into our business?" asked the Hatter, feeling some of his confidence returning.

"I traced him to somewhere in Puyallup."

The Hatter spluttered as he choked on his tea.

"It could be a coincidence," said the decker. "But dataline access in Puyallup is so unreliable that I don't think he'd risk diverting through there."

"What would Ratatosk be doing in a squat like that? He doesn't get out of bed for less than five figures!"

"I don't know. He may not be there, just somewhere in the area. Is there anything else in Puyallup worth taking?"

"The company doesn't have any interests there that I know of, unless the mages are getting stuff out of the wastelands. The area pretty much belongs to the Nishidon-Gumi and the Yellow Lotus: Ratatosk's supposed to have cojones the size of basketballs, but I don't think even he would take on either syndicate unless the payoff was huge, and it wouldn't explain him checking our garage. Have you ever hired him, or met him?"

"No, but I think Valdez has; I'll see if I can get anything useful out of him without giving too much away."

Hare nodded. "I've bumped up the security on the sign-out sheet as high as I can without drawing undue attention to it, though I don't think he'll be back. But there is one other possibility."

"What's that?"

"What if he's working with your mercs?"

The Hatter blinked. "You think Wallace is double-crossing us?"

"He may be wondering why he's there."

"I've hired Wallace before. There are plenty of gunmen I could have gotten for less, but he likes to think he's an honorable man in an honorable profession. That sort of delusion can be very useful, if you know how to exploit it."

"Maybe it's not him. Maybe it's somebody else in his company who thinks he should be cut in for a percentage. It's just a thought."

"Not a very pleasant one," said the Hatter, scowling. He pushed his ham sandwich and the cup of tea aside, unfinished. "I don't know of any links between Wallace and Ratatosk, but there's never more than two or three degrees of separation between shadowrunners. I'll do a more thorough background check on his team members, as well as Ratatosk. I may want to use Wallace again, so I don't want to kill him unless there's evidence against him. Let me know what you find."

The metal detector—a simple beat-frequency oscillator— had been cobbled together from Didge's portable stereo. It had taken Lankin longer to persuade Didge to part with it than it had taken Zurich to convert it into a clunky-looking but serviceable device that not only detected the edges of the metal rectangle beneath the assorted improvised floor coverings and the thickness of concrete, but could still play CDs. "Three meters by six, nearly enough," he said, after several minutes walking through people's living quarters.

"About the size and shape of a shipping container," suggested Crane. "Or something else meant to go on the back of a truck."

"Or a coffin for a small dragon," said 8-ball darkly.

"Or some sort of bunker. Whatever it is, it probably won't be easy to open," said Zurich. He looked around the group and shrugged. "Where should we start digging?"

Yoko's refuge in the Crypt was a standard-sized cubicle along the west wall, containing only an elongated futon bed with surprisingly clean sheets, a weapons rack (empty), a medium-sized suitcase (locked) on a folding stand (stolen), a lantern with a hand-cranked battery charger, an incense burner and a few half-melted candles. Ratatosk sat on the bed with his Novatech Slimline in his lap; the light from the fold-out vidscreen and the LEDs was enough to dispel the darkness but not the gloom.

Ratatosk knew better than to completely ignore Doc Czarnecki's orders about diving back into the Matrix—not that there was a jackpoint in or near Yoko's room—but the data in his online memory was potentially useful, maybe even valuable, and curiosity had long been Ratatosk's greatest weakness. Even his obsessive pursuit of women was driven as much by an intellectual fascination with what made them all different and desirable, as it was by a craving for physical pleasure. If he lived long enough, he hoped to one day come up with a Grand Unified Theory of sexual attraction . . . and even if he failed, he was enjoying the research.

The elf's long fingers danced across the keyboard, but he still found the process agonizingly slow compared to the way he usually glided through the Matrix, effortlessly moving at the speed of thought. Scrolling through the corrupted data from the partially downloaded file felt more like trying to wade through fast-drying concrete. Eventually, though, he managed to re-create a readable copy of the datafile's front page, a time sheet for that day's activity in the garage. He found the listing for the Nomad with the matching registration, and looked at the name of the employee who'd checked it out. Thomas Mather. It was vaguely familiar, and Ratatosk found himself wishing he was back in his apartment among his well-ordered archive of datafiles he'd copied from the different corps.

The roster said that Mather's office was on the sixty-fourth floor, which Ratatosk remembered as being the lair of their security staff and security-related middle management. He looked down the list of Step-Vans that had been checked out, and found that one of these, too, had been requested by Thomas Mather.

Ratatosk was sure it had to mean something, but his headache was too intense for him to think clearly, and staring at the small vidscreen for as long as he had hadn't helped matters. Reluctantly, he powered down the cyberdeck and closed his eyes.

*   *   *

Pierce swung the pick, wondering why it was that any-time a job came up that required muscle rather than brains, it seemed to land in his lap. Still, he had to admit there was something comfortable about the rhythm he was starting to settle into. He started to whistle in time with the *chunk* the pick made as it bit into the concrete, and while this didn't seem to please his workmates, none of them actually voiced an objection.

When they'd made a big enough hole in the concrete floor of Pike's quarters to clearly see something orange that obviously *wasn't* concrete, Zurich had knelt beside the pit and tapped cautiously on the object, then reached for his improvised metal detector. "Well?" asked Sumatra, his voice muffled by his filter mask.

"Fiberglass, I think," said the dwarf. "Or some sort of very tough, hard plastic or ceramic, with similar properties. But there's some metal underneath it, probably stainless steel."

"How thick?"

"A couple centimeters, at least—probably three or four. How much of that is metal, I can't tell yet. Maybe half a centimeter, maybe twice that."

"Great," muttered Pierce. "You mean it's a fraggin' safe. How're we going to hack our way through *that*?"

"I think the real question is, *are* we going to hack our way through that?" added Sumatra.

Pierce raised his pick and brought it down on the plastic with all his strength. It bounced off with a flat *thud*.

"Stop, you—" Zurich began, then looked up at the orks and sighed. "This is some sort of secure containment facility. That's why it was buried under a quarter meter of concrete. I don't know what it was meant to contain, but until we have some idea . . . Besides, there has to be some better way to open it than trying to smash through the top. Locks. Hinges. Some other weak point."

Pierce looked at the unblemished surface and shrugged. "Suits me. I didn't like its tone, anyway. So what do we do now?"

"Clear away the concrete until we find an edge. If the top opens, we should be able to find a way to open it. The ramp's over that way, so it would make more sense to have the hinges on the far side. Or if it's one of the ends . . ."

"We do even more digging?"

"Yeah," said 8-ball, taking up his entrenchment tool. "Guess we try to find the northeast corner." They all went back to work, but with less enthusiasm than before.

Ninety minutes later, they'd uncovered enough of the corner to get a clearer picture of the shape of the object. The lid was recessed slightly from the corner, and sealed with a gasket of nonbiodegrading plastic. "Looks like a fraggin' big freezer," said Pierce.

"It may be," said Zurich, and glanced at the digital clock on his wristcomp. "Three and a half hours before the deadline. Can we get it open by then?"

Chen's face hadn't gotten any prettier since the last time Lankin had seen it, nor was his broad smile any more convincing. "Hello, hello. How may I help you?"

"I thought we might be able to help each other, Chen," Lankin replied smoothly. "I know you're a man who can find almost anything a man could want, and at a good price."

"Could be. What is it you want?"

·"It's not for me, you understand. I'm trying to retrieve something taken from an associate of mine. He thinks the people who took it may have tried to sell it to you . . . not that I'm suggesting that you would knowingly buy stolen property, of course. But if you happen to remember anybody from the Crypt coming to you with medical equipment . . ."

"Medical equipment?"

"Laboratory equipment. Medical research." He watched Chen's face closely. "Biological. Biohazard containment. Anything of that nature. We'd pay for its return, of course—and the sooner it's returned, the less the risk of, ah, contamination."

A hint of alarm cracked Chen's masklike composure for

an instant. "I don't remember anything like that coming in recently," he said after a brief pause. "Can you be more precise?"

"Not exhaustively. I can't give you all the details, but Az . . . ah, my associates, sent a mobile research facility to the Puyallup area, near Hell's Kitchen, after hearing some rather alarming stories. It was set up rather hastily, and the only complete inventory of the equipment was in a computer that the thieves also took—along with its backup disks. We're trying to compile a new list, but it could take a while, and we really can't afford to wait."

"What sort of stories?"

"You haven't heard?"

"No."

"That's a relief: the fewer people know, the less the chance of panic. And that also suggests that it hasn't spread . . . though the incubation period is . . . anyway, we need to find the equipment. Urgently."

"When did this robbery take place?"

Lankin wasn't sure whether Chen was calling his bluff or was genuinely worried. "Three days ago, though they may have managed to pilfer some of the stuff from the stores before then without it being noticed."

Chen shook his head. "I've not seen anybody from the Crypt in more than a week," he said. "And no scientific or medical equipment in months. The stuff you're after hasn't come here."

Lankin paused, trying to think of a sufficiently subtle way of asking whether the Hatter or any of his associates had come around trying to *buy* scientific or medical equipment that might have come from the Crypt. "Can you ask around and see if anybody else has seen it?"

"Not without more details," said Chen, spreading his hands in a gesture of helplessness. "If you're looking for a specific item, and you're able to pay more than . . . any other bidder . . ."

Bingo! "That shouldn't be a problem," replied Lankin, smiling slightly. "Though I'd want to be sure I wasn't bidding against myself. The other bidder . . . did he say who he was working for?"

"I can't reveal that sort of detail about my client . . ."

"Corp?"

"He might have been. He didn't say."

"Well dressed?"

"Very. Why?"

"Damn. We may have had a communications failure; I told him *I* was going to call you, because we'd had dealings before. He must have forgotten, or misunderstood. Can you excuse me for a second? I have another call, and it's flagged urgent." He put the fence on hold, and looked out into the corridor. Spotting a child, he yelled, "Get Zurich! *Now!*"

14

Ratatosk coughed hard enough to wake himself up, and sat up suddenly and sniffed cautiously. Smoke? No, not smoke. Dust of some sort . . .

"Are you okay?" came a female voice from outside.

He coughed again experimentally. "Just a bad dream, I think. What's happening? Are we being bombed?"

"They're tearing up the floor. Most of us are wearing our filter masks. I came by earlier to tell you. I looked in, but you were asleep."

"That must have been the good part of the dream," said Ratatosk automatically, as he recognized the voice.

Leila pushed the curtain aside and stepped into the room. She was dressed in black jeans, T-shirt and boots, and there was so little light in the room that even Ratatosk's dark-adapted metahuman eyes could see little more than her eyes and the filter mask covering her nose and mouth. "Are you sure you're okay? Mish said you'd just had your brains burned."

"I've felt better," he admitted. "They told me I should stay in bed, so that's what I'm doing. But I wouldn't mind some company."

She sat on the foot of the bed. "Yoko's my sensei," she said, looking around the tiny room. "She's told me a lot about you." Her tone suggested that most of what she'd heard was good, but Ratatosk decided it was safer not to reply. "She's why you're here, isn't she?"

"Yes."

"She means that much to you?"

"Yes."

"Me, too. I wish I could be more like her, but I don't have the knack. No magic at all. I can't even pull a rabbit out of a hat."

Ratatosk blinked. He had the strange feeling that she'd just said something incredibly important, but why should the mention of rabbits and hats start sounding alarm bells somewhere in the back of his brain? "We all have different knacks," he reassured her. "The best way to be like Yoko is to find out what you do best, and keep doing it. And find a good teacher—but you've already done that."

"Is that what you've done?"

"Yes. I can't punch through a wall or dodge bullets the way she does, but she can't sleaze her way through ice, either. From each according to his or her abilities."

Leila's mouth was hidden by her filter mask, but Ratatosk could see the smile in her eyes. "Yoko's told me about some of the other things you're good at, too."

"I've had good teachers."

"And lots of practice?" she murmured, leaning over and touching his thigh.

Ratatosk's smile widened until it matched hers, and he sat up and reached toward her to stroke her blue-black hair, then the delicate fur on her long, lovely neck. She removed her filter mask and slid closer to him. They kissed, and her hand moved up the inside of his thigh. She broke off the kiss to murmur, "I hope your mouth isn't making promises that your body's not healthy enough to keep."

"My mouth doesn't make any promises that *it* can't keep," Ratatosk assured her.

She laughed, and pulled her T-shirt up over her head and threw it onto the floor, then did the same with her neck knife. Another two knives clattered onto the floor as she pulled off her boots. She unbuckled her belt and slithered out of her jeans as Ratatosk stood up to remove his lined coat and his smartgun. She turned her back on him as she admired the gun, and he stroked her back, noticing that the fur didn't actually cover her entire body. She turned to face him and reached for his belt buckle.

"How long before they throw us out of here?" he murmured in her ear.

"About three hours," she replied, smiling. "That's why I decided not to waste too much time on small talk."

Zurich came running into the medicine lodge, and Lankin apologized to Chen and put him on hold again. "What gives?" the dwarf asked, panting slightly.

"Can you tap a tridphone call from here?"

Zurich snorted. "With the equipment I have on me? No way. If the other end hasn't answered—if he's had to send voice mail or text—Ratatosk might be able to deck into his service, but if it's live, it's lost. Sorry." He looked at Lankin's sour expression and grimaced in sympathy. "We might be able to *trace* a comcall, but not a tap, not from here."

"A trace would help," said Lankin. "Somebody's offering to buy medical or scientific gear that comes from the Crypt. If I know Chen, he'll call that buyer as soon as I'm off the line."

"What's his number?"

"It's 4206 31–6748. And he'll be using the cheapest service-provider available."

"Good; that'll make it easier. I'll get Ratatosk, just in case . . . Do you know where he is?"

"Someone at the clinic should know," said Pierce, when Lankin didn't answer.

"Can you get him? I'll be at the jackpoint." They both retreated from the lodge, while Lankin took Chen off hold. "Sorry about that," Lankin said, smiling. "Another deal going down. You wouldn't be in the market for some drones and a case of slightly used assault rifles, would you?"

Ratatosk, barefoot and shirtless, was still fumbling with his belt buckle as he ran into the library. "What's so fraggin' urgent that you had to get me out of bed?" he demanded.

Zurich, jacked in to his Novatech Hyperdeck, didn't look up. "Trying to trace a call," he said.

"Do you want me to try?"

"You're still injured from last time," said Mish, who'd been sent to wake him and was still blushing.

"Not badly."

The shaman muttered something uncomplimentary in Russian, and her elfin features became strangely mouselike as she cast a healing spell on him. Ratatosk took out his own deck, and waited for the dwarf to log off.

"I've found it," said Zurich. "It's a cell phone downtown." Reluctantly, he unplugged his deck from the jackpoint. "You want to take it from here?"

Ratatosk nodded, sat down on the floor and logged on, while Mish hovered over him anxiously. "Got it," he said a moment later. "Corner of John and Fifteenth. Triangulating . . ."

"The hospital?" asked Mish.

"Aztechnology Pyramid," said Ratatosk. "He's—drek. He's hung up." He rubbed his eyes. "Okay, trying to trace the number. It *may* be listed."

He was silent for more than a minute; then he swore again. "Pocket secretary with a silent number, from a batch of numbers issued to—guess where?"

"One of the shops in the Aztechnology Pyramid?" replied Zurich.

"Right. It might have been bought by an outsider, it might have been stolen . . . but the odds are against it. And—hold on a second. Frag, I *thought* it seemed familiar."

"What?"

"I downloaded a booking sheet for the vehicles in the Pyramid's garage. This same number is listed as the cell number for the guy who checked out the Nomad outside and a Step-Van. Thomas Mather. Name ring any bells with you?"

"No. Should it?"

"I don't know. I can't help thinking I've heard it before, or read it . . . it'll come to me."

"Is he the decker you ran into there? The rabbit?"

Ratatosk blinked. "I don't . . . I don't think so." He gritted his teeth as he stood. Part of him wanted to go back to bed to resume his interrupted encounter with Leila. Much less of him wanted to call a meeting, especially as that would require him to talk to Lankin, but he knew that was the rational part of his being. Or maybe his instinct for self-preservation—the part of his brain that was also telling him that sleazing his way back into the Pyramid's system and trying to download staff files was a very bad idea. Either way, it probably shouldn't be ignored. "Where is everybody?"

"Still here."

"Oh, good. Is Yoko . . ."

"She's still unconscious," said Mish, "but she's out of danger. At least—"

"At least until there's another attack," said Ratatosk. "Got it. I think we need another war council."

Wallace had changed the guard after relieving Lewis, even though it meant reducing the number of watchers from five to four. Kat and Dutch were still recovering from the sleep spells that had been cast on them, Lori was resting, and Griffin was watching over all of them through the rotodrone's cameras. Wallace was concentrating on watching King, hoping that he wasn't about to go on a rampage to avenge his brother, who was still in surgery. Wallace's own wound had been healed, but it still itched, and now that it had begun raining in earnest, he found himself regretting that last cup of coffee. Lewis' idea of quitting to become a security guard was sounding better every time he thought about it.

His phone demanded his attention, and he managed not to snarl; he knew it had to be the Hatter. "Yes?"

"We've just had a decker try to download the vehicle roster, and now somebody's asking the local fences about squatters bringing in . . ." Despite his obvious irritation, he paused. "Loot from Hell's Kitchen. What's happening there?"

"Well, it's raining," said Wallace with mock levity. "No one's moving—not above ground, anyway, unless they're invisible. All quiet on the western front."

"Do you know who's down there? Or how many of them there are?"

"Not without going in. We tried sending the mage in astrally, but she couldn't get past their defenses. Neither did that troll who brought that drekheap of a van down here. They've dumped his body above ground, but I'm not going to pick it up without a good reason. There's only a couple of hours to go before sunset. Do you need to know before then?"

"Have you questioned your prisoners?"

"They're only kids!"

"They may still know who's down there. Have you ever heard of a decker named Ratatosk? Or an elf named Lankin?"

"No."

The Hatter was silent for a moment. "The negotiated position was that they didn't have to evacuate until an hour after sunset, correct?"

"Yes."

"Did you say that you wouldn't be going in before then?"

"Not when I first made the deal, no, but after the drek hit the fan, we had to change the terms. The sun'll be setting in a couple of hours; they should all be out in three—"

"You'll have to send men in anyway after that, won't you, to make sure the place is empty and secured? Or were you planning on taking their word for it?"

"I'll send my men in when I think there's a decent chance of them coming out alive again," said Wallace coldly. "The fewer of them there are down there, the better the odds are. And I'm going to send some drones in first, if that's okay with you?" He didn't sound as though he were asking permission.

"Of course," said the Hatter blandly. "So why not do it now? You'll get a better idea of what they might be plotting down there—and some sort of warning of how well they're armed if they're not intending to evacuate as arranged. Wouldn't that be a sensible precaution?"

Wallace clicked his teeth while he examined the idea for traps. "They're your drones," he said a few seconds later.

"True," said the Hatter. "Let me know what you find."

"Anything in particular you think I should look for?"

"No . . . just send me a full status report, and a copy of the video. I probably won't have time to look at it today, but it may be useful later."

"Will do," he said, and signed off, his suspicions largely confirmed. *There's something valuable down there,* he thought, *and the bastard doesn't trust me enough to tell me what it is.*

The Hatter stared at his pocket secretary until the screensaver—a stock ticker—kicked in. He idly wished he'd thought to put bombs in the Step-Van and the Nomad as well as that rusting heap of drek he'd given the squatters as transport. Better by far if everybody else who knew about this died. Except for Hare, of course, and sometimes the Hatter even wondered if he could trust *him.*

Maybe trust was the wrong word, he decided. He could *rely* on Hare to act in his own best interests. And he was useful. No, Hare should live. At least until he found a replacement.

Ratatosk looked around the lodge at the tired and dusty team gathered there—Leila, 8-ball, Zurich, Crane, Sumatra, Mute, Pierce and Lankin—and cleared his throat. "We've confirmed that the man behind this is working for Aztechnology," he said, with a slight nod at Zurich. "His name is Thomas Mather, and he's in their security section, probably fairly high up. Has anyone had any contact with him before?"

"This is the fragger who Chen phoned?" Pierce asked.

"Yes."

"Uh-huh. Sounds like the same guy who sent that snooper here to tell us to leave. Least, they both wear a top hat."

Crane blinked. "Human?"

"Yeah. Why?"

"I was hired by a Johnson a couple of years ago who

wore a top hat. Maybe it was part of his camouflage, because I don't remember much about his face. I don't know who he was working for, but he wanted me to extract a scientist from Renraku. About the only other thing I remember is that he said that if we couldn't extract the target, we'd get half the payment for killing him. Real cold."

Pierce turned to Sumatra. "You were there when Boanerges talked to the snoop. Do you remember anything else he said about 'im?"

The rat shaman hesitated, then shook his head. "Just that he was well dressed for a Johnson. It might not be the same guy."

"Whether it is or not," said Lankin, "he's been dealing with Chopsticks Chen and asking what he's bought that might have come from the Crypt, so there's definitely something here that he wants. Unfortunately, Chen wouldn't give me any details, or tell me what this Mather had offered to pay for it. Does anyone have any contacts in the Pyramid?"

Lankin hesitated, then nodded stiffly. "I know someone. This isn't his department, but he has a good security rating; he may be able to dig something up. And speaking of digging up, how is the excavation going?"

"Slowly," muttered 8-ball. "I don't think we're going to be able to open the whatever-it-is before the deadline. Of course, it'd help if we knew what we were looking for."

Sumatra nodded. "Just because it seems to be a hazmat container doesn't mean there's anything of value inside. It could just be computer parts that weren't worth recycling."

"An old hard drive might contain useful information," said Ratatosk.

"Maybe, if you had time to search through the files," the shaman replied. "I'm not saying we should stop digging—but I don't think we should get our hopes up too high, either."

"What if you had an earth elemental?" asked Leila.

The dwarf blinked. "I don't know. Can we get one?"

"Magnusson could summon one, if we had the materials," she replied. "And we probably do. There's a lot of stuff in the workshop we sell to talismongers, or use to train students. It probably won't be very powerful, but it might help."

8-ball nodded. "Any help would be appreciated. Is that all?" He looked around the room, but no one seemed to have any more to say, so he stood. "Okay. Leila, can you go talk to Mag—excuse me." He looked at his wristphone, which was vibrating, and flipped the screen up. The readout told him that he had an incoming call from Griffin. "8-ball."

"Hoi," came the reply. "Hope I didn't wake you."

The dwarf smiled. "I wish. 'S'up?"

"I've been ordered to send a drone down into your cellar there to look around," said the rigger, a hint of apology bleeding through his Louisiana accent. "It's just a Gaz-Niki Snooper. No weapons, standard sensor package. I just thought I'd warn you, and let you know that I've only got the one."

"Thanks."

"So if anything bad happens to it, I don't have a lot of options for replacing it," Griffin continued. "Just a Doberman patrol vehicle with twin machine guns. And the fraggers only issued me one belt of gel rounds, too . . . but you know what fraggin' supply sergeants are like."

"I understand," said 8-ball dryly. "I'll tell the sentries to let it pass, and warn people not to step on it. Ahhh . . . it doesn't weigh enough to set off a land mine, does it?"

"I hope not."

"Uh-huh. Catch you later." He flipped the vidscreen down and looked around the room. "Sounds like they're on to us."

"It could be a coincidence," said Ratatosk uneasily.

"Yeah, it could be. They could be trying to count the guns, or the wounded, or anything like that. I guess we'll know if they head straight for the dig."

"What do you want us to do?" asked Pierce. "Fill the fraggin' hole in again?"

Zurich shook his head. "The standard sensor package for a snooper doesn't include anything like a seismograph, does it?"

"No," said Crane, "but the sniffer might detect the dust

if it gets close enough, and the mics will pick up the sound if we keep digging."

The dwarf looked straight up. "How reliable are the sensors? Will they be surprised if they lose the signal? After all, we're inside a big metal grid."

Crane shrugged. "They're designed for use in rebar concrete buildings like this; there may be some interference, a little signal loss, but if their rigger's any good, he'll allow for that. After all, we can still use our cell phones in here without too much trouble, even though I don't know where the nearest relay station is. I think he'll smell a rat if we try to jam him."

"He will," said 8-ball. "And if he thinks we disabled the snooper, he might program the next patrol drone to fire at any humanoid target if the signal is disrupted for more than a few seconds. I'm not saying he *will*, but I know he *can*, and he knows I know. And then he'll come and fix it, with half the squad to back him up."

"What if we set up some sort of obstacle course so this drone only goes where we want it to go?" suggested Leila. "It can't open doors, can it?"

"Not this one. But a couple of linked machine guns can open most doors," replied 8-ball.

"It could buy us some time," said Zurich. "Crane, you have your deck here, don't you?"

"Yes, but no drones—"

"So we borrow theirs. 8-ball, do you know what radio frequency they're likely to be using?"

"Yeah, but—"

"We can send a stronger signal from inside this box than their rigger can from outside, and we have the transceiver from the drone Mute shot down, which should tell us what sort of encryption he's using." He smiled. "So we should be able to send it new orders. Turn left instead of right, turn down the gain on the mics . . . nothing too obvious, but it should be possible to keep it out of sensitive areas. Right?"

"We can try," said Crane. "Leila, can you and Pierce stop it getting in here, into the clinic, into the dig . . . anywhere else?"

"The latrine?" suggested Sumatra, standing. "And while we're on the subject, is this meeting over? I've got to go. I don't know what was in that MRE I just ate, but I think they were supposed to feed it to the enemy."

8-ball waved him away, and Sumatra ran toward the chemical toilets. Zurich stood and stretched, then turned to Crane. "I'll go get my tools. Do you have what's left of that drone?"

"In my room."

8-ball nodded. "Mute, can you ask Magnusson about the earth elemental? Lankin, can you call your guy in the Pyramid? Okay, I think we're finished."

Lankin watched them leave, then grabbed his pocket secretary and muttered, "Esquivel."

The phone rang twice before Jose Esquivel's face appeared on the screen. "Yes?" he said, then paled slightly as he recognized Lankin. "What is it?" he asked warily.

"I need some information," said Lankin. "What can you tell me about an Aztechnology employee named Thomas Mather?"

Esquivel's expression didn't change, but he looked around his expertly decorated office before answering, as though trying to calculate how much he had to lose. "Why do you want to know?"

"Does it matter?"

"Let's put it this way," said the exec carefully. "If it affects the corporation, it affects me. Yes, we do have a Thomas Mather working here. He's the champion on our competitive pistol-shooting team, as well as one of our best bridge and chess players. I can tell you that much for free. He doesn't have much to do with my department, and I've only met him a few times, so I don't know much more than that. But if you're planning on blackmailing him . . . be warned. Word is that he's extremely clever, unpredictable and a worse bastard than you are. He's also wired like a Christmas tree, with the best alphaware and biotech he can afford—reflexes, smartlink, headware and God only knows what else. He and his partner are supposed to be Cruzan's pets: she brought them with her from HQ."

Lankin smiled. Maria Cruzan was head of Aztechnology's electronics division in Seattle, and frequently employed shadowrunners for industrial espionage and extractions. "Who's his partner?"

"His name's Herrera, but he calls himself the March Hare."

"A decker?"

"That's right. Do you know him?"

"Only by reputation. Do you know what they're working on?"

"Not really. Mather's usual job is head-hunting, vetting new employees for security clearances, that sort of thing."

"Recruiting supplemental resources?"

Esquivel smiled slightly at his use of the corporate euphemism for shadowrunners. "If someone has particularly valuable talents, and is proving difficult to relocate, he *might* occasionally hire employees on short-term contracts to assist with the . . . transport. But I've never had to make use of his services: I understand he mostly works for the R & D people."

Lankin nodded. Esquivel was a middle manager dealing with sales and distribution of the food and home appliances; the only use his division had for shadowrunners was the occasional datasteal from their competitors. "Can you access his personnel file?"

"No, but he probably has one on you."

"What?"

"He and Hare keep dossiers on unofficial assets—those who've worked for the corp, and as much information as they can get on those who've been hired by our competition. It's their forte. I don't know if the Hatter still does the fieldwork himself, but he's usually consulted when any supplemental resources are needed."

"The Hatter?"

"That's what most people call him—and what he calls himself, I understand. He wears a top hat most of the time, even indoors." There was a hint of a sneer on his face; Esquivel's own clothing was conservative, not flashy, and mostly bought from Aztechnology's own stores at wholesale prices. The only hint of color in the ensemble came from the small Aztlan flags on his tie.

"Can you get copies of those dossiers?"

"I don't think so. I'd have to submit an application for temporary staff, with a budget and a timeline and a detailed set of objectives, and the applications are prioritized according to profitability as well as urgency. I can recommend particular individuals for a job, but I doubt my division could afford your services," he said, showing his teeth for an instant. "I'm also sure the Hatter would want to know why I'd chosen you, and that might be difficult to explain."

Lankin nodded. "Where does your wife work?" he asked casually.

Esquivel froze. "You wouldn't—" He studied Lankin's face, realized that he *would*, and changed tack. "She can't help you either. She works in accounts, in payroll, but she doesn't have the security clearance to look into payments for supplemental resources. Certified credsticks usually come out of research costs, not salaries."

Lankin looked at his eyes and decided that the exec was probably telling the truth. "Do you know why Aztechnology R & D might be interested in Puyallup?"

"No, but I don't know what R & D is working on—and I have nothing at all to do with the magical division's research."

"Thanks. Good-bye." He hung up and stood, wishing the ceiling wasn't so low. The only hunch he had was in his shoulders, to prevent him banging his head on the ceiling. Grudgingly, he walked over to Yoko's room and knocked on the doorframe, then pushed his way through the curtain without waiting for an answer. The decker was lying on the bed with his eyes closed; Lankin was disappointed to find him alone, but he consoled himself that at least he could disturb his rest. "It was a waste of time," he said. "All he could tell me is the name of the decker who fried you. He calls himself the March Hare, but his real name's Herrera. A real hotshot, apparently. Cruzan brought him up from Aztlan when she was transferred."

Ratatosk opened an eye. "March Hare?"

"Right. And Mather's known as—"

"The Mad Hatter?"

"Right again. They're characters from *Alice in Wonderland*, right?"

"*Alice's Adventures in Wonderland*," Ratatosk corrected him, closing the eye again. "And they return in *Through the Looking Glass*. And . . . and I've just remembered where I've heard of them before."

"Where?"

"A file I reconstructed a year ago. Did you know Mandy Mandelbrot?"

"No."

"She managed to partially download some files from a sealed system inside the Pyramid before her team had to slot and run. She brought the files to me to see if I could recover them; I was recovering from surgery." He raised his cyberarm slightly, then let it fall back to the mattress. She liked excitement, never had the patience for the tedious stuff. She went on another run a few weeks later, and died."

"Another one of your harem?"

"Briefly, yeah, but that's not . . ." He drew a deep breath. "One of the files was about something called the Balcony Project. Pet scheme of Cruzan's. They were deliberately hiring people with personality disorders for certain positions. Paranoids. Self-mutilators. Surgery addicts. Obsessive-compulsives. And psychopaths.

"The file listed two of the most promising case studies—a decker with narcissistic personality disorder, a borderline psychopath, and a company man who was a full-blown sociopath. Their full names weren't listed, just their initials and their street names. The March Hare and the Mad Hatter."

"They deliberately hired these people?"

Ratatosk shrugged. "As long they know what they are, they obviously think they can control them. And do you think they're the only psychopaths working for the corporations? Frag, if the megacorporations were individuals, most of them would fit the definition of a sociopath perfectly."

"Spare me the psychobabble," said Lankin, yawning. "Does knowing this help us in any way?"

"It tells us that we can probably rule out negotiating with

Mather, if you were thinking of trying," the decker replied. "What else did your contact say?"

Sumatra looked at the walls of the Porta-John and decided that the soundproofing probably wasn't good enough for him to risk speaking. And sending a watcher spirit with a message would be pointless; it might succeed in leaving the Crypt without being detected, now that the only guards capable of astral vision were his own watchers, but it wouldn't get through the magical security on the Aztechnology Pyramid. He took out his cell phone, flipped it open and began composing an e-mail.

It had been nearly a year since Sumatra had done a job for a Mr. Johnson who wore a top hat, but he'd never figured out who the man was working for. Now that he did know, and knew the man's name and had some idea of what it was he wanted and—best of all—what he might be prepared to pay for it . . . well, they'd done business before, and while the relationship had been brief, it had also been profitable. This could be even more so. Much more.

15

Quinn leaned over Griffin's shoulder, looking at the vid-screen as the rigger guided the drone between the sentries. The fixed camera showed darkness ahead; the turret-mounted rotating camera revealed that one of the rifle-toting sentries, a female dwarf with purple hair, was watching the drone while the other, a scrawny ork missing both ears and one hand, looked up at the entrance. "Recognize them?" she asked.

"No. They both look a little young to have been in the army," said Griffin dryly. "D'you think I know every meta-human in Seattle?"

"No."

"I've never even been here before. Flew a Banshee into Cascade Ork territory once to nab some smugglers, but that's as close as I've come." He adjusted the brightness and contrast settings on the low-light camera until he could see two taller figures standing amid the clutter at the end of the ramp. The studs and rings in the ork's face and ears reflected the available light, forming a constellation, while— Griffin swore in surprise. "That's a Night One there—the one that's basically a misty silhouette."

"Lot of crap on the ground," said Quinn. "Do you think they're trying to slow you down?"

"Probably; do you blame them?" The exec didn't answer. "There's a lot of crap in the air, too. I wonder how they breathe in there."

"What is it? Smoke?"

"Not sure. I'm not getting anything on infrared to say there's any big fires down there, but it could have been hanging around for a while—the place can't be that well ventilated. The sniffer says it's inert, and it's not getting through the filters, so it's not any chemical weapon I've heard of. It's reducing visibility by a little, but not enough to make a real difference." He shrugged.

"We'll find out when we go down there," said Quinn darkly, and glanced at the clock on the dashboard. 1624. A little over two hours before sunset.

The Hatter looked at the message on the small screen of his pocket secretary, and examined it carefully for traps. MR. MATHER, it read, I AM INSIDE THE CRYPT, UNABLE 2 TALK 4 FEAR OF BEING HEARD, BUT CAN LISTEN THROUGH EARPIECE. I HV INFORMATION THAT MAY INTEREST U.

He thought for a moment, then swiveled around in his chair and downloaded the file on Sumatra. It had been nearly a year since he'd last hired the rat shaman, and the run had been only partially successful—though that seemed to have been the decker's fault, not Sumatra's. The file refreshed his memory. Sumatra was an initiate, capable of reflecting hostile spells; he was also observant, sneaky, greedy, and accomplished at preserving his own warty hide at any cost, all qualities that the Hatter admired greatly. The photo looked vaguely familiar, and on a hunch, he called up Foote's fuzzy snap of the ork hiding in the shadows of the Crypt and ran both pictures through his facial recognition software. *Match possible, but insufficient reference points to confirm.* The Hatter drummed his fingers on his desktop for a moment, then said, "Convert voice to text."

"Converting."

"Who else is down there, question mark, end, send."

Magnusson examined the material components that Jinx had gathered from the enchanting kit, assessing their purity, and finally nodded. "You'll need to draw a new circle," he told her quietly. The four reusable circles he'd created for teaching purposes—one for each type of elemental—

were upstairs, in the garden, where there was natural earth, clean air and water on good days, and enough room for a bonfire. "If they see you performing any sort of ritual, their mage might try to stop you. She'll certainly know what you're doing, and she may work out why. Now, there isn't much material here, and even if there was, we don't have time to summon anything very big or powerful. Can you draw a meter-wide circle in your room?"

"Me?"

"I'm needed here," he said. As well as healing, he was using a clean air spell to minimize the level of dust in the clinic. "You know the ritual, don't you?"

"Yes, but I've never done it without you watching me! What if I frag up?"

"Tell me when you're ready to begin the actual summoning, and I'll come and look at the circle and make sure you have it right. If the elemental gets away from you, which I'm positive it won't, I'll take control of it myself."

She nodded, but it was obvious that she was nervous. Czarnecki watched as she walked out of the clinic, then walked up behind Magnusson and murmured, "You're sure she can do it?"

The mage raised an eyebrow. "Are you suggesting that I can't teach a simple procedure to one of my most gifted students? Anyone who wants to pass Hermetic Conjuring 101 has to be able to do a one-hour summoning."

"What happens to the ones who flunk?"

Magnusson's expression didn't change. "If it's an earth elemental, usually a premature burial. Brief and nonfatal, of course. All the examiners have to know healing spells as well as banishment rituals."

"What if it's a fire elemental?"

"The university stopped us using that as a question in the first year practical exam back in 2052," the mage admitted. "The insurance is too expensive. But please don't tell my freshman class. I'd hate them to think they didn't have to know it."

The Hatter looked at Sumatra's reply to his question, and his eyes bugged slightly. He began reading out the names, and his computer pulled dossiers out of the database. Most of the names drew blanks, but there were enough elite shadowrunners among them to make the Hatter feel as though he'd just seen an opponent in a chess game turn all of his pawns to queens. He made a quick estimate of what it would cost to hire this team for even a day, and paled.

Only two possible explanations occurred to him. One was that they'd learned about GNX-IV and were trying to beat him to it. Or alternatively, they didn't know what they were looking for, but were working for someone else who did—a fixer, perhaps, or one of the corps. He might still be able to win a bidding war, but that would eat into his already depleted budget—and if they demanded quick payment, he was sunk.

The other possibility was that there was something else in the ruin that he knew nothing about. Something else that Monolith had stored, perhaps? Or maybe something magical. The Hatter glanced at the list of names again, wondering why the name Magnusson seemed vaguely familiar. He was prepared to admit that he didn't know much about magic, except for its monetary cost . . . but he was well aware of the resale value of items such as foci, or raw materials such as orichalcum or radical gold.

He thought for a moment. Negotiating seemed to be his best option, and he had contact details for several of the shadowrunners in the squat, but how to contact them without letting them know that he had an informant on the inside? He stared at the dossiers on the screen before him, then called Wallace. "You've been negotiating with somebody inside that squat, haven't you?" he asked.

"Yes."

"I'd like to talk to him myself. How do I contact him?"

8-ball scooped a handful of grit out of the hole in the concrete, and looked down. "Definitely another hinge," he told the squatters. "I think we're—hold on." He flipped up the vidscreen of his wristphone and said, "Yeah?"

"Am I speaking to 8-ball?"

He glanced at the screen, which was blank except for a

line of text saying that the caller's phone number was unlisted. "Yes," 8-ball replied, sliding an opaque cap over the camera lens. "And who am *I* talking to?"

"You may call me Fedorov."

8-ball blinked, then turned to Mute, who ran out of the room. "Thank you," the dwarf replied, as he walked slowly toward Boanerges' medicine lodge. "What do you want?"

"I'd like us to be able to resolve the current situation and stop wasting each other's time and resources."

"Can you be more specific?" asked 8-ball dryly, reflecting that even a lawyer might find it difficult to be *less* specific.

"You've agreed to evacuate that ruin by seven fifteen, is that correct?"

"It may not be that simple. Three of our people have been killed since I said that—two of them teenagers. And two young children who left here are still being held by your gunmen, last I heard. Not everyone here is feeling cooperative." He kept his voice calm with an effort. "Can you give us any reason why we should?"

"What do *you* want?"

"What're you offering? I'm guessing you don't have the power to raise the dead."

"Unfortunately, no. But if you'd left when I first asked, those people would still be alive."

"Maybe," said 8-ball, picking up his pace slightly. "But there are some history buffs here who remember what happened to people who gave up their homes because some fragger says he bought the land. Common law says we own this place—and you didn't buy it from us."

"That was a mistake," said the Hatter smoothly. "One that I'm now attempting to correct. The van that you asked for is outside; consider that a first installment. I repeat, what do you want?"

8-ball hurried toward the medicine lodge, where he found Lankin reclining on Boanerges' bed. Lankin looked up, and 8-ball removed his wristphone and handed it to him. "It's the Hatter," he said quietly. "He wants to negotiate."

Lankin snatched up the phone as Mute burst into the room, with Zurich a few steps behind her. "First, we'd need to know your plans for this site," Lankin purred. "Could the squatters return here at some time? Or perhaps work here? Considering the location, I gather you're not planning to build luxury condominiums."

"Not exactly, but I can't go into details."

"Can you provide some alternative accommodation, then? Or maybe we should put this on a percentage basis. Say, ten thousand nuyen down against a twenty percent share of the net profits?"

The Hatter laughed. "I suppose you want to audit the books every year, too? Let's say I thrown in another van, and . . . How many of you are down there?"

"Why do you need to know?"

"So I can be sure we provide you with enough transportation. And rather than a certified credstick for a lump sum, I can provide everybody there with things they'll find useful immediately. Food and drink. New, clean, warm, dry clothing. Backpacks or duffels. Other survival equipment. Maybe even some boots. But for that, I'll need to know numbers."

"I'll have to do a head count, and call for a vote. I can't guarantee that everybody will be satisfied with those terms. Can you hold on for a moment?"

"No. I'll call you back in . . . about thirty minutes."

"Wait, please. What are *you* asking?"

"No more dead soldiers, no more damaged equipment and you evacuate peacefully at the agreed time. You can keep any weapons you may be carrying, but not ammunition. If everybody leaves as arranged, and agrees to a search, they'll be compensated. If not, nobody gets anything." He hung up.

"Frag," muttered Zurich. "I nearly had him. I'll go see if Ratatosk did any better."

"He'll call back," said Lankin. "And I've recorded his voice. We can play it to people, see if any of them recognize it."

"He's clever," said 8-ball. "A lot of people are going to want to take that offer, especially if the alternative's a body bag. I'd like to make the fraggers pay for the people here they've killed and wounded, but when you're a squatter, justice looks like a luxury you can't afford. Frag, ten years ago, I probably would've accepted myself."

"This place is worth much more than that," said Lankin. "To somebody, anyway. If we don't blink, we can drive the price higher. Maybe much higher."

"Then you're going to need to offer them something a little more concrete," said the dwarf. "And I don't mean the stuff we've got to hack through before we find whatever it is we're looking for . . . if it's down there at all, *if* we can recognize it when we see it, and *if* we can move it when we do."

"We can," said Lankin confidently. "At least, the Hatter is sure we can move vital parts of it—given time, of course."

"What makes you so sure?"

"It's why he's gone to the local fences, asking them to let him know if anybody from the Crypt tries to sell any scientific or medical gear—and why he's started asking for people who're leaving to be searched."

8-ball did a double take, then whistled admiringly.

"He knows we're looking for it now," Lankin continued, "because Chen told him we were, and he's worried we'll find it before the deadline, which means that it's possible. I was hoping he'd say something that would give me some other hint as to exactly what it was, but he's too careful for that." He nodded at 8-ball. "I'll need you to keep telling me how the people here think, but I've cut deals with enough people like the Hatter to know how *he* thinks."

Ratatosk pushed the curtain aside and walked in. "The call came from the same cell phone that Chen called," he announced. "I couldn't get a fix on it, because it was moving too fast—so fast he was either on the Intercity, or flying. He was moving south, but whether that's because he's coming here or whether he's just trying not to be traced back to the Pyramid . . ." He shrugged. "I've got a subroutine running to try to trace any more calls he makes from that phone—maybe even let me tap it. What've I missed?"

8-ball recounted the conversation. "I'll have to call a

meeting before this Hatter calls back. A full meeting, not just the war council."

"What?" Lankin spluttered. "What if they decide we all have to go?"

"Then we go. If you want to stay, you'd better have a pretty good counter offer."

Lankin stared at him, then looked entreatingly at Zurich and Mute. "Are we just going to give up that easily?"

Neither replied. "If we're going to have a meeting," said Ratatosk, "I think it's important that the Hatter doesn't get to listen in. What's happening with the drone?"

"Crane's still working on overriding it," said Zurich, looking even more uncomfortable. "It's the same frequency as the Condor that Magnusson brought in, not the one 8-ball remembers them using, but there's some pretty good real-time encryption that we haven't cracked yet. We can jam it, and we've kept it away from the dig and the clinic by setting up little tank traps, but at present, that's it. Leila's following it to make sure it doesn't go anywhere we don't want it to."

"Can we jam the audio without being too obvious about it?"

The dwarf nodded. "The farther it gets from the ramp, the worse the interference will be anyway. There's plenty of devices in a kitchen that could mess up the signal without making them too suspicious."

"And the digging?" asked Lankin.

"The container seems to have a number of compartments with separate lids," said 8-ball, glancing at Boanerges' clock. "Six or eight, at a guess. Should have the first of them open in a few minutes; I'll tell you what we find at the meeting. Seventeen hundred hours. Spread the word."

Sumatra looked at the sturdiest of the tables in the dining hall, hoping to find a relatively clean spot large enough to sit on, and decided to stand. It was difficult to tell the food crumbs from the concrete dust, and there was something off-putting about the red splodge—Tabasco sauce or ketchup—with the small boot prints in it. Normally, the kitchen and dining hall were two of the tidiest rooms in the Crypt, because everyone who ate there was required to clean up after themselves: the mess suggested that at least some of the denizens were preparing to abandon the place, and might already have abandoned hope. Sumatra looked at the worried faces amid the crowd, and listened as 8-ball addressed the assembled residents.

"The person who bought our land is offering to compensate us if we get out of here soon after sunset," said the dwarf. "He also wants us to submit to a search, and give up any ammunition we may be carrying. In exchange, he's talking about giving us clothing, food and another van for transport, but the details haven't been worked out yet. He could be fragging with us, but he might be on the level. He's calling back in about twelve minutes, so there isn't much time to debate this before we need to vote."

"What have the diggers found?" asked Mish, standing at the edge of the crowd, only a few steps from the clinic.

"We've opened one locker, or bin, or whatever it is," said the dwarf, without much enthusiasm. "There's some sealed containers inside with biohazard labels. All the same make—Monolith. The labels say they came from hospitals more'n thirty years ago, and that the stuff inside couldn't be sterilized or destroyed on site . . . but beyond that, we've got no way of knowing what's in them, much less what they might be worth. Doc Czarnecki is looking at them to see if he can identify anything valuable, and Ratatosk and Zurich are continuing to search the Matrix for any clues to what might be hidden here, but we don't have anything yet. We're hoping to have another two lockers open within an hour." He shrugged, and turned to Lankin.

"Even if we do find something in the lockers," said Lankin, "I don't think *anything* will enable you to keep this place indefinitely. The new owner is going to want it searched thoroughly, and he won't want any of you around while he does it. *Maybe* in a week, or a month, he'll pull out and you can return, if there's anything left standing.

"That leaves you with two options. One is to get the best offer out of him that I can, and for everybody to accept it. The other is to stall for time in the hope that we find something before he sends the mercs in to drive us out—dead or alive." He looked around at the crowd and the squalid, crumbling building. "If we stall and find whatever the owner is looking for, I may be able to find another buyer who'll give us more, maybe even enough for you to start a new Crypt, and who'll protect us from the mercs as well . . . but I can't promise that."

"How much do you think this thing is worth?" asked one squatter.

"The new owner must have spent at least thirty thousand already, so he must think there's a good chance of finding something worth more than that. Now, maybe he should have come to you in the beginning with thirty thousand, that's about a thousand each . . . but he didn't, and I don't know how much he has left. But I'm going to ask for two thousand each, for all of us, draw out the negotiations if possible, and see if I can get him to agree to at least half that much . . . if that suits everybody here?"

"Boanerges wouldn't have sold!" an ork said, her voice shrill. "And if he dies, it'll be their fault! Their mercs shot at our kids, their toxics attacked our people in their sickbeds . . . and you expect us to cut a deal with these fraggers?"

"Is there a third possibility that I haven't considered?"

"We fight!"

Lankin shrugged eloquently, then turned to 8-ball. "I've watched you try to shoot, Ulla," said the dwarf dryly, addressing the ork who had spoken up. "You flinch *before* you pull the trigger, and you can barely see past the end of the gun. Why do you think you weren't put on sentry duty? Any soldier in that squad could kill you before you knew they were there."

"We can't just give up!" said Ulla. "They've killed two of our people. We should—"

"Kill two of theirs?" 8-ball finished the sentence for her. "Or more? Do you think that's what Boanerges would want?"

"Whose side are you on? I know they're friends of yours out there! Who's fragging side are you on, shorty?"

There was some muttering at this, and 8-ball shook his head, unable to think of an answer that would prevent an argument. Sumatra looked at him anxiously, then cleared his throat. "Okay," the shaman said, "maybe there is a third possibility. Winner takes all. We get killed. The mercs get killed. And the fragger who set this up gets the place and whatever's in it for the cost of a few body bags."

The muttering died down to a faint murmur. "I say we give Lankin until sunset to see what he can get out of this fragger," Sumatra continued, sensing that he was on a winner, "and we don't go anywhere until he's delivered. And we keep digging until then. And even if we find frag-all, at least we'll get *something*."

He noticed many heads nodding, though Ulla's wasn't among them. "So, what're we going to ask for? Certified credsticks work for me." He listened to the hubbub as people volunteered ideas, then slipped away to the toilet.

The Hatter looked at the text message on his pocket secretary, and smiled. LANKIN 2 ASK 4 60K, it read. R U SERIOUS ABOUT SEARCH?

"Yes, of course."

I HV MAGIC STUFF I WANT 2 KEEP. NOT AMMO, & NOT FROM HERE.

"If it isn't what I'm looking for, I'll tell the mercs that you can keep it."

& MY FEE?

"You'll be paid your percentage. But the more I have to spend getting the others out of there, the longer you'll have to wait. Understood?"

Cutter Czarnecki hadn't meant to doze off, but it had been twenty-two hours since he'd last slept, and he hadn't worked a shift that long since his student days. He'd sat down on the floor, leaning up against the wall, and closed his eyes for a moment . . . and by the time Mish returned from the meeting, he'd begun to snore. Magnusson placed a finger over his lips as the mouse shaman entered. "Don't disturb him," he murmured. "How was the meeting?"

"Lankin's haggling over terms now." She shrugged. "I guess I should start taking down my lodge and packing it away. Maybe I'll find somewhere else to set up."

"If you're willing to teach magic, I might be able to find you some students who'll pay to learn some of the spells you know."

"Pay? Money?" She shook her head. "Boanerges always told me our totems meant magic to be free."

"Do they mean you to starve—" He looked around as he heard a moan, and dashed over to Yoko's bed, Mish close behind him. The adept's eyes were still closed, but her aura suggested she was starting to revive.

"You did it!" Mish squeaked. "You healed her!"

Magnusson shook his head. "I can't take the credit," he said. "Boanerges—" He looked up as Ratatosk walked in. "Yes?"

"Can I talk to you for a moment? In private?"

The magician raised an eyebrow, then shrugged. "One minute," he said. "Mish, if anything happens, I'll be in the library." He followed Ratatosk into the next room and asked, "Well?"

"You have a mind-reading spell, don't you?"

"Mind probe, yes. Sumatra knows one that compels truth, and Jinx knows one that detects lies. Why?"

"I think we have a leak."

"What?"

"A traitor. I've been tracing the Hatter's calls. Someone from here called him before he spoke to Lankin."

Magnusson raised both eyebrows at that. "You're sure it was someone in here? Not one of the mercs?"

"Not absolutely sure," Ratatosk admitted. "It was only a short conversation, a few text messages either way, and I didn't get the complete number—but I got most of it, and it doesn't match either Wallace's phone or Griffin's. Or 8-ball's—and he was in the meeting the whole time—or mine. Of course, anyone can have more than one phone . . . but I'm going to try to keep tracing it, and see if I can recover any of the messages. They might be enough to tell me who it is."

"Do you suspect anyone?"

"No . . . but I don't know any of the squatters. The only people here I've run with are 8-ball and Yoko. But if we catch anyone acting suspicious, we're not going to have time for much in the way of due process."

"Do you want to collect everyone's phones?"

"No, that'd tell whoever it was that we're onto him or her. And I wouldn't want to stop people getting information from their contacts—or even taking calls from their fixers. I was hoping there might be some simple magical way of finding a traitor."

"A mind probe is exhausting," said the magician. "I can't do one and be sure of having enough energy to keep healing people."

The elf frowned. "Frag," he muttered a moment later. "How is Yoko?"

"Better. She may be able to walk out of here herself, if Lankin can buy us enough time."

"That's great. Okay, don't tell anyone about the drain. We might be able to bluff."

Magnusson gave him a crooked smile. "Who else have you told?"

"Only 8-ball. Can you let me know when Yoko wakes up?"

"One complete outfit for everyone," Lankin announced to the group gathered in Boanerges' medicine lodge. "Waterproof jacket, securetech vest, pants, T-shirt, boots, socks and underwear. It'll be cheap stuff, probably Aztlan army surplus or something like that, but clean. Plus a prepaid handset phone, a transit pass, a backpack and ten days worth of ration bars each. Anybody with no money should be able to sell the phone and the vest to a pawnbroker and get enough for a few nights at the Y or somewhere similar. That only comes to a few hundred each, but he's also providing another small truck. I know it doesn't sound like much," he said before anyone else could speak, "but it may buy us a few more hours while we measure people and the Hatter tries to get things that fit."

8-ball snorted. "You've never been in the army, have you, college boy? They only make stuff in two sizes—too small and too big."

"That's why I asked for boots as well. If the mercs are going to search us, that'll also slow them down and give the diggers more time. I suggest whoever goes out first packs as much crud in their bags as they can carry, so they take even longer to search."

"Your list also lets him know how many of us there are," said Mute.

"Not really," said Lankin, smiling. "I inflated the figure by about forty percent. It hides our numbers, and will give the squatters more stuff to sell."

"And what's in it for you, Lank?" asked Ratatosk. "Somehow I can't see you in khaki and army boots."

Lankin scowled. "Like you, I'm gambling on the possibility that we'll find something valuable in that container before the mercs come storming down the ramp. If we don't, we all come up dry, but I'm sure that's not a new experience for any of us. Anyway, the Hatter said he'd call back again soon after five. Do I tell him we accept this offer?"

This was greeted with nods and a few shrugs. "What if we *do* find something?" asked Sumatra. "Those boxes are a bit big to put in your boot, and fraggin' heavy. How're you goin' to get 'em past the mercs?"

"We can't make any plans until we know what there is to find," said Mute. "Do we know what was in that first lot of cases?"

"We haven't opened them," said Zurich, "but if the labels are to be trusted, they're stuff that isn't safe to try to sterilize or destroy in the usual ways, and isn't worth recycling. Medical radioisotope capsules with a short half life. Power packs from old-fashioned cyberware. That sort of thing."

"Why didn't they sterilize it magically?"

"Maybe no one on staff knew the spell that long ago: you'd have to ask Maggie. But I can't see what use any of it could be to Aztechnology. We'll just have to keep looking and hope that we recognize the stuff when we see it. It might just be data that we can copy. Or it might be something too big to hide in a backpack, in which case we'll just have to think of something else."

"If it's small enough for one person to carry," said Sumatra, "I know an invisibility spell—one that'll get me past any drones without being detected, as well. And I haven't been casting as many spells as the healers, so I should be able to maintain it until I'm well out of range."

Lankin nodded. "That makes sense. We might be able to fool the mercs, but getting past the rotodrone . . . that won't be easy. Crane, how long can one of those things stay up?"

"At cruise speed, like that one? About five hours, five and a half. They put it into the air in midmorning . . . they must have taken it down to refuel at least once, about three thirty at the latest. They'll probably refuel again before sunset, to make sure it'll stay up while we're bugging out."

"Could we shoot it down?"

"With an assault cannon, yes; it would be in range. But you'd only get one shot."

No one spoke for a moment, and then Lankin nodded. "Thank you, Sumatra. That's the best plan I've heard in a while. We'll keep it in mind."

Wallace and Griffin walked outside the Step-Van, leaned against its side and watched the sky shade through gray and scarlet to a somber muted mauve, to the grim shade of blued steel. The synchronized digital clocks in their retinal displays said 1825.

Wallace sighed, and turned to his old friend. "Call 8-ball; ask how soon he'll be ready. I'll call Fedorov, see if he's got an ETA for that truck."

The elemental pounded away at the concrete as though determined to get back to the real earth beneath the vault. Pierce swung the pick to the same beat, pausing occasionally to move chunks out of the way to reveal more of the container. "That's both hinges clear," he said. "You going to open her?"

8-ball nodded, and Jinx ordered the earth elemental to move over to the next compartment. Zurich bent down to examine the old-fashioned lock, then removed a drill from his tool kit. 8-ball didn't notice his phone vibrating until after the drilling had stopped; then he flipped the screen up and looked at the caller ID. "Hold it 'til I get back," he said, and walked down the corridor to an empty room— one decorated with pinups of huge-breasted female fomori and giants. No accounting for tastes, he thought. "Yeah, Griff?"

"Chief wants to know whether you're ready."

"We'll start moving people out when the stuff arrives. No point in doing a strip search if you're going to put the same clothes back on, is there?"

"Uh-huh. I'll tell him. See you soon."

The dwarf nodded, pressed the Disconnect button and left the room. He turned at the sound of someone running, and saw Magnusson, his face pale and . . . wet? " 'Sup?"

"DocWagon just called me," said the magician, talking quietly as though every word had to be forced around the lump in his throat. "Boanerges is dead."

16

Griffin returned to his seat in the back of the Step-Van and plugged himself into his control rig. It had started raining again almost as soon as the sun had set, and he checked to see that the rotodrone was still maintaining the correct altitude and path. It was, and the infrared didn't show any movement except for their own sentries.

No sign of the bus that Fedorov said he'd hired, either. He just hoped it was in better condition than the piece of drek that troll had driven up. *That* didn't look as though it'd get to the nearest junkyard without breaking down. At least the drones were well maintained, as were the Step-Van and the Nomad. The snooper was still rolling around the mess of underground rooms and corridors, functioning pretty well apart from a hazy picture and sound that dropped out occasionally, but it wasn't giving him much data except for reminders of just how little the squatters had, and just how difficult it would be for invaders to take the place. The small rooms and narrow twisting corridors meant that they'd have to fight for every meter they advanced, and keep an eye on their satnav or compass readouts to make sure they weren't walking in circles and coming up behind their own people. It was almost as if the Crypt itself was determined to keep them out, and resisting them as best it could.

Wallace's voice traveled through the bones of his skull

to his ear. "The Dobie prepped? Fedorov wants it sent in as soon as they say the last of them is out."

"Dead?" 8-ball repeated.

Magnusson nodded and grabbed hold of the wall for support. "They've stopped trying to revive him. No EEG readings, no aura, no pulse. They want to know what I want done with the body." He gulped. "I asked about Patty. They said she's out of surgery, but not out of danger. She's on a respirator, and they may have to grow her new lungs. Lungs that big, they don't keep in stock." He turned as Jinx stepped into the corridor.

"We've found something," she said. "At least, it may be something. It's not from the hospital, anyway."

"What is it?"

"It's another hazmat container. Same make, looks a lot like the others, and it's sealed just as thoroughly . . . but it weighs almost nothing and there's no radiation hazard trefoil on the label. And it's addressed to the biotech R&D lab at ORO Corporation, in Tenochititlan."

"ORO." 8-ball blinked. "That's what Aztechnology . . . What else does the label say?"

"Zurich's looking at it now. There's some sort of declaration on the back, in English and Spanish, but it's pretty cryptic. You don't have a clairvoyance spell, do you?"

"No. Remind me to learn that one when we get out of here." He waved at the curtain. "After you."

"Are you going to tell her about Boanerges?" 8-ball murmured when Jinx was out of earshot.

"Later."

After some hurried discussion and a hasty distribution of chemsuits and filter masks, it was agreed that Zurich and Magnusson would take the box to the improvised pistol range while Mute stood guard and kept everyone else a safe (they hoped) distance away—on the ramp, if need be. Zurich began carefully breaking the tamperproof seals, and Magnusson stood by ready to cast a sterilize spell. The dwarf didn't inhale until the box was open, revealing two vials sealed inside multiple layers of transparent packing material and an old-fashioned optical computer disk. Zurich whistled as he gingerly picked the disk up by the edges and examined the shiny surface. "Seems okay," he said. "Wonder what's on it."

"No bioweapons," said the magician, examining its aura for signs of toxicity. "Nothing *intended* to kill . . . Can you read it?"

"Depends on the formatting. I haven't seen a data disk this size since I was a kid. It won't fit any of the equipment I have on me: I'll have to jury-rig something. Get Ratatosk, and tell Didge I'll need her CD player again—and tell the others to keep digging. This may not be it."

Magnusson walked out, returning two minutes later with Ratatosk and the makeshift metal detector. "8-ball just had a call from their rigger," said the elf. "The transport's just left the freeway. ETA ten to fifteen minutes. Wow, an antique."

Zurich smiled behind his respirator mask. "I just hope I can read it and copy it into memory. What do you want to bet it's encrypted?"

The decker snorted and sat opposite him, folding his limbs into a lotus position. "If you can read the disk, I can crack the code."

"In fifteen minutes?" asked Magnusson.

"The code isn't the problem. Even an old disk that size could hold a few gigs of data. If I don't have some sort of clue as to what I'm looking for . . ."

"There's a label on the vials," said Magnusson. "GNX-IV. Does that mean anything to you?"

"No," said the decker. "But it's a good place to start."

8-ball was helping Leila and Sumatra pack the library, enchanting kit and telesma when Griffin called to say that the bus had arrived with the clothing and other supplies. "Thanks," the dwarf replied awkwardly. "We'll start sending people out as soon as we can. How many can you search at a time?"

"Four, and no more than two of them female. Okay?"

"Copy. I'll get 'em organized." He looked over at Leila. "I'll be back in a few minutes."

"We can manage here," said Sumatra.

8-ball nodded and walked to the clinic, where Doc Czarnecki greeted him with a grunt. "Did you hear about Boanerges?"

"Yeah. Magnusson told me. Where's Mish?"

"Taking apart her medicine lodge."

"Okay. Do you need any help packing up here?"

"No chance of a reprieve, huh?"

"I wish. The bus is outside. Do you want to move the wounded first, last, or . . ." He looked at the bodies on the beds and mattresses. "How are they?"

"Yoko's doing well. The others . . ." He shrugged. "Akira's out of danger and stable, as long as we can keep him somewhere reasonably safe and clean. Angie has a SIN, so they should be able to find room for her at Good Samaritan. I don't know whether Rove has a SIN or not, but he's young enough that they won't just let him go: either they'll find his parents, or they'll send him to some other home. And if he can't come back here, I don't know where he'll end up . . ."

"Look, do you have to be in Puyallup to do this work?"

"What? No, I suppose not, though I think we can help more people if we are. Why?"

"Crane's paid the rent on a garage in Redmond for the next few weeks. You might be able to set up there as soon as we convince a Seoulpa Ring that he's not coming back anytime soon. It isn't as big as this place, but there should be room for a few beds and the library and the other stuff. Call it Boanerges Memorial."

Ratatosk stared at the lines of gibberish and swore under his breath. "It *should* be a simple scramble program, easy to decrypt with . . . Oh, frag. I'm an idiot."

"What?" asked Zurich, his tone suggesting that he agreed with the assessment.

"It's in Spanish. I'm using character frequency algorithms for English, and the numbers are all wrong . . . What did you say this was called, again?"

"GNX-IV."

"Okay, that's . . . Okay, it's starting to come together.

Give me another minute. How's your Spanish? My translation software might not handle some of the jargon, and I know just enough to get my face slapped by waitresses."

"I know a little more than that," said Magnusson, "and I have a translation spell, but I'm no biologist either. Should we get Czarnecki?"

"Not yet. Okay, some of these things are turning into words, I think. Does . . ." He stopped, then swore again. "Get him."

Yoko opened her eyes a few seconds after 8-ball had walked out, and waited for things to come into focus. "What happened?" she croaked through cracked lips.

Doc Czarnecki rushed to her side. "Hey, welcome back. How do you feel?"

"Like drek. Did I just hear someone say something about Boanerges?"

"He's dead," said the street doc gently. "He cast a stabilizing spell on you after that toxic attacked you, and the drain was too much for him. DocWagon picked him up, but they couldn't help him. How many fingers am I holding up?"

"Three," she said muzzily. "I'm still in the Crypt?"

"For another few minutes. We've begun evacuating."

"What?"

Czarnecki filled her in on the events of the past few hours as succinctly as he could. He was recounting Sumatra's plan for removing whatever they found when Zurich burst in. "Doc! Do you speak Spanish?"

"Yes, but I can't leave the clinic while—"

"Then we'll bring the disk here. Ratatosk thinks he knows what GNX-IV is . . . but he's having trouble believing it."

8-ball watched as another four people—a human man and woman, their ten-year-old elf son, and a teenaged ork girl with the pallor of a severe heliophobe—walked up the ramp, moving slowly because of the weight of their bulging bedrolls. The dwarf shrugged, then turned to Leila. "Okay, you're in charge until I get back," he said. "Keep them moving out—but not *too* fast. And don't let anyone touch my car. You two, stick around," he instructed Pierce and Ulla. "We're going to need stretcher bearers. Okay?"

He didn't wait for them to answer, but hurried to the clinic, where Yoko was sitting up on her bed. Czarnecki had refused to leave his patients, so Lankin, Crane, Zurich, Sumatra, Magnusson, Mute and Ratatosk were all crammed into the small room with him. "Okay," said 8-ball. "What's in those vials?"

"They called it GNX-IV," said the street doc. "It's a virus, and seems to have naturally mutated and been discovered by chance, rather than being engineered. The ORO Corporation thought it might be turned into something that could reverse goblinization." He paused. "They tested it on fifty subjects here—orks and trolls, most of them homeless or prisoners, but technically volunteers. ORO wanted to test it on even more subjects in Aztlan."

"Did it work?" asked Sumatra, fascinated.

"After a fashion. It caused their outer layers of skin to liquefy, along with any dermal plating, and also loosened their teeth until they were easy to pull out. Unfortunately, nearly all of the subjects died before their skin could finish growing back. In fact, it killed all of the orks, and all but two of the trolls, both of whom made it through the last two rounds of testing. Those trolls survived long enough to contract HMHVV. After that, the lab here decided to hand the whole thing over to head office.

"The scientists had tried combining the virus with drugs they'd hoped would give the subjects a chance to survive while their skin regrew. None of them worked, unless you count the two trolls. Even if you count them, the mortality rate of the project is still 96 percent. The volunteers were never told that. They were never given any idea of just how risky it was."

Lankin smiled evilly. "No wonder Aztechnology wants this stuff back. If that leaked out, and the families sued, it would cost them millions—maybe billions, if you factor in what the bad publicity could do to their share price. Are the names of the subjects on that file?"

"I don't know," said Czarnecki. "I haven't looked for them."

"I think we should call the Hatter and say the price has just increased slightly. He gets the vials and the disks, and you get to keep this place, free and clear, and . . . shall we say five thousand each?"

Czarnecki stared at him.

"Or instead of cash, would you prefer a stabilization unit and a case of slap patches? Something like—"

"Hold on a fragging second!" said the street doc. "You're talking about giving them back a virus that has a hundred percent fragging fatality rate among orks!"

Lankin was silent for a moment. "What makes you so sure this is the only sample? They might already have it."

"I don't think so," said 8-ball. "If they did, they would've used it against the rebels in Campeche by now. Or just to clear out some slums. How is this virus transmitted, Doc? Airborne?"

"It could be, though it doesn't survive long in an inhospitable environment: you'd have to spray it directly onto the skin. The subjects were mostly vaccinated, or given infected slap patches."

"But you could use it as a weapon?"

"Yes. And we haven't found anything on this disk to say whether it was ever tested on humans, elves or dwarves. It might be safe for them, or it might be just as lethal."

Ratatosk nodded. "Doesn't sound like something I'd want the Azzies to have. I say we destroy the vials, and send the data to the newsnets. Or direct onto the Matrix. And we might mention that they sent toxics in to kill squatters, while we're at it."

"Are you crazy?" asked Lankin. "This could be worth millions!" He looked around the room, then drew his Fichetti and aimed it at Ratatosk's forehead. "Put down the deck until we've sorted this out."

"He's not jacked in," said Zurich heavily. "And he doesn't have the original disk. I do." He popped it out of Didge's much-abused CD player and placed it alongside the vials on a rickety soy milk crate that served as a table.

Lankin's gaze followed it for an instant—just long enough for Ratatosk, Mute and 8-ball to draw their own guns and Yoko to pick up a scalpel. Lankin looked around, inhaled slowly and lowered his pistol until it pointed at the floor. The other guns didn't waver.

"This is pointless," Lankin said. "You're assuming they're just going to hush it up. What if they've made advances, found a way of keeping the patients alive?"

Magnusson and Yoko glanced at Czarnecki, who shrugged. "That's possible," he conceded. "But after what they've done to try to get their hands on this stuff, I don't feel like trusting them. And what if the treatment's only fifty percent effective—or only ten percent? Even if it's *ninety* percent, how many orks and trolls do you think are going to die trying it, just so they can look human?"

There was a long, uncomfortable silence. "Well, that's their choice, isn't it?" asked Lankin finally.

"Do you think so? How many will do it to please their parents? Or to improve their chances of getting a job? I think Ratatosk's right about sterilizing the vials—but not about the disk. I'd be happy to see Aztechnology lose a few million for what they've done, but I'd much rather *none* of this data got out, in case it inspires someone else to kill orks and trolls in search of a cure for goblinization."

"We're talking about millions of nuyen here!" Lankin protested.

"We don't all have your expertise when it comes to blackmail," said Mute dryly. "What if the Hatter decides he could save millions by having us all killed?"

"There are ways of guarding against that," said Lankin. "But if you have a better idea, I'm willing to consider it."

"We sell it to someone else and let *them* use it to blackmail Aztechnology," said Mute. "Another corp. I have contacts in Mitsuhama . . ."

"No," said Yoko coldly. "I think Ratatosk and the doc are right about the vials, and I don't trust Mitsuhama. Even giving them the data would be dangerous. There might be enough information in there for them to engineer the virus with nanotech."

"Yamatetsu?" suggested Crane.

Czarnecki shook his ugly head. "Not if I get a vote," he said. "You want to give a Japanese corp something else they can use against metahumans? Maggie, you've been quiet. What do you think?"

"I hate the idea of destroying data," said Magnusson, "but I think you're right—about the vial, at least. Even if I gave it to the biotech department at the university, it'd end up in corp hands before long. They sponsor so much of the research we do, it's inevitable they'd find out about it before long. Same with all the hospitals with the facilities to deal with something like this, even the Centers for Disease Control. And I'm not sure that goblinization is something we should be trying to *cure*. To me, it sounds a lot like the old experiments where they tried to assimilate non-white children into white societies by separating them from their parents, or make them look Aryan by injecting blue dye into their eyes."

"People buy blue eyes every fragging day," said Lankin. "Do you object to that, too?"

Sumatra stood. "We don't have time to spend arguing like this," he declared, "and none of it's going to matter if we can't get the stuff past the guards. I say we take it outside now and meet up later, and *then* we can decide what to do." He looked around the room expectantly.

"That makes sense," said Ratatosk slowly. "You said you had an invisibility spell, right?"

"Yes."

"Okay. Before you disappear, can I ask one small favor?"

"What?"

"Can I see your cell phone? All of them, if you have more than one."

Sumatra hesitated. "What . . . why?"

"I just need to know the number," the decker replied. "Check the address book and log, any saved messages, that sort of thing. Someone in here has been calling the Hatter and telling him what's going on. I just want to be sure it isn't you."

Sumatra stared at him, trying to smile. "What makes you think it's me?"

Ratatosk shrugged. "Nothing in particular. But if you expect us to trust you with data worth millions of nuyen and a virus that can kill thousands . . ." The muzzle of his gun swung away from Lankin and toward the shaman. "I think this is a small thing to ask in return."

The ork looked around the room. Some of the people seemed startled by the suggestion, but not outraged. The ork looked at the phone on his wrist, took a step toward Ratatosk, then vanished from sight.

17

Zurich was the first to react, making a grab for the vials and the disk—but they disappeared an instant before he reached them. Yoko leaped off her bed, arms outstretched, hoping to make contact with the invisible Sumatra, but he eluded her grasp. Crane, who was nearest the exit, tried to block the doorway, then fell backwards as the shaman head butted him and punched him in the stomach. He grabbed the curtain on the way down, but the thin plastic tore. Sumatra stepped on the rigger's chest and face as he ran out. Crane rolled out of the way as Yoko and Mute came running out of the room, with 8-ball close behind them. Magnusson began praying in Aramaic as he conjured up a watcher spirit and sent it toward the ramp at the speed of thought.

Mute stopped as soon as she was in the corridor, tossed her pistol into the air and grabbed it with her right hand while she drew her narcoject pistol with her left. She listened for the sound of Sumatra's footsteps and the distinctive rhythm of his breathing, but there was too much background noise for her to pinpoint it. Dropping to one knee, she fired four shots along the corridor at about a meter above the ground, fanning them out in the hope of hitting her invisible target.

"Did you get him?" asked Yoko.

She was only murmuring, but Mute hurriedly cranked down the sensitivity on her amplified hearing. "Assume I didn't," she said. "Is there any way out other than the ramp?"

"The stairwell's still blocked," said 8-ball. "He could get out that way, but not quietly. You head for the ramp; I'll check out the stairs."

Yoko had sped away before the dwarf had quite finished speaking; he shook his head and began running toward the blocked fire escape. Mute headed off after Yoko, pausing briefly to check for any signs that her darts might have hit the shaman. Magnusson was the next to come sprinting out of the clinic, already breathing hard. Crane watched them go and decided to stay where he was as Lankin emerged from the crowded room and ran toward the ramp, his long legs enabling him to easily outpace the magician. A moment later, Czarnecki ventured out and crouched beside the rigger, examining his wounds. "Where does it hurt?"

Crane groaned, waving a hand over his belly, chest, nose and forehead. The street doc nodded, helped him to his feet and guided him back into the clinic. Ratatosk and Zurich were standing guard over the wounded—and Ratatosk's deck, which held the only decrypted copy of the data from the disk. Crane looked up at the elf wonderingly. "How did you know Sumatra was talking to the Hatter?" he asked.

"I didn't," said Ratatosk. "I thought it was Lankin. If Sumatra had handed his phone over, I would have asked Lankin next."

Leila turned around as the watcher spirit materialized near the foot of the ramp. *"Message from Magnusson!"* it yelled. *"Invisible enemy! No one and nothing to enter or leave! Block the ramp!"*

"What the—" Pierce spluttered, but didn't object as Leila grabbed his arm and that of the elf on her right, forming a human chain across the ramp—the first of many. By the time Sumatra reached the bottom of the ramp, there were several chains of humans and metahumans of all sizes blocking his path.

The shaman paused for breath, concentrating on maintaining his invisibility spell, and shoved the vials and the disk into one of the many pockets of his filthy armor jacket. Then he drew his silenced Fichetti and shot the nearest target through the eye. The ork slumped as the back of his head sprayed across Pierce's jacket. Ulla, who was holding him up, flinched—but she didn't drop him.

"Out of my fraggin' way!" Sumatra shouted, trying to drown out the persistent watcher spirit. There were only a dozen people between him and freedom, and he had twenty-nine shots left without needing to reload. *"I can shoot all of you if I need to!"* He backed up the threat with a mass agony spell, and watched as most of the crowd let go of each other and cowered—all except Pierce, Leila, Didge, Ulla, and the corpse that Ulla was still propping up. Feeling himself slow down as the drain from his spells sapped his strength, he aimed at Ulla, and felt something sting the back of his neck. He turned to see Mute standing behind him, a narcoject pistol in her hand. Yoko stood beside her.

"You talk too much," said Mute, smiling. Sumatra tried to aim his pistol at her, but it seemed far too heavy to lift, and his target was fading into the shadows that were closing in on him. He didn't see Yoko grab him as he fell face forward toward the concrete, or feel it when Ulla stepped forward and kicked him in the groin.

Mute aimed her pistol at the ork's head, but Yoko kicked it out of her hand. "No," she said softly.

Mute looked at her incredulously, and Ulla growled as she reached for her knife. "No," the adept repeated. "Not in cold blood."

"We can warm his blood up first," suggested Pierce. "There's a microwave in the kitchen."

"We take him with us," Yoko repeated. "Lankin can interrogate him later, or Magnusson can do a mind probe. He may know something useful." She lowered the shaman's body to the floor and patted it down, searching for the disk and the vials. Mute untabbed his jacket to look for concealed pockets, and gasped as she saw the pendants hanging around his neck. Most looked like talismans, but one was horribly familiar.

Yoko looked over her shoulder. "A peace sign?" she said, as Mute grabbed one of the pendants.

"No. Mercedes Benzene wore a pendant like this." She bit her lip. "Just like this."

The adept decided not to ask. She found the vials in one of his bulging pockets—to her relief, they were still intact—and the disk a second later. Holding these, she walked back to the clinic.

"What should we do about this guy?" asked Didge, crouching beside the dead ork and closing his remaining eye. "Does anyone know his name?"

No one replied for several seconds. "He's been here only a couple of weeks," said Pierce. "Hiding from someone. Boanerges woulda known—he knew everyone's name—but I don't."

This was followed by another lengthy silence, which Pierce finally broke by saying, "I'll take him up to the morgue, okay?"

Mute nodded.

"What about Sumatra?" Pierce continued, looking covetously at the shaman's boots. "Should we keep searching him?"

"Go ahead," said Mute. "Take whatever you like. He won't be needing it."

8-ball examined the pendant, then handed it back to Mute. "It *looks* like Mercy's," he admitted. "You think he's the one who betrayed us?"

"He was prepared to sell a bioweapon that he knew killed orks," she replied dryly. "It's in character."

8-ball shrugged and followed her back to the clinic, where Czarnecki was bandaging Crane. Apart from the still-unconscious patients, the only other people there were Yoko and Magnusson. "Where's everyone gone?" he asked, looking around the room.

"Packing," said the doctor. "We just had a call from Didge. The merc who searched her wouldn't give her back her pocket computer. It's years old, and it was cheap when it was made, but she talked to their commander— Wallace?—and he said it was their orders. Any medical gear, and anything with a memory, they take back to their boss. It'll be returned after it's been searched—at least, that's what they're saying. But they'll also want to search your car, 8-ball, and take Ratatosk's deck, the disks from the library, and everyone's pocket secretaries and medkits and that sort of thing. And if they take my equipment away from me for a few hours, I don't think our patients are going to survive."

8-ball winced. "You think there's something else in the vault that we haven't found yet?"

"Maybe. Whether or not it's worth anything, I wouldn't know. And I don't think the Hatter really knows, either . . . or if he does, he's not told the mercs."

"And even if this drek is all there is, since we can't trust Sumatra to turn anyone invisible, we have to think of another way to get it past Wallace," said Crane.

Yoko opened her eyes and glanced at Magnusson, who seemed to be praying softly. She blinked and peered into the astral, and saw a spell fly from the magician and circle the vials. She hastily closed her eyes again.

"Could we hide it in one of the body bags?" Mute suggested.

"They've probably thought of that one—or the Hatter has," said 8-ball. "And they're soldiers, so they won't be squeamish. Maggie, do you know any invisibility spells?"

"No," said Magnusson. "The closest I have is a physical mask. The best we could do would be for Mish to call up a city spirit and hope that its concealment powers were enough to get it past the sentries and the eye in the sky. It's the latter that worries me."

Crane nodded. "It should. If they've upgraded the sensors in that the way they did in the Condor, I don't think you'd have a chance."

"Could you or Zurich jam it?"

"Not at that altitude."

"You're saying we're fragged."

Crane shrugged. Mute looked at him, then asked, "Where is their rigger?"

"In one of the vans," said 8-ball. "Why?"

"Crane, if you had his rig, could you take over the roto-drone? You're not too badly injured?"

"I'm fine," Crane replied, "but how'm I supposed to get ahold of his rig?"

"Hijack the van."

"*What?*"

Mute turned to 8-ball. "Will it be guarded?"

"There'll be some guards," said the dwarf cautiously. "Not many. Most of the soldiers who're still standing will be searching people who're coming out. Didge will know how they're positioned. What do you have in mind?"

"I should be going, not you," said Mute, as Yoko washed her face and looked into the bathroom's ancient, cloudy mirror. "You're still not fully healed."

The adept shrugged. "I feel better than I look," she said, examining her cracked and blistered skin critically. She was wearing Leila's track pants and a T-shirt she'd borrowed from Ratatosk, but had kept her own black armor jacket, wrapping duct tape around the elbows and cuffs to make it look secondhand. Her feet were bare. "And yes, I know that's not difficult at the moment, and it's a pity we can't *both* go—but they said only two women at a time, and one of them has to be Mish." She wiped her face and hands on a tiny but rapidly expanding microfiber towel, which she then wrapped around her head like a bandana. She led the way out of the bathroom, then stopped and turned to face Mute. "And I think Leila's going to do a better job of creating a diversion. She's a good actress with a fine pair of lungs, while you don't like drawing attention to yourself. That's why you're called Mute, neh?"

"It's short for Mutant. I have twelve toes."

"Oh. But since it *is* your plan . . . if you really want to go, I'll toss you for it."

Mute stared at her, then shrugged. "Okay, if you—" The next thing she knew, she was flying through the air into one of the empty bedrooms. She landed on her back on an old army cot, which collapsed under her weight. Before she could move, Yoko was straddling her and had pinned her wrists to the cot.

"If you go, neither of your guns will be loaded," said Yoko, her tone mild. "If you reach for a gun instead of a knife, by the time you've remembered you have no ammunition someone might have shot you. Or they might have shot Crane, because unlike me, you're not tall enough for him to hide behind, and then we wouldn't have a rigger and your plan—and it's a very good plan—wouldn't work. Neh?"

"Wakarimasuka," Mute whispered.

"Good. Let's go." She took a step back, helped Mute up, and they walked to the dining hall, where Magnusson, Mish and Crane were waiting. "Everyone ready?" the adept asked.

Wallace looked at the four people who walked up the ramp and across the rubble to the sidewalk—two well-dressed middle-aged human men, and two elf women who looked as though they'd taken their clothes from a trash can. Lori, standing behind him, inhaled sharply as she peered at them in astral. "What?" Wallace murmured.

"Three of them are Awakened." she said. "Two have auras you could read by. And the man on the right is heavily cybered."

"What sort of cyber?"

"I can't tell, but it's all through his body, not just his head. Could be wired reflexes, or skillwires."

Wallace nodded, studying the man's face. He was beardless, his black hair was cut short revealing a widow's peak and two datajacks, and his cheekbones and nose hinted at Native American ancestry. Apart from that, and a slung Ingram smartgun, he was as devoid of distinguishing features as a custom-made federal agent.

The older man was slender and pale, with long silver hair gathered into a ponytail, and a neatly trimmed beard and mustache. His long coat was open, and he didn't seem to be wearing a gun—at least, not a large one. He walked up to Wallace, his hands held palm forward, his long fingers fanned. *We come in peace; shoot to kill*, the mercenary thought sourly, and patted down the outside of the coat. "We'll need the wristcomp," he said. "You'll get it back. What's this?"

Moving slowly and carefully, the man pulled out his

pocket secretary and handed it to him. Wallace glanced at his hands, then at his hiking boots. "You're no squatter," he said neutrally. "What're you doing here?"

"Just visiting friends."

"Uh-huh. Take off the coat and turn around." He noticed the man's neck knife and asked him to remove it. The blade was sharp, but seemed too short to be much use as a weapon, and it wasn't balanced for throwing. He was about to hand it back when Lori made a sound. "What?"

"It's a weapon focus," she said, taking it from him.

"Dangerous?"

"Only in astral combat. But beautiful work." She looked at the mage with even more respect. "I noticed the circles in the garden. And the herbs, and the background count. There's something magical here, isn't there? Something about the place itself."

"It's a school, and a hospital, and these people's home," came the reply.

Wallace grimaced, but Lori nodded. "I know what you mean," she said. "I was an army brat. Moved from base to base a lot; never really found a home." She returned the ritual knife to its owner. "You come here to teach?"

"When I can. Good students are a treasure."

She smiled and glanced at the others. Lily had finished searching the elves, but was rummaging through the huge improvised backpacks. "No computers, nothing medical," she said after a moment.

"Likewise," said Hartz, who was examining the tarot deck and collection of calligraphy pens he'd found in one of Yoko's pockets.

"Okay," said Wallace. "Pick up your gear and get on the bus."

"We have our own car," said the man with the datajacks.

The commander turned and stared at him for a moment. "That one in there?" he asked, with a nod toward the Crypt.

"No. That's 8-ball's. Mine's parked a few blocks away, behind the saloon."

"You left a car unguarded in this area?"

"The saloon's a gang hangout. Orks and trolls, but we

have an understanding. They won't touch it, and no one else would dare."

Wallace shrugged. "Okay, then. Good luck."

"Thanks."

The four picked up their gear and headed north, past the Step-Van, the Nomad and the rusting van. Lewis was sitting on the steps of the bus with a pile of canvas rucksacks on his right, cartons of clothing and a collection of jungle boots on his left. He looked them up and down before grabbing two of the olive-drab rucksacks. "Your phone, your food and your transit pass are in there," he said, handing them to the women. "And let's see—one elf medium, one elf small . . . what size shoes do you take? They're all in men's sizes, I'm afraid."

One elf blinked, startled, but the other bowed slightly. "It doesn't matter, as long as they're not too small," she said. "I can always wear lots of socks."

Lewis smiled, looked at her feet and chose a complete outfit for each woman. "What about you?" he asked the men. "They're free."

The man with the ponytail shook his head. "We don't need them," he said.

The merc smiled crookedly. "No, I suppose not." He watched as the elves pulled their socks and army boots on, then bundled the rest of the clothing into their rucksacks. "Wait!" he said as they set off. "Where are you going?"

The man with the ponytail looked over his shoulder without breaking his stride and repeated the story about the car behind the saloon. None of the four spoke again until they were well out of earshot.

Mish shrugged her backpack off and lowered it carefully to the sidewalk, laughing awkwardly. "Seems like a nice guy," she said quietly. "I almost feel bad for not telling him the truth."

Yoko snorted. "I think he was hoping he could watch while we changed."

"I saw three sentries," said Crane. "Assume there's a fourth on the far corner . . . five doing the searches, including their mage . . . one on the bus . . . that'd make ten.

Including the rigger, that leaves no more than six in the van, and since at least some of them are wounded or stunned . . ."

Magnusson nodded. The shaman reached into the pack for the securetech vest, which she put on over her once-black sweatshirt. Yoko dropped her rucksack and removed her boots, and Mish summoned a city spirit. A small pile of garbage appeared and shaped itself into a vaguely human form, with an asthma inhaler for a nose, condom wrappers for eyes, and a Nerps box for a mouth. "Yes?"

"We need concealment. All four of us."

The spirit nodded, and followed them as they returned to the Step-Van, walking as quietly as possible around the far side of the bus. Crane pressed a button on his wrist-phone, sending a message to Leila. The four of them watched as four squatters walked toward the bus, and waited until they heard a shriek: as Mute had said, it was all in the timing. "No one said anything about a fraggin' cavity search!" Leila shouted.

The mercs and the bus driver turned to see what was happening, and Yoko dashed forward and opened the door of the Step-Van, with the others following close behind her.

There were two mercs sleeping in the back of the van—a spectacularly ugly ork with pendulous ears, and a young human woman curled into a ball. The ork opened one eye at the sound of the door opening, then the other. He sat up and reached for his rifle, and Yoko ducked, enabling Magnusson to see past her and cast a stunball into the back of the van. The ork fumbled, dropping the gun, and when he bent down to pick it up, Yoko lunged and hit him in the temple. The merc fell to the floor, unconscious, and the adept looked around cautiously. The human woman, lying on the bench seat, continued to snore softly, unaware that anything had happened.

Magnusson, Crane and Mish dashed into the back of the Step-Van. Mish released the city spirit, and Crane slammed the door shut and locked it. Griffin, in the driver's seat, turned around to see Yoko standing behind him. She pulled the plug out of his datajack with one hand, and touched a nerve cluster in his neck with the other, and he slumped forward over the steering wheel. *"Crane!"* she shouted as she hauled the merc out of his seat. *"Get your butt in here!"*

Crane hurried forward, and grabbed Griffin's control deck, while Magnusson picked up the fallen rifles. "Do you know how to use one of these?" he asked Mish.

"The bullets come out of that hole, right?"

"Actually, I think that's the grenade launcher," said the mage uneasily. "But which trigger is—" He stopped, hearing someone thumping on the Step-Van's door. "Yoko?"

"For frag's sake," said the adept, returning to the cargo compartment. "They're AK-98s. They're designed to be used by drunken peasants in a raging blizzard! They're almost draftee-proof." She shook her head at their expressions. "You've used handguns?"

"I have," said Magnusson.

"Fine. Give me that and take one of the sidearms. You have a spell for locking doors, don't you?"

"Yes."

"Get ready to use it."

The bus driver looked around, bewildered, as Lewis ran toward the Step-Van, leaving four squatters standing by the heap of rucksacks and clothes. Didge, who had already boarded the bus and was standing next to the driver, grabbed the Roomsweeper from his belt and jammed it into his side. "You, in here!" she barked at the squatters. She waited until they'd scrambled inside, then turned to the driver and pointed the shotgun at his face. "Shut the doors. And no tricks."

Trembling, the driver obeyed.

"How tough is the window glass?"

"Shatterproof," he whispered. "It's a school bus."

Didge nodded, then looked down the aisle. "Everyone get down," she snapped. "Don't let them see you." She turned her attention back to the driver. "Who're you working for?"

"McAlister High," he whimpered. "We're allowed to use the buses after hours for a little extra cash . . ."

"Who hired you?"

"I don't know. My boss took the call and told me where to go. *Please don't kill me!*"

Didge looked at the terrified man. He was on the wrong side of fifty years and ninety kilograms, and his pale face was starting to turn red. She wasn't sure whether he was about to cry, or go into cardiac arrest. "Do exactly what I tell you, and you'll be fine. You got kids?"

He nodded. "Three. And a grandson. He's two."

Didge smiled crookedly. "Get out of that chair, and lie down in the aisle. Facedown. You'll be a lot safer there than you would be outside."

Crane looked through the patrol vehicle's cameras and activated the flashpak fitted into the firmpoint. He was sure that the mercs would have flare compensation built into their helmet visors, if not into their eyes, but it would startle them and provide a harmless demonstration that the drone was no longer under their control. He activated the vehicle's loudspeaker, and yelled, *"Drop your guns! You near the van, step away from that door!"*

The mercs looked around, but none of them put down their weapons. Wallace opened a channel to Griffin and murmured, "Griff, if this is a joke . . ." There was no reply, and he turned to Lori. Before he could speak, Crane's voice blared out, *"You have five seconds to throw down, or I will start shooting. I control all of your drones; I can see all of you!"* This was a slight exaggeration, but it was enough to make all the sentries look up anxiously.

"Can you hear us, too?" Wallace snapped.

"Loud and clear," Crane replied, at a more normal volume, then, *"Three seconds!"*

Leila slipped a knife out of her sleeve and touched it to Hartz' belly. "You heard the man," she said.

"State your terms." said Wallace.

"You can have the land. We leave, take the vehicles and whatever else we want. No more searches. You get to keep your weapons and one of the vehicles, but no ammo," replied Crane. *"Two seconds!"* The indicator on the rotodrone's panel said that its machine gun was loaded with nearly a full belt of gel rounds. He rotated the camera, looking for a suitable target, and decided that the troll standing on the northwest corner would be the best demonstration. Wallace, Hartz, Lori and Lily were too close to Leila and three other squatters for him to be sure of not hitting his own people—and 8-ball had warned him to avoid taking out Wallace, as this would leave the unpredictable Quinn in command.

Wallace hesitated. As much as he hated the idea of allowing himself to be disarmed, there didn't seem to be a good alternative. "What's happened to my rigger?" he asked.

"He's stunned, but stable. Same with the other people in here—both of 'em. *One fragging second!*"

"Throw down," Wallace muttered into his throat mic. He couldn't quite bring himself to say it aloud; even subvocalizing the command hurt. "That's an order. Put down your guns. Now." He popped the clip out of his rifle, squatted, carefully placed the gun on the pavement, then stepped back from it with his hands in the air.

Crane watched anxiously through half a dozen camera eyes as all but one of the mercs obeyed the order . . . the one 8-ball had tagged as Quinn. "Captain," she subvocalized on a private channel. "Permission to speak freely?" Without waiting for an answer, she burst out, "This isn't right! We have hostages, too, and if we go underground, the drones can't—"

"Mow us down before we reach the ramp? Don't bet on it. And there are still shadowrunners down there. You have your orders, Lieutenant." He closed the channel.

Quinn looked up at the cloudy moonless sky, locating the rotodrone by its heat signature and zooming in. She switched off her radio, then looked at the broken ground between her and the ramp, calculating quickly. She took one long breath, then hurtled toward the entrance at a speed so great that Crane barely had time to turn the drone around and aim at her as she leaped over the trip wires and traps.

Wallace drew his pistol, but froze for an instant, unable to shoot one of his own squad in the back. Leila had no such issues and threw her knife; it hit the commando between her shoulders, but barely penetrated her armor jacket. Crane fired a burst of gel rounds from the drone, hitting the merc in the arm, side and leg, but Quinn kept running until she reached the eastern edge of the ramp. She paused just long enough to fire a neurostun grenade into the middle of the small crowd: she knew her filter mask wouldn't protect her from the gas for long, but it might be long enough to even up the score. The squatters scattered, and Quinn somersaulted onto the ramp and rolled down into the Crypt.

A bullet hit her in the leg while she was regaining her feet, and she looked up to see one of the shadowrunners aiming a pistol at her. The dark-skinned human fired again, and Quinn dodged, then returned fire. Two rounds hit the woman in the torso, and she staggered backward and fell. Quinn waited for a few seconds, then crept forward and looked at her opponent. There were two bullet holes in her abdomen, but Quinn was unable to tell whether the runner was dead or merely paralyzed by the gas. She shrugged, and was about to set off down the corridor when a small, squat, dark figure stepped out of a doorway.

"Quinn?" said 8-ball politely, raising Beef Patty's assault cannon to his shoulder and aiming at the commando's chest. "Good to meet you at last. You've earned yourself quite a reputation: I hear you've never lost a fight."

Quinn dropped to the ground, simultaneously spraying the corridor with autofire—but the dwarf fired an explosive shell into the ceiling above her, and falling lumps of concrete and earth thudded onto her helmet and knocked the rifle from her hands. Her ears ringing, she reached for her sidearm. "That's right. And I'm not going to start now."

8-ball fired again, hitting Quinn in the right arm and reducing it to a stump. She glanced at the wreckage—a mass of twisted wires and vat-grown skin—and swore viciously.

The dwarf smiled. "Boanerges told us not to use this baby on people," he said with mock cheer. "Unfortunately, Boanerges is dead, so I don't feel too guilty about disobeying his orders. You, on the other hand—what you're doing is mutiny."

"He's right," came a voice from halfway up the ramp. The Doberman patrol vehicle rolled down into the basement, followed closely by Wallace and Lori. "On your feet, soldier."

Quinn stared at 8-ball with hatred, and hauled herself to her feet, standing to attention and turning to face her captain. "Sir."

"Looks like you could use some medical attention," said Wallace, with a glance at Lori. The mage nodded, and cast a stunbolt spell. Quinn pitched forward, unconscious.

The three stared at her for a moment; then Wallace shook his head. "What will you do with her?" asked 8-ball.

"Drop her off at a hospital, I guess," the ork replied sadly. "Call it a medical discharge. Your friend looks in worse shape than she does." He looked around at the maze of makeshift walls. "So this is where you grew up?"

"Yeah."

"No place like home, huh?"

"No," said the dwarf. "No, there isn't." Then, to his embarrassment, he started to cry.

18

It was after eleven when they finished loading the last of the gear from the Crypt into the vehicles. Zurich had disabled the tracking device on the Nomad, which had been pressed into service as an ambulance, and made three runs to Good Samaritan. Czarnecki was finally asleep, lying on the stretcher and snoring like a sawmill in a thunderstorm. Haz's rusting van had become the hearse, on the assumption that it might be able to reach the Salvation Army Fortress without breaking down. "What are you going to tell the Hatter?" 8-ball asked Wallace as he handed him a rucksack full of empty clips and loose ammo.

"Who?"

"Mather. The Aztechnology suit who hired you."

The merc shrugged. "He called himself Fedorov when I talked to him, and I didn't know which corp he was from. I'll tell him that we finally secured the premises after one hell of a fight, the drones were destroyed, and the last of the survivors escaped in the Nomad. The fragger probably won't pay us the rest of the fee, but it could've been worse. Want to show you something," he said, leading the way to the Step-Van.

Once inside, he opened a tool kit and handed a metal cylinder to the dwarf, who examined it carefully. "Is this what I think it is?"

"Pipe bomb," said Wallace. "Griff found it under that piece of drek the troll drove up in. Fedorov didn't want you getting out of here alive, but after the fight you put up, we figured you all deserved better'n that.''

"Thanks," said 8-ball, staring at the explosive. "Now I'd *really* like to hang around here and ambush the fragger."

"I don't see him walking into a trap like that," the merc replied. "He probably pays some other poor frag to take that sort of risk for him. 'Sides, it seems to me that the best way to hurt rich people is to turn 'em into poor people."

"You're probably right," said the dwarf. "Well, we'll be seeing you, Wallace."

Wallace smiled. "What're you going to do now?"

"We've found another place where the squatters can stay for a few weeks, maybe set up the hospital again . . . 'course, the Seoulpa are there now, so that might not be as easy as it sounds."

"We're not flying out until seven thirty hours. Give me a call if you need any help, and I'll ask for volunteers."

Mish cast a catalog spell on the magical gear, making sure that nothing had been left behind. She turned around at the sound of heavy but tentative footsteps approaching, and saw Pinhead Pierce walking toward her with his huge fist clenched. "What—"

"Shh," said the ork, looking around furtively before opening his hand. "You know how Leila and I were searching Sumatra's body? Well, I found this in one of his boots, and it seemed sort of strange. Leila thought it might be magical, and seeing as how you do all that stuff for talismongers . . ." He showed her a bar of orange metal the size of a postage stamp. "Leila thought it might be valuable, too."

Mish stared, then reached out to touch the fragment almost reverently. "If it's orichalcum—and that's what it looks like—then yes. Magnusson would know better than I would, but a piece this size would be worth a fortune. Do you want me to ask him?"

The ork grinned. "Yeah, why not? I was just going to take it to my piercer and see if he could turn it into a couple of rings."

Mish blinked and looked at his face. "Can you do me a favor?"

"Sure. What?"

"*Please* don't tell me what you were thinking of getting pierced."

"You got everything you need?" 8-ball asked as he stopped at Royer Station to let Crane out.

"I think so," the rigger said, hauling his bags out of the back of the dwarf's Land Rover. "Good working with you all. And thanks for the ID," he said to Lankin.

Lankin shrugged, mildly embarrassed. "I've transferred your money into the credstick, but get rid of both of them as soon as you can. And have a good trip," he replied. The rigger had discarded almost everything that might be used to identify him, giving a few personal items to 8-ball to put into secure storage, destroying some and handing the rest over to Lankin for resale. The elf had paid him a more-than-adequate advance, but asked him not to tell anyone that he had been generous.

"Call me if you need anything," said Ratatosk. "And use the secure line. Even *I* won't be able to tell where you are."

"Thanks." Crane popped the clip out of his smartgun, putting the gun into the suitcase and emptying the bullets into his carry-on luggage. "Give my regards to the Seoulpa. And good luck."

"It's orichalcum, all right," said Magnusson wonderingly. "Where would he have gotten this?"

"Someone stole a load of telesma meant for Mitsuhama Research Unit 13 last week," Yoko replied. "I've heard it included a few grams of orichalcum. I don't know who was involved, and I wouldn't have thought Sumatra had the guts to do anything like that, but maybe the others took the risk and he provided magical backup. Or he lied to them about what this was worth. Or stole it from his buddies, which would explain why he was hiding in the Crypt with at least a hundred thou of magical gear hidden in his boots and his pockets. He was either waiting for a buyer, or hoarding the stuff—but I guess you can ask him when he wakes up." She looked at the ork, who sat between them on the backseat of Beef Patty's Superkombi. He was gagged and heavily bound, and both of them were watching him in astral, ready to respond if he cast a spell or attempted a summoning. "Can I ask *you* a question?" she asked, speaking in Sperethiel. "You cast a spell on the vials, didn't you?"

"Yes. I sterilized them. I thought the stuff was too dangerous to keep. I'm not sure what to do about the data from the disk, though."

"Zurich gave me the original, but Ratatosk has the decrypted copy," said Yoko. "He still wants to leak the data to the newsnets, but I'm pretty sure I can persuade him to erase it instead."

Magnusson smiled. "You know, after all this, the faculty meeting on Friday is going to seem even more boring than usual. I might not even bother wearing armor."

Kwan yawned and looked at the street samurai sleeping next to him with more envy than lust. Carla was an attractive woman, if you weren't turned off by shaved heads, but she was more likely to inspire fear than desire among those who knew her by her Korean street name—Myondo Kal, the Razor. Kwan wondered what *she'd* done to get a lousy job like this: camping out in the back of a light armored van, watching over an empty warehouse in Hollywood—Komun'go turf—in the vain hope that the owner would come back to pick up his gear. On the other hand, the frag in question had been dumb enough to help steal a boat belonging to the leader of the Divine Revenge Ring, complete with its cargo of smuggled military weapons, so he obviously had more guts than brains. Kwan, who'd been aboard the boat when it was stolen, was hoping for a chance to decorate a wall, Valentine's Day–massacre style, with the aforesaid guts and brains and maybe redeem himself in the eyes of the leadership.

Kwan blinked as he saw a small convoy pull up outside the warehouse: a Land Rover, a Superkombi, a Nomad, and a Saab Dynamit. A redheaded elf in a long coat emerged from the Land Rover and jacked into the security system, while a bald dwarf and a tall hooded figure stood guard. The dwarf was carrying a submachine gun; the other didn't seem to be armed at all. Kwan turned and grabbed Carla's wrist, careful to avoid her spurs. "Wake up!" he hissed. "We've—"

"I wouldn't do that, if I were you," said an unfamiliar voice behind him. Kwan spun around and saw a young elf woman standing inside the van, cut off at midshin by the floor.

"Who the frag are—"

"Shh," said the elf. "The man you're looking for? Crane? He's left town—probably the country, too, by this point. You're wasting your time here."

Carla opened her eyes and looked over her shoulder. "What's—"

"We've had a *very* bad day," the elf continued. "You have ten seconds to drive away. Miss that deadline, and you'll have to walk back to your own turf. If you're still here in thirty seconds, you can either crawl away, or spend the rest of your lives here—which will be another thirty seconds, if you're extremely lucky. So ka?"

"Do you know who we are?" demanded the street samurai.

Kwan glanced forward through the tinted window, and his jaw dropped. The elf had managed to get the door open in a few seconds—a job that had taken their best cracksman more than ten minutes. The hooded figure stepped inside, and Kwan waited to hear the clatter of the automatic-weapons fire that had greeted their thieves. And waited. And waited.

Silence.

"Five seconds," said the elf politely.

The doors of the other vehicles opened, and another six people stepped out; orks, humans, and an elf almost as tall as a troll. Three of them wore military-issue helmets. One carried an assault cannon. Kwan started the car.

"Is Crane there?" asked Carla.

"Crane has left Seattle," the elf woman repeated. "Two seconds."

The street samurai opened the door and leaped out of the van just as it pulled away. Kwan stopped, and Carla drew her smartgun and ran into the street, firing a burst at the ork with the assault cannon, then shooting at everyone who seemed roughly the right size to be the elusive Crane.

Yoko stood inside the garage, looking first at the autonomous gun system mounted on the ceiling, then at the other hardware stored there. Crane had warned them that he'd rigged the entire security system, and that several of the drones had their weapons fully loaded and were connected to the main power and the backup solar cells in the roof. Some high-velocity blood spatter on the floor near the doorway bore this out. Yoko took another step toward the sentry gun, but it neither tracked her nor fired, and she smiled. She'd volunteered to go in first because she was protected by a quickened deflection spell that Boanerges and Joji had tattooed onto her back, but it was good to know that Crane had given Ratatosk the right codes. "It's safe—" she began, then flinched as she heard shots. An instant later, she realized they were coming from outside the room, not inside, and ran back toward the doorway.

An Asian-looking woman with a shaved head was running across the street, a smartgun in one hand, a spur extended from the other. Yoko reached into the pocket of her armor jacket, grabbed the first object to come to hand, and threw it like a shuriken. The tarot card sliced off the top centimeter of the razorgirl's left ear before embedding itself in the side of the van stopped in the middle of the street.

The woman ducked, touched her wounded ear, and turned to see what had done the damage—giving Yoko enough time to look around and see what had happened to the rest of her team. Ratatosk was lying on the ground, protecting his head with his hands and his deck with his body. Pierce was crouching on the other side of the doorway, fumbling with his Roomsweeper. Lankin, Magnusson, Leila and Lori had ducked behind the cars. She couldn't see Wallace or Griffin, but she didn't have time to worry about them. The street samurai fired a burst at Yoko's chest, and stared as the adept stood there, unharmed, without even flinching.

"Drop the gun!" Yoko shouted, reaching into her pocket again and grabbing the first object she touched—a data disk. She knew that it would take her nearly a second to get close enough to the street samurai for a kick, and that would give the razorgirl enough time to shoot someone who didn't have the benefit of a protective spell.

The street samurai glared at her, then lowered her gun and fired a burst at Griffin, who was lying on the near side of the Nomad. Yoko threw the disk, aiming at the woman's throat. It tore through her carotid, jugular and windpipe before being stopped by her reinforced spine. She fell backward onto the street, the smartgun continuing to fire until the clip was empty.

The razorgirl's partner watched in horror through the window of the van, then drove away, keeping his foot on the accelerator until he could no longer hear shooting. Magnusson picked himself up from the sidewalk and began examining their wounded, while Yoko and Ratatosk walked over to the street samurai's body. The decker plucked the disk—the one with the data on GNX-IV—from her throat, and glanced at the adept.

"You were right," he said softly. "This thing *is* dangerous."

19

Lankin returned to the warehouse late in the afternoon, by which time the windows had been covered with metal foil to keep the interior dark and Mish had already begun reassembling her medicine lodge in one corner. The makeshift Boanerges Memorial Hospital already had its first three patients—Griffin, Wallace and Mute, who were still unconscious despite the best efforts of Czarnecki and the magicians. Lori had rescheduled her flight to enable her to stay in Seattle and continue treating them until they were well enough to travel, and was resting on a nearby cot. Mute seemed unlikely to recover in time for Lankin's run against Federated-Boeing, but he'd decided not to replace her: the original plan had called for a team of four, and while it was riskier, it also meant there were fewer people to share the money.

Lankin opened the unlocked door cautiously, and stepped into a vestibule of improvised blackout curtains. He pushed these aside, walked into a large open space and stared at the people sleeping among the chaotic array of high-tech vehicles and old gear salvaged from the Crypt. Pierce glanced up from his MRE, muttered, "Hoi," and returned his attention to the soy spaghetti.

Lankin shook his head. "Haven't you even posted a guard? And where is everybody?"

"Gone home, most of 'em who have homes. The rest're still at the Y," said Pierce. "I guess they'll show up when their money runs out, but the beds are better there, and we only got one shower. Which is where Yoko is, if you were wondering.''

"As for the guards," said Yoko, emerging from the bathroom wrapped in a damp towel, "this place is meant to be a hospital and a school, not a fortress."

"What about the Seoulpa?"

"They're too scared of her," said Pierce, jerking his head at Yoko and grinning. "They know what she did to that Divine Revenge razorgirl, and what she's done to yaks—''

"—and they think the enemy of their enemy is a potential ally," said Yoko with a shrug. "They don't have friends, and they're not good at gratitude, but I think we've come to an understanding . . . and they know that if anything happens to me, the coven will avenge me. Isn't that how you work?"

Lankin nodded stiffly. "I've been talking to some fixers. No one of them had enough money to buy all of the salvage, but I've got an offer of fifty thousand for the orichalcum, and Crane's fixer thinks he can find buyers for all the vehicles."

"Not *all* the vehicles," said Ratatosk, emerging from the bathroom, also clad in a towel. Lankin did a double take, and gritted his teeth. "At least, not immediately. We need the Nomad."

"What for?" asked Lankin, his tone sour.

"It has Aztechnology registration chips; it'll make it into the Pyramid without being stopped or searched."

"They'll have listed it as stolen," Lankin pointed out. "That'll set off the alarms."

"Easy to cancel; give me three seconds in their system, and it's done," said the decker. "Creating a fake registration from scratch takes *minutes* and is much more difficult to hide—much more likely to be discovered before you can get out."

"Why're you going into the Pyramid?"

"Because that's where the Hatter is."

"You're going to kill him?"

"I'm going to find out who was giving the orders. Whether it was the Hatter, or someone higher up, I'm going to make him wish he'd listened when Boanerges told him to stay away from the Crypt. Then I'm going to make him very sorry he sent toxics in to kill us. After that, I may kill him: I haven't decided."

"Revenge doesn't pay the bills," said Lankin.

"He has a Toyota Elite and shops at Lacy's."

Lankin considered this for a moment, then looked at Yoko. "What do you think?"

"I think if we want justice for Boanerges and everyone else who was killed in the Crypt, we'll have to arrange it ourselves," she replied. "No one else is going to take on Aztechnology for their sake. Taking on corps is what we do. And I think we're still alive because we have a reputation for avenging our dead. If it gives us money to build a hospital and a school, so much the better. So I'm in. And we have the support of the rest of the coven—except for Sumatra, of course."

Lankin looked around. "What've you done with him?"

"Magnusson took him somewhere where he could probe his mind. It just confirmed what we already suspected— he'd betrayed us to the Hatter, he robbed the rest of his team after they stole that shipment of Mitsuhama's magical gear, he betrayed Mandy Mandelbrot and Mercedes Benzene to Brackhaven . . ."

"You should've let me interrogate him."

"What would you have found out that Magnusson didn't?"

"Nothing, probably," Lankin admitted. "But it would have been much more painful. Is he dead?"

"No. He would be if he'd been in on it from the beginning and was responsible for killing Boanerges . . . but he wasn't. And Sumatra was a member of the Coven, and we all swore an oath of fraternity. We stripped him of his membership, but we've kept material links that will enable us to find him at anytime."

"On the other hand, 8-ball and I would be happy to kill him," said Ratatosk conversationally. "We're not members of the coven, so not bound by any oath. And Mute probably feels the same. And there's the last team that he ripped off, which I hear included Genocide George."

Lankin winced. You didn't work the Seattle shadows for long without hearing at least one story of the outrageous, consistently vicious behavior of Genocide George.

"And Mercy Benzene was a former member of the Blood Rumblers, so they're after him too. If Maggie does decide to let him go, he'll probably go hide and wait for one of those many groups to catch him. I doubt he'll enjoy the rest of his life very much."

"And if he calls the Hatter and tells him we have the virus? Does he know where you are?"

"He might have worked it out," Ratatosk admitted, "but I don't think that the Hatter will believe him even if he has told him. I borrowed Sumatra's phone. As far as I know, they only communicated by text messages, so whether or not the Hatter knows the sound of Sumatra's voice, he should recognize the number. And I've sent him a few messages telling him where we hid the vials. First, it was Forever Tacoma's grease pit. Then it was the Rat's Nest. Then the Ultra Club, then the arcology, then a few more places, just in case he wasn't exhausted from all the running around. It's probably time I called him again. You have a voice modulator, don't you? Do you think you can do Sumatra?"

Lankin smiled. "Yeah," he grunted, using his cyberware voice modulator to create a near-perfect imitation of the ork's accent. "Where you want me to send the fragger? I know this farm and lab up in Snohomish where they're trying to cross hellhounds with barghests. Give me the phone."

The Hatter stood on the pile of concrete and rubble in the middle of the abandoned ruins of the Monolith warehouse, and stared at the stacked containers, his fists clenched so tight that his manicured nails dug into his palms. The entire underground storage container had been exposed by a couple of trolls armed with jackhammers, and each compartment emptied. The Hatter had sent the trolls away and examined all the containers twice. None bore the ORO Corporation logo; all apparently came from local hospitals. "They took the damn thing," he muttered.

Hare shrugged. "Or it was never here," he suggested. "It was always a long shot. If long shots paid off every time, what would we do for fun?"

"Sumatra told me they'd found it. They must have gotten it past the mercs . . . or maybe they were in on it, too . . ."

"Or maybe Sumatra was lying," Hare replied. "Look at their dossiers, and you tell me which is more likely. If it *was* Sumatra."

The Hatter glowered at him, but didn't argue the point. "Nguyen told us he'd brought the stuff here."

"Doesn't prove it was *still* here when the vault was sealed. Unless we can find out who was working for Monolith at the time, and find some of them still alive, I guess we'll never know what happened. What're you going to do now?"

"Get somebody in to level this place," the Hatter replied savagely. "A few shape-charges around those support pillars should bring the roof down and fill in this hole. Then start covering up that lost equipment. Can you edit the vehicle sign-out sheets?"

"Edit how? I can get rid of your name, but I can't replace the truck or the drones, and somebody's going to notice them missing eventually. If they find out what's happened, you could end up being transferred to Campeche to run informants."

The Hatter thought for a moment. Campeche was still a trouble spot for the Aztlan government, and being posted there was regarded as a death sentence, especially for intelligence and security officers. "Change the record to say that Morales booked them. Can you do that?"

"Yes, but it won't stand up to any sort of serious scrutiny if they've made offline backups."

The Hatter nodded, his expression still grim. "Do it anyway, and find out when the file is backed up. Then I want you to update the dossiers on the shadowrunners who Sumatra told us were down there. I don't think he was lying about *that*. I know 8-ball was down there, and I'm fairly sure about Ratatosk and Lankin. And keep looking for Sumatra, too. I've invested too much in this scheme to give up now."

* * *

Lankin's apartment was approximately half the size of Crane's garage, but it offered more privacy and had much better security. Lankin's chair had been custom-made to comfortably fit his angular 2.76-meter frame, and it dominated the huge living room by virtue of its position and the lighting as well as its size. Ratatosk assumed that there were weapons concealed in the arms, and that the high back was well armored. There were other chairs and sofas in the room, some broad and sturdy enough to accommodate giants, others small enough for 8-ball and Zurich to sit in without needing to dangle their feet above the floor, all strategically placed so that no one's head was higher than their host's. Ratatosk sat between Yoko and Mute, and tried not to stare at what seemed to be an original Degas sketch on the opposite wall. "I've found the files on Project Balcony that I decrypted for Mandy Mandelbrot a while back," he told the group. "They're a couple of years old, but there's stuff here that you wouldn't normally find on a personnel file. The stuff on the Hatter's routine isn't much help—according to this, he rarely leaves the Pyramid except for work, and has a habit of leaving all social engagements after about four hours. Apart from that, he seems to delight in being unpredictable. Extremely status conscious, not a team player . . . nothing we couldn't have worked out." He shrugged. "The schedule from the Aztechnology garage confirms this, for what it's worth. His car's left the building only once in the past four weeks, and the only others he's signed out were the Step-Van and the Nomad. The schedule ends on the twelfth, and there's not enough data there for me to predict when he might leave again.

"On the bright side, Hare actually seems to have a pattern. The psychoprofile says he likes to go to the casino once a week to play blackjack. He picks up two women if he wins, one if he loses. Doesn't lose often, but can lose badly when he does. The schedule seems to confirm this: he leaves the Pyramid every Monday night between ten and twelve, in his own car, returning four to seven hours later."

"Which casino?" asked Lankin. The theft of the

Federated-Boeing Commuter had gone off without a hitch, enabling him to pay off some of his more insistent creditors and relax for a while.

"The file doesn't say. Do any of you have any contacts in the casino biz?"

"I know a few people at the Gates and the Seward Club," Lankin replied.

"Escorts?"

"No, of course not," said Lankin, sounding wounded. "Hat check and bar staff."

Yoko sighed. "I've heard how you blackmailed your contact in Aztechnology. I don't believe it's the only time you've pulled that scam. You must know some madams, at least."

"Yes, but not the ones who work the Gates; they're all run by the Finnigan family. Or any based near the Seward Club."

"What about the others?"

"No, but I might know somebody who knows somebody. I'll see what I can do. Do you have a photo of Hare?"

"No," Ratatosk replied. "I'll try to access his personnel file, but I'm pretty sure it'll be well protected."

"What does he drive?"

"A Jackrabbit, believe it or not."

"White?"

"Silver. Electric, three-door, fifty-nine model. The files say that the Hatter goes with him occasionally. But here's what I don't get. The Hatter has a Toyota Elite. Even unmodified, it has enough headroom and legroom for elves. Why wouldn't they take that?"

8-ball shrugged. "So if we hit the place any night but Monday, we know the Hatter's likely to be there, and so's his car. Sounds good to me."

"No," said Yoko. "Hitting him in the Pyramid is too risky. If anything goes wrong, we'll have to deal with the Leopard Guards, magical security . . . If we can catch him outside, we have a much better chance of getting away alive."

"She's right," said Ratatosk. "We wait until Monday night, put a tail on Hare when he leaves, see where he

goes and who's with him. It'll also give you two more time
to heal."

"I'm fine," said Mute. Czarnecki had removed the bullets
from her gut and dosed her with drugs, and a healing spell
had done the rest. The mercs had finally left a few hours
before, in fair health—once Magnusson had cured their
hangovers from the farewell party with a detox spell.
Yoko's skin still looked raw in a few small patches, but her
wounds didn't seem to be troubling her.

"Then it'll give Maggie and Doc Czarnecki time to catch
up on their sleep in case we have casualties," said Ratatosk.
"And if Hare's alone, then okay, we try Plan B."

"What's Plan B?"

"I don't know yet; ask me after I've found out more
about the Hatter . . . his schedule, the location and layout
of his apartment, that sort of thing. Anything else that your
contacts can tell you will be much appreciated, because if
I have to go back into the Pyramid's system, I'd like to be
in and out of there as quickly as possible: I really don't
want to have to go up against Hare on his home turf again.
While I'm there, I'll change their vehicle register so that
the Nomad's no longer listed as stolen, so we can drive it
in. After that . . ." He shrugged.

"We might be able to lure the Hatter out some other
way," suggested Lankin. "There's a missing Dali bronze of
Alice in Wonderland; if somebody told him they'd located
it, he might be tempted. I know forgers who could fake
one in a couple of weeks."

"Weeks?" 8-ball repeated, aghast.

Ratatosk glanced at the Degas sketch again. "I don't
know if he's a collector," he said. "That's something else
to ask our contacts, but I think it's better to move quickly."

Mute nodded. "We'll need four cars. *Inconspicuous*
cars," she said, looking pointedly at Lankin.

"At least one big enough to act as a roadblock, if we
need it," said 8-ball. "A courier van, or something like
that."

"Shouldn't be a problem," said Lankin. "I can get them
from the people who bought Crane's collection, and sell

them back the next day. So, what do we need in the way of weapons?"

Like the living quarters in the Crypt, the shantytowns in the Rat's Nest were made from whatever materials could be scrounged from the junk—largely crates, cartons, pallets and discarded furniture, but also old refrigerators and freezers, Dumpsters too thoroughly rusted to be worth patching and vehicle bodies. A large cargo container, intact and relatively clean, was a mansion; the inverted hull of a fiberglass boat, a palace. Sumatra had managed to wheedle crash space in a corner of the medicine lodge belonging to Nicodemus, a fellow rat shaman—one with walls and a roof and a locked door that kept out the weather and other unwelcome intruders—by promising to teach him his magic fingers spell. He'd wrapped himself in a relatively clean garbage bag and used his jungle boots as a pillow: they were cheap Aztlan army issue, all rubber and canvas, but being new, they didn't smell remotely as bad as the rest of the Rat's Nest. Unlike the Crypt, which Czarnecki and Mish had insisted be kept as clean as possible for the benefit of patients in the clinic, the junkyard reeked of rotting food, dead bodies and worse. The devil rats and other scavengers were tolerated mostly because they helped dispose of the corpses: besides, most of them tasted so bad that they were scarcely worth the effort of catching.

Sumatra stayed in the lodge during the day, only venturing out after sunset—usually concealed and guarded by a city spirit. The squatters who'd searched him hadn't left him anything of his own apart from his stained cargo pants and his socks. His oversized parka, jungle boots, fatigue pants, T-shirt, underwear and new socks had all come from the load they'd extorted from the Hatter; Magnusson had given him these before pushing him out of his car on the edge of the Rat's Nest. He hadn't left him a weapon, a phone, or even the ration bars, secure vest and rucksack that everybody else had received. Before venturing along the junkyard's main drag, aptly known as Ammonia Avenue because of its stench, Sumatra had found a length of metal pipe that would serve as a club, in case he ran across more scavengers than he could deter with his powerbolt and mass agony spells, and searched for signs of magic. By the time he'd found the lodge, he'd scored a handmade shiv, a Portland Lords baseball cap, a disposable lighter, a guide and a little extra confidence. The next night, he'd wandered around until someone had challenged him, then looted their shelter after leaving them unconscious, coming away with a space blanket, a water purifier, a small cache of food and a reputation as somebody not to be fragged with. He decided that after two weeks, when he'd finished teaching Nicodemus the magic fingers spell, he might be the boss of this corner of the Rat's Nest. The prospect thrilled him not at all.

What galled him most was the knowledge that it was his own greed that had landed him here. If he'd resisted the urge to take the orichalcum from that package when Genocide George and his brother Elwood weren't paying attention, he wouldn't have needed to hide in the Crypt. If he hadn't tried to cut a better deal for himself with the Hatter, he could've snuck out of the Crypt with the virus and the data disk and gone to a fixer who would've gotten him the best deal possible—maybe even enough for him to buy the club he really wanted, the sort with a bar, a kitchen, some dancers, maybe some sloppy soy wrestling occasionally, and a few private rooms upstairs and out the back for business and pleasure . . .

He looked up as the door opened. The man silhouetted in the doorway was too tall to be Nicodemus, but his blocky shape and flattop haircut were familiar. "Sumatra?" the man asked, pointing his smartgun at the huddled shape.

The shaman looked around the lodge, seeing nothing and nobody large enough to hide behind. "Hello, George," he said cautiously, wondering what the best move would be. Probably a stun spell; Genocide George Sequoia was stubborn enough to resist most mana-based spells, but his natural toughness was enhanced with dermal plating, bone lacing and damage compensators. The armor he wore wouldn't help him against a powerbolt or any other spell that damaged living flesh from within, but his bodyware and constitution would. Once stunned, he'd be easy prey: if he'd been foolhardy enough to come here alone, then Sumatra could murder him at his leisure before he revived; if not, then he could take his guns (George always carried more than one gun) rather than consume energy casting more combat spells. And George was bound to have a phone, a car, and various other essentials. Sumatra could barely stop himself from grinning.

"I knew I shouldn't have trusted a rat shaman," George grumbled as his left hand moved down toward his belt, "but Elwood said you were okay, and you knew the spells we needed. He even said we should let you live if you give us back the drek you took. So where is it?"

"Kill me and you'll never find it," Sumatra replied.

"Fair enough," said George, and fired a burst from the smartgun into the shaman's belly. "One more question, though." He flicked the switch on the flashpak on his belt. The flare compensation in his cybereyes kicked in automatically, canceling out the strobe effect, and he reached for the Roomsweeper on his belt. "Is it true magicians can't cast spells at things they can't see?"

Sumatra gritted his teeth, trying to ignore the pain from his wounds, and peered into the astral. Genocide George remained clearly visible—he had little cyberware apart from his eyes, some bone lacing, and smartlinks in both hands—but the light from the flashpak was gone. He cast a stunbolt at George, then an invisibility spell on himself, concentrating on keeping drain to a minimum. Then he rolled away from his bed in the corner and scrambled to his feet. A moment too late, he remembered his shiv, checked his pockets, and finding them empty, looked around. The clumsy knife lay between his boots, three meters away.

If George was startled by his target vanishing, he recovered quickly, despite the fatiguing effects of the stunbolt. He watched and listened for sounds of movement, then fired from the hip at Sumatra's improvised bedding. When the shaman didn't reappear, he walked a burst along the far wall, aiming low and carefully spacing the shots a quarter meter apart so that at least one or two would hit his target. Sumatra squawked as one round blasted a bloody hole in his right thigh, then another amputated the ring finger from his left hand. George drew his Roomsweeper with his left hand and looked at the filthy floor, hoping to see signs of fresh blood, maybe even footprints. Sumatra froze, and despite his wounds, managed to concentrate for long enough to cast another stunbolt.

George reeled, dropping the smartgun as he leaned against the wall. Sumatra considered casting another stunbolt, but the energy drain of the invisibility spell meant that he was as likely to knock himself out as the merc. Instead, he watched George's gun as he crept back toward his boots, nearly silent in his stocking feet. The merc was wearing bullet-resistant dark glasses, which prevented anyone seeing his eyes, and his face was as expressionless as a leather mask, but Sumatra was reassured by the way the barrel of the Roomsweeper was beginning to droop, as though the effort of holding it up was becoming too much for him.

George stared woozily at the floor, still looking for traces of blood, but all he could see was evidence of where the ork had been, not where he was now. The lodge wasn't much more than three meters square, and at that sort of close range the shot wouldn't spread enough for him to be sure of hitting his target. Fighting to remain conscious, he waited, and listened, and watched, and as soon as the knife disappeared from view, he squeezed the trigger. Some of the buckshot blasted a hole in the lodge's makeshift wall, but enough hit Sumatra's left arm, leg and chest to send the ork staggering backwards. Sumatra let the invisibility spell drop and prepared to cast another stunbolt, but even as badly fatigued as he was, Genocide George was quicker; he fired at the shaman's head, removing most of his face. Sumatra fell against the wall, then slid to the floor.

George reached into one of his pockets for a maximum-strength stimulant patch, peeled off the backing, then slapped the patch onto the back of his opposite hand. Cautiously, he bent down and picked up his smartgun, then returned the Roomsweeper to its holster, and sat down while he waited for the stimulants to kick in. Once seated, he grabbed a spare clip, reloaded his smartgun, and fired a single shot at Sumatra's knee. The ork didn't even flinch.

George searched Sumatra's corpse hastily, finding nothing of value, then quickly returned to his car before the effects of the stimulant patch wore off. He barely had time to set the autopilot before his eyes closed, and he slept peacefully all the way home.

The building directory in the Aztechnology Pyramid's system had been designed to look like its physical counterpart—a lobby of intricately carved stonework, with a three-meter-high model of the Pyramid in the center. Two icons—a man and a woman, both human in scale but with a distinctly elflike beauty—sat behind a counter to one side of the Pyramid. Ratatosk approached the woman, but instead of asking her where he could find the Hatter or Hare and risk alerting them, he distracted her with a deception utility while downloading the entire directory for later reading. He left the datastore and hurried along the datalines back to the Pyramid's garage.

Their programmers had upgraded the scramble IC on the sign-out sheet, as he'd expected, as well as adding tar pit IC, but it was still easy enough to cut through without triggering any alarms. Inserting the subroutine he'd written into the datafile took another few seconds, but he was jumpy enough for the wait to seem like minutes. It was a simple logic bomb, a once-only order to switch the lights in the northeast corner office on the forty-second floor on and off when Hare's car left its bay It was harmless, and impossible to trace back to the decker, apparently nothing more than a prank, and simple enough that Hare probably wouldn't spot it . . . but in case he did, Ratatosk had inserted another subroutine into the database, one that would periodically check to see if the first was in place, and turn off all the lights in the Pyramid if it failed to find it. If *that* happened, the team was to leave the area at top speed, and hope that the confusion prevented the Azzies from chasing them.

Once the logic bomb was in place, Ratatosk found the

database entry for the missing Nomad. He blinked, seeing that the record had been changed to say that the vehicle had been checked out not by the Hatter, but by a Dr. Morales—and two days earlier than on his copy of the data.

The vehicle was still listed as missing, and there was an unfamiliar symbol next to Morales' details. Ratatosk studied this for a moment, then made a hasty exit and headed for the recruiting office. Another woman, just as beautiful as the one in directory assistance, smiled at him as he pretended to read a pamphlet on opportunities in their security forces. He sleazed through their security to the personnel records, and looked uneasily at the IC clustered about all the files. Moving carefully to avoid a screamer program, he found the index, which was protected by probe IC and the ubiquitous scramble. He hesitated, then retreated from the datastore and looked at the directory file he'd downloaded, in the hope of finding where Dr. Morales worked. To his surprise, he found that the scientist's contact details had been struck through, and his apartment listed as vacant.

Ratatosk chewed his lower lip for a moment, then slipped out of the Aztechnology system and into the RTG where he'd set up a secure comcall conference network. "The software's in place," he said. Magnusson and Mute were waiting in a Jackrabbit in the parking lot of Seattle General with a clear view of the Pyramid. 8-ball and Jinx were orbiting the Pyramid in another Jackrabbit, staying at least three blocks away at all times. Yoko and Lankin were parked near northbound and southbound highway entrances in an Americar and a discreetly armored Leyland-Rover personnel carrier. Crane's fixer had been helpful and efficient, even throwing in a box of magnetic rubber logos for the carrier at no extra cost.

"Did you find anything?" asked Lankin.

"Not much. I'm not going back in until Hare leaves. After that, even if I get caught, it won't tip him off. One strange thing, though. They've changed the sign-out sheet to say that the Nomad was checked out by someone else. Just that one, not the Step-Van; I haven't checked the inventory for the drones. But it looks to me like they're covering their tracks."

"What?"

"I don't get it either. There's been no report of the vehicle being used in a crime, or anything like that, so why bother trying to set up some sort of plausible deniability just for a car?"

"Unless they weren't authorized to use it," Lankin responded. "Or the job went so badly over budget that they're trying to shift the losses onto somebody else's books. Who do they say took it out?"

"A Dr. Morales. Software R & D. But he's—"

"Disappeared?" said Mute softly.

"Yes."

"I helped him disappear."

"The Hatter must have heard about it . . . of course he would have. He works in security for R & D." Ratatosk's icon slapped its forehead. "He went voluntarily?"

"Yes."

"If they're trying to hide something like this, on a secure system," said Lankin, "then they're trying to keep it from their own people, and that could make it difficult for them to call for backup. And if they're bothering to conceal a loss like that, they don't have unlimited resources, either."

"That doesn't do us much good if the cream of the security team is also in on the secret," Ratatosk countered. "Even if it's something they're doing on the side, we'll still be up against the Leopard Guards, as well as their deckers . . ."

"The job wouldn't have needed mercs if he'd had any Leopard Guards on the side; they'd have come storming in wearing plain clothes, on their day off. And the Leopard Guards wouldn't bother concealing the loss of one vehicle; have you ever seen the way they drive, even when they're sober? No, I think this is a small group with their eye on a nice little earner; the more people know, the less each of them gets."

"That sounds reasonable," said Magnusson, "but if we're thinking of going into a secure facility crawling with troops, I'd rather err on the side of caution."

No one argued with that, and the line was silent for several minutes, until Mute said, "The lights just blinked.

We're on." She pulled out of the parking lot and drove around the block until they saw a three-door silver Jackrabbit heading along Broadway away from the Aztechnology Pyramid. Magnusson astrally projected into the car and looked around. The only occupant was an elf with some headware, who seemed to be enjoying a trideo while the car ran on autopilot. There was no sign of any magical security on the vehicle, or any magic about the passenger, so Magnusson conjured up a watcher spirit and told it to sit on the roof of the car, without manifesting, to help identify it from the hundreds of identical boxes on the road. The watcher obeyed, making a great show of turning its head blue and spinning it around like the kids in *The Exorcist XIII*.

Magnusson returned to his meatbody, still assensing the watcher. "Signal in place. Looks like Hare, but he doesn't seem to be paying much attention to the road. No sign of the Hatter. Following south on Broadway." They continued shadowing Hare for several blocks until Mute saw 8-ball's car ahead; then they slowed down.

"He's headed across the lake," said 8-ball a few minutes later. "Probably going to the Gates. I don't think we should try to intercept him anywhere on the way: Lone Star would be there in a minute."

"Agreed," said Yoko. "Ratatosk?"

"You're not going to ask me to hack in to the Gates' system, are you?" said the decker, putting a plaintive note into his voice. "They've got enough IC to sink the *Titanic*. I'd be safer in the Pyramid."

"I know people there," said Lankin. "I'll see if they can tell me anything."

"Fine. I'll try to access the Hatter's personnel file. I've found his apartment, if that helps, and Hare's. The Hatter's is going to be a problem. It's on the fifty-eighth floor, with a window, right next to the express elevator for the security teams—and they're slaved to the off-line security CPU in a cold vault, not the main system. I can't do anything with them without physically going inside and jacking in there."

"What about Hare's?"

"Much better. Fifty-second floor, just a few doors down

from the main elevator shaft. It won't be easy, not by a couple of decimal places, but if we can get inside the garage, the main problem is security cameras. All we'll need to do is look as though we belong. It's not a heavily restricted area."

"What about the lock?" asked Mute.

"Fifty-second floor . . . probably a retinal or voiceprint scanner, slaved to the security CPU. I'll see if I can get that data from the personnel files. Have fun at the casino."

The hatcheck woman, a pretty elf with hair as red as Ratatosk's, smiled at Yoko when she introduced herself as a friend of Lankin's. "He told me you'd be here. What're you after?"

"Anything you can tell me about the elf at the blackjack table—the one with the big teeth, looks as though he sleeps in a wind tunnel."

"Herrera? He comes here once or twice a month. Secure coat, off the rack, Fichetti pistol. Gets very friendly and tips well when he wins—sometimes more than he wins. Bad loser, though."

"How bad?"

"I've heard rumors that he's hit people, but I've never seen it happen. One time the pit boss told me to lose his gun and have it sent back the next day by courier. He'd lost more than enough to make up for the expense."

Yoko nodded. "Does he come here alone?"

"Usually. Sometimes there's a man with him, occasionally a woman. Always the same man, but I don't think it's ever been the same woman twice."

"Tell me about the man."

"Human, well dressed—beautiful secure coat, and even wears a top hat. Slivergun, palm pistol, sometimes a smartgun as well. English accent. I'd know him if I saw him again, but I couldn't tell you much more about him. Might be his boss."

"You said he gets friendly when he wins. How friendly?"

The woman looked wary. "Depends how much he's won, how good-looking the woman is and what she'll let him get away with in exchange for the tip. When he actually leaves

the tables, he goes for the professionals. Doesn't like to
waste time."

"No!" Lankin snapped.

"The yakuza started training me as a geisha before the
mamasan decided that my true calling lay elsewhere,"
Yoko reminded him. She was sitting in one of the soundproofed toilet cubicles, but spoke into the phone quietly
anyway. "I know I'm not dressed for the part, but there
are boutiques here. I think I can get him interested."

"No. The Mafia runs the escorts in there, they vet them
thoroughly and they have a zero-tolerance policy when it
comes to freelancers. And what if he recognizes you?"

"He won't recognize *me*," said Mute before Yoko could
respond. "And I can get you a photograph, even a
voiceprint."

"That'd be useful," said 8-ball.

"Okay," Yoko replied. "I'll keep an eye on him, but I
won't get too close. See you when you get here."

Mute walked in a few minutes later. She still wore her
black leathers and running shoes, but they were stylish
enough to meet the casino's dress code, and she'd opened
the jacket to reveal a distractingly low-cut saffron top beneath it. Yoko watched from the half-nuyen slot machines
as she approached the blackjack table and stood opposite
Hare. The decker was losing, and so intent on the cards
that he didn't seem to notice her at all. Mute hovered
around the table for a few minutes, photographing him
from several angles and recording his voice, then retreated
to the powder room. She slotted a chip into her head,
downloaded the picture and audio files of Hare from the
headware memory connected to her camera eyes and cyber-
ears, then removed the chip, inserted it into her wristphone,
and sent the data to the rest of the team. Yoko was waiting
by the sinks as she emerged from the cubicle. "Any
problems?"

"Not for me, except that he didn't say much and I
couldn't see his eyes well enough to get a shot of his retinal
prints. *He's* losing fairly badly, and raising the stakes to

cover his losses. They're not very high yet, but he's not happy."

Ratatosk analyzed the probe IC that encased the index of personnel records and carefully deflected it using his deception software, then began decrypting the scrambled text. A quick search gave him the system location for Hare's and the Hatter's personnel records, but he paled when he identified the IC that surrounded the datafiles. He made a quick sensor test to make sure there were no other deckers in the datastore, then tried to decrypt the Hatter's file while avoiding the tar pit. He had just begun downloading the dossier when he felt a shadow pass over him, and looked up to see an icon approaching—great black skeletal form, the image of the Aztec death god Mictlantecuhtli. Ratatosk hit it with a slow program that enabled him to evade the incoming attack, but he knew he had no chance of defeating such high-rated black IC, nor of holding it off for long enough to copy the complete file. He logged off as deftly as he could, and found himself in the back room of the Big O, surrounded by Leila, Pierce, Didge and Zurich. "Slot and run," he said quickly. "I don't think they traced me, but I don't want to stick around." He hurried out with barely a glance at the strippers on the catwalk, leaving the others in his wake. The five of them piled into the Nomad and Ratatosk's Jackrabbit, and headed for the alternative jackpoint, an illegal tap behind a Stuffer Shack a few kilometers away.

"Hare's put extra IC on his own file, and on the Hatter's," Ratatosk explained to Lankin and 8-ball when he phoned to apologize for the temporary loss of their secure comcall network. "They're probably better secured than the CEO's. When he gets back to the Pyramid, it won't take him long to work out where I've been or who we're after."

"Will he know it was you?" asked Lankin.

"No, but depending on how many other people are gunning for him at the moment, he might guess. Or he might just be arrogant enough to think it's headhunters hoping to recruit corporate deckers . . . but I wouldn't count on it. I think it'd be better if he never returned to the Pyramid— at least, not until after we've tackled the Hatter. I suggest we go in tonight."

"And *I* suggest we wait until we know more," Lankin countered. "He must have some sort of weakness we can exploit—and this decker may not be the only friend he can call on. He's in security, so he's probably wired from the eyes down, and he must know some mages as well. It's too risky."

"He's not going to lower his guard anytime soon," replied Ratatosk, "and if he thinks we have GNX-IV, *he* may already be gunning for *us*. We know Sumatra told him our names. He has dossiers on any of us who've worked for Aztechnology. 8-ball? How do you vote?"

"I think you're right," said the dwarf. "And I've never gone for that 'revenge is a dish best served cold' drek. Sorry, Lankin."

Lankin shrugged. "I think it's a mistake, but I'll go along with the majority. Let me know when the network's back up, and I'll see whether my contacts have come up with anything useful." He hung up.

"Any damage to your deck?" asked Zurich from the backseat, to break the silence.

"I don't think so, but I'll run a medic program now." He plugged himself back into his deck, letting the autopilot drive until they reached the Stuffer Shack's parking lot. Pierce, in the Nomad, pulled in beside them a moment later, and headed for the stuffers while Ratatosk busied himself reestablishing the secure comcall link.

Lankin phoned back a few minutes later. "I have something," he said. "Yoko, are you there?"

"Yes."

"Is he still losing?"

"I think so," replied Mute. "Magnusson's watching him. He has his phone switched off, but I can ask him to leave the tables."

"It can wait. I've been speaking to a contact in what is euphemistically known as the Seamstresses' Guild. They have a fat file on Mr. Herrera: they won't let me read the whole thing, but they've given me a summary of the highlights. He gets nasty when he loses, and likes to leave bite marks and welts. They're bad enough that most professionals won't go near him—certainly not those at the Gates. So he's made a deal with a few of the brothels. They get some chiphead or other addict who doesn't feel pain, somebody desperate, clean her up a little, make sure she can't feel pain or remember too much, and let him go to town while another woman watches to make sure it doesn't go too far."

"What do you mean by 'too far'?"

"If any of them die, he has to dispose of the bodies himself. My contact tells me that none of them *have*, so far, but they think it's possible."

"Is this just to discourage me from trying to pick him up?"

"No. There are very few brothels willing to offer that sort of service, and my contact gave me the name of the only one in the area. It's called Nero's; I'm on my way there now. I've had to pay for the information—well, offer to pay—but if Hare loses, we'll know where he's headed next, and can be waiting for him. Ratatosk, can you check out their security system?"

"What if he wins?" asked 8-ball .

"Then we'll have to think of something else."

"I have an idea," said Mute. "You said he hires two women when he's winning, right?"

"Yes, but—"

"How well is he likely to play if he's distracted?"

Hare looked down at his cards—an eight and an ace—then at the deck. The casinos had taken steps to prevent people with headware memory from counting cards, as well as more obvious measures to stop magicians from using spells such as magic fingers on the roulette wheel or analyze truth in the poker tournaments. Hare's own memory and his ability to calculate probabilities were good enough to give him an edge at the game despite the frequent and seemingly random changing of the deck, without diminishing the thrill.

He looked up as he heard a woman ask for another card,

and his jaw dropped slightly as he saw an unnervingly beautiful elf sitting a few seats away, next to a dusky-skinned human woman in black leathers and low-and-behold top. The dealer gave her a six to add to her pair of sevens, then turned to him. "Another card?" he asked.

He nodded, and the dealer gave him another eight. He winced, and the women laughed as the dealer passed them their chips. The elf wrapped her arms around the human and lifted her up until their faces were on the same level, then kissed her. Hare stared as the kiss seemed to go on forever, then tried to turn his attention back to the table.

His next hand was a four and a five; the women were dealt a pair of jacks and a six and a nine, respectively. He stared at their cards, trying to remember what cards had already been dealt from the deck, and found that he couldn't concentrate on any of the numbers. After losing the next two hands, he left the table, cashed in his remaining chips and called for his car.

According to its license, Nero's was a tavern and restaurant that offered live entertainment. Ratatosk's quick search of guides to less-than-legal Seattle turned up descriptions of the quality of the table dancers, a schedule of its prices for private shows, and a mention of the restaurant's soup kitchen and shelter for homeless women. It was officially owned by a shell company, but security and many other services were provided by well-known Finnigan family fronts . . . which he knew meant that the business' computer systems would be online, to enable the mafioisi to keep an eye on the business and make sure the profits weren't being skimmed too heavily. The security camera network was protected by ripper IC, which could crash his deck, but nothing as dangerous as the countermeasures he'd encountered in the Aztechnology system. "Okay, I'm in," said Ratatosk. "What's the plan?"

"I don't want to try putting anybody inside the place," said Lankin. "Too risky, and there's no time. But if you can put the cameras in their parking lot on a closed loop, we can ambush him there. The lot should be a bit out of the way, so it's much safer than doing it on the street."

"Piece of cake," said the decker.

"I'm following his car," said 8-ball. "He's headed in the right direction."

"He's there," said Ratatosk a few minutes later. "Getting out of the car, walking up to their back door . . . He's in. I don't have to watch him while he's in there, do I?"

"Just keep an eye on the exits. All of them."

"I am. Who's going to pick him up?"

A little over an hour later, Hare walked out of the back door of Nero's with a grin that showed his large teeth. He opened the door of his Jackrabbit, climbed in and squawked when a bald black dwarf leaned over the seat and pressed something into the back of his neck. "Not a sound," 8-ball warned him. "Just take out your pistol and your phone and give them to me, then set the autopilot for Montlake."

"Who are you?" asked Hare, handing over the Fichetti and removing his wristphone. He grabbed a cable that was plugged into the dashboard jack, but froze when 8-ball growled.

"I'm the guy pointing a gun at your head," the dwarf reminded him. He saw no need to mention that the pistol was a narcoject dartgun. "And if you've got a phone in there, or anything like that, don't bother trying to call anyone: I've got a jammer back here. The autopilot recognizes your voiceprint, doesn't it?"

"Yes," said Hare.

"Good. Tell it where to go, then shut up."

"What do you want? The car? It's yours. Money? I don't have much, but what I have is—"

"I didn't tell you to ask questions," said 8-ball. Hare closed his eyes, muttered, "Montlake Boulevard," then shut up. The car pulled out of the parking lot, and the Jackrabbit parked next to his followed a moment later.

"Thanks for the offer," said 8-ball, when they were two blocks away from Nero's. "Yes, we will take the car, for a start. Most of all, though, we want information. Anything you can tell us about Tom Mather, the Hatter."

Hare's eyes widened. "What do you want with him?"

"Just a moment of his time. He killed some friends of mine."

"If you're planning on killing friends of his," said Hare around a lump in his throat, "think again. He doesn't have any. He doesn't care about anybody but himself."

"Not even you?"

"Well, not enough to risk his life. Or even his car. So if you're thinking of asking him for a ransom for me, better not go over five figures."

8-ball grinned. "Thanks for the tip. Now, we can do this one of two ways. Tell us what we need to know, and you wake up tomorrow morning. Fail to cooperate, and you never wake up again. What's it to be?"

"I'll cooperate," gulped Hare. "What do you want to know?"

"How do we get into the Hatter's apartment?"

"I don't know. I mean, even if you can get into the Pyramid and get up to that floor . . . I know there's a credstick lock and a voiceprint lock, but I don't know the password, and I don't think he would have told anybody else. He probably has the same sort of sequence I do—it asks him a question that most people wouldn't know the answer to, and it only accepts the answer in his voice. The same for his office, I think. I'm sorry if that's not the answer you want, but it's true."

The dwarf grimaced. "Any overrides?"

"In theory, but the doors are controlled by a red-level system in a cold vault. You're not a decker, are you?"

"No. Could you do it?"

"Yes, but only from inside the system. Inside the Pyramid."

8-ball shook his head. "I don't think so, chummer. Is there anywhere else that the Hatter goes where we might meet up with him?"

20

Lankin was the first to arrive in the university's car park, and he sat in the van until he saw Yoko and Mute climb out of the Americar. "My contact in the Pyramid has just sent me some interesting mail," he told them by way of a greeting. "Aztechnology has a monthly unrestricted-pistol-shooting event. The Hatter just won for the third time in a row, beating members of the Leopard Guard as well as others in security."

Unrestricted, Mute knew, meant that there were no limits on the contestants' cyberware or their choice of pistol: unlike the Olympics and other games, unrestricted contests could be as much a test of new technology as they were of pure skill. She shrugged. "We didn't think he'd be a push-over," she said.

"He also says the Hatter's applied for a job in the head office. If he gets it, he could be leaving by the end of the week. It looks like waiting for more information would have been a mistake, after all." He sounded almost apologetic.

"Do you think he might be expecting us?"

"I suppose we'll find out."

"Do you trust your informant?"

"I think so. The Hatter *could* be trying to take control of the timetable, but the job is apparently real, and it pays better."

Mute shook her head. "He wouldn't leave unless he's given up on GNX-IV. Do you think that's likely?"

"He may not have given up," said Yoko. "The container we found was addressed to their head office. If he knew that, then he may have decided to look there when he didn't find it in the Crypt. In any case, now that we have Hare, we're committed. It's tonight or *we* give up."

"We probably *should* be committed," muttered Lankin. He looked around as more vehicles arrived—first 8-ball and Hare in Hare's Jackrabbit, then Mish in another, and Magnusson in a third. Hare emerged from his car reluctantly, and 8-ball handcuffed him to a tree before joining his teammates.

"Here's his retinal prints and a voice sample," he said, handing a chip to Mute. "And everything else I could get out of the sorry sack of drek. I told him we wouldn't kill him if he cooperated, and he sang like a bird. What should we do with him?"

"Get his clothes when Ratatosk arrives," said Yoko. "It's probably safest to knock him out and leave him in the van with Lankin and Pierce. We can release him when this is over, and let him decide whether he returns to Aztechnology or looks for work elsewhere. Did you get a description of the Hatter?"

8-ball nodded. Magnusson stepped out of the black Jackrabbit and donned his top hat. "How do I look?" he asked.

The Pyramid's gates opened automatically as Hare's car approached, and Ratatosk breathed a sigh of relief. The gate closed behind them again almost instantly, and he drove on until they were stopped by a boom gate. A security guard was watching a trideo in his booth, and looked away reluctantly. "ID?" he asked.

Magnusson, muttering softly in Aramaic, cast a physical mask spell on the decker. Ratatosk opened the window and leaned toward the camera and microphone. "Marc Herrera, computer security."

The guard nodded, then glanced at the monitor. "I'm reading four bodies in the car."

"Thomas Mather, resource co-ord for R & D," came a

male voice from the backseat, with the careful intonation of the mildly drunk, "and two visitors."

"Okay. Have a good one."

"Thank you." Ratatosk raised the window, and Magnusson let the spell drop.

"What happens if they check and see that the Hatter hasn't left the building?" asked the mage.

"We have to hope that they won't," replied Mute, still in Mather's voice. "Someone with the Hatter's job has to be free to come and go without needing to check in or out. It's magical security that worries me."

No one and nothing stopped them as they drove down to the lowest sublevel of the garage. Ratatosk, who knew the layout from the computerized model in the system, led the way to the elevators. Magnusson concentrated on maintaining the physical mask spell while still chanting quietly in Aramaic to reduce the drain. He was careful not to look at any of the cameras, hoping desperately that the hired top hat and new lined coat would be enough of a disguise to fool casual observers into mistaking him for the Hatter. As they approached the doors, a monitor between the elevators lit up, showing the face and shoulders of a man wearing the butternut-and-blaze-orange uniform of a security guard. "ID, please."

"Marc Herrera, computer security; Thomas Mather, resource co-ord for R & D; and two visitors," Ratatosk intoned. "Fifty-second floor."

"Further ID required for visitor passes. Visitors please approach the monitor and stand on the red line, one at a time."

Ratatosk stepped aside, slightly anxious but mildly relieved that the system hadn't asked Magnusson to confirm that he was the Hatter. Mute stepped onto the line and looked at the monitor. "Name, please."

She looked at the monitor, trying to guess whether the face was real or a computer simulation. "Devi," she said, her voice modulator programmed with a synthesized voice borrowed from a Bollywood musical star.

"Full name, please."

"Devi Khan."

"Height one point six-six meters, voiceprint and facial scan registered. Temporary visitor pass issued for Devi Khan." A plastic card emerged from a slot beneath the monitor. "Next, please."

She took the card and stepped aside, and Yoko took her place. "Yumiko Arisake."

"Height one point eight-nine meters, voiceprint and facial scan registered. Temporary visitor pass issued for Yumiko Arisake. Thank you." The lift doors opened, and the four hurried inside.

"Fifty-second floor," Ratatosk repeated, glancing at Magnusson. The mage was still muttering softly in Aramaic to minimize the drain of maintaining the physical mask spell. "You holding up okay?"

Magnusson nodded, and no one else spoke until the lift doors opened again.

Diaz gazed at the bank of monitors, yawned through clenched teeth, then turned and glared enviously at the fat wagemage lying on the couch behind him. Security mages could close their eyes for a couple of hours at a time, supposedly prowling the pyramid in astral form in search of intruders, but Diaz suspected that many of them were actually asleep; meanwhile, he sat between the door and their unconscious bodies while watching a dozen changing but eternally boring views of the corridors. Diaz looked back at the screens, caught a glimpse of a top hat and blinked.

Standing next to the top-hatted figure was an attractive human woman in leathers and a low-cut top. He looked at the entry register and grinned. So the Hatter and his pet decker had brought home a couple of women, had they? Diaz swiveled his chair back and looked at the two gorgeous women again, then called up that night's roster. He'd never forgiven the Hatter for putting him on the graveyard shift in this dead-end post after Morales had escaped, and a chance to land him in the drek with his tasty blond squeeze was too good to pass up. "Station two, this is station four. Is Elena Vargas there?"

"Her body is; the rest of her should be back soon."

"Great. Ask her to check out elevator B-nine when she does, can you?"

Ratatosk inserted Herrera's credstick into the socket next to the door and waited. "Pawn to king four," said the speaker.

"Pawn to king four," Mute replied in Hare's voice.

"Knight to king's bishop three."

Ratatosk tried to visualize a chessboard. "Knight to queen's bishop three," Magnusson murmured. "It's Giuoco Piano." Mute repeated this, and the door slid open. The four hurried in, and the door shut behind them, leaving them in darkness.

"No magical defenses," said Magnusson, looking around the room astrally. He dropped the physical mask spell. "Lights." He staggered over to the nearest chair, while Ratatosk ran toward the coffee table and grabbed Hare's deck bag. As soon as the bag was opened, he whistled.

"What is it?"

"An Excalibur!"

"Valuable?"

"A million, easy, and that's without the software, not to mention any Aztechnology codes it has in memory . . . Oh, man, this is—"

"Can you use it?" asked Yoko as she disappeared into the bedroom to make sure no one else was in the apartment.

"*Can* I?"

"Immediately?"

Reluctantly, Ratatosk closed the bag again, and slung it over his shoulder. "I'll look at it later." He glanced at the telecom in the corner near the door, examined the jackpoint, and opened his own deck bag. "Okay," he said a few seconds later, "this is the secure system. Needs a retinal print—Mute, can you take care of that? Can't find anything monitoring this room apart from the standard safety devices, none of which can ID us. I'll see if I can override the Hatter's lock."

"Can you scrub our facial scans, first?" asked Mute,

changing the retinal pattern of her cybereyes to match
Hare's. "And Yoko's voiceprint?"

"Not yet, not if you're going to be walking the corridors," said Ratatosk, and thought for a moment. "I can
write a logic bomb that'll erase your records as soon as the
Hatter's car leaves the garage. Will that do?"

"How long will it take?"

"I'll just have to change a few lines of code . . . two
minutes? Another minute or two to set up an ID for 8-ball
so he can drive the Nomad in. Then I'll take care of the
cameras in the garage, then the elevators, then the main
door, and *then* I'll get to work on that lock."

Diaz snatched up the phone as soon as it rang. "Station Four."

"This is Vargas. There's nobody in B-nine."

"You must have just missed them. They've gone into
Herrera's place."

"Missed who?"

"Mather, Herrera and two female visitors."

"Mather didn't go out tonight."

"He didn't *sign* out, but according to the log, he came
back in at three oh eight."

"That's . . . did you see him?"

"Not his face," Diaz admitted. "He was looking down
the . . . he was looking down."

Vargas was silent. She could hear the malice in Diaz's
voice; she knew he had no reason to think there'd been
any breach in the security and part of her wanted to give
her lover the benefit of the doubt, but she'd learned to not
trust too easily. "Did Herrera check out?"

"Yes, at ten fourteen, but he *has* to."

Vargas nodded. She'd left the Hatter's bed just before
twelve to begin her shift. "I'll look into it," she said, and
hung up. She sat there fuming for a moment, then lay back
on her couch and sent her astral form down to the Hatter's
apartment. Unlike the Pyramid's exterior, the inner walls
had no magical security: in theory, the mages were supposed to respect employees' privacy, but Vargas felt that
until the Hatter revoked his invitation into his bedroom,

she was free to check on him. To her relief, she found him fast asleep in the large bed. Her astral form hovered over him for a moment, then returned to her meatbody. The armed guard sitting between her and the door looked around as she sat up, and asked, "Everything okay?"

"I'm not sure," she said quietly, and reached for her phone.

8-ball smiled as he closed the window of the Nomad. The guard hadn't shown any surprise when he'd identified himself as Dr. Morales, nor had he questioned the IDs given to his passengers. They drove down to sublevel nine, stopping briefly so that Zurich, Mish and Leila could continue down the ramp to the bottom level where the Hatter's Elite was parked, then headed for the bay assigned to them.

"What now?" asked Jinx, who was watching for magical security.

"We wait," said 8-ball. He picked up his Ares launcher and checked that the grenades were loaded in the correct sequence.

The architecture of the security system was a stark arrangement of straight lines and right angles, mostly in shades of metallic gray. Colors were used sparingly, and only for identification purposes. The only icons that showed any hint of imagination were the IC programs—feathered serpents, skulls and the symbols of the more bloodthirsty Aztec gods. Ratatosk stared at the reactive IC around the slave node for the lock on the Hatter's door, wondering whether to abandon subtlety and just blast it away with his attack utility, when he heard Magnusson swear. "Company!" he said.

Mute looked around, and listened, but the apartment was so well soundproofed that she couldn't hear anything outside. "Where?"

"An astral form just went through the room. I think someone knows we're—"

The door slid open, and the Hatter stepped in, his Ingram smartgun blazing. The burst hit Mute in the chest and the arm, knocking her backward and sending her pistol flying across the room before she could return fire. A second later, the beautiful blond woman behind the Hatter cast a stunball spell. Magnusson automatically reflected the spell back at her, and Elena Vargas staggered, seriously fatigued by the power of the spell combined with the drain of casting it. Moving with the superhuman speed of his wired reflexes, the Hatter grabbed the wagemage with his free hand and dragged her into the room behind him, then fired a burst at Magnusson. The door slammed shut.

Yoko came running out of the bedroom, but the Hatter had already jumped over Mute and grabbed the wire that connected Ratatosk to his deck. He pulled the plug out of his datajack, leaving Ratatosk reeling in dump shock, then slipped behind him and put his gun to the decker's temple, using his long body as a shield.

"Drop your weapons, and don't move!" he snapped. "Any of you!"

Yoko stopped in midstride and dropped to a crouch with her arms spread wide. "I'm not armed," she said.

"She's magically active," said Elena, drawing a small pistol. "Some sort of quickened spell. Don't trust her."

"I wasn't about to trust *any* of them," replied the Hatter sourly. "Now, I know this must be the famous Ratatosk, but who are the rest of you? No, let me guess. You're Yoko Aruki, the ninja who killed those yakuza bosses. Am I right?"

Yoko bowed slightly.

"And you," he said, looking at Magnusson. "You don't look like the photos I've seen of Boanerges, so you must be the other one. Magnusson."

"Boanerges is dead," said the mage. "That toxic shaman you sent in killed him."

"And one of you killed the toxic. Seems fair to me. And the one with the sucking chest wounds is Mute. Am I right?"

Mute, fighting to breathe, didn't answer. "And you're Thomas Mather," said Yoko. "The Mad Hatter."

"Just the Hatter, please. I'm glad we meet at last. I thought I might have to come looking for you, but you've saved me the bother. I hope you brought the data with you?"

"Data?" asked Magnusson.

"On GNX-IV. You did find it, didn't you?" He smiled. "Is it in this deck?"

Zurich whistled as he saw the cars: Toyota Elites, Mitsubishi Nightskys, Eurocar Westwinds, even a gleaming white Rolls-Royce Phaeton. "Ever get the feeling we're in the wrong line of work?" he said, as he pulled out his maglock passkey.

"If Ratatosk hasn't fixed those cameras, we're going to be in the line of *fire*," said Mish uneasily.

"Ratatosk knows what he's doing," said the dwarf. "Technology's not like magic. It always follows the rules . . . Frag," he muttered as the Elite's door failed to open. He braced himself, waiting for the car alarm to start blaring and the lights to start flashing. "Ah, keep an eye on the lift doors, will you? Just in case?"

"In that deck?" Yoko repeated and smiled. "Exactly how stupid do you think we are?"

"Some of it might be in his headware memory, though," said Magnusson quickly. "I know he's been reading the files."

The Hatter glanced at him, then at Vargas, but his gun didn't waver. "So you do have it? What about the virus itself?"

"I destroyed the virus. Sterilized it magically," said Magnusson. Vargas cast an analyze truth spell, being careful to minimize the drain, and nodded. "Ratatosk had a copy of the data, but I don't know where it's stored. If you kill him, you may never find it."

"Besides," said Yoko, "we have *your* decker."

Vargas nodded again. "Hare was useful, but I can live without him," the Hatter snarled. "Your teammate there isn't going to live without some sort of medical or magical help, and none of you are getting out of here until I have that data."

"What will you do with it when you have it?" asked Yoko.

"Sell it."

"It's not worth much," said Magnusson. "It killed nearly all of the subjects; the survivors came down with vampire virus. Who's going to buy a goblinization reversal that kills all the patients?"

"If it only kills orks and trolls, the bioweapons department can find a use for it. If not . . ." He shrugged.

"You're going to test it on a wider range of subjects?"

"It's not up to me. Management can decide. But I spent a lot of money on finding GNX-IV, and I want that data."

Yoko looked at Ratatosk, seeing his eyes refocus as he recovered from the dump shock. "No," she said. "You're not getting it. Even if you have to kill every one of us."

The Hatter smiled and aimed his smartgun at her head. "If you insist," he purred, and fired. Yoko instantly leaped toward him, and the bullets were diverted by the deflection spell tattooed on her body. One ricocheted from the coffee table and smashed the pendant light, plunging the room into near darkness. Yoko, Ratatosk, Mute and the Hatter recovered almost instantly as their eyes—elven or cybered—adjusted to the low light, but Magnusson and Vargas were briefly blinded. Ratatosk ducked, extended his cyberspurs, and stabbed the Hatter in the side. The Hatter squawked with the pain, but didn't release his grip on the elf's collar. Vargas stared into the astral and cast a powerbolt spell at Yoko, then immediately passed out from the drain and collapsed on top of Mute.

Magnusson saw the astral form of the spell and quickly blocked it, protecting Yoko from its effects. The Hatter fired another ineffective burst at Yoko, then turned the gun on Ratatosk again and squeezed the trigger—but Magnusson cast a magic fingers spell, pushing the select switch back to safety, then popped the clip from the magazine holder. The Hatter threw the gun away with a curse, pushed Ratatosk away from him toward Yoko and snapped the fingers of his left hand. The hidden compartment in his left index finger popped open, releasing a monofilament whip.

The Hatter slashed with the wire, slicing through the back of Ratatosk's lined coat and armor clothing, leaving a long shallow cut below his bottom rib and narrowly missing his spine. The decker hit the floor face first, and Yoko jumped back outside the weapon's reach, waiting for an opening. The Hatter stared at her for a moment, realizing that her reflexes were as good as his own wired ones and possibly better, then swiped at Magnusson, who ducked just in time to save his head, though not his top hat.

"Well, this is interesting," said the Hatter, still grinning. "A Mexican standoff in the Aztechnology pyramid. How apt."

"Standoff?" queried Yoko, as Ratatosk rolled out of range and drew his smartlinked slivergun. "You're outnumbered, outgunned, outclassed—"

"But not out of my element," the Hatter replied. "And I have something better than a gun. I have a headware phone with a direct line to security. I can seal this entire floor, seal every exit of the building, call for a whole squad of Leopard Guards . . . and my biomonitor is linked to the system here. Kill me, and you'll be lucky to outlive me by as much as a minute.

"Of course, if it comes to that, we all lose. Even if I survive, I'll be down some sixty thousand nuyen with nothing to show for it. So I'll make you a deal: I'll buy the GNX-IV data from you. I can't offer much up front, unfortunately, but once I've recouped my expenses, we can split the proceeds fifty-fifty. What do you say?"

"We don't have the data on us," said Ratatosk quickly.

"That does complicate matters," the Hatter admitted, "but it needn't be a deal breaker. I could let one of you go and keep the rest of you here until I have the data. I could even get medical help for your friend on the floor." He glanced at Mute and saw that she was looking back at him, Vargas' Beretta pointed at his head. He slashed at the gun with his monofilament whip, foolishly taking his eye off Yoko for a fraction of a second. The adept leaped toward him, and before he could turn to face her, she had hit him in the temple, throat and the top of the spine.

Yoko looked down as the Hatter collapsed at her feet and stomped on his left hand. He didn't flinch or utter a sound.

"Is he dead?" asked Ratatosk.

"No," said the adept. "He might have been bluffing about the biomonitor, but I couldn't take the chance. Magnusson, can you—" She looked at the mage and saw that he was already kneeling over Mute. He began chanting in Aramaic as he cast a healing spell.

"I'm sorry," Yoko murmured. "I should've been the one watching the door."

"Could you see through it?" asked Ratatosk as he removed his slashed coat, then opened Hare's deck bag. "And what if there'd been something nasty in the next room instead? Something magical that she couldn't have seen?"

Yoko shrugged. "What are *you* doing?" she asked as he plugged himself into the deck and walked toward the telecom. "You're bleeding all over the place, and we have to get out of here!"

"This should only take a minute," said Ratatosk, jacking in. "And even if that drekhead managed to alert security, and I hope he has, we've got at least three minutes before they get here. Probably five. Maybe more."

"What?"

"Their express elevators won't stop until they get to the lowest sublevel, and then they'll go straight back up to the Temple. They'll keep doing that until one of their deckers finds the little bug in the software that's causing the problem. I *told* you I'd take care of the elevators. Don't worry, *we'll* still be able to get out."

"And what are you doing now?"

"Transferring a million nuyen from one of their slush funds into the Hatter's account."

"What?"

"Don't worry, I'll transfer it out again. My fixer has some numbered accounts in Konigsberg for this sort of thing."

Mute started laughing, though the bubbling from her bullet-riddled lungs sounded disturbingly like a death rattle.

"He'll take his cut, of course," Ratatosk continued, "but

we should be able to set up a pretty decent hospital and school somewhere in the Barrens with half a mil. Can you put some tranq patches or something on the Hatter? I'd hate him to escape."

21

8-ball sighed with relief as his phone rang. "We're on our way down," said Yoko. "Mute's badly hurt, so we'll need you to pick us up by the elevator. Otherwise, proceed as arranged."

Diaz yawned again, reached for his coffee cup and found it empty. He was about to get up and get a refill, because he was having difficulty keeping his eyes open, when the wagemage reclining on the couch behind him sat up and said, "Can you check the elevators? There's a woman in one of them who looks like she's sick or injured."

Diaz stared at the monitors. "Can't see anything. Which one?"

"B-nine, I think. Heading down, probably somewhere in the thirties." Despite the magical R & D division's best efforts, navigating in astral space was still more of an art than a science.

"B-nine's heading for the basement, all right," Diaz confirmed, "but it's empty. Exactly what did you see?"

"Two mages, two mundanes. Two elves, two humans; two male, two female. Human female mundane lying on the floor; male human mage was casting a healing spell on the male elf."

"No group like that in any of the elevators," said Diaz, glancing at the clock. He thought for a moment, then called up a readout. "Okay, this says B-nine is carrying close to three hundred kilos. Something's wrong somewhere. Do ghosts weigh anything?"

"Could there be a problem with the cameras? A crossed wire, or something?"

"They've been working all right until now." He thumbed the switch for the microphone and said, "This is Security. Do you require medical assistance?"

There was no answer. "Did you try talking to them?" Diaz asked.

"Yes. I manifested, asked if there was a problem. They said no—"

"Did you recognize them?"

"No, but I'd know them if I saw them again—the mages, anyway."

"All right. Better to be safe than sorry. See if you can find them again, find out who they are. I'll make sure there's somebody to meet them when they get to where they're going."

"This is Security," said the voice over the speaker. "Do you require medical assistance?"

Ratatosk looked up at the indicator above the elevator doors. Twenty-third floor; twenty-five to go. Magnusson was nearly exhausted from the three healing spells he'd cast and didn't have the energy to maintain any physical masks, and they hadn't taken any countermeasures against magical security . . . and now, thanks to a random astral patrol, Aztechnology knew where they were.

Yoko leaned close to the decker's pointy ear. "Any ideas?"

"Tell the others to slot and run, not to wait for us?"

"Do you think they will?"

Mute turned her head to stare at them. "Didn't you say you'd trapped the security teams in their elevators?"

"Only the Leopard Guards. Not all of them." Ratatosk stared at the indicator. "We'd better hope they don't do the same to us."

8-ball looked around as he heard the elevator doors open, and swore as six men hurried out. All six—three humans, an ork, a troll and an elf—wore Aztechnology security uniforms, complete with helmets and sidearms: two were pushing a long cart that reminded him weirdly of Snow White's glass coffin. "What is that?" asked Jinx.

"It can't possibly be what I think it is," replied 8-ball, as four of the guards positioned themselves in front of the door of the next elevator and drew their pistols. He flipped up the vidscreen on his wristphone, angled the camera so that it showed the group and their equipment and called Ratatosk. "You've been spotted," he said. "There's a team down here, and you're not going to *believe* what they've got waiting for you."

"You're kidding," replied the decker, grinning as he recognized the box on the cart as a deluxe stabilization unit. "That's . . . looks like two medics and only four guards. Can you take care of them?"

"Sure. How long before you get here?"

"About twenty seconds."

"Okay." He turned to Jinx. "What spells do you know?"

"Treat wounds, analyze truth, and glue strip. No combat spells."

"Glue strip . . . that sticks people to the ground, right?"

"Yes. Why?"

"Fine. Get ready to cast it . . ." He reached for the grenade launcher and lowered the window of the Nomad just far enough to create a gun port. "Now!"

The grenade landed under the cart, and released a cloud of gas. Jinx cast her spell just as the security men hurriedly began backing away; the elf and one of the humans fell over almost instantly, and the ork stumbled while turning around to see where the attack was coming from. 8-ball closed the window. "Good thing those are dart guns," he said. "Or we'd be—*drek*!" He ducked as the troll dropped his narcoject pistol and drew an Ares Predator from his belt. A bullet smacked into the windshield, crazing the shatterproof glass as 8-ball started the engine and reversed out of the parking bay and away from the elevator doors.

"What are you—"

"Getting out of range! That's neurostun! Just try to keep those fraggers inside the cloud! Maggie, can you hear me?"

"Yes."

"Get ready to cast that clean air spell as soon as the doors open. And have your guns ready just in case—two of these guys haven't fallen . . . okay, make that one of these guys . . . " he said as the ork hit the ground. The troll continued to run toward them, apparently unhindered by Jinx's spell.

The elevator doors opened, and the gas dissipated. The troll turned around, and 8-ball slammed the Nomad into forward gear and drove at him. The guard stumbled aside, and the car hurtled past him. The troll fired at the Nomad's back window, then fell over as Magnusson hit him with a stunbolt. Ratatosk scrambled out of the elevator and opened the lid of the stabilization unit.

"Just what the doctor ordered," he breathed, as Yoko placed Mute into the unit. "Nice of them to send paramedics as well as guards."

8-ball drove the Nomad up and opened the back door. "The Hatter?"

"Still alive," said Magnusson.

The dwarf looked at their faces, then shrugged. "Boanerges would be proud of you. Okay, chummers, let's go go go!"

The guard at the gate looked up as he heard the unmistakable roar of a Westwind approaching along the narrow ramp, then stared as it was followed by a black Toyota Elite, a white Rolls-Royce Phaeton, a silver Jackrabbit, and a dark gray Nomad. The Westwind accelerated and smashed through the boom gate, and continued toward the street entrance. The guard hit the button to sound the alarm, and continued to pound at it when the klaxons failed to sound. Ratatosk, who had rewritten the software so that hitting the alarm button would open the main gates, nonetheless heaved a sigh of relief as all the cars made it out onto the street and split up. He just hoped Zurich had been as successful in removing the tracking devices from the cars.

A few minutes later, the Rolls and the Westwind pulled up in the parking lot of the YMCA. Leila stepped out of the sports car, looking at it wistfully. "Are you sure I can't keep it?" she said as she climbed into the Hatter's Elite.

Zurich shook his head. "It'll give the Azzies something to chase," he said as the Westwind, on autopilot, headed out of the parking lot bound for Seattle Center.

Mish waved good-bye to the Rolls as it drove off toward Council Island, then slid in next to Leila. "Home," she said, and giggled.

The Hatter did his best to keep his face impassive as he walked into his section head's office. "Tom," said Martinez warmly as he stared out of the window at the ocean. "That was good shooting in the tournament this morning. Well done."

The Hatter did his best not to blink. "Thank you, sir."

"May I see your gun?"

"Certainly." He drew the Fichetti out of its shoulder holster and handed it to his boss. Martinez looked at it with mild interest, then placed it on his desk.

"Now," he said, "about your application for a transfer . . . I'm afraid it's been declined. What with the Morales incident and now your friend Herrera disappearing . . ."

"He wasn't a particularly *close* friend," said the Hatter quickly. "We just played chess together. And bridge."

"Of course. I understand. Still, with him using your account to launder that money he stole from the pension fund . . . you have to understand that it doesn't look good."

The Hatter nodded. "Yes, sir."

"However, the board has decided that it probably would be for the best if you were relocated," Martinez continued. "Somewhere closer to head office. A job where you have a better chance of being . . . noticed by the people at the top. A vacancy has opened up for an intelligence officer in our office in Campeche."

The Hatter turned pale. "Sir, I . . ."

"A job I'm sure is well suited to a man of your abilities and . . . interests, shall we say? You'll be starting immediately. There's a helicopter waiting on the roof."

"Immediately? But . . ."

Martinez picked up the Fichetti and aimed it between the Hatter's expensive eyes. The office doors opened, and two Leopard Guards walked in, both in full armor with rifles at the ready. "No," said Martinez softly. "You won't need to pack. The suit you're wearing should be fine."

Beef Patty walked out of the hospital, moving under her own power for the first time in weeks, and inhaled cold December air into her new lungs. Pinhead Pierce led the way to an old red Eurovan and threw her bag into the back. "So," said the troll as she fastened her seatbelt gingerly, "what's the new place like?"

"Quiet," said Pierce as they headed east. "Used to be a motel and a restaurant until the Universal Brotherhood took it over. When they cleared out, some ghouls moved in. Maggie's been cleansing its aura, or whatever it's called, but it still has a bad rep, and a lot of people from the Crypt haven't come back. Or maybe that's 'cause the Gravedigger's turning the parking lot into a fraggin' garden and started her classes again.

"But Akira's back, and so's Joji, and Hook and Ulla and a lot of the others. But Leila moved out, stayed with Ratatosk for a while, then started studying with Mute. Didge and Jinx have started taking some classes at the university. The Crypt is still close enough to Hell's Kitchen that Doc Czarnecki and Mish are usually busy, and Maggie's students still find their stuff for the talismongers, and Zurich tapped us into the Matrix before he left, so we've got a jackpoint again. And the coven owns the building, all legal, so no one's likely to try to throw 'em out this time. But the place just isn't the same without Boanerges."

Patty took another deep breath and realized that the smell emanated from the ancient van, not from Pierce or his clothes. "It has hot showers, too? And a laundry?"

"Yeah," said the ork. "Why?"

"I just wondered. I'm not expecting to stay long."

"Don't blame you," said Pierce. "I moved out a few weeks ago, myself."

"You did?"

"Yeah. I'm going to miss some of the people, but it was too far to go to work."

"You have a *job*?"

"Inna band. I even had to say no when 8-ball and Mute asked me to go on a shadowrun last week because I couldn't let down the band."

Patty took another look around the van. "You're a roadie?"

"Drummer," said Pierce proudly. "Something Mute said made me think about the way I was playing, and I realized what I was doing wrong."

"Something *Mute* said?"

"Yeah," said the ork. "Apparently, it's all in the timing."

About the Author

Stephen Dedman is the author of the novels *The Art of Arrow Cutting*, *Shadows Bite* and *Foreign Bodies*, and nearly one hundred short stories published in an eclectic range of magazines and anthologies. He also wrote the RPG sourcebook GURPS *Dinosaurs* and two *Villains and Vigilantes* adventures, co-authored GURPS *Martial Arts Adventures* and GURPS *Deadlands*, and has been shadowrunning since 1990. He lives in Western Australia with his wife and a finite number of cats. For irregular updates, see stephen-dedman.livejournal.com.

SHADOWRUN #5

Aftershock

by Jean Rabe and John Helfers

The troll known as Hood and his fellow
Shadowrunners steal some biological agriculture
from the Plantech Corporation—only to find
themselves framed for murder and tied to an
even greater conspiracy.

0-451-46101-0

**Available wherever books are sold or at
penguin.com**

Roc Science Fiction & Fantasy
Available November 2006

SHADOWFALL:
Book One of the Godslayer Chronicles
by James Clemens
0-451-46050-2

Four millennia have passed since the gods came to
Myrillia, creating the nine lands of peace as a haven
from the nightmarish, accursed Hinterlands. In all
this time nothing has disturbed the harmony of the
nine lands.

AFTERBURN
by S.L. Viehl
0-451-46117-7

After driving a mutual enemy across the border ter-
ritories, the Allied League of Worlds gathers for a
peace summit on K-2, the homeworld of the
underwater dwelling 'Zangians. With the Bio
Rescue team assigned to protect the delegates,
Sub-Lieutenant Burn mu Znora's attention is
placed on Liana, the daughter of one of the ambas-
sadors, who possesses information vital to the fate
of four worlds.

Available wherever books are sold or at
penguin.com